In the Steamy Texas Heat

Silence engulfed her, so loud it roared in her ears. Rays of brilliant June sun pressed down hotly on her shoulders, and the vast blue sky made her feel small—a noteworthy accomplishment on the sky's part, since very little made her, the only daughter of the powerful J. D. Strayhorn, feel small.

A breeze gusted past and swirled her long hair around her face, pressing fine strands to her lips. She combed it back with her fingers, gathering it at her nape while she walked toward the house, still looking for the Silverado's owner.

Then she saw a man—a big man she didn't recognize. He came around the corner of the house. She could tell he had seen her. He paused for a second, then came directly toward her, long legs eating up the space between them.

He was wide shouldered but lean. He was clean and wearing a bright blue torso-hugging T-shirt that showed off muscles in his arms and shoulders. The shirt was neatly tucked in to starched and creased Wranglers. He had on cowboy boots, not worn-out, but well used. He looked like a cowboy, all right.

Lone Star Woman

SADIE CALLAHAN

A SIGNET ECLIPSE BOOK

SIGNET ECLIPSE
Published by New American Library, a division of
Penguin Group (USA) Inc., 375 Hudson Street,
New York, New York 10014, USA
Penguin Group (Canada), 90 Eglinton Avenue East, Suite 700, Toronto,
Ontario M4P 2Y3, Canada (a division of Pearson Penguin Canada Inc.)
Penguin Books Ltd., 80 Strand, London WC2R 0RL, England
Penguin Ireland, 25 St. Stephen's Green, Dublin 2,
Ireland (a division of Penguin Books Ltd.)
Penguin Group (Australia), 250 Camberwell Road, Camberwell, Victoria 3124,
Australia (a division of Pearson Australia Group Pty. Ltd.)
Penguin Books India Pvt. Ltd., 11 Community Centre, Panchsheel Park,
New Delhi - 110 017, India
Penguin Group (NZ), 67 Apollo Drive, Rosedale, North Shore 0632,
New Zealand (a division of Pearson New Zealand Ltd.)
Penguin Books (South Africa) (Pty.) Ltd., 24 Sturdee Avenue,
Rosebank, Johannesburg 2196, South Africa

Penguin Books Ltd., Registered Offices:
80 Strand, London WC2R 0RL, England

First published by Signet Eclipse, an imprint of New American Library,
a division of Penguin Group (USA) Inc.

First Printing, January 2009
10 9 8 7 6 5 4 3 2 1

*As always, this is for
my husband, George, and my daughter, Adrienne,
my biggest fans and strongest supporters*

ACKNOWLEDGMENTS

I want to thank Sherry Patterson. Sherry is the owner of Triple "S" Quarter Horse & Paints, in Alba, Texas. Though she doesn't know me from Adam, she was very generous in answering my questions, about paint horses in particular, and their history. If you go to her Web site, mysite.verizon .net/resvyjgr, you can see a picture of Harley, the black-and-white Tobiano paint stallion I used as a pattern for Jude's horse, Patch. Harley's full name is Heza Hollywood Harley, and he is so pretty!

I also want to acknowledge the big, old West Texas ranches. They and their histories are the stuff Texas legend and spirit are made of.

And a special thanks to my good friend and superb critique partner, Laura Renken.

1

The West Texas sun had peaked in a bright blue sky, and Judith Ann Strayhorn had already wasted more than half the day. Behind the wheel of her Dodge pickup truck, she raced along the highway on her way from Lockett to Abilene, a hundred miles away. Her mind was on Harley Beall, the state cop who had stopped her earlier for speeding. He hadn't been sympathetic when she told him she was on a mission. He had looked at her with cold eyes, his mouth set in a grim line. He must have been having a bad day because this time, he hadn't given her the usual warning. *This* time, he had given her a ticket. *Damn*. Now Daddy would try to badger her into going to driving school.

Since the first time she had been allowed to drive the twenty-eight miles from the Circle C ranch to the town of Lockett all alone, Jude had found adhering to the speed limit a burden. Today, after getting the ticket, she forced herself to drive slower while she considered whether to go to court and plead not guilty to driving eighty in a sixty. The judge would probably be accommodating, given that her grandfather and father allowed him hunting privileges on the family's rangeland. But in the county where Strayhorn wealth and influence overshadowed everything, Jude was cautious about throwing her family's weight around. She would never deliberately put Grandpa or Daddy in an awkward position.

Still debating the pros and cons of taking the matter to

court, she drew near the old 6-0 ranch, the thing that had her rushing toward Abilene. The ranch's cattle-guard entrance lay just ahead on the right, and at the end of the driveway, she saw a tan pickup truck. What was *that* about?

She lifted her foot from the accelerator, slowed and pulled partially off the highway onto the shoulder for a closer look. Not recognizing the tan pickup, she eased all the way off the pavement and stopped. She shoved the gearshift into park and sat a few seconds, studying the trespassing rig and pondering the best way to find out who owned it.

Her attention veered from the pickup to the old two-story house. Of Victorian style, rising from the middle of a sun-drenched Texas panhandle pasture, it couldn't have looked more out of place. It sat at the end of a quarter mile of caliche driveway, its fancy carved wood trim and much of its clapboard siding bare of paint and weathered to gray. The slatted shutters that had once framed two of the front windows in white had been missing for a while now.

Her eyes traveled to a two-story barn standing five hundred feet behind the house, canting to the east in sad shabbiness. In a coil the size of a car, rusted barbed wire leaned against the barn's east wall. Other outbuildings of both metal and wood in various stages of dilapidation baked in the brittle early-afternoon sun.

As far as Jude was concerned, the buildings were an inconsequential part of Marjorie Wallace's estate. The valuable part was the fifteen sections of land the buildings sat on—9,600 acres of prime, rolling bluestem grassland that had been ungrazed for months. Enough land to run at least two hundred head of cows and calves. The very thought was enough to make her heart sing.

Jude wanted to own that 6-0 rangeland more than she had ever wanted to own anything. And she had the wherewithal to buy it. She hadn't yet made an offer, but without her father and grandfather knowing it, she had already started the wheels rolling to take the money from her trust fund. She had an appointment this afternoon to meet with the banker in Abilene to discuss it further and sign documents. No doubt when Daddy and Grandpa learned what she was up to, another family explosion would occur.

She could hear Daddy now: *Jude, why don't you spend your energy on finding a husband?*

And Grandpa: *Why, Judith Ann, that trust fund is for your future and the future of the children you should be concentrating on having.*

And the discussion wouldn't end there. Hadn't they already tried to marry her off twice?

But at the moment, she couldn't think about a hypothetical. The unfamiliar pickup had her curiosity jumping up and down. She shifted out of park, made a right turn and jostled and bumped up the neglected driveway until she came to a stop behind the newer-model Chevy Silverado. Its bed was filled with household furnishings: a mattress set, a cabinet-like thing that looked to be a dresser, some chairs and a table. Having been here several times, she knew the house and all the outbuildings had hasps and padlocks on the doors. Had the Silverado's owner broken in and taken that furniture from inside the house?

From where she sat, she couldn't see whether the lock on the front door had been removed. A sudden jolt of anxiety hit her stomach. She thought of her cell phone and her cousin Jake Strayhorn, who was the Willard County sheriff. She thought of her pistol, which she knew how to use and had a permit to carry. It was locked in Daddy's gun cabinet at home. *Damn.*

She pulled closer to the Silverado's back bumper and angled across the driveway's two tracks. The pickup could get out, but only with some skillful maneuvering. Without killing her engine, she continued to study the unfamiliar vehicle. It was clean and neatly kept. No dents, good tires. Not a rig she would associate with a burglar. The license plate holder said, COWTOWN CHEVROLET. The only city in Texas known as "Cowtown" was Fort Worth. Jude's ever-present curiosity began to outweigh her anxiety.

Jake would be able to find the pickup owner's name easily enough. His office could log in to computer networks that knew everything about everyone. She pulled a small spiral notebook from behind the sun visor and jotted down the plate number. As she returned the notebook to its place, she glanced around but saw no one. She switched off the motor and slid out, her boot heels cushioned by clumps of assorted weeds that had overtaken the driveway.

Silence engulfed her, so loud it roared in her ears. Rays of brilliant June sun pressed down hotly on her shoulders, and the vast blue sky made her feel small—a noteworthy accomplishment on the sky's part, since very little made her, the only daughter of the powerful J. D. Strayhorn, feel small.

A breeze gusted past and swirled her long hair around her face, pressing fine strands to her lips. She combed it back with her fingers, gathering it at her nape while she walked toward the house, still looking for the Silverado's owner.

Then she saw a man—a big man she didn't recognize. He came around the corner of the house. She could tell he had seen her. He paused for a second, then came directly toward her, long legs eating up the space between them. A squiggle of anxiety zoomed through her stomach again. He was at least as tall as Daddy, who was over six feet. He was wide shouldered but lean. He was clean and wearing a bright blue torso-hugging T-shirt that showed off muscles in his arms and shoulders. The shirt was neatly tucked in to starched and creased Wranglers. He had on cowboy boots, not worn-out, but well used. He looked like a cowboy, all right, but not a cowhand. Having spent her entire life around both, she knew the difference. Now she was sure he was no burglar.

But what was he? A shot of panic surged for a reason other than concern for her personal safety. Good Lord, could he be a buyer for this place? She summoned the boldness for which she was notorious. "Hey," she called to him.

His step didn't falter as he continued walking toward her. "Something I can do for you?" His voice was deep, but soft.

As he neared, she strained to see his eyes, but they were

hidden in the shadow of a purple ball cap. It had the TCU logo, embroidered rather than stamped, so it was one of the better-quality caps. *TCU. Humph.* She no longer held so much as a shred of fear. TCU, Texas Christian University, was a sissy school in Fort Worth. Like her father, Jude Strayhorn was a proud graduate of the only college in Texas—or the whole United States, really—that mattered: Texas A&M. "This is private property," she said.

"I know," he replied almost absently, as he continued to look around.

"Then what are you doing here?" She had to raise her chin to look him in the eye. And those eyes, sitting above wide cheekbones and a lean jaw were as blue as the Texas sky. He didn't answer her question, but she felt the intensity of his head-to-toe assessment, as if he were seeing through her clothes, all the way to her skin. She had been observed by men before, was used to not reacting. What she wasn't used to was the electricity in the air between them and the strange flutter agitating inside her midsection. She stood there sweating in the heat, waiting for him to explain himself.

His gaze moved to her pickup, parked across the driveway, blatantly displaying her intent. He looked back at her, his jaw and body taut. "What are *you* doing here?" His tone would have frozen water on a July day.

"I'm a neighbor from up the road."

"That doesn't tell me why you parked crossways and blocked my exit. Who the hell do you think you are?"

She flinched at his sharp tone, but didn't back down. "I stopped by, being neighborly. But I'll damn sure get out of your way. If you don't feel like telling *me* who you are, I guess you can tell the sheriff." She turned and willed herself to saunter toward her pickup as if she hadn't a concern in the world, but her heartbeat drummed in her ears. "He's my cousin," she added over her shoulder.

"Hold on," he called. She stopped, turned back and faced him.

He came to where she stood, the corners of his mouth tipping into a hint of a smile that fell somewhere between friendly and smirky. Whatever its meaning, it sent another odd reaction through her stomach. He stuck out his right hand. "Brady Fallon."

He said the name as if it should mean something to her, but she couldn't place it. She had a feeling she had seen him before, but she couldn't think where. Still, she gave him her hand. His big, rough hand engulfed hers in a strong, palm-touching grip. Startled by another odd little disturbance darting through her, she pulled her hand away and stuffed it into the back pocket of her jeans. "So, uh, I don't think I've seen you around here."

"Haven't been around here . . . lately."

Lately? Who *was* he? Was he kin to someone local? She thought she knew every living being in Willard County, all 1,653 of them.

She had to know what he was up to. Striving for nonchalance, she said, "The, um, owner of this place passed away recently. Are you looking to buy it?"

A faraway look came into his eyes and he glanced back over his shoulder toward the outbuildings. She wished she could read minds. His attention returned to her, his eyes intent on her face. "Nope," he said.

"You're leasing?" The question was no sooner out of her mouth than she thought she knew the answer. "No, you're a bird hunter." By the hundreds, game-bird hunters ventured from the Fort Worth/Dallas metroplex to shoot the abundant quail and dove on the West Texas high plains. Fewer came to Willard County than to the surrounding counties because Strayhorn Corp owned more than half of the rangeland and Daddy and Grandpa gave only a chosen few permission to hunt. Years back they had been more generous in allowing hunting, but after too many unfortunate incidents with livestock and fences, they substantially cut back hunting by outsiders.

The stranger chuckled, a deep, friendly sound. He flashed

a boyish grin loaded with charm. "I never met a bird that deserved killing."

She couldn't keep from staring at his wide mouth and his even white teeth. "Actually, me neither. Personally, I don't like the taste of game birds. These dudes who come out here and use hunting as an excuse to get drunk and show off the shotgun they got for Christmas, it's a wonder they all don't shoot each other."

He shifted to a cock-kneed stance and propped his hands on his hips. "You didn't say your name."

"Jude Strayhorn. I live on the place that butts up to this one."

His chin lifted and his brow arched. "Ahh." His annoyance seemed to dissipate, as if he knew who she was.

But then, who in West Texas didn't know or hadn't heard—good or bad—of the Strayhorns? "So, what are you doing here?"

Those laser blue eyes fixed another steady look on her. Though the temperature had to be above ninety, she thought of icicles. Okay, so he didn't want to discuss it. Maybe she was being nosy. And maybe a little pushy.

A long pause. "This place belonged to my aunt Margie and uncle Harry." He looked down and appeared to study his boots. "Now I guess it belongs to me."

Jude barely halted a catch in her breath and willed her eyes not to bug. *Nooooo*, she wanted to scream, but she said, "What do you mean?"

He lifted his cap and reset it, revealing golden brown hair, bleached by the sun and darkened by sweat. "They never had any kids to leave it to. They sort of favored *me*."

How could she not have heard about this? Jude wondered. She hadn't known Marjorie Wallace personally, but everyone in Willard County knew that a few weeks before her death, she had suddenly sold her cattle herd and taken up residence in the town of Lockett's only nursing home. Only then did she reveal she had terminal cancer. Jude had assumed the 6-0 would be put on the market when its owner passed away.

Jude rarely found herself at a loss for words, but this unexpected news left her scrambling for what to say next. She gave the deceased woman's nephew a nervous titter. "Want to sell it?"

"I don't think so. I'm making this my home."

Now her heartbeat became a bass drum in her ears. She glanced at the furniture in the Silverado's bed, then the house, then him. "Margie Wallace didn't have any money to leave anybody, unless she kept some buried in the backyard. You rich?"

Frowning, he tucked back his chin. "That's no business of yours."

"Mister, I'm just saying, it's going to take a bunch of money to make this place even a little bit livable. I'd be surprised if the water well's even any good." She lifted her shoulders in a shrug and opened her palms in a show of feigned indifference. "But, hey. Like you say, it's none of my business."

She turned and started to her pickup again, drawing measured breaths to calm herself. She needed this land, had been planning to buy it for weeks. Owning her own place would give her a chance to try her ideas in cattle breeding without Daddy and Grandpa criticizing her every move and bellyaching about why she didn't just get married. And now the best chance she had run across lately to prove the points she constantly argued with her father had been snatched from her by some damn . . . *heir.*

The only thing that kept her from breaking down and bawling was that Jude Strayhorn didn't cry.

What the hell was that about? Brady wondered. He watched his visitor walk back to her shiny black truck, his eyes on her butt, which was molded into skintight denim. With tomboy agility, she climbed into the driver's seat and slammed the door. A one-ton was a big rig for a woman to be driving, but it was one good-looking truck. And she was one good-looking woman, like something out of a magazine, all neat and polished and gleaming. Hell, her boots could make his next month's child-support payment. The price of those big-ass sunglasses would buy his groceries for the week. He knew plenty about the cost of women's fashion. He had learned it in a hard lesson from his ex-wife.

Jude Strayhorn. Judith Ann, all grown up and curved in all the right places. He knew her. Sort of. She was a cousin to one of his best friends growing up, Jake Strayhorn. Brady had spent part of his youth hanging out with Jake and another of Jude's cousins, Cable Strayhorn. In those days Judith Ann had been a little kid, always throwing fits and getting in their way.

Without giving him another look, the full-grown woman fired the engine, expertly backed in an arc and turned the big shiny truck around in the narrow driveway. He noticed a fifth-wheel hookup in the bed. A horse-hauling rig. God knew he had seen enough of those. North central Texas, where he had come from, was known for being competitive cutting-horse country. There, half the pickup trucks on the road pulled luxurious horse trailers filled with high-value horseflesh.

The daughter of one of the wealthiest ranching families in Texas was a woman who just might own both of those things, the last woman a man of modest means should ever give a second glance. Rich and spoiled. He knew her type too well, had married it and paid the price. And because he had paid dearly, no woman would ever grip him by the balls again.

Even with that dismal reminder and resolution, he watched until she reached the highway, made a right turn and disappeared. She had affected him in an unexpected way. The image of her athletic body and storm of hair whipping around in the wind lingered in his mind. He had always liked the look of long, lean women with thick, luxurious hair. It made him think of something wild and primitive.

Common sense told him to forget it. She was further out of his league than the queen of England. He knew the Strayhorn family owned most of Willard County and had probably lost count of all the cows, horses and oil wells they possessed. Besides that, there were too many close connections from years back. For once, he listened to that voice of caution—something he hadn't always done when it came to the fairer sex—and forced her out of his mind. He had more important things to think about anyhow.

He returned to his inspection, now starting to wonder if his inheritance was a boon or a boondoggle. He ambled back toward the outbuildings, which were surrounded by tall grass and assorted weeds. Grass burrs stuck on his jeans like miniature cacti. Before going into the big barn, he stopped and picked the prickly little bastards off, then dug a heavy key ring from his pocket and unlocked the padlock on the barn's double doors.

Inside the barn's silent murk, slivers of sunlight seeped through cracks in the weathered wood siding and lay in stripes on the dirt floor. Dust motes floated in the narrow sunbeams. Brady stood in the center of the huge room and turned in a circle, remembering the day his uncle Harry had given him his first saddle on this very spot. He had been around eight years old. His uncle had known that in the Fallon household, there was no extra money to spend on something as extravagant as a saddle. Brady's throat tightened with emotion.

For several years, he had spent summers here at the 6-0 ranch. Back then he hadn't questioned why his aunt and uncle had taken to him in a way they had not taken to his younger sisters and brother. Not that they had been unkind to his siblings, but they had treated Brady as if he were their own kid. Later, after he was grown, his mother had told him that Margie and Harry had been unable to have children.

They had always wanted a son. Thus, they had formed a special attachment to Brady from the day he was born.

Seeing the condition of the buildings reminded him that he had been negligent in regards to his benefactor in recent years. After his marriage, he had been caught up with his own life—becoming a father and building his business. A few years later his uncle died from a stroke. By then Brady had become preoccupied with his crumbling marriage, his bitter divorce, the nasty custody battle for his son and finally the altogether collapse and liquidation of his business.

After his uncle Harry's death, Brady hadn't kept in touch with his aunt as he should have. He hadn't visited her, hadn't even known of her declining health and desperate circumstances until her last days. For that matter, his mother, Aunt Margie's own sister, hadn't known, either. Aunt Margie had always been an independent and private person. When he heard she had left him everything she owned, a nagging guilt had settled within him, and it hadn't gone away yet.

He forced his mind back to the barn, studying it, applying a professional eye to the buckled walls, the sagging roof supports, the collapsed stalls. The building was older than he was. Back when Uncle Harry had given him that saddle, the barn had been hell-for-stout and whitewashed. It had withstood decades of extreme West Texas weather. Now it was rickety and the paint had weathered away. But having been in the construction business for years and knowing a little about building things, Brady had already determined that all the outbuildings could be saved, including this big old barn.

He moved on to the outside. Attached to the barn were corrals of rusting steel-pipe fencing. Salvable, too, he judged. They needed only some cleaning, some antirust treatment and some new paint. The other outbuildings, mostly all metal, needed the same.

And all *he* needed was money.

And therein lay his biggest problem today.

He turned his attention to the barbed-wire fencing that stretched as far as his eye could see. Tumbleweeds filled the space between the strands of wire. The pesky thistles might have been accumulating for years. Mounds of tan sand had formed a berm against them. Clearing all of that could be a huge, if not impossible, task.

He scanned the expanse of pasture searing in silence in the blistering sun, its wild grass pushed east by blusters of westerly breeze. It was a landscape raw and treeless except for new junipers and burgeoning mesquite trees threatening to overpower the grass. In an unirrigated pasture in a part of the world where rainwater was scant, those parasites competed with grass for every drop of moisture. The mesquite thorns scratched livestock, leaving wounds that were open invitations to blowflies, and thus worms. The thick brush gave the pests and predators a place to hide. The brush and mesquites would have to be poisoned or dug out by the roots and burned. Or all of that.

A blossom of gloom opened in Brady's chest, threatening the optimism he usually felt. He had just come from the courthouse, where he had spent damn near his last spare dime catching up the taxes on the place. The lawyer who had called and informed him of his inheritance had said his aunt had sold everything not nailed down to pay off debt against the land and pay for her last days in the Lockett nursing home. Almost as an afterthought, the guy had added that there had been no surplus funds for paying the taxes.

After filling his truck's gasoline tank, Brady still had a few hundred dollars in his pocket. He had some money, hard earned, in a bank in Stephenville. Most of it was earmarked for child-support payments that automatically went to his ex-wife every month. And that was as it had to be. If so much as a hiccup occurred in the timely arrival of those checks in her mailbox, Brady Fallon would find his ass in jail. His former spouse came from a wealthy family, but she exacted penance from Brady every chance she could find.

The child-support payments were more than a stay-out-of-jail card, though. They were his ticket to seeing his nine-year-old son, Andy, two weekends of every month. The restricted access was as painful as a slash from one of those mesquite thorns.

As for his need for money in the long term, he felt confident that even with the scars his divorce and the liquidation of his company had left on his credit, he could take his deed for the 6-0 to the bank and borrow against it. He might have to do just that at some point if he intended to get this place in shape, but he would let bankers touch his property only *if* and *when* he had to. He'd had some experience with bankers. Big-time. He was well aware of the pitfalls of thinking a banker was a buddy, especially if the banker was better buddies with somebody more powerful than Brady.

No, he didn't need a banker at the moment. What he needed was a job, and he needed it in a hurry. A way to earn a living until he thought through his options and made decisions. But all wasn't lost. The guy at the service station had told him the Circle C ranch, a place he had known in his childhood, was hiring ranch hands. That had to be an omen. But was it good or bad?

2

On the road again, Jude couldn't keep from chastising herself for how clumsily she had handled the encounter with Margie Wallace's nephew. She just wasn't good in situations that called for finesse. She functioned better in an environment where everything was open and up front, where she could freely speak her mind.

An heir to the 6-0 ranch popping out of the woodwork meant Jude would no longer be making an offer to buy the old place with money from her trust fund. Her intended trip to Abilene was no longer necessary. She now had nowhere to go. Still off balance and disappointed, she picked up her cell phone and keyed in the number to the direct line of Bob Anderson, the Abilene banker who managed her trust fund. The Strayhorn family had had a relationship with the Mercantile National Bank in Abilene for decades before Jude was born. When the banker, a man approximately the age of her father, came on the line, she told him she no longer planned to make a real estate purchase and to halt the transfer of money from her trust fund. She heard relief in his tone as he replied that he was happy to comply with her request.

Mr. Anderson was glad to see her abandon the liquidation of trust fund assets because he knew she intended to use the money to buy Willard County land in her own name. He had told her all along he thought it a foolhardy idea for her to purchase grazing land separate and apart from Strayhorn

Corp, the entity that owned the Circle C ranch. In fact, he had almost forbidden it, until she reminded him that he wasn't her father.

Jude knew she had put him in a delicate position. She only hoped he would be discreet enough never to tell Daddy or Grandpa of her intent. Ethically, he shouldn't, but that didn't mean he wouldn't. Mr. Anderson, her daddy and her grandpa were well acquainted, having done business together for years.

She had kept her activity with the bank a secret because Daddy and Grandpa would be hurt that she hadn't, at the very least, discussed her plans with them. They would never understand—or accept—that she couldn't discuss *anything* with them that wasn't something *they* wanted her to do. Since both of them were clueless about their own autocratic attitudes toward her, she had seen no point in stirring up a hornet's nest by even bringing up the subject of the purchase of land that would be hers alone.

She spent the rest of the trip to Lockett stewing over whom she should visit first—her cousin Jake, who, with his finger on the pulse of the county, might be able to tell her what was going on with the 6-0 ranch and Mr. Brady Fallon, or her best friend, Suzanne, on whose shoulder she could cry. Not exactly cry real tears, for to do such a thing would be out of character for a Strayhorn. Jude could think of no time when she hadn't dealt with her emotional setbacks on her own, though this one might be harder than any she had faced since leaving college. She chose to see her cousin first and made her way to the sheriff's office.

Among the many things Willard County's two-man sheriff's office did not have was a marble monument to law enforcement. The entire department was housed in a low-slung frame building, the sheriff's residence on one end and the jail on the other, with the office sandwiched between the two. Attached to the jail, enclosed by a tall chain-link fence, was an exercise yard a quarter the size of a basketball court. A coil of concertina wire spiraled along the top of it as if it had been added as an afterthought, which, in fact, it had. The whole setup looked so flimsy, Jude suspected a determined criminal would have little trouble fleeing the jail or the exercise yard.

Bars on the windows and razor wire on top of the fence were not the most effective security measures in place at the Willard County jail. The deterrent against prisoner escape was the sheriff himself. Jude was as sure as sunrise that if the .45 attached to Jake Strayhorn's belt didn't cause a criminal to think twice before attempting to run, one look into Jake's eyes did. He had been an MP in the army, then a Dallas cop. He had seen and handled everything and anything that might be required of a keeper of the peace. Nowadays, as the sheriff of virtually crime-free Willard County, he was as good as retired.

She found her cousin in his office, engrossed in paperwork. Ever the gentleman, he rose when she entered and propped his hands on his belt. People often commented on how much alike Jude and he were in appearance. He was tall and lanky, but solid of body. He had thick reddish brown hair, similar in color to hers, but his had a few strands of gray. Instead of brown eyes like hers, though, his eyes were distinctly green and as clear as bottle glass. And she had yet to see them give away so much as a scintilla of his deeper thoughts.

He dressed in the manner of many county sheriffs in rural Texas—jeans and a starched, long-sleeve white shirt that contrasted with his suntanned skin. He wore his gold badge hooked in his left breast pocket, but more than the badge bespoke his authority. The man had a presence that filled a room. He was tough, independent and canny, a package of strong Scots-Irish genes, the stuff pioneer West Texans were made of. He was one of the few people who could intimidate Jude Strayhorn if he chose to. The fact that he had never chosen to was, in Jude's opinion, a mark of his character.

"Jude. How are you, girl?"

He always had time for her, no matter how busy he might

be. He always asked about her welfare, but he never asked about the Circle C or anyone else associated with it. Jacob Campbell Strayhorn was the son of Jude's father's brother and, like most of the Strayhorns, a namesake of the original founder of the Circle C ranching empire. By blood, he was as much a part of the family as Jude, but he had distanced himself from all of them except for her and their cousin Cable.

"I'm okay," she said. "You?"

He invited her to sit and offered her coffee. She declined the coffee. She had never understood why people had hot drinks when the thermometer registered a hundred degrees, but Jake seemed to thrive on coffee. It was a cop thing, she assumed. "A hot drink raises the body temperature," she told him with a laugh as she took the seat he offered.

"Something's on your mind," he said, sinking into his own chair behind his desk.

Remembering that he was as good as John Edward at reading minds, she managed a laugh, intending to put him off his game. "Why would you think something's on my mind? I just stopped by to say hello."

He grinned. "Jude, honey, if I ever decide to take up poker playing, I hope you're my first opponent."

Okay, so she was a little obvious. She sighed. "It's disconcerting having a conversation with someone who sees right through you. But honest, Jake. Nothing's on my mind. I'm on my way to Suzanne's and I just stopped by. No kidding."

"Uh-huh," Jake said.

Dammit, he didn't believe her. And he knew her too well. She raised her palms in surrender. "Okay, okay. I'm being nosy. I just met the new owner of the 6-0."

Jake leaned forward in his seat and rested his forearms on his desk blotter. "Brady Fallon? Where'd you run into him?"

Brady Fallon. The name still sounded as if it should mean something to her. "At the 6-0. Why didn't you tell me Mrs. Wallace had left her place to her nephew?"

"I didn't know it until I saw him at her funeral. He told me then that he'd be heading out here."

Margie Wallace's funeral had taken place two weeks back. Jude, her father and her grandfather had been present, too. Now she knew why Brady Fallon *looked* familiar. He had been a pallbearer. "You know him?"

"He's an old friend, though I haven't seen much of him lately. He's been living in Stephenville. You know him, too, if you think about it."

She racked her memory but came up with zero. "Why should I know him?"

"He used to spend summers with Margie and Harry when he was a kid. He ran around some with Cable and me." Jake picked up a pen and began turning it with his fingers, his eyes leveled on her face. "What were you doing at the 6-0?"

A glimmer of recollection started to glow in Jude's brain, but she refocused on answering Jake's question. No way did she intend for him to find out about her plans that had just been smashed. She ducked his gaze. "I just happened to be driving up the road on my way to town and saw a strange pickup parked at Mrs. Wallace's house. I thought it might be a thief."

His brow arched, Jake stopped playing with the pen. "And you *confronted* him? Jude, how many times have I—"

"So he inherited that place, lock, stock and barrel, huh?" she asked quickly, sensing a lecture coming. "He told me he's going to live there."

Jake leaned on an elbow on his chair arm. "Maybe. But I wonder. I think he's taking on a handful. That house is so run-down, I don't know if it can be brought back. And I don't know what shape the other buildings are in. And the pasture . . ." He shook his head. "I just don't know."

Jude had given only a fleeting thought to the possible cost of restoring the buildings at the 6-0, though she had looked closely at the pasture. It called for some work, for sure. But she couldn't let Jake know she had afforded it so much as a glance. "I guess I haven't looked that closely."

"It's too bad what's happened to that place. It was pretty once. But it's reached the point of no return, in my opinion."

"From what I knew of Margie Wallace," Jude said, "the appearance of the place would have been the last thing to concern her. I still can't figure out how I missed hearing someone had inherited it. Holy cow, gossip's more prevalent than air around here."

Jake's mouth tipped into a grin. "Sometimes there's a dead branch in the grapevine."

Jude leaned forward and braced her palms on her thighs. "So this Brady guy has got some money, huh? To fix it up, I mean?"

"I don't know. He made good in Fort Worth in the construction business, but he got a divorce a couple of years ago. From the way he talks, I'm guessing he got skinned."

New hope flickered in Jude's heart. "You think he might sell the 6-0, then?"

"He says not. At least, not at this point." Jake leaned forward again, his eyes intently on her face. "Why are you so interested?"

For an instant, Jude wondered how it would feel to be a criminal guilty of something and to be interrogated by Jake Strayhorn. "Oh, just being nosy. You know how I am. When you're a native, you just like to know what's going on."

If she'd had any doubt about the legitimacy of the inheritance and the new heir's intentions, this brief conversation with Jake had erased it. Time to change the subject. "And speaking of what's going on, Jake, I heard Chuck picked up Jimmy Wilson for DUI the other night." Chuck Jones was Jake's only deputy.

"Lemme guess. Jimmy was one of your students."

Jude had been teaching biology and science and helping coach the girls' sports at Willard County High School since returning from A&M five years ago. With the total high school population at fewer than a hundred kids, she knew most of the teenagers as well as the young adults who had chosen to stay in Willard County rather than move elsewhere to make a living. She had a protective attitude about her students and former students. After all, she had graduated from Willard County High School herself. "Last year. I heard this wasn't the first time for him. Is he in a lot of trouble?"

"Not for me to say. It's up to the judge."

Jude knew she would get nowhere questioning Jake, but she felt a need to stand up for someone she believed to be a good person, someone who deserved a chance. "He was one of my best students. He's a real smart kid. He has a real interest in science."

"Hangs out with the wrong people," Jake said. "If he's gonna have a future, he needs to get his act together. He probably should get out of Lockett."

Well, that was more than Jake usually said about people his office dealt with. "Easier said than done, coming from the family he does," Jude replied. "You should talk him into joining the army or something." In a worse mood than ever, and not wanting to discuss the influence Jimmy's alcoholic parents had on him, she got to her feet on a big sigh. "Well, I'm on my way to Suzanne's."

Jake, too, rose. She started for the exit but stopped in the doorway and turned back to reassure herself of the answer to one of the questions that had brought her here. "So we aren't kin to this Brady, then?"

She could barely keep all the members of the Campbell-Strayhorn clan straight. Grandpa talked about the dead ones as if they were still alive, which only added to her confusion. And she sometimes ran into distant cousins she didn't know she had.

"No. He's just an old friend from back when we were kids. Before the . . ."

Jake ducked his chin and a long pause followed. Jude knew he had almost said something about the scandalous incident no one discussed, the tragedy that had separated Jake and his mother from the Strayhorn family. Jude personally hadn't been so affected by what had happened between

Jake's father and her own stepmother or their deaths. She had been too young to be greatly emotionally impacted, but Jake had been fourteen when the accident occurred, and he had been closer to the whole affair. No doubt he still remembered much of it.

"Well, when we were kids," he said, raising his head and hooking his thumbs into his belt, obviously recovered.

Jude had been a kid, too—a seven-year-old to be exact—when Brady Fallon would have been hanging out with Jake and Cable. Her memory of those days was spotty.

Since Jake chose to avoid the subject by not even naming it, Jude did, too. She was still distracted by the encounter with Brady Fallon. On one level, she felt relief. For some reason, she didn't want him to be a relative. She laughed, attempting to lighten the mood and slide past Jake's uncomfortable moment. "What I remember is y'all used to shut me out. You never let me go anywhere with you."

Jake laughed, too. "You were a pip-squeak back then. And a mouthy one at that. The mouthy part still applies."

Half an hour later, Jude found her best friend, Suzanne, in her barn lot currying her horse. That woman had a regular romance going on with a buckskin gelding she called Buck.

Though Jude and Suzanne Breedlove had been friends since kindergarten, their lives had gone in two starkly different directions. Suzanne had participated in small-time rodeos forever, riding barrels, but not often winning and never owning a horse good enough to take her to championships.

She hadn't had wealthy parents to help pay her way through college. Having at best a strained relationship with her mother, she had left home right after high school and struggled to both work and go to college in Lubbock. The summer after her second year, at a rodeo, she met a Pro-Rodeo bull rider from Wyoming and hit the rodeo trail. Jude knew a few professional rodeoers, including her cousin

Cable. Chasing rodeos was a hard life. Being adrenaline junkies, bull riders in particular had a reputation for fast and hard living.

Suzanne had returned to Lockett two years ago after having been so out of touch with her family, she hadn't even come home for her mother's funeral. She showed up at her dad's house in the middle of the night with a black eye, a dislocated shoulder and numerous scars. To this day, she hadn't said specifically what had happened between her and her Wyoming bull rider. Now she lived with her widowed dad, Truett, a long-haul trucker. In her father's almost constant absence, Suzanne kept the Breedlove hearth and home and worked in town at Lucky's Grocery. Other than the Circle C's supply house, Lucky's was the only grocery store in Lockett and one of the few employers besides the Circle C.

Suzanne was something of a free spirit and claimed to be content with her present life. If that was true, Jude envied her. Jude couldn't recall the last time, if there had ever been one, when she had felt content. She walked over to Buck and ran a palm down his smooth neck. He was damp with sweat. "So what's going on with Buck?"

"We did some exercise this morning over at Pat Garner's. He told me I could use his arena anytime I want to. Can't let my horse get out of shape."

Pat Garner was a local small rancher who worked with cutting horses, his interest so high he had built his own arena. He was an excellent horse trainer who sometimes did work for the Circle C, but he was a shy man who had been divorced for several years. Jude believed he harbored a crush on the flamboyant Suzanne. Evidently unable to find the nerve to actually ask her out, he would use any excuse to see her.

"I'm surprised you aren't sleeping with Pat by now."

"He's willing, but I'm still thinking about it. I'm still sizing him up."

"He's a nice guy. I like him. He's good with horses. What

are you doing in his arena with Buck? Why does he need to be in shape?"

"You never know when I might take up barrel racing again."

That was empty talk. Jude knew horses. Buck might be pretty and have a sweet personality, but he was no champion barrel horse. Nor was Suzanne a champion rider. She was thirty years old, twenty pounds overweight, out of shape and out of practice for years. Her barrel-racing days were as far gone as yesterday's passing tumbleweeds. At different times here and there, Jude had heard Suzanne say all of that herself.

When Jude didn't reply, Suzanne asked, "What's on your mind?"

Though she didn't feel like laughing, Jude managed a chuckle. "I must be as transparent as cellophane. You're the second person who's asked me that today."

Suzanne laughed. She had a lusty, infectious laugh. She gripped her horse's halter and started him toward the gate. "Who was the first?"

"Jake." Jude walked alongside Buck on the opposite side, her palm on his shoulder.

"Naturally," Suzanne said. "That pretty man's got eyes like a hawk. Just one time I wish he'd train them on me. Honey, I'd give him a ride for his money." She opened the gate and Buck clumped through into the sunny pasture.

"Good luck with that," Jude said, stuffing her hands into her back pockets and watching the horse lower his head and start munching. "If I didn't hear about him taking someone out on a date every once in a while, I'd think he doesn't even like women."

Suzanne closed the gate and latched it, then pulled off the blue scarf that held back her hair. Layered bleached-blond curls fell past her shoulders. "Doesn't matter. I'm just mouthing. You know I'm through with men."

They began walking back toward the barn. "Yeah, yeah," Jude said. "Until the next one comes along. You love men.

And sex. It's just a matter of time before you're in bed with Pat."

Suzanne grinned impishly. "What can I say, girlfriend? Sometimes a girl just needs to get laid. Without getting involved, know what I mean?"

Jude's brow tugged into a frown. "You know, I can't recall a time when I've ever felt an urge to *just get laid*."

"Oops," Suzanne said, laughing. "I should have said except for you. I forgot you're not human."

Jude was more human than Suzanne, or anyone, would ever know. She simply had more control over her urges than most people. But more importantly, she had different priorities. She had a legacy to consider, a fact that lurked in the farthest recesses of her mind without letup.

Though no one had ever told her so, she believed with all her heart that the day would come when she would take Daddy's position as manager of the Circle C or even Grandpa's seat as the president of Strayhorn Corp. The conviction influenced and shaped every facet of her life. Meanwhile, she had no desire to create an environment where former sex partners and even scandal would come out of the woodwork to embarrass the family.

But beyond all that, she didn't categorize sex as recreation. As a biologist, she knew of too many possible negative consequences. "Yes, I am," Jude said, irked because she felt as if she had to justify not sleeping around.

"It can be just for fun, you know."

"Not for me."

They had reached Suzanne's small tack room. Jude leaned on the steel-pipe corral fence while Suzanne went inside. "You know what your problem is?" Suzanne said from inside the tack room. "You've never had it when it was really, really good. If you ever did, you'd be just like the rest of us poor deprived souls. You couldn't leave it alone."

Suzanne's favorite topic was sex. She could talk about it all day. "You don't know what I've had," Jude said, now even more annoyed. This wasn't the conversation she had come to her friend's house to have.

"Yes, I do. You've told me about the two losers you were engaged to."

Jude had never called Webb Henderson and Jason Weatherby "losers." That was Suzanne's word. Jude might not admire or respect either of her former fiancés, but she had always been guarded in what she said about them. Their families were still friends of Daddy's and Grandpa's. "They aren't losers. Webb's a partner in his daddy's law firm now. And Jason's an officer in his daddy's bank."

A snort came from inside the tack room. "I rest my case." Suzanne came back outside and closed the tack room door. "What would they be without their daddies?"

Jude had wondered the same thing but never said it.

"I thought you were going to Abilene to meet with the banker today," Suzanne said.

"That fell through. I came by to let you talk me into a good mood, but so far, you aren't doing a very good job."

Suzanne gave a thumbs-up. "But I can do it. I'm the queen of good cheer. They expecting you home for lunch?"

"No. They think I'm in Abilene."

"Wanna go up to the house? I'll find something in the fridge. Believe it or not, they started stocking Boar's Head in the meat department at Lucky's. I brought home some great ham. I'll feed you and you can tell me what's bugging you."

Jude shrugged. "Okay." They began the trek toward the Breedlove house, a redbrick sixties-vintage ranch. "Suzanne, when we were kids, did you ever know a guy named Brady Fallon?"

"Nope. Who is he?"

"The new owner of the 6-0."

Suzanne made a little gasp. "You are shitting me. He bought it? Or what?"

"Inherited it."

Suzanne clasped Jude's arm, halting their progress. "You are shitting me. I thought Margie Wallace had no heirs."

Jude shrugged. "Yeah, well, she had one apparently."

Suzanne removed her hand and they resumed walking. "Damn, girlfriend. That screws up your plans. We knew the guy as kids?"

Jude shoved her hands into her back pockets. "Yes and no. You might not have run across him, and I was too young to remember him. He didn't go to school here. Jake says he ran around with him and Cable for a few summers."

"Huh," Suzanne grunted.

"Looks like I'd better tell the school I won't be quitting my job after all," Jude said sourly.

"Oh, my gosh, Jude. I didn't know you'd told them you were quitting. I thought you liked teaching those kids."

"I thought I would get the 6-0. If I had, I was afraid I wouldn't have time to do a good job teaching. So I said I *might* not be back next year. We left it sort of open. They're waiting to hear from me."

Suzanne flicked her hand. "Oh, well, school won't start 'til the middle of August. That's more than two months away. You've got a little time to think about it."

"Not really. I can't just leave them hanging. Angela's waiting for me to tell her if I'll help her with girls' sports next year. If I don't, they need to have time to find someone else. If I do, I'll have to start planning before mid-August."

"You don't have to do it, you know. It's not like you *need* a job."

To Jude's dismay, everyone—Daddy, Grandpa, even her friends—trivialized her accomplishments and efforts to be a responsible citizen. Her family's wealth and position trumped everything else in people's minds. "I do have to, Suzanne. I have to be productive. I couldn't look myself in the mirror if I weren't."

Suzanne sighed. "I know, Jude. You're such a hardhead."

"Maybe so, but I couldn't stand living my life on a free

ride. Where's the satisfaction in that? And as you say, I kind of like teaching those kids. They look up to me."

"And I admire you for wanting to be something more than the idle rich. How's this? Since you can't get the 6-0 land, why don't you forget about the whole thing? If you've just got to have a job experimenting with something, move someplace where you can do what you've educated yourself to do. I'd hate to see you leave, but if you'd be happier . . ."

Jude shook her head. "The only people left to bring in some new ideas and keep the Circle C alive are me, Jake and Cable. Jake's a career cop. He couldn't care less about ranching. And Cable . . . Hell, who knows what Cable cares about. He never even comes around."

"Earth to Jude," Suzanne said, making a twirling motion at her temples with her fingers. "It doesn't make any difference what those cousins do. Your grandpa and your daddy have already proved they aren't about to let you and your ideas loose on that ranch. You're your daddy's little girl. And that's what him and your grandpa want you to be."

"What they *want* is for me to find a husband and become a birthing machine. Like one of the cows."

Suzanne hooted. "What they want is for you to produce an heir."

"*I'm* an heir."

"But they want a *boy* heir."

This was information Jude didn't need to be told. "This isn't medieval Europe, forgodsake." She exhaled a deep breath of frustration. "Can I help it if I was born without a penis dangling between my legs? Sometimes I feel like saying that to Daddy, but he might not recover from the shock."

They reached the house and stomped barn dirt off their feet on the back stoop. "How many times have we had this conversation?" Suzanne said, opening the back door and leading the way into a utility room. She began washing her hands in the deep utility sink. "As long as your daddy and your granddaddy are alive and well, and as long as you continue to live at that ranch, you're stuck with what you're doing. Unless you find a husband all of you like."

Jude leaned a shoulder against the wall, watching Suzanne wash up. "Don't I know it. That's why I wanted to buy the Wallace land. I wanted . . . well, you know what I wanted to do."

Indeed, Jude had told Suzanne often enough. She wanted to buy some Angus cattle and other crossbreeds. She wanted to raise some calves that she wouldn't ship to be fattened in a feed lot. Grass-fed beef was the coming trend. It was healthier. At the ranch, they ate only grass-fed beef themselves.

Suzanne tore off sheets of paper towel and dried her hands. "I saw some of that organic beef in Albertsons down in Abilene. It costs more." She stepped aside, giving Jude access to the sink.

Jude began washing her own hands. "But consumers are buying it. They're proving they would rather pay more to get the healthier meat."

"Well, you aren't gonna change any minds at the Circle C," Suzanne said. "There probably isn't a living soul out there who wants to fool with grass-fed steers. They'd probably have to hire more cowboys."

Jude didn't disagree. Leaving the spring calves on the range to graze longer would require more care by the hands.

"So stop fighting it, girl," Suzanne said. "Get in J.D.'s fancy plane and fly over to Fort Worth."

She was referring to the small jet the ranch owned. It was housed at the airport in Abilene. A landing strip and hangar had been built on the ranch when the plane was purchased years ago, but keeping a jet airplane at the Circle C was a maintenance and logistical challenge. Daddy had eventually decided it made more sense to let the plane stay in Abilene and have the pilot fly the hundred miles to the ranch and pick him up when he wanted to travel somewhere. Jude could use it anytime, of course, and occasionally she had.

"Pick up some guy you like and try him out," Suzanne

went on. "He might turn out to be *the one*. Get a bottle of wine, rent a room, get naked and wallow in hot, unbridled sex for a couple of days."

Jude's curiosity had always been aroused by Suzanne's remarks about sex. She usually said just enough to generate questions she never answered. Jude shook water off her hands and reached for a paper towel. "Something tells me you've done that."

Staring out the window above the washing machine and dryer, Suzanne gave a low chuckle. "Yeah. I've done that."

Jude could see that Suzanne's mind had traveled somewhere else. Something about the plaintive ring in her voice made Jude say, "What could you possibly do for two days? I mean, the whole thing only lasts a few minutes."

Suzanne looked at her with a Mona Lisa smile and shook her head. "Jude, Jude, Jude. For a thirty-year-old woman, you are so dumb."

Jude threw her paper towel in the trash. "I'm not thirty. Yet."

Suzanne walked into the kitchen. "Well, you're close. My question is, were those two dudes you were engaged to really that stupid?"

Jude followed her. "I don't know. I just wondered what you'd do for two whole days in a hotel room."

Suzanne reached into the cupboard for two tall glasses. "What you do, girlfriend, is screw like rabbits and come about a dozen times. Then you start over and do it again."

What Jude knew about sex surfaced in her mind. Her brow furrowed. "But no male animals can—what I mean is, men can't—"

"But *you* can."

The heat of embarrassment crawled up Jude's neck. Feeling Suzanne's eyes on her, she didn't look up.

"Can't you?"

Now Jude's cheeks were flaming. "Of course I can. It's just that . . ." She stopped talking. She had never come a dozen times. Often it hadn't happened at all. She knew ex-

actly how sex worked, but she didn't know how it was supposed to feel. One thing she had always suspected, though,
was that she had missed something.

"I'll bet you've never come with a man inside you, have
you?"

"Suzanne!"

"Seriously, didn't they want you to? Didn't they try?"

"Maybe . . . I don't know."

"Then how did they make you come? With their fingers?
Tongue?"

"Tongue?"

"Of course, tongue. You know damn well people have
oral sex." Suzanne turned to the refrigerator door and filled
the two glasses with ice cubes. "But not you, huh?"

Jude gave an exaggerated sigh, too embarrassed to admit
her limited experience. "Suzanne, are you going to feed me
lunch or what?"

Suzanne set the two glasses of ice on the counter, then
opened the refrigerator. "I'm serious, Jude. You never had
oral sex with either one of those guys?"

"No. Well, Webb did, but I didn't. And Jason and I hardly
had sex at all. We were only together three months. And I
didn't see that much of him."

Suzanne came out of the refrigerator with her arms and
hands loaded with jars and packages. She pushed the refrigerator door shut with her foot. "Wait a minute. You're telling
me you gave Webb blow jobs, but he didn't return the favor?"

Jude closed her eyes and sighed, wishing now she had
never asked Suzanne about her past experiences. In fact,
Webb had been interested only in his own gratification. And
because Jude hadn't figured that out right away, she had put
up with it for nine months.

"That's just like a friggin' lawyer," Suzanne said fiercely,
thrusting a jar of mayonnaise and a sealed carton into Jude's
hands. "I dated a lawyer in Lubbock. We hung out with all
of his lawyer friends. Self-centered fuckers, every one of
them."

Jude leaned on the counter, watching as Suzanne began opening packages and cartons. "Webb thought it was unsanitary," she said.

Suzanne made a little huff of disgust. "And he thought you sucking his dick wasn't? See what I mean? Self-centered. I'm telling you, what a guy does for you in bed says a lot about him."

"It wasn't a big deal. I can't believe men really like to do that anyway."

"Well, they do. It makes them hot. And it shows unselfishness on their part. Shows they want you to have a good time, too." She frowned and cocked her head, holding a knife and a slice of bread suspended. "Then again, maybe it's not unselfishness. 'Cause they probably figure if they do it to you, you'll do it to them. But on the other hand, that doesn't count if it's a one-sided deal." She slathered mayonnaise on the bread and placed it on a plate. "Just take my word for it, Jude, when you find a guy who does it all, you'll be so hungry for it, you'll beg him."

Jude made an unladylike snorting noise. She couldn't imagine the day she would be so hungry for sex she would beg. "No doubt all that's why you hung on to some character in Wyoming who beat you up."

"A good lay's hard to find, girlfriend. If you've got one, it's worth trying to hang on to it if you can."

3

After walking the fence lines closest to the barn and house, Brady's frustration and worry had only deepened. So much work needed to be done. So much money needed to be spent. Brush removal alone would cost a small fortune. Most troubling of all, he didn't know if a living could be made in this day and age on fifteen sections of West Texas pastureland, even under the best circumstances.

His practical businessman side told him he was caught in a dubious enterprise. But the eternal optimist that had kept him going through the many highs and lows of his life told him he was a lucky man to have been given free land and he had to honor that.

Needing a diversion from the enormous tasks he saw, no matter where he looked, he turned his attention to the house. He approached it, eyeing the tumbleweeds that had collected in a corner where the wooden front porch jutted from the house. The porch roof that wrapped around three sides of the structure sagged across the front. He stepped up onto the wooden porch with caution, putting pressure on one foot and springing a couple of times to test the plank's stability. When he didn't fall through, he walked across, unlocked the padlock on the front door and entered the living room. The house was empty, just as Aunt Margie's lawyer had said.

In the stifling, hot room, lit only by daylight filtering

through paper window shades, a hollow silence prevailed. An odor of dust and disuse hung in the air. He looked overhead at a vintage light fixture, the opaque bottom shadowed with what was probably dirt and dead insects. He had called a few days earlier and had the electrical power turned on, so he tried a toggle switch on the wall. A dim glow showed through the fixture's yellowed glass. He was home.

He walked slowly through the living room into the kitchen, his boot heels thudding against the linoleum floor. In the square room, its walls painted a Christmas green now dingy with age, he found two items that had not been sold: an aged refrigerator and the freestanding gas cookstove. These were the same appliances that had been here when he was a kid. His aunt had cooked hundreds of meals on this stove. When he switched on the refrigerator, it started to hum like it was new. What else did a person need? To Brady, function had always been more important than form.

Comfort, on the other hand, was extremely important. Having sweated through his T-shirt, shorts and even his jeans outside, in the hot house he was wringing wet. A swamp cooler hung in one of the living room windows. He hadn't lived with a swamp cooler since the summers he had spent in this house.

Before plugging it in, he studied all the controls, then walked outside to check the outdoor part of it. A flurry of wasps circled the unit's gray metal housing. He remembered his uncle Harry removing a wasp nest from the air conditioner and telling him swamp-cooler housings were perfect places for wasps. When Brady left Stephenville early this morning, he hadn't considered flying varmints. He hadn't brought chemicals to deal with them.

He returned to the tack room in the barn, where he had seen an assortment of cans and jugs, and found a wasp-killer bomb. At his truck, he dragged a long-sleeve shirt from behind the seat and shrugged into it, covered his head and neck with a bandana, then secured it with his cap and shoved on his sunglasses. Ready, he lifted his toolbox out of the truck bed and tackled the swamp cooler.

Half an hour later, without being attacked or stung, he had removed the cooler's housing and bombed a wasp nest the size of a softball. While wasps expired all around him, he tore loose the nest lodged in the corner, then reassembled the cooler.

Now able to closely examine the unit, he found jagged holes peppering the housing. They were surrounded by red rust and white corrosion. Age and hard water explained both. On the ground, he spotted a rubber garden hose. Once red, it had been faded to pink by the sun. It crossed a pitiful smattering of dried grass between the air conditioner and a stand faucet ten feet away. He turned the spigot and listened as a spew of water flooded the cooler's interior straw lining. At least that part of it worked.

Back inside the sweltering house, he plugged the old thing in and switched it on. Cool, damp air roared into the living room, along with a gust of dust, sending him into a coughing fit. When recovered, he breathed a sigh of relief that the swamp cooler, too, worked. He returned to his truck for the cleaning supplies he had brought with him.

Soon the swamp cooler had cleared itself of dust and cooled the house. He had swept a gallon of sand from the old linoleum floors. With the help of a rented dolly, he had unloaded some household items and the pieces of furniture he had bought at a Salvation Army store in Fort Worth. A used table and two chairs now sat in the kitchen, a small sofa, a reclining chair and a small TV almost filled the living room, and he had a dresser and a queen-size bed with a good mattress in the bedroom. His six feet and two inches didn't fit comfortably on anything smaller.

Having consumed all the drinking water he had brought with him, he strode to the kitchen and dug a clean glass out of a box of dishes sitting on the table. He ran it full of tap water, sipped and found the taste slightly salty and heavy with minerals, but passable. He plopped onto a kitchen chair, the first time he had sat down since arriving this morning.

Golden afternoon light streamed through the small bare window above the kitchen sink, highlighting dust floating in the air. Except for the low hum of the refrigerator and the roar of the swamp cooler from the living room, an eerie silence surrounded him, created by the absence of the human being who had always been present in this room with him. Distinct smells from childhood came to him— animal medications Aunt Margie had kept in the refrigerator, Pine-Sol she had used to mop the floors, myriad cooking aromas, like frying bacon, black-eyed peas stewing with ham hock, fresh peach pies and lots of other desserts.

Brady looked around him at the linoleum nailed onto the countertop with galvanized roofing nails; the faded linoleum floor, its pattern worn away entirely in front of the sink and stove; a large sheet of yellowed plastic thumb-tacked to the dingy green wall as a grease shield above the cookstove's back. He could envision his chunky aunt, her jeans covered by a canvas butcher's apron, the heels of her cowboy boots clomping on the kitchen floor.

An outdated setting hadn't prevented Aunt Margie from being a great cook. She had baked *tres leches* cake, one of his favorites, before fancy restaurants added it to their menus. She just called it "cake and pudding." As a boy, he thought her chocolate brownies with fresh pecans and thick chocolate frosting were the best things he had ever tasted.

Thinking of his childhood brought up thoughts of his own son, and a deep anguish gripped him. Now that he owned land and would soon own cattle, he longed to share the rural ranch life with his boy, wanted to teach him stewardship of the land, and how to ride and rope and handle livestock. Giving up his Fort Worth home and everything in it to his ex-wife had hit Brady hard, but losing custody of his son had hurt more than a blow from a two-by-four. Even worse, the pain was constant, like a thorn endlessly pricking his gut.

He had spent money he couldn't afford fighting Marvalee for Andy. He gave up only after his lawyer told him little else could be done. The judge favored mothers. What the judge didn't know, and what Brady hadn't been able to prove, was that the average alley cat had better parenting skills than Marvalee Fallon and probably more interest in being a parent. Brady suspected Andy was spending more time with babysitters than with his mother.

Marvalee was so bad at relating to Andy and Jarrett, her twelve-year-old son from a previous relationship, that the day Brady had packed his clothing and left the house, Jarrett had come into the bedroom, his face wet with tears, and begged Brady to take him. Rarely ever seeing his real father, Jarrett called Brady "Dad." And why not? The boy had been a toddler when Brady married Marvalee, and Brady had always treated him as if he were his own kid. Brady would have taken Jarrett, would still take him if possible, right along with his own son.

When he began the fight for custody, he figured Marvalee would willingly, even eagerly, give up both boys. Then her father and his millions entered the fray. The person Brady had battled for custody wasn't Marvalee. The person he had gone against indirectly was his ex-wife's father. Fighting Marvin Lee Erikson had been a David-and-Goliath match. But with a less favorable ending for David.

Brady forced that mind-numbing crap out of his head. He had to get going. He had land, free and clear. What more could a man ask for in this life than almost ten thousand unencumbered acres? And he intended to have a job before dark. He drained his glass of water and got to his feet.

As the day waned, Jude said she had to go home, and Suzanne walked with her outside. "What about this for an idea?" Suzanne said. "Get a reservation down at Lake Austin Spa. Go down and lose yourself in decadent attention. Get a facial and a massage. Do yoga. Commune with nature and feed the ducks." Suzanne closed her eyes and lifted her shoulders. "That day down there last year was sheer heaven."

For Suzanne's thirtieth birthday, Jude had treated her to a day of beauty at the posh Lake Austin Spa and Resort. Suzanne mentioned it often. Jude would do more for her best friend, but she knew Suzanne wouldn't take her charity. A birthday present was different.

"I don't have to go to Austin to commune with nature," Jude said. "I can look out my window."

"The point is, change your scenery. Just screw off for a week. That's exactly what I'd do if I had your money."

A day idling at a spa held no appeal for Jude. "Yeah, I could do that," she said. "And then what?"

Jude had rarely passed a day doing as little as she had done today, but her mood had improved. Suzanne's off-the-wall approach to life always lifted her spirits.

She left the Breedlove house early enough to reach the Circle C in time for supper, conscious that showing up late would cause Daddy and Grandpa to worry. Beyond that, she disliked arriving after supper was over. Her father and grandfather started their days so early, they went to bed with the chickens. Without them awake to greet her in the Circle C's barnlike house, the old dwelling, with its hard floors and plaster walls and high ceilings, felt hollow and too silent.

Soon she reached the limestone rock stanchions that marked the Circle C's entrance, made a right turn off the highway and followed a winding two-mile driveway to the house's wide wrought-iron gate. She keyed in the security code, and the gate's two halves, each marked with the welded-in Circle C brand, silently crept open.

Another half mile put her in front of the garage adjacent to the house. The ranch house had been built in 1899, before homes had attached garages. Though its size made her feel lonely at times, she loved the old house. Some people called it a mansion, others called it an albatross, some even called it haunted, but to her, it was simply home. Constructed on a bluff looking to the west over a far-reaching red rock canyon, it was a massive three-story structure veneered with red limestone quarried from the ranch's land. It loomed like a fortress among ancient live oak, chinaberry and black walnut trees that a groundskeeper carefully nurtured. Behind it, a fruit orchard grew, as well as a garden maintained by the kitchen help.

In the hundred and nine years since the house's construction, it had been updated, redecorated and remodeled. Nowadays, it consisted of four three-room bedroom suites and six guest bedrooms, ten bathrooms and two living areas. There was an octagonal-shaped sunroom that had been added on to the house by Grammy Pen, a breakfast room brightened by the morning sun, a large formal dining room, as well as a large laundry room, a mudroom, a pantry and a cooling room that was no longer in use. For that matter, more than half the house was no longer in use, though in Jude's youth, the entire Strayhorn family had lived in it.

That had been before the accident.

Except for the years she had been in college, Jude had never lived anywhere else, had never *wanted* to live anywhere else. Though she had followed in her father's footsteps and gone to college at A&M, nearly four hundred miles away, she had never wanted to "go away to school." She had never wanted to reside on either the East or West Coast to rub shoulders with the beautiful people and dabble in liberalism, had never wanted to wander through Europe. Even when she had traveled to Australia once on a study trip, she had been restless to return to Lockett.

Many of her peers thought that in her devotion to the Circle C and Lockett, Texas, she was a throwback of some kind. She often heard, "If I had your money, I'd do this," or

"I'd do that." But Jude paid those attitudes little attention. She was a Texan to the very marrow of her bones, but more than that, she was a *West* Texan and a part of a family that had made Texas history. From the day of her birth, she had been surrounded by that history and the power and responsibility of ownership and wealth. Through osmosis she had come to believe she was a woman of destiny.

She arrived at home early enough to allow herself time to freshen up and change her clothing before going to the dining room. Grandpa complained if she or Daddy came to the table sloppy and dirty. The only people for whom he relaxed the dress expectation were the ranch hands he often invited to supper. If anyone in the family truly was a throwback, it was Jefferson Davis Campbell Strayhorn. In many ways, he behaved and talked as if he lived in a generation even older than himself, and he demanded respect from those younger than he.

Entering the house through the back door, Jude heard no activity except for Windy and his Mexican helper, Irene, talking in the kitchen. The aroma of onions, garlic and Tex-Mex spices was potent and tantalizing. Supper was under way.

Their latest house cook, Windy Arbuckle, had been a chuck wagon cook until he slipped on some ice last winter and broke his hip. The aging widower had recovered but was left with an awkward limp, and Grandpa and Daddy would no longer allow him go out on the chuck wagon to distant parts of the ranch. Now he and his limp were confined to thumping around the Circle C's kitchen in his cowboy boots. He cooked in the chuck tent only during roundup.

Some outfits would have let Windy go when he became unable to perform the job for which he had been hired, but generations back, it had become the Circle C's custom to take care of its hands. Many of them, like Windy, had spent decades in the ranch's employ. Besides that, Windy and Daddy had been friends their whole lives, and Windy had a proprietary attitude about the ranch. He had whittled wooden dolls for Jude when she was a child. Once he had whittled her a "cowboy toothbrush" from a skinny mesquite limb and taught her how to use it to clean her teeth. The Arbuckle children had been Jude's playmates, and she still called them friends, though all of them had left Willard County long ago.

Jude passed through the kitchen, said hello, then made her way to her second-floor suite, passing paintings of some of the Circle C's majestic stallions hanging along the stairway. The Circle C was as well known for its fine horses as for its fine cattle.

She changed into a brown broom skirt and a pale green sleeveless T, freshened her makeup and pulled her hair back with a leather barrette at her nape. She dabbed a few drops of Interlude behind her ears and between her breasts. It was an old-fashioned fragrance, but it had been Grammy Pen's favorite. For as long as Jude could remember, her great-grandmother had moved through her life in a cloud of the musky scent. By wearing it, Jude could keep the only female relative she had ever known close to her.

She added a turquoise squash-blossom necklace and silver earrings to her earlobes. She didn't mind dressing for supper. Doing it held a kind of old-world appeal. She spent quite a lot on her Santa Fe–style wardrobe. With her lack of social life, if not to dine with Grandpa, where else would she wear the clothing and jewelry she bought?

Jude returned downstairs to the cavernous galley-style kitchen to see Windy wreathed in a cloud of steam and smoke curling up from the grill. The mouthwatering aroma of searing meat and onions filled the kitchen. "Hmm-yum. Whatcha cooking?" she asked, her voice echoing. When the original Circle C ranch house had been built, everyone, including the ranch hands, ate in the big house. For ease of cleaning, the kitchen's walls as well as the floors were covered with tile. That, coupled with the room's huge size and high ceiling, created the hollow-sounding acoustics.

"I'm grillin' up some o' yore granddad's beef into the best dang fa-*hee*-tas you'll ever eat," Windy said.

Windy was a superior cook of basic food, much of it spicy with Tex-Mex flavors. But his traditional American frontier food, like Dutch-oven buttermilk biscuits and sourdough bread pudding, had won prizes at fairs. He even kept a crock of sourdough starter in the refrigerator, to which he regularly fed potatoes.

Jude laughed. "I don't doubt it for a minute. They're low cal, right?"

"I wouldn't know about that. All I know is I'm using prime lean beef from this ranch and fresh, homegrown vegetables I picked out of the garden just yesterday. We've got some fine sourdough biscuits and a few fried Idaho taters and onions. You know yore granddad's got to have his fried taters and onions."

"I know," Jude said with a grin. Jefferson Davis Campbell Strayhorn ate fried potatoes and onions with every meal. An old friend in Idaho shipped him the fresh-from-the-field vegetables. Jude often teased him, telling him those two items in his diet were responsible for his long, healthy life, which was a fact as much as a joke.

Jude had had something on her mind all week that she wanted to discuss with her father. "Is Daddy here?" she asked Windy.

Both his hands were busy, so Windy's head tilted toward the dining room. "He went off to fix hisself a little toddy."

Daddy's custom was to retire to his study up the hall from the dining room for a drink before supper. Jude left the kitchen and made her way there. She tapped on the deep brown oak door and at the same time stepped inside the room onto rust-colored Mexican tile softened with cowhides. On the walls were heads and horns from game animals, most of them bagged on the ranch. She called the room's emphatically masculine Western decor a wolf's lair.

The office had a compact but full-service bar, and sure enough, she found her father standing at it. Wearing clean Wranglers and a fresh short-sleeve snap-button shirt, he had cleaned up for supper. From his appearance, unless someone noticed the custom-made boots he wore, no one would ever guess his financial worth.

Jude had always thought him handsome. He was a tall and sturdy man whose body, as a result of a lifetime of physical work, belied his age. His face, on the other hand, was overtanned to a permanent russet brown and deeply creased around the eyes from spending every day in the Texas sun. But his forehead, constantly shaded by his hat, was pale white. His hair, once a reddish brown like hers, was now white, but it was still thick. He kept it cut short.

Jude had wondered often whether he was lonely. She had never known of him having a female companion except for a couple of local "friends." Occasionally he invited one of them out to dinner or to some function, but as far as Jude knew, that was the extent of his romantic life.

The scent of cigar smoke lingered in the air, and she saw a stub in his left hand. His head turned her way and he smiled. "Hi, punkin. Just having a little Crown before supper. Want some?"

Mentally, Jude clenched her teeth at hearing him call her by her childhood pet name. Long ago she had given up asking him not to do it. The habit was too ingrained, she supposed. She walked over to the bar, which hid behind slatted bifold doors when not in use. A hint of Aramis, the cologne she had always associated with him, commingled with the fruity aroma of his cigar. "Sure. But don't forget to fix mine with lots of water."

He chuckled, dropping ice cubes into a second tumbler. They clinked softly in heavy crystal. He poured a generous portion of Crown Royal into each glass, then added ice water to hers from a stainless-steel pitcher. "Haven't seen you since this morning, sugar. Whatcha been doing?"

"Oh, this and that."

He handed her the glass of whiskey. She carried it to a large leather wing chair in front of his desk and took a baby sip, shuddering as the alcohol burned her throat and hit her empty stomach. A whiskey guzzler she was not and never had been, even in college.

Sitting in the wingback chair put her at eye level with the credenza behind her father's desk. There, among photographs of sleek horses and massive Hereford bulls in their curly-faced maleness, was an assortment of photographs of Jude at various stages in her life. Tucked among them and partially hidden was one from eleven years ago of her and Webb Henderson at an A&M/UT football game. Webb was a graduate of the University of Texas law school. Daddy and Grandpa had viewed him as excellent husband material. Proof of how much they thought of him was the fact that Daddy kept that picture on the credenza with his favorite bulls and horses.

She had been introduced to Webb when she was eighteen and a freshman at A&M. Grandpa and Webb's father, an Austin lawyer and politician, had known each other for years. Mr. Henderson had insisted that his son and Jude meet. Webb's marriage proposal came almost at once, as if preordained. She accepted because she had been too young and too sheltered to know her own mind, and she thought that by planning marriage to a family friend, she was doing what her father and grandfather wanted. But as the engagement progressed and Jude grew smarter, she came to see Webb as a money-grubbing pain in the neck, too eager to marry into her family. Daddy and Grandpa, having spent almost no time around him, had never seen that greedy quality in him. She assumed they had been so eager for her to marry, they had been dazzled by Webb and his father's brownnosing.

Beyond greed, Webb Henderson had other traits that had both shocked and appalled her, among them, control issues and selfishness and a streak of willfulness. No one had ever tried to control her in the ways Webb had attempted. But her Strayhorn stubbornness had won out, and in spite of her family, she had managed to free herself of Webb.

She didn't think about him much these days. She had ended the relationship, to Daddy and Grandpa's chagrin, without discussing it with them. They might not realize it, but she had saved them, as well as herself, from future pain and consternation. She had no doubt she had done the right thing.

She steered her eyes away from Webb's picture. She could scarcely stand to look at him.

4

"I was in town for a minute," Jude said to her father. "Then I went to Suzanne's." Even to her own ears, her day sounded boring and empty.

She rarely told Daddy when she visited Jake, though she knew her father didn't hate him. The Strayhorn family had supported his run for sheriff and contributed heavily to his campaign. And Jake hadn't turned down their money or changed his name. Still, very few words about him ever were voiced in the Circle C house.

"How's Truett Breedlove doing these days?" Daddy asked. "Haven't seen him around town lately."

Jude swallowed another baby sip of her strong drink. The ranch had an intermittent relationship with Suzanne's father in that he sometimes hauled Circle C cattle. "On the road a lot, I think."

Daddy came from the bar, sat down on a nearby chair and drew on his cigar. He shook his head as a swirl of sweet smoke encircled him. "He spends so much time in that truck, somebody'll find him dead in it one of these days."

Could be, Jude thought. "It's what he's done all his life, Daddy."

But Suzanne's father wasn't what was on Jude's mind. "Listen, since I'm sort of at loose ends until I have to get ready for school, I thought I might ride with you next week and help with the weaning. I could help separate the calves."

The weaning process would start on Monday. Calves born in February and March now weighed six hundred pounds or so. Old enough to graze, they would be parted from their mothers, loaded into trailers and relocated into their own pasture miles away. Allowing them to continue nursing was a drain on the strength and health of their pregnant mothers.

Some of the larger ranches used helicopters to round up the cattle, but Grandpa and Daddy believed it was more expensive than manual labor and caused undue stress on the pregnant cows. With the price of fuel skyrocketing, she didn't disagree about the cost. She had opinions that conflicted with theirs on several facets of the cattle operation, but she understood their preference for using men on the ground for roundups. She, too, liked the idea of good cowboys on good horses flushing the cows and calves out of the brush and arroyos, then driving them from remote corners of the ranch. They were preserving a practice that was more than a hundred years old. It also provided the chance to "see" the ranch. With 469 square miles under fence, there were many parts of the Circle C no one went near for months, even years.

Daddy sipped his drink before answering. Jude had discussed ranch chores with him often enough to know he was framing a rebuttal. She had tried a dozen approaches to making a case for being allowed to play a greater role in the ranch's operation and had made no inroads into Daddy's and Grandpa's thinking. But she refused to give up.

"Why spend all day on a horse out in the hot sun?" he said. "If you need something to do before school starts, darlin', go up to Santa Fe and go shopping. Take the plane and go over to Dallas for some R and R."

"I haven't done anything to exert myself since school was out," she said. "I don't think I need R and R. I wish you'd let me work the cows with you. I can be of some help."

Her father sighed and adjusted his silver wire-rimmed

glasses. "Jude, I just don't understand *why* you want to do that. It's man's work. Most girls don't—"

She interrupted him by leaning forward and looking him in the eye. "Daddy, I'm not a girl. I'm twenty-nine years old. Why did you teach me to ride and rope if you never intended for me to do it?"

His eyes lowered to the contents of his glass, an indication his mind was closed to the idea. "Most young ladies, then. Most don't want to get on a horse and spend a day sweating in the sun with a bunch of cowhands." He swirled the ice cubes in his drink, looked up and gave her a smile. "They'd rather get prettied up and go out on dates."

Jude studied her father's profile as he tilted his head back and drained his glass. She had often wondered if that had been his perception of women his entire life. That description apparently fit the two he had married.

His first wife and Jude's mother, Vanessa, had spent most of her time getting "prettied up," according to Jude's great-grandmother, Penelope Ann. Even Grandpa had said Vanessa had an obsessive preoccupation with her appearance. The story Grammy Pen had told was that Daddy met Vanessa O'Reilly when she came from Connecticut to interview for a teaching job. The woman took one look at the Strayhorn holdings and decided to stay. Grammy Pen also said Daddy was lucky she left. Jude's great-grandmother had never minced words.

If Daddy felt the same about his first wife as Grandpa and Grammy Pen did, he had never said so in Jude's presence. If he knew where she was or what had happened to her, he hadn't mentioned that, either. The rough life in West Texas was too much for her to bear, was the excuse he gave for Vanessa O'Reilly abandoning her husband and infant Jude forever.

To Jude's knowledge, the bitch had never been in touch with Daddy again. Or with Jude herself. That was just fine, Jude thought. She had grown up perfectly well without her. Daddy and Grandpa and her other grandparents had provided all the parenting she needed. Long ago she had labeled her mother an irresponsible nitwit, a coward and a pantywaist, and a few more choice names unfit for use in public.

Then there was Daddy's second wife, Karen. She spent her time going out on dates all right. Dates with Daddy's youngest brother, Ike, who was Jake's father. Ike and Karen Strayhorn had died together in a drunken, grinding car wreck on a desolate rural road when Jude was seven and Jake was fourteen. A generation later, the family was still recovering from the pain and scandal that had ensued.

Another mark chalked up to the Campbell Curse, Grammy Pen had stated. According to her, the incident had been caused by excessive undisciplined behavior by two people who kept no check on their appetites. Jude was grown before she figured out that Grammy Pen hadn't been talking about food.

Water over the dam, Jude thought now. She missed her great-grandmother, who had passed at age ninety-five, just four years ago. "I want to feel useful, Daddy."

"But sweetheart, you're useful. You help me buy good bulls. Your research and knowledge are more help than you'll ever know."

"That's no big deal," she said.

And it wasn't. It wasn't even a challenge. Her knowledge came from her education in biology and genetics. Most of her research and her contacts all over the Southwest and West came via her computer and the telephone. If she decided to go outside the ranch to acquire a bull, she could locate him and spot his quality as a sire with a glance at his registration papers and his statistics. She could make deals to buy with one eye closed and one hand tied behind her back. She kept such thorough records on premium bulls, rarely did she ever have to actually see one standing in a pasture somewhere to know if he was worth considering.

The corners of Daddy's mouth lifted into a smile that led to a chuckle. "You might not think so, but if I didn't have you to do it, I'd have to do it myself. And as you keep reminding me, I'm a klutz on the computer."

Jude smiled and shrugged. "You just haven't tried to learn to use the computer."

"If managing the bull herd isn't enough, look at the work you do at the school, teaching these harebrained kids around here a little science. You work with your horses. You've got ol' Patch in the best shape he's ever been in. The paint horse show's coming up in Fort Worth. Why don't you take him over there and show him off a little?"

He referred to her paint stallion. Patch's snow-white coat was marked with large black patches so perfect, he looked as if he had been painted with a brush. A tobiano paint, his bloodline went all the way back to the 1870s and one of the original Circle C stallions her great-great-great-grandfather had purchased from the Comanche. If not for Patch's illustrious bloodline, he would have been gelded and sold as some dude's pleasure horse. He was a fine horse all right, and he met the ranch's criteria for being a good using horse, except for one fact. Ranch hands preferred solid-color horses.

"He is in good shape, but he can't compete in those events. I haven't trained him to be a show horse."

"Don't they have a team penning round? Why, smart as Patch is, he could do that one on three legs."

The team penning event required a team of three riders who had practiced together. Jude laughed, rising to her feet. She carried her glass to the bar's small counter and dumped her ice cubes into the sink. "Oh, Daddy. What am I going to do with you? I can't compete in team penning. I'm not part of a team. Patch is a cow horse and he knows it. He wants to do real work." She returned to her father's chair and wrapped her arms around his shoulders from behind, taking in again the scent of Aramis and cigars, now mixed with good whiskey. "Let me help with the weaning and I'll show you just how good he's gotten at cutting calves."

Her father patted her forearm. "Jude, honey, weaning's a hard, dirty job. And sometimes it's dangerous."

Jude didn't disagree. At the Circle C, weaning was an age-old, fast-moving process that cowhands, under Daddy's direction, had made as efficient as it could possibly be while dealing with dimwitted animals that had a powerful instinct to bunch together in herds. She had never dwelled on the dangerous part of ranch chores. It was a given that riding or handling animals that outweighed humans several times over carried an element of risk. "Getting dirty has never bothered me, and I'm not afraid."

"I know you're not," Daddy said. "I didn't raise you to be afraid of anything. But it makes an awful awkward situation having you out there with the hands. They feel like they need to look out for you and protect you. I don't want you putting yourself or one of them in harm's way."

The sentiment touched Jude, as it always did. She could even see his point. No ranch had ever had a better manager than J. D. Strayhorn, and no daughter had ever had a kinder, better father, she was certain. And because she was certain, she would go far out of her way never to hurt him. Giving up, she sighed. "Okay. I get the point."

A soft rap sounded on the door. "Come in," Daddy said.

The door opened and Windy's kitchen helper announced supper.

Daddy stood, and his thick, solid arm hooked around Jude's shoulders, a symbol of the protected life he had provided her. "Let's go eat, punkin. I've had a long day. I'm tired."

She didn't doubt it. He got up at four a.m. every day, seven days a week. They walked side by side through the wide tiled hallway to the dining room, his shielding arm still around her shoulders.

The dining room was a large, open room, with a high ceiling, a tile floor and rough-finished white plaster walls decorated with original watercolors and oil paintings. The collector of Western art was Jude's father. He owned origi-

nals from many of the better-known Western artists. Some
of the canvases had been painted on this ranch as well as
other well-known Texas ranches. A few of the artists had
dined in this room.

A long oak table with a dozen leather chairs sat in the
center of the room. Above it, a custom-made wrought-iron
chandelier gave off a soft golden light and warm ambience.

Supper at the Circle C was often a surprise—not the
menu, but the company. Daddy and Grandpa were always
present, but half the time, one of them invited one or several
of the hands or someone from town. Or some old friend
would stop by just in time for supper.

Jude believed both Grandpa and Daddy invited people
in for supper because they were lonely men. Nowadays,
they were lonely *old* men. They were both in great shape
physically, but Daddy was sixty and Grandpa was eighty-
four.

They heard footsteps, and Grandpa came into the room
alone. Tonight it appeared only the three of them would be
eating. Jude walked over and kissed her grandfather's crin-
kled, weathered cheek. "Hey, Grandpa."

The patriarch slid an arm around her waist. "Judith Ann.
Have you had a busy day? I noticed your truck was gone all
day long."

Not much gets past Grandpa, Jude thought with amuse-
ment. "Yes, sir," she answered. She had always addressed
him as "sir." Most people did. She straightened his bolo tie.
It was a gold horseshoe design. "I was visiting friends in
town."

They took their seats. Grandpa sat at the head of the
table. She usually sat on Grandpa's left and Daddy sat on his
right, unless one of the hands dined with them. In that case,
she gave up her seat to the hand.

Behind Grandpa hung an enlarged blurry and grainy photograph of Jude's great-great-great-grandfather, Jefferson
Davis Campbell, standing shoulder to shoulder with the legendary Comanche chief Quanah Parker. Her ancestor wore a

three-piece suit, a tie and a big hat. The Comanche chief wore Native American clothing typical of the day and a long braid. Her ancestor had done something the U.S. government never succeeded in doing—negotiating in good faith and ultimately doing business with the fierce Comanche. Jude had looked upon the photograph every day she had spent in this ranch house, and seeing it never failed to give her a few seconds' pause.

The three of them bowed their heads and closed their eyes, and Grandpa gave thanks in his gravelly drawl and asked the Lord to provide rain. None of them were regular churchgoers, but that didn't mean they were ungrateful for the bounty that had been bestowed upon them. Long ago, Jude's great-great-grandfather, Roslyn Shaffer Campbell, and his siblings had built the first church building in Lockett.

After the prayer, Windy and Irene brought out hot platters of sizzling sliced beef, grilled vegetables and condiments, including hot peppers and sliced jalapeños, and they started filling their plates. Grandpa might be old, but he hadn't lost his taste for spicy food.

"I heard you hired a new man," Grandpa said to Daddy as they dug in to the meal.

Jude was constantly amazed that even at his age, Grandpa continued to concern himself with the ranch hands Daddy hired. For that matter, she was amazed Daddy didn't allow the wagon boss to hire the help. Strayhorn Corp had all sorts of management types doing different things—an accountant in charge of the money, a wrangler in charge of the remuda, a chuck wagon boss in charge of food and stores, a vet with a sophisticated clinic and lab to oversee the care and insemination of horses and treat sick livestock, and a wagon boss in charge of the ranch hands and the work with the cattle. Yet for some reason, Daddy and Grandpa involved themselves in the hiring of every individual who worked at the ranch. She couldn't fault the policy. Many cowhands stayed with the Circle C for years, even lifetimes.

"Where'd you find him?" Grandpa asked, using his knife to arrange his meal in different sections instead of rolling it into a tortilla the way most people ate fajitas. Ever fascinating to Jude, Grandpa ate with his knife.

"Margie Wallace's nephew," Daddy answered.

Jude's stomach lurched and she dropped her fork. It clattered against her plate and fell to the floor. She scooted her chair back quickly and picked it up.

Daddy held his fajita halfway between his plate and his mouth. "You okay, sweetheart?

She got to her feet. "Yes, uh, I'm fine. I'll just go to the kitchen and get another fork."

Her heartbeat had kicked up, and she was glad to remove herself from the table. In the kitchen, Irene handed her a clean fork and she drew a quick deep breath before returning to the dining room. Suddenly supper had become more interesting than usual. Typically Jude listened only casually to the conversational back-and-forth between Daddy and Grandpa about the ranch's employees. Tonight, she intended to take note of every word.

"He isn't going to work her place?" Grandpa was asking as Jude reclaimed her seat, the image of Brady Fallon's smile and perfect teeth vivid in her memory. Her earlier conversation in town with Jake jumped into her mind.

"Says he is," Daddy said. "Don't know how it's gonna work out. He's strapped for cash."

"He wouldn't be the one who was around here as a boy, always with Ike's boy—"

"Uh, yessir," Daddy said, laying his fajita on his plate and looking intently at Grandpa. "I didn't know if you'd remember him."

A loud silence followed. Jude waited, almost holding her breath. She couldn't recall ever hearing her father say his youngest brother's name, and had rarely heard Grandpa say it. She had never heard a discussion of Ike Strayhorn and his family or of Daddy's second wife, Karen. Other than the scant information gleaned from Grammy Pen, Jude had no idea what kind of relationship Daddy and his brother might have had before the fatal accident that had altered life at the Circle C.

"We want to be sure to keep an eye on what happens there," Grandpa said after a long pause. "Margie damn near let that place go to brush. It'll take some doin' to clean it up."

Jude had the same opinion of the 6-0 pastures. Fighting back the insidious juniper and mesquite was a job the Circle C's brush-removal crew worked at year-round. But obviously Margie Wallace hadn't been able to stay on top of it.

"The old house ought to be torn down," Grandpa said.

"He's gonna live in it," Daddy replied.

"Is he a family man?"

"No, sir. Says he's divorced."

"Then why isn't he moving into the bunkhouse? It's more convenient, Jasper, if the unmarried hands live in the bunkhouse."

"I offered that to him," Daddy said, "but he says he'll drive over every day."

Grandpa shook his head, his eyes hard. Jude had seen the look many times when something displeased him. "Jasper, those hands get their breakfast, pick their mounts and are horseback before daylight. It'll be a bad situation if they have to wait for somebody to come to work."

Her grandfather's attitude struck Jude as odd and even more narrow-minded than usual. Most of the hands were married, with families. They didn't live in the bunkhouse. They either lived in one of the ranch's many houses or drove to work from some other home every day. Some even lived in town. Though breakfast was served at four forty-five a.m., she had rarely heard a complaint about someone being late and holding things up.

"Dad," her father said, "I'm on top of it, okay? Just let me handle it. If it becomes a problem, I'll simply tell Fallon he has to move on. But I think he'll make a good hand." He picked up his fajita again, prepared to go on with his meal.

"He's been doing some cowboying off and on for a couple of years over in Stephenville, so he's not afraid of the work. And he's a college man. Graduated from Tarleton with a BBA. Got some smarts between his ears. He asked me for an opportunity and I gave him one." Daddy bit into his food again.

"Just remember this, Jasper," Grandpa said. "If he decides to sell, we want to be the buyer. That fifteen sections would square up our line on that south side. I tried to buy it from Margie after Harry died, but the cantankerous old woman wouldn't sell it to me."

A light came on in Jude's mind. This was the root of Grandpa's displeasure with Daddy's hiring Brady Fallon and with him not living in the bunkhouse, where Grandpa might be able to keep tabs on what he was doing. Land acquisition was so much a part of the Circle C's history, Jude supposed it had become almost like a gene. She felt the corner of her mouth quirk at Grandpa calling Margie Wallace an old woman. At her death, she was younger than Grandpa.

"I know, Dad," Daddy said.

"You keep on top of the situation, you hear, Jasper?" Grandpa tapped his forefinger on the table as he talked.

Jude could see that if she had been the one to acquire the 6-0's land, it would have caused a much bigger family explosion than she had imagined. A part of her was glad the transaction had fallen on its face.

"I will, Dad. I understand," Daddy said.

And what did *that* mean? Exactly *what* did Daddy understand? Did Grandpa want the 6-0's new owner to fail so he could get the land? The notion wasn't far-fetched. Time and again Jude had seen him prove his pragmatism. For all of his reputation for doing good works, contributing to the community and being a caring employer, she had seen him be downright ruthless when it came to something that affected the Circle C's holdings.

Daddy's assurance to Grandpa was unclear, but one thing Jude knew was that he and Grandpa were like-minded. She believed her father was a fair man, but if Grandpa wished it, Daddy did it, sometimes even before Grandpa made his wishes known. She also knew that Grandpa and Daddy, though they might appear to be low-key, were both powerful and influential men, with tentacles crawling into unlikely nooks and crannies. And not just in Texas.

Jude had lost her appetite. What did her grandfather's attitude really mean? She felt an inexplicable concern for Brady Fallon. Anyone could see he had his hands full trying to put the old 6-0 ranch back together. But now he was facing another harsh reality without even knowing it and an adversary not of his own making.

5

At the end of supper, Daddy followed his usual routine by retiring to his suite for some reading, then his usual early bedtime.

Grandpa invited Jude to accompany him on his evening stroll around the barns and the barn lots. She liked walking with him. Often they walked with long but comfortable silences between them. But sometimes Grandpa would be in a talkative mood and their evening strolls would be rife with information. She traded her sandals for boots, he put on his Stetson and away they went.

He walked with his wrists crossed behind his back, his step slow and careful. She had noticed lately that he had become smaller in his old age. Once she had thought him as tall as a giant, but now his shoulders slumped and he was the same height as she. She plucked a tall blade of summer grass and adjusted her own step to his, as together they ambled across the backyard, across the wide caliche driveway and on toward the barns.

The sinking sun had lost some of its heat and light. It painted the sky in slashes of purple and gold and cast the landscape in soft amber. A bank of deep blue clouds bloomed in great billows in the west. "Cloud's got a bellyful of rain," Grandpa said. "Looks like it's coming our way."

Spring and early summer often brought violent storms, but along with them came the precious rain that plains ranchers and farmers prayed for and cherished. Grandpa never relied on TV or radio for the weather forecast. He simply looked at the sky and smelled the air. "I see that," Jude said, hoping to someday be able to look at the sky and sense the oncoming weather.

Beneath the clouds and off in the distance, long twin mesas rose from the flat plain, a deep gray silhouette at this time of day. Grandpa had told her many times that those tablelands had been sacred sites for the Comanche. Willard County was located well within what the Spanish explorers had called Comanchería and had been the home turf of the Quahadi, Quanah Parker's band.

Though the legend of Quanah Parker's Anglo mother, Cynthia Ann Parker, and his Comanche chief father, Peta Nocona, was a tragic one, Jude loved it. She thought it a true love story that had produced a mighty leader. She might teach high school science rather than history, but if her students hadn't heard the story, she always told how Cynthia Ann Parker had been kidnapped as a child by the Comanche, then later had fallen deeply in love with Peta Nocona, and how she had starved herself to death after the army's rescue separated her from him and their son Quanah. Jude believed people should know and respect those who had lived here before them.

The storm cloud chased a cool breeze toward them that brushed Jude's cheeks, ruffling her skirt and swirling her hair across her face. It carried the scent of summer grass and unsullied air and even the hoped-for rain. With a pop and a screech, the windmill fan shifted, catching the oncoming wind. The fan began to race, driving the well's sucker rod frantically up and down, pumping a gush of water from deep within the earth.

A fierce love of all that surrounded her filled Jude's chest, like nothing else ever had. She drew a deep breath, as if she could take every sight and sound and smell into her body and her brain and save them forever.

"It's a good time of year," Grandpa said, a dramatic pronouncement from a man of few words.

Jude knew the love of the land was in her blood. It had come from her grandfather and all of the Scots-Irish family preceding him. She looked over at him, knowing he would soon leave them, and she felt bereft.

As they neared the fenced pasture behind the barn, the longhorn cows he kept as pets stood near the fence. The waning sunlight showed the wide spans of their horns as golden. Two of the cows thrust their noses through the fence rails in curiosity. Grandpa walked over and talked to them in a low voice as he gave their faces a good rub with his gnarled fingers, his affection for them palpable. "Cattle like these were the beginning of everything, Judith Ann."

"I know, Grandpa." Jude, too, rubbed their faces. The cows and their three- and four-foot racks of horns looked frightening, but these were gentler than pet dogs.

"Without their strength and toughness, there might've been no such thing as a cattle industry and our family wouldn't be blessed with all we have."

Jude had heard him say this many times. "I know, Grandpa."

But longhorn cattle and their contribution to the cattle industry were of little interest to Jude this evening. After visiting Jake in town earlier and hearing the exchange between her grandfather and father at the supper table, Jude had Brady Fallon on her mind, and Jake and her cousin Cable and the days of their childhood. The urge to say what she was thinking overcame her. "Grandpa, did you not want Daddy to hire Brady Fallon?"

"Jasper has been hiring our hands for years, Judith Ann. He can hire anyone he wants to. Why do you ask?"

"I just got the impression at supper that you were unhappy that Daddy hired Mrs. Wallace's nephew."

"No. I have nothing against young Fallon."

"But you said you wanted the 6-0 land to square the Circle C. Were you mad because he got the land?"

"No. The 6-0 was Margie's to do with as she saw fit. But not selling it to me at the market price when she had the chance was poor judgment on her part. Her young nephew would've been better off inheriting the money. He can't do what he's set out to do with that old ranch. No man without resources could."

Resources. When Grandpa used that word, he meant money. Grandpa thought in terms of dollars most of the time.

"But no matter," he said. "He'll figure out he has to sell. We'll be ready to buy him out when the time comes. Strike while the iron is hot, Judith Ann. I learned that from my father, who was a brilliant businessman. I've already alerted Bob Anderson at the bank in Abilene."

Jude angled a startled look at her grandfather, thinking of what she had heard of her great-grandfather, mostly from people outside the family. Many in Willard County viewed Franklin Bennett Strayhorn as something less than a brilliant businessman. Greedy ruthless shyster was the more common opinion. A few said his early demise from heart failure had been a blessing. "I thought Grandpa Frank was a lawyer."

"He was that, too. And he eventually became a stockman."

By marrying lucky, Jude thought. That's what the local old-timers said, and she believed them, even if Frank Strayhorn *was* a blood relative. Grandpa's mother, Penelope Ann Campbell, had met Frank Strayhorn when she went away to school in Dallas. She was a sheltered young woman who left a devoutly religious home. Handsome and persuasive, Frank Strayhorn swept an unsophisticated girl off her feet and married her. Eventually he persuaded her God-fearing father, Roslyn Shaffer Campbell, to tell the only other living Campbell heir, Grammy Pen's aunt Martha Alice, who had married a Dallasite and rarely returned to Willard County, that the family's West Texas land was worthless.

Frank Strayhorn then brokered a deal whereby Roslyn

Campbell purchased Martha Alice's interest in the land and cattle for pennies. If Martha Alice had ever realized the falsehood that had fostered the dispossession of her hereditary right, she never acknowledged it, and she never returned to West Texas again in her life. Upon Frank Strayhorn's death, Penelope Ann Campbell Strayhorn stood as the sole heir to the three hundred thoudand–acre Campbell ranching empire and its thousands of head of cattle and horses.

And now, as Grammy Pen's only offspring, Grandpa had inherited all of it.

This story had been told to Jude by none other than their cook, Windy Arbuckle, and embellished by a few of the other older hands who had worked on the ranch for years. There was a benefit to not holding yourself above the people who were loyal to you, and that benefit was that they felt free to communicate with you.

"But Grandpa, how can you know Brady Fallon has no resources?"

"I know his mother and his father, Judith Ann."

At some point in the course of this conversation, a dawning had crept up on Jude. Now she realized why the Abilene banker had been so nervous about *her* attempting to buy the 6-0. The banker's concern had nothing to do with fearing she might make a financial blunder with her trust-fund money. It had everything to do with the fact that Grandpa intended to acquire the 6-0 himself. How could she have been so naive as to not figure that out?

Her offer for the old ranch would have been a million dollars, a substantial chunk of her trust fund. It was a fair offer for neglected rangeland in Willard County. If Brady Fallon found himself in financial straits—and Jude didn't question her grandfather's and father's qualifications to make that determination—Grandpa and Daddy would be waiting to pounce like cougars. To get what they wanted at the price they wanted to pay, all they had to do was wait—wait and patiently watch Brady Fallon twist in the wind until the rope that held him broke.

Who had spoken to her more often of the virtues of patience than the two men who had raised her?

A sour taste formed in Jude's mouth and a slow anger began to crawl around within her. It wasn't fair. Brady Fallon had to be a good person or Jake wouldn't call him a friend. Sympathy for the 6-0's new owner flew through Jude, warring with family loyalty, and she couldn't explain the conflicting emotions even to herself.

"I know the Fallon family," Grandpa went on. He picked up her slim, smooth hand with his knobby one and patted it, smiling. "Never forget, Judith Ann, the apple doesn't fall far from the tree."

She thought of the many stories she had heard of Frank Strayhorn's underhanded shenanigans and wondered just how true that old saying might be. She leveled an assessing look at her grandfather. More important than what he had said about the 6-0 ranch and its new owner was what he hadn't said.

The longhorns moved away from the fence and began to snuffle through hay on the ground. She and Grandpa circled the small pasture in silence, then started back toward the house. Her mood had changed. She no longer felt quite as conciliatory to her grandfather's age as she had been inclined to earlier, no longer felt like biting her tongue so as not to offend him.

The way Daddy had cut off the conversation at supper when Grandpa mentioned Uncle Ike nagged at her and reminded her of things that had piqued her curiosity for years. If not for Grammy Pen, she would have precious little knowledge of the affair between her stepmother and Daddy's brother. It was possible she wouldn't even have known the circumstances of their deaths if Grammy Pen hadn't told her. The locals might blather on about Frank Strayhorn, who had been dead for thirty years, but when it came to Grandpa and his three sons, they talked less freely.

"I wish I could remember more about my uncle Ike," she said, lifting her hand and letting the breeze take the blade of grass she had been toying with from her fingers. "And my stepmother."

Long moments passed before Grandpa spoke. "When it came to the work, when he set his mind to it, Ike was as good as there was. But he could be as bad as there was if he wanted to. He had a wildness to him. He wasn't a steady hand like your daddy."

Jude waited for him to speak of her stepmother, Karen. Or of Jude's mother, Vanessa. Or of someone. But he kept his silence.

"Did Daddy and Uncle Ike get along before . . . you know, before the—"

"Not well," her grandfather answered before she could finish asking her question.

No one ever answered a question or finished a sentence when it came to conversation about her uncle and stepmother. "They were too different," Grandpa added. She waited again, but he said no more.

Dark had descended by the time they returned to the house, and the sounds of crickets had risen in a steady rhythm in the nighttime emptiness. Grandpa said good night and shuffled to his ground-floor suite. Jude checked the doors and windows, preparing for the coming storm.

She made her way upstairs, her thoughts continuing to trouble her. She tried to imagine what it must have been like for Daddy and Grandpa living in the same house for the past twenty-four years. Neither of them was great at communicating feelings. The death of a son and a wife, their lives ended while engaged in an illicit tryst, had to have caused some kind of schism between her father and grandfather. But if so, they kept it well hidden. She assumed they succeeded in getting along so well due to having a mutual interest in the ranch and the Campbell-Strayhorn legacy—and the fact that the family history was more powerful than they were. From what she had seen, the history had usually proved itself to be more enduring than mere mortals.

Thunder had begun to rumble in the distance by the time

she reached her room. She usually spent quiet evenings reading or watching TV. This evening, she changed into her pajamas and selected a book published in the forties about the great old ranches of the rolling plains of West Texas. She settled into the overstuffed chair where she always read, but couldn't concentrate on the book. Seeing Brady Fallon, followed by learning who he was from Jake, then trying to extract information from Grandpa about Jake's father and her own stepmother—all of it had pushed into her thoughts and wouldn't relent.

She closed her eyes and rested her head against the chair's back, letting the past take over her mind. She had only shards of memory of those days following the fatal accident. She had a vague image of Grandma Ella, Grandpa's wife, weeping and screaming. Grammy Pen had taken Jude into her room and made her put on a dress and black shoes—and white socks with lace on them. In her mind's eye, Jude could still see her feet in those shoes and socks but had no recollection of the color of the dress. Someone had taken her out of the house and given her cookies and sat with her on the back porch. All these years, she thought it had been Jake, but could it have been Brady Fallon?

She remembered melancholy hanging in the house like a heavy black curtain, people coming and going. Tears and woeful cries. A service in the church in town and the preacher talking forever. Grandpa weeping. But perhaps that memory was confused with Grandma Ella's passing unexpectedly from complications from gall bladder surgery a few months later. Another funeral and a lot of food.

The clearest memory she had of her father from those days was of a loud and fierce argument he'd had with Grandpa and Grandma Ella over where her uncle Ike should be buried. In the end, he had been laid to rest in the family cemetery. To this day, Jude didn't know what the alternate choice might have been. Her stepmother had been buried somewhere in Abilene by her own family. Jude had never known where.

After Ike's funeral, Jake and his mother faded away, almost as if they had never existed, and Jude had lost touch with them until Jake returned to Lockett a few years ago. She was aware he had joined the army at a young age and later worked for the Dallas Police Department but knew little else about him.

Thinking of how unforeseen events altered life in dramatic ways and sent people on irreversible courses, she drifted to sleep.

The tempest arrived at midnight, rumbling and blowing and throwing rain against the windowpanes in great slaps. She loved storms, loved nature's display of power and might. She awoke with a start, crawled into bed and listened. She dozed, but the storm kept her adrift in a state of half wakefulness.

The next thing she knew, it was daylight. She had missed the end of the thunderstorm and had overslept. But that didn't mean she didn't have a plan for the day.

After the storm, expecting humidity along with the heat, she dressed in jeans and a camisole with spaghetti straps and made her way to the kitchen, where she found Windy and Irene already at work on the noon meal.

"Mornin', Judith Ann," Windy said without looking up from his task. With hands the size of hams, he was doing something delicate with Jell-O. The creation under construction looked fragile.

Irene came to her, smiling and wiping her hands on a towel. "*Buenos días*, Yudee." She pronounced Jude's name as if it had two syllables, replacing the hard American *J* with a soft spanish *Y*. "You want the breakfast?" She spread her arms wide as if encompassing the world. *"Bien grande?"*

Jude regarded their Mexican help with great affection. In broken English, a Mexican housekeeper had explained menstruation to her. A different Mexican housekeeper had taught her to braid her hair. Her daily life was filled with small tasks she might not have learned to perform well, if at all, without the Mexican housekeepers who had always been employed by the ranch.

Jude couldn't keep from laughing at Irene's pronunciation of her name, knowing the letter *J*'s sound wasn't commonly used in Spanish. Trying to speak English was Irene's attempt to be like other Americans. She had grown up in a non-English-speaking home, so what little English she knew had come from taking lessons at the church in town and working with Windy. Since Windy probably hadn't gone past eighth grade and had been a ranch hand at the Circle C for more than forty years, his speech was mostly rural cowboy slang and a litany of cusswords. Exactly what Irene might be learning from him, Jude didn't dare guess.

"No, thanks," she told Irene. "I'll just have a bowl of cereal." She prepared a bowl of corn flakes with milk and sugar and backed against the counter edge to eat it. "Who's coming to eat dinner?" she asked Windy. The noon meal had always been "dinner" and the evening meal had always been "supper" at the Circle C.

"Clary Harper and Doc Barrett got some AQHA folks coming down from Amarillo today."

Ah, politics and horse breeding, Jude thought. Clarence Harper was the horse wrangler who took care of the remuda, and Dr. John Barrett was the ranch's vet. With someone from the American Quarter Horse Association present, the dinner meeting, she suspected, would be about quarter-horse breeding, thus artificial insemination and embryo transfer. She knew the Pitchfork had a couple of highbred mares they wanted Sandy Dandy to breed with. And by now, some of the other ranches with breeding programs might have ready mares, too. Sandy Dandy was the ranch's latest superstud. He was a powerful, award-winning stallion with a good disposition except when it came to the mares. With them, he was tough and dominant and brooked no rebellion.

Jude had mixed emotions about transferring embryos from impregnated mares into surrogate mothers. She appreciated the advancement of the science and the positive benefits, but the whole process flew so blatantly in the face of what nature intended that it made her uncomfortable.

And it made her even more uncomfortable knowing that, usually, the motive for doing it was making more money off the horses' bloodlines.

She often wondered if Thoroughbred horse owners were the ones who had the right idea, allowing highbred horses to be registered only if reproduced as a result of live cover. Every time she had those thoughts, she accused herself of being as old-fashioned as Daddy and Grandpa. With live cover, bacteria and disease could more readily be introduced into a mare's reproductive tract. Stallions were aggressive and could be mean during copulation. If a mare resisted, live cover could turn into a violent event and cause injury to both stud and mare. Artificial insemination was safer all around.

Though the Circle C's breeding program had produced several famous horses, money wasn't what drove it. The primary purpose had always been to produce the best and strongest ranch horses possible and maintain the ranch's remuda at approximately a hundred head. Consequently, most of the male horses were gelded and the best of the fillies were added to the herd of broodmares. But if a male foal had outstanding bloodlines or looked as if he might grow to be a superior animal, he was kept as a stud. The Circle C couldn't keep every horse that was born, so no one balked at selling a colt or a filly for racing or cutting or rodeo, or even pleasure.

After the breeding conversation, the men would sit at the table and smoke cigars and probably get into a more pointed discussion of breeding the stallion Sandy Dandy to some particular mare. Several of his offspring had been doing well in various cutting competitions.

She told Windy to include her in lunch. No one had invited her specifically, but she lived here. She didn't need an invitation.

She finished her cereal and placed her dish in the sink. Just in case someone later wondered about her whereabouts, she told Windy, "I'm going to town to run some errands."

Twenty minutes later, she rumbled across the 6-0's driveway.

6

The old Wallace house had no attached garage, but Jude saw the new owner's pickup parked under a metal shed that was rusting from the ground up and the roof down. It was located across the driveway from the house. The battered metal roof looked as if it might collapse onto the truck at any minute. She parked her own pickup near the house's sagging front porch and slid out. She could hear thumps and thuds from behind the house and loud country-western music. She recognized Gretchen Wilson's voice belting out "Redneck Woman."

"Hellooo? Anybody home?"

When no one answered, she walked through the weedy side yard toward the barn, her boots rustling through the springing grass, the morning sun warming her bare shoulders. June was a great time to be alive in West Texas. She saw Brady Fallon walking away from the barn, carrying several long, wide boards.

"Morning," she called out, stuffing her hands into her jeans' back pockets as she walked toward him.

He didn't stop but continued a few more steps to a neat stack of long weathered boards similar to those he carried. He dropped his load on the ground, bent over and began to pick up the boards one at a time and lay them on the stack.

She stood in silence, unable to not watch him—the raw-boned lankiness of his body, the ripple of powerful muscle under the faded blue T-shirt he wore, his taut efficiency and smooth agility as he worked. The whole package exuded the epitome of energy and masculinity and sent a shiver all the way to her toes. She appreciated physical perfection in all animals, including humans.

He straightened. "What's up?"

She sensed the same edginess in him she had detected yesterday. With his eyes shadowed by the bill of his cap, she couldn't seem them clearly, but somehow she knew they were focused like lasers on her. The thought left her speechless for a few seconds. She hesitated, but then got around to saying, "Nothing much. I just came to talk a minute."

He pushed his cap back, yanked a red bandana from his back pocket and wiped his perspiring forehead. "About what?"

She removed her sunglasses and squinted up at him. "I sort of want to start over. When I came—"

"Hey, you've got brown eyes." He grinned as if he had discovered a secret.

"My whole family's eyes are brown, except for Jake. Does it matter?"

"I wondered. You had on those sunglasses yesterday." He gave a nod toward the sunglasses in her hand.

He had wondered about her eye color? What else had he wondered about her? The question threw her off track again. "Uh, when I came by yesterday, I thought you were a burglar. I didn't know Mrs. Wallace had left her place to someone."

"What did you think would happen to it?" He readjusted his cap, shadowing his eyes again.

"I don't know. I didn't think about it at all. I just saw the strange rig and . . ." *And what?* She was still distracted by his comment about her eye color and what it meant. She lifted her shoulders in a shrug. "Anyway, we're neighbors, so . . ." She shrugged again, the words she wanted to say still not coming to her. So she smiled. "And now I know who you are."

As he peeled off his leather gloves and stuffed them into his jeans' back pocket, his mouth eased into a near smile. "I have to admit, I didn't know who you were, either, until you said your name. Guess I should apologize."

She laughed, though nothing was funny. "No need. I didn't know you at all, even *after* you said your name."

"Not your fault. It's been about twenty years since I was around your folks' place." He planted his hands on his hips. "You probably would've been what, six or seven the last time I saw you?"

She couldn't say why, but she liked him. Was drawn to him. And it had nothing to do with his being the best-looking stranger who had shown up in Willard County in a while. Or maybe ever. "Jake refreshed my memory about those days."

Brady nodded. "Good guy, Jake. Known him a long time."

Jude looked around, trying not to be obvious in her scrutiny of the place. From where she stood, she could see the need for so much work, she wouldn't know where to start. No way could Brady Fallon—or anyone—cowboy five or six days a week for the Circle C and at the same time accomplish much on this old place. Even if he had the money, when would he find the time or energy? The Circle C hands worked long, exhausting days, many of them horseback all day long. She agreed with Grandpa. Brady's situation looked hopeless.

A hole had appeared in the side of the barn since she had seen it yesterday. She gestured toward it. "Whatcha doing?"

He looked back over his shoulder toward the leaning barn. "I'm gonna replace some of the studs. Probably put up some new siding. Try to keep it from collapsing."

"You're a carpenter, huh? Jake told me you used to be in the construction business."

He turned to her again, but she still couldn't see his eyes. "Yeah, I was in the construction business. But I'm not a carpenter. I think I can fix this barn, though."

Okay, if he was in the construction business but wasn't a carpenter, he had to be a management type. Daddy had said he had a BBA. She longed for him to mention his going to work as a cowhand at the Circle C. She did not want to be the one to bring it up.

"You, uh, need some help? On the barn siding, I mean."

"You volunteering?"

"Sure."

He didn't reply for a few seconds. He glanced away, then back at her. "Now, why would you do that? I'll bet you've never hammered a nail. Or done much work of any kind."

She bristled at the criticism. Another person who thought her an empty shirt. She had done plenty of work around the ranch, but she didn't want to debate the issue. "Look, before you just dismiss me, I can see you need help. I'm a capable person. And a fast learner. Besides, what have you got to lose? I don't see anyone else lined up to help you." She winced mentally at the tactless words.

He chuckled. "You got *that* right."

She lifted her arms and let them fall to her sides. "So put me to work."

"You're not dressed for work."

"This is what I wear all the time."

"You got any gloves? Got a long-sleeve shirt?"

"Not with me. You're not wearing a long-sleeve shirt yourself."

"But I'm tough."

She didn't doubt that.

He chewed on the inside of his jaw for a few beats, as if he were deciding what to do. "Okay. Be right back." He strode toward the house.

She had only a short wait before he returned carrying a plaid shirt and a new pair of leather gloves. While she shrugged into the shirt, he said, "I'll tear off the siding. The boards that are fit to keep, you can carry 'em over and stack 'em, okay? That'll save me a few steps. The ones that are too far gone, just throw over on that burn pile." He pointed toward a pile of debris.

The shirt smelled of laundry soap and the hem fell to just above her knees. The cuffs covered her fingertips. She began rolling them up, past her wrists. "Great." While he watched in silence, she finished the last cuff and pulled her hair from underneath the shirt collar. "Let's do it," she said, probably more brightly than necessary.

He continued to stare at her. "Yeah, let's do it," he said eventually. "Don't forget the gloves."

As the gap in the barn wall grew larger, the stack of salvable boards grew taller, the sun climbed higher and the temperature rose to blistering. Wearing a long-sleeve shirt, Jude was close to melting. Her whole body was damp with sweat, and her stomach had begun to feel empty.

She didn't know the time, but she could tell by the sun's position that it was near noon. She thought about dinner at the Circle C ranch house and wished she hadn't told Windy she would be there to eat. If he set a place for her and she didn't show up, Daddy and Grandpa would wonder where she was and what she might be doing, or worse yet, would fear she had run into some kind of trouble. She appreciated that they loved her and had always taken care of her, but sometimes their attention could be suffocating.

Beyond that concern was her internal debate over whether she should continue helping Brady Fallon after dinner and on into the afternoon. Though she wanted to stay, she also wanted to hear the dinner conversation among Daddy and Grandpa, the Circle C's vet and the representatives from the AQHA. Because she had tracked and studied the genetic history of many of the Circle C's horses, the breeding program was of great interest to her. But all of that seemed less important now than it had been earlier today, so she continued to stack boards.

Soon, Brady came over, removing his gloves. A sheen of sweat covered his face, and moisture showed in darker patches on his blue T-shirt. "You getting hungry?"

She straightened and pressed her own damp brow with her shirtsleeve. "Uh, well, kind of. All I had for breakfast was cereal."

"That's what I thought. You didn't leave home expecting to do any real work."

Her spine stiffened. There it was again. That subtle mockery and skepticism of her motives. She couldn't expect anything different, she supposed, when she didn't even know her motives herself. "I didn't know if you'd welcome my help."

"I can make us a sandwich."

If she were facing a firing squad, she couldn't explain the mysterious allure that made her say, "Okay."

The dinner decision made just that simply, she removed the gloves. "I need to get my purse out of my pickup, okay?" She didn't add that she also needed to call home.

"Just come in the front door," he replied, and started for the back door, leaving the boom box on. All morning, they had listened to a steady blare of country-western music, everything from Patsy Cline to Toby Keith.

"Would you like for me to turn off the radio?" she called to his back.

"Nah," he answered, and kept walking. "We're not gonna be gone that long."

She tramped to her pickup, pulled her cell phone from her purse and called the Circle C. The housekeeper, Lola Mendez, answered, and Jude told her she was tied up helping a friend in town and wouldn't be home for dinner after all. Daddy would assume she was helping Suzanne do something and wouldn't worry.

As she tucked her cell phone back into her purse, she acknowledged that her interest in Brady Fallon had now caused her to, uncharacteristically, fib to her family for the second time.

She stepped into the living room gingerly and found the air so cool against her heated body, she shivered. Her hearing followed a dull roar to a swamp cooler in the window.

She had never been inside the Wallace house, but she had been in the homes of many of Willard County's citizens. The county and the town were less than prosperous, with many of the residents elderly or Hispanic, living on incomes below the national poverty level. Most of the homes that weren't mobile homes reflected that. They were outdated and worn-out. Jude saw that the interior of Marjorie Wallace's house was no different.

Brady's voice came from the adjoining room. "Hope you like baloney and cheese."

She walked toward the voice, into the kitchen, and saw him soaping and washing his hands in the sink. A bare window over the sink let light into the kitchen and onto his face and hands.

"That's mostly what I eat these days," he said. "It's easy and it's cheap." He went to a refrigerator that had to be forty years old and laid his cap on top of it beside a radio.

"That's fine," she said, but she couldn't remember the last time she had eaten bologna. She felt a pinch of conscience. She had never had to consider the cost of food.

He gathered a jar of mayonnaise and a jar of mustard, a package of cheese, a package of lunch meat and a jar of pickles from the refrigerator and carried them to the counter in one load.

She thought of the meal Windy and Irene would be serving. With company there, it would probably be steak and all the trimmings. "I, uh, need to wash up, too." In fact, she had needed a stop in the bathroom for a while.

"Oh, sorry." He walked into the living room and pointed to his right. "This house just has one bathroom. It's up that hall."

He started back into the kitchen and she started into the living room. They nearly collided as they both tried to pass through the doorway at the same time. "Oh," she gasped, her shoulder brushing his chest as she dodged him.

"Oops." He stiffened, his back flat against the doorjamb.

"Sorry." For an instant, she felt the heat of his body and

smelled his scent, a mix of sweat and some kind of cologne. In that same instant she became even more acutely aware of his big, solid body, and she fought not to look down. Instead, she willed herself to look up, her face no more than a foot from his. His eyes locked on hers. Uncertain what she saw in them, she ducked her chin and stared at the heartbeat steadily pulsing at the neckband of his T-shirt. "I'll be back in a minute," she said.

A swarm of butterflies fluttered in her stomach all the way to the bathroom.

The bathroom had a lemony cleaning product smell and she noticed that everything—fixtures, walls and counter— appeared to be freshly scrubbed, though she saw abundant evidence of the wear and corrosion caused by hard water. Bad water was a West Texas blight. She had lost track of how often plumbing had been replaced in the Circle C ranch house, but she knew that to most Willard County residents, frequent plumbing replacement was an unaffordable extravagance. Most people just lived with plugged fixtures or perforated pipes until the inconvenience became an emergency.

When she returned to the kitchen, she saw two sandwiches sliced into neat halves on two plates on the table. A roll of paper towels lay in the middle of the table.

"Have a seat," he said. "Want a glass of milk?"

"Yes, please." She eased onto a chair at the table, relieved to sit down. Already, she was sore everywhere and the day was only half over. He was right in that she had never before done the kind of work she had done all morning. The boards were wide and heavy. Because they were also long, they were awkward to manhandle.

He poured two glasses of milk and set them on the table, then took a seat adjacent to hers. He tore two paper towel sheets from the roll and handed one to her, smiling. "Sorry, no napkins. This is the best I can do."

Jude had been a teacher in an underfunded public school full of students from low-income families that could scarcely afford paper towels, much less napkins. If Brady hadn't brought the substitution to her attention, she would hardly have noticed, though she had never seen the Circle C dining table without napkins. "No problem," she said, and looked into his face for a few extra seconds.

At last, she could really see his eyes and take the time to study them. And they were most interesting: sky blue irises surrounded by a navy blue ring. She found herself thinking of long lines of women and wondered why he and his wife divorced. Had he been unfaithful? Had he had a girlfriend? With his looks, he could have had a harem. The quality about him that fascinated her came to her in a eureka moment. He had a confidence that had nothing to do with his good looks, but everything to do with his maleness. He reminded her of a testosterone-driven stallion that just knew by instinct he was the boss horse the mares wouldn't reject.

"What do you hear from Cable?" he asked.

"Very little. I'm surprised you haven't run into him. He bought a rope-manufacturing company somewhere near Fort Worth. Lariats, you know?"

"There's several of those."

She was growing more impatient, waiting for him to reveal that he had hired on as a Circle C cowhand. Finally, she couldn't take it anymore, so as she usually did, she decided to appease her curiosity. "Daddy said you're going to work for the Circle C."

He sat back in his chair, just looking at her and chewing, as if he were peering inside her. She could see that tinge of mockery in his eyes again. He picked up his glass, and her eyes fixed on his corded neck as he swallowed a long drink of milk.

He set the empty glass back on the table but looked at his sandwich instead of her. "I was wondering when you were gonna get around to saying something. So that's what you're doing here. Being nosy."

"I'm not nosy. To tell you the truth, I don't know what I'm doing here. Daddy said you aren't starting until Monday."

"I told him I need to get over to Stephenville tomorrow and pick up my horses and the rest of my stuff."

"But the ranch will furnish your mounts. You don't have to ride your own horses."

"I don't intend to. But I want my horses here with me. A friend's been pasturing 'em for me. Now that I've got a place to keep 'em, I want to get 'em out of his way."

"How many horses do you have?"

"Three."

"Ranch horses?"

"Yep. Good ones."

They *would* be good ones. He just looked like the type of man who would have good horses. "I can't remember the last time I was in Stephenville."

He stopped chewing and looked at her again, wiping his mouth with a sheet of paper towel. "Don't tell me you're volunteering to help me move my stuff from Stephenville."

"Why not?"

He laughed.

"What's so funny?"

"Darlin', I appreciate the offer, but it's a job I can do easier by myself. Besides, even if I needed the help, J. D. Strayhorn would can me before I ever get started if he thought I hauled you with me over to Stephenville. Hell. I'm wondering what he might do if he knew you were here right now."

"He doesn't tell me what to do."

"Maybe not, but I'd bet my best saddle he doesn't want you fraternizing with the hired help."

Her father could never be called snobbish in his attitude about the men who worked for the Circle C, but he and Grandpa condoned her mixing with the male help only to a point. Daddy had always told her to stay away from the bunkhouse and not to invite trouble. She hadn't understood that as a child, but now that she was grown, she had to acknowledge that the practice was a good one. Other than the families who lived a distance away from the main house and the Mexican household help, all of whom were married, she was the only female on the place. Brady Fallon's insight into Daddy's and Grandpa's attitudes left her without a rebuttal.

"I've got the time right now," she said, "but in a few more weeks, I'll have to get ready for school."

"I thought you were out of school."

"High school. I teach biology. And help coach girls' sports."

"The hell you say."

"What's wrong with that?"

"Nothing. I'm just surprised is all."

"I have to do something. I don't want to be worthless. Look, I can see what you're trying to do here will be hard. I just think you can use all the help you can get." Just in time, she kept herself from saying, *I know you don't have any money. I know you can't afford to hire anyone.*

All at once she realized she had to be careful about what she said. She did want to help Brady Fallon. Her whole life, she had rallied around underdogs. But after what Grandpa had told her about his own plans for the 6-0, she couldn't betray his trust. *Damn.* She had put herself in a delicate position.

"This is gonna be a nonstop working trip, darlin'. I've got to clean out the trailer house where I've been living so somebody else can move in. That'll take me most of tomorrow. Sunday morning, I'll load up my horses and gear and come back."

She opened her palms and held his gaze, as if it were perfectly normal and usual for her to agree to an overnight trip with a cowboy she hardly knew. Well, it wasn't entirely true that she didn't know him. There was a childhood connection, and Jake had said he was a good guy. That was enough for her.

"Look, you're a grown woman," he said. "If you say your dad doesn't care what you do, I accept that, though I'm not sure I believe it. I guess you're welcome to go with me if you want to, but I don't mind telling you, I don't want your dad and granddad to know about it. I need that job at the Circle C. At least until I can figure out what to do next."

As if a stranger had taken control of her tongue, Jude said, "Great. And don't worry. Daddy won't know. I'll figure out something to tell him."

7

Jude dragged herself home from the 6-0 just in time to shower and dress for supper without a minute to spare. There was no time to drop into her father's office for a drink before the evening meal. She met him and Grandpa in the dining room. A mix of mouthwatering aromas wafted from the kitchen and made her stomach rumble. Having eaten nothing more than a bowl of cereal for breakfast and a bologna and cheese sandwich for lunch, she was starved.

"Looks like you got some sun today, punkin," Daddy said, pulling out her chair at the table.

She had worked without sunscreen. A cap had done little to prevent the merciless sun from cooking her face. Luckily, she'd had Brady's shirt to wear, or her neck and shoulders would have been as red as a boiled lobster. She took her seat, then pressed a palm to her cheek. The skin felt warm against her hand. "There isn't much shade around Suzanne's barn," she said.

She winced inside, facing that the small fib was an extension of the greater lie in which she had participated since this morning. Guilt was an unfamiliar and burdensome emotion for her. Until she had become obsessed with the 6-0 ranch, she had lived her life openly and honestly, and hadn't needed to lie about anything, large or small.

Windy and Irene began bringing out dishes of food. Part of supper was obviously leftovers from dinner. "Sorry I missed dinner," she said, heaping her plate with slices of grilled sirloin, mashed potatoes and brown gravy. "What did y'all talk about?"

"Sandy Dandy, mostly," Daddy answered. "Looks like we'll be transferring quite a few sperm samples. I'm especially interested in that mare Pitchfork brought up from South Texas. We all think she's a perfect match with Sandy Dandy. Who knows? Might get another Dash for Cash."

He grinned and Grandpa chuckled. The legendary record-setting Dash for Cash was a Texas-bred quarter-horse stallion that had sired two generations of prizewinners.

"And the Triple D's got several mares, too," Daddy added.

"Wish I'd been here," Jude said. And she sincerely did wish it. Before today, nothing could have caused her to miss a dinner conversation about horse breeding. Unfortunately, she couldn't be in two places at once.

"What were you and Suzanne up to?" her father asked as Windy and Irene fussed around the table.

Jude's stomach muscles tightened at the prospect of telling yet another untruth. "She's, uh, giving the barn a good cleaning and doing some work on the corral."

It was a lame excuse and didn't even come close to being a good reason for Jude to miss an important dinner. Daddy knew she would have been interested in talk about breeding Sandy Dandy. His head cocked and a look of curiosity came her way. *Oh, hell.*

Grandpa saved her with a gravelly *heh-heh-heh* as he spooned green beans onto his plate. "If you want to clean barns, Judith Ann, we've got a few around here."

"I know, Grandpa. I just wanted to do Suzanne a favor. She doesn't have any help and she's got a full-time job." Then that same alien force that had taken hold of her tongue at Brady's house said, "I, uh, we're going to take a break, though. We're going over to Fort Worth tomorrow to spend the night. Do some shopping and go out for some of the downtown nightlife."

"Good," Daddy said. "Glad to hear you're taking my suggestion to heart."

"Well, you know, school will be starting the middle of August. I'm going to have to start making my lesson plans before long. The next thing you know, teachers' meetings will begin and I might not get a chance to go anywhere. It's been ages since either Suzanne or I ate at Reata."

"Will you be seeing Jason while you're in Fort Worth?"

"No, I'm—"

"You should drop in on him and surprise him. I know he'd be glad to see you."

Jason Weatherby. Her most recent fiancé. His wealthy family had given him everything money could buy. That fact was the one and only thing Jude and he had in common. She had known the relationship was a sham mere weeks into the engagement, but Daddy and Grandpa so desperately wanted her to find a husband, she had wanted to try to please them. Again. She had endured the engagement for three months, all the while trying to make herself believe she could have a happy life with Jason.

It had been impossible from the start. Besides being a snob, Jason couldn't think his way out of a sack. Physically, he was a wimp. Didn't have a muscle anywhere. She could outrun him, outwalk him and outwrestle him. He was afraid of horses and cows. "Daddy, Jason and I aren't friends anymore."

"I know, but he still keeps in touch. I talk to him or his dad every couple of weeks. You know, we've known his family for years, punkin. You'll be having a birthday in another couple of months and Jason will soon be thirty-five. His dad would like to see him marry and start a family. I've been hoping—"

"Please, Daddy. If I broke our engagement because I didn't enjoy his company, I sure don't want to have his children. I don't want to spend time with him, either."

"Oh, I understand, punkin," her father said, chewing and swallowing.

This was how all of these conversations ended. Despite what he said, Jude knew he didn't understand. His and Grandpa's wishes for her to get married and have kids overrode understanding.

"By the way," he said, "since you're going to be in Fort Worth, there's a new Boren watercolor at Sid's museum. You might drop in and take a look at it."

Damn. How can I get past this? The Sid Richardson Museum of Western Art was a downtown Fort Worth landmark. If her father went to Fort Worth for any reason, he rarely left without visiting the museum. If he requested she go see a painting, how could she refuse? "I hadn't heard that."

"I've been trying to find the opportunity to get over there," her father said. "I'm told it's one of his better works."

Jude nodded.

"You girls planning on staying at the Worthington?"

Oh, damn. Another lie. "Um, yes. That's the easiest."

"Are you taking J.D.'s plane?" Grandpa asked.

"Oh, that isn't necessary," she said. "We'd rather drive. We can listen to music and talk and not have to fool with renting a car."

Daddy nodded again, and Jude wondered if he could tell her heart was pounding. She had told him more lies in the past half hour than in her entire life.

Soon Windy ended the meal by bringing out a fresh lemon meringue pie, and they all had generous slices. "Good pie," Grandpa said, scraping his plate clean. "After this, Judith Ann, we'll need a good long walk."

Jude suppressed a groan. She was so physically spent, she had barely managed to climb the stairs for a shower. The very thought of strolling around the barn lots sounded like pure agony. "No, thanks, Grandpa. There's a show on the science channel I need to watch."

As soon as was gracefully possible, she made an excuse to leave the table, then chastised herself all the way to her room for being a liar.

She logged on to the Internet and calculated the trip to

Stephenville. A three-and-a-half-hour drive. Longer coming back since they would be hauling three horses. She fell into bed, barely mustered the energy to turn on the TV and quickly went sound asleep. An hour later, she awoke to a program about Mars. She hit the power button on the remote and switched off the lamp, expecting to fall quickly back to sleep. Half an hour later, she found herself wide awake and worrying. Where would she sleep in Stephenville? If Brady was moving out of his dwelling, there would be no bed. Should she rent a motel room? Should she take a sleeping bag? And if so, where *was* her sleeping bag? She hadn't seen it in months. She drifted to sleep again.

She awoke a short time later arguing with herself. What would be wrong with simply telling Daddy and Grandpa she had helped Brady Fallon all day and she intended to go to Stephenville with him to help him further?

But her grandfather's words from just the previous evening popped into her thoughts. Grandpa had his own ideas about the future of the 6-0 ranch. He would never understand her reasons for helping Brady. She still didn't understand them herself. Added to that was the agreement she had made with Brady not to tell Daddy they were traveling to Stephenville together.

She slept again only to awaken a short time later. While drifting in and out of a sleepy haze, she had made a decision. As soon as the sun showed on the horizon, she would call Brady and say she had changed her mind. Problem solved. Worry gone.

She rose before daylight, stiff limbed and sore muscled and almost as worn-out as when she had gone to bed—and reached for her cell phone. As she flipped it open, it dawned on her that she couldn't call Brady. She didn't have his phone number. She hadn't seen a phone in the house, so he probably had only a cell phone. Or maybe he didn't even have a cell phone. She hadn't seen one of those, either. Hell. Just hell.

She debated what would happen if she simply didn't

show up. Would he wait for her, thus delaying his leaving? Of course, even if he waited for a while, he would eventually go on to Stephenville without her, but no doubt he would be mad. She hated the idea of leaving a bad impression on him.

Resigned to lying in the bed she had made, she dressed in older jeans and a knit tank and packed a small duffel with toiletries, pajamas and a change of clothing. She braided her long hair into a single queue, pulled on a denim jacket and went downstairs.

There, she ran into her father on his way to the cookhouse. Most mornings, he ate breakfast with the hands. She walked with him, grabbing an orange from a bowl as they passed the harvest table in the entry. At her pickup door, they hugged, and he told her to drive carefully and to have a good time. The urge to tell him the truth of her weekend plans tempted her, but she couldn't forget she had promised Brady she wouldn't.

She drove away from the ranch house with guilt pinching at her like a skinny-fingered old crone. All the way to the 6-0, she debated if she should call Suzanne and alert her that she was suddenly part of a conspiracy, but decided against it. Suzanne would ask questions. And the possibility that Daddy might call her was remote.

Approaching the 6-0, even from a distance, she could see the house's porch light glowing as bright as a lighthouse in the predawn darkness. When she reached the driveway, she saw Brady's truck parked in front of the house, its bed covered by a dark tarp. As she came to a stop, he came from inside the house, obviously in a hurry and ready to go. He was wearing a straw cowboy hat and carrying a thermal mug with a lid.

She buzzed down the window to say good morning, but before she spoke a word, he said, "Put your truck in the shed and I'll close the door. The last thing I need is for somebody to see it and tell your dad."

Now she was glad she had overcome the urge to discuss their trip with her father.

She complied with Brady's request and walked back to his pickup carrying the orange and the duffel, doing her best to clear her mind of worrisome thoughts and what-ifs. The childish conspiracy had grown into a two-ton elephant in her mind.

Brady's head tilted toward the duffel. "What's that?"

"My things."

"Put it up front. The bed's full of empty boxes they gave me at the grocery store." He walked across the driveway, closed the shed door and locked it. When he returned, he said, "I've got another mug if you want some coffee to go."

Jude rarely drank coffee, especially in the summertime. But she would if it was heavily laced with cream and sugar. "Do you have cream?"

"Armored cow."

"Pardon?"

"Canned milk. I've got some canned milk."

Then she remembered she had seen the ranch hands use canned evaporated milk instead of cream. She had even tried it a few times. "Okay, great," she said, though she wasn't sure she really thought it was great. "Sugar, too," she added as he strode back into the house.

He came out a few minutes later carrying a second mug with a lid and handed it to her. "Let's hit the road." He opened the passenger-side door and held it for her. "Be nice to get down there and get some of the work done before it turns hot and the humidity reaches the strangling point."

"Right," she said. As a native West Texan, she considered North Central Texas, with its lower elevation and wetter climate, a swamp. Maybe he felt the same. As she climbed onto the passenger seat, her shoulder brushed his firm chest, and that little stir she had felt yesterday returned. She deliberately didn't look at him.

She placed her duffel on the crew cab's backseat. He closed the door behind her and she watched him shrug out of his canvas jacket as he rounded the front of the pickup. He scooted behind the wheel, filling the small space with the scent of a fresh shower, shampoo, even toothpaste, and that same woodsy-smelling cologne she had noticed yesterday. He laid his jacket and his hat on the backseat beside her duffel, fired the engine and changed gears, his short-sleeve T-shirt revealing his biceps flexing and bunching under his tanned skin. She forced her eyes back to her cup.

They rode in silence for what seemed like a long while, both sipping their coffee and staring at the ribbon of highway stretching before them. The early morning's blackness began to fade to gray, and she couldn't keep from sneaking glances at his strong profile and golden brown hair. It was sun streaked and had a slight curl. It looked soft and thick. Without oil. The color reminded her of Jason Weatherby's, but that was where the resemblance ended. Brady Fallon had the same suntanned, lean and rangy look the Circle C's ranch hands had, a look that came from years of physically demanding outdoor work. It was a look that had been familiar to her all of her life, and until this moment, she had been unaware of just how appealing she found it.

His strong-looking body sat relaxed, one large hand on the steering wheel. His hands and fingers were scarred, like those of most of the working cowboys she knew. His fingers were freshly nicked and cut from yesterday's demolition work. A Band-Aid was wrapped around his left forefinger.

Jude puzzled over how this particular man had caused her to behave in a manner so impulsive and totally out of character for her. Looking for something, anything, that might lead to conversation, she said, "I checked the distance on MapQuest."

"Two hundred and eight miles to Stephenville," he replied, his eyes fixed on the highway. "Durham's place, where I was living, is twenty miles on farther south, between Stephenville and Hico."

"Ah." She nodded once. More silence. She searched

for more to talk about. "Daddy said you graduated from Tarleton."

"Yep."

Surely he knew Tarleton was a part of the Texas A&M system. "I went to A&M down in Bryan. So in a way, we're brother and sister. Schoolwise, you know."

"I guess so."

"I got the impression you're from Fort Worth."

"Nope."

"But you had on that TCU cap. And your license plate said 'Cowtown Chevrolet.' "

"I lived in Fort Worth a long time."

"But you didn't to to college there. . . . There are half a dozen colleges in Fort Worth. Why did you go to Stephenville?"

"I'm not from Fort Worth. And I didn't live in Fort Worth back then. I lived in Stephenville."

"Oh. I just assumed . . . So are you *from* Stephenville?"

He angled a glance in her direction. Though the morning light was creeping over the horizon, the pickup's cab was dim. Still, she could see a hint of a smile tweak the corners of his mouth. "You're just plumb nosy, aren't you?"

"No, I'm really not. I'm just making conversation."

"I grew up in Stephenville. I didn't move to Fort Worth 'til I got out of school. That answer your question?"

"Ah." She nodded. "Can I ask you something else? And I'm not being nosy," she added quickly.

His mouth lifted into a full grin. "Long as it's not personal."

Unable to tell if the remark was a joke, she blurted a laugh. "Well, I suppose it's sort of personal. What kind of conversation between two people isn't personal? Why did you agree to let me go with you today?"

"Damned if I know. All night long, I wished I hadn't."

Did that mean he had spent a sleepless night, too? And had he spent some time thinking about her? She let out a tiny huff. "Gee, thanks."

"It has nothing to do with you personally. I just think this could cause me trouble I don't need."

"As you said yesterday, I'm grown and so are you. I suppose we can do what we want to."

"Nothing's ever that simple."

She, of all people, knew that to be true. "Jake said you're divorced."

"Yep."

"Do you have kids?"

"Yep."

She waited, but he offered no more. "They, uh, live with your ex-wife?"

"Yep."

She waited again for him to say more, but he didn't. She couldn't remember the last time she'd had to ask a man so many pertinent and leading questions to get him to talk about himself. Brady Fallon had sidestepped almost every one of them.

And they still had more than a hundred miles to go.

Just shut up, she told herself and stared out the side window, pondering again why she was doing this. Soon she nodded off to sleep.

8

Brady still couldn't believe J. D. Strayhorn's daughter was riding to Stephenville with him to help do grunge work. When it came to women, he had done some dumb things, but what he was doing now just might be the dumbest yet. Why hadn't he made himself say "no, thanks" when she volunteered to help? Was it because of who she was?

He glanced across the cab at the passenger seat. Jude's head leaned against the headrest as she slept. Her scent, something soft and flowery, drifted to him. He had noticed it yesterday morning, too.

Thank God she had dropped off to sleep. He needed to escape her questions and think. But he wasn't thinking very well because he kept sneaking glances at her from the corner of his eye—at the shape of her breasts in a body-hugging top, peeking from behind a denim jacket and gently rising and falling with deep breathing. With her hair pulled back in a braid, he could see her delicate profile and skin so smooth it didn't have as much as a freckle, though it was a tinge pink from yesterday's sun.

Her dark, thick eyelashes lay against her cheek like little brushes, and he thought about how, a long time ago, before everything went sour, he used to kiss Marvalee awake, starting with her eyelids.

But it was Judith Ann Strayhorn's lips, now slightly

parted and vulnerable in sleep, that got to him. *The color of ripe berries. And probably taste just as sweet.*

Yesterday, even with his shirt covering a tight little top with skinny straps and tight jeans fitting her firm bottom like a coat of paint, she had distracted him. Then his agreeing to let her accompany him today had kept him awake half the night. What had he been thinking?

Of all of the obvious lures, he had to acknowledge, none of them were what had persuaded him to allow her to come along with him. What had kept him from saying "no, thanks" was more mysterious. She had touched an instinct buried so deep within him, he couldn't even identify it. It was something he couldn't define and wasn't sure he wanted to.

Hands off, dumb-ass, he told himself.

And he intended to heed that warning, though she was a damned tempting woman.

The next question, then, was what the hell would he do with her tonight? At his trailer, unless he gave her his bed, there was no place for her to sleep.

Oh, he knew what he would *like* to do, what any normal, red-blooded male would like to do with a woman who looked like her. But that was neither possible nor sane.

He had never been more baffled about a woman. What did she want from him? And what was she up to? She had to want something and had to be up to something. But what could somebody like him ever have that somebody like her would want or need? He hoped to hell she wasn't looking for some damn boy toy.

Nah. Don't be any dumber than you already have been. Hell, with her looks and connections, she probably had a string of rich dudes chasing her.

He was still blown away by the fact that he had known her when she was a little girl, younger than his son's age now. Other than a thick mop of sun-bleached reddish hair that had always been a tangle, he recalled no resemblance to the woman she had become.

His thoughts turned to the work she had done yesterday, stacking boards. Busywork. Any average twelve-year-old could have done it, but she had tackled the chore as if the survival of civilization depended on the job she did.

She had shown herself to be a good hand, had kept up with him all day without complaint. In his judgment, that made her a helluva fine sport. An image of her at the end of yesterday filtered through his anxiety. When he had said, *Let's wrap it up,* she had looked up at him with straggly hair, a dirty face and a wide, white-toothed smile. *We got a lot done, didn't we?* she had said, as if she were bursting with pride.

Her face had been red and sweaty, her eye makeup smeared and her lipstick gone, but he had thought in that moment she might be the most beautiful woman he had ever been close to. And he had known some fine-looking women, too, had been married to one. Weird to be thinking thoughts like that about a woman he feared being seen with.

He couldn't figure any of it out.

For all of his confusion, one thing was for sure. He had to take damn good care of her. If something happened to her, he suspected J. D. Strayhorn could and would have him horsewhipped, tarred and feathered, then lynched.

"Oh, my gosh," she said, her voice startling him. He swung a glance her way in time to see her yawn and squint against the morning sun. "I fell asleep. This looks like the interstate."

He forced a smile that probably looked as pitiful as it felt. "Good nap?"

"I didn't get much sleep last night." She yawned again and lifted her arms in a stretch, shoulders back, breasts thrust forward, nipples raised, their shape showing through her clingy shirt.

And just like that, something caught in his gut. The intimacy of seeing her wake up curled low in his belly, and a hundred carnal images sprang into his mind.

"Where are we?" she asked, rubbing her eyes with her fingertips.

He cleared his throat, striving for a normal voice. "Not too far from the exit."

"Gosh, we're almost there? I slept a long time." She leaned forward and shrugged out of her jacket, a movement that emphasized her flat stomach and the graceful arc of her hip. He cleared his throat again and willed the devil in his pants to cool it. "Wanna get something to eat?" he asked. "I didn't have breakfast and I'll bet you didn't, either."

"That'd be great. You're right. I missed breakfast."

"There's a McDonald's at this next exit. We'll stop." He slowed, made the exit and pulled into the lane leading to the drive-through window.

"We aren't going to get out?" she asked. "To stretch our legs?"

Going inside to eat would take at least thirty minutes. If she weren't with him, he would grab something and eat it on the road. "Don't have time."

"But they probably have a restroom inside."

He did a mental eye roll. Women must have bladders the size of a robin's. "I'll park over there," he said, nodding toward a row of parking places. "You can run inside."

At the order intercom, he gave her a questioning look, waiting for her to make a selection. She peered past him at the menu on the electronic board. "Uh . . . hmm, let me see. . . . Well . . . okay, I'll have an egg, sausage and cheese biscuit."

He stared at her a few seconds. There just weren't that many choices. Maybe she didn't eat at fast-food places much. He placed an order for three of the same and added a cup of milk.

He gave her the questioning look again.

"Yes, milk will be fine. You drink a lot of milk, don't you?"

"It's good for you." He added another cup of milk to the

order and asked for extra napkins. He didn't want grease on his truck's upholstery.

"I don't eat at McDonald's very often," she said. "It's cheap, isn't it?" She reached down and lifted her purse from the floorboard.

Did she think he expected her to pay for their breakfast? He put a hand out and stopped her. "I know you're rich, but if I ask if you wanna eat, I'll pay."

She shook her head and opened her purse. "It's no big deal."

He might be damn near broke, but no way was he going to let her buy him food. "It is to me."

"But I always pay. In fact, I do it without even thinking about it."

"Maybe you ought to start thinking about it," he told her. "Put your purse away."

She shrugged, her lips twisting into a scowl, but she returned her purse to the floorboard.

After they received their order, he pulled into a parking spot. She grabbed her purse and scooted out. As soon as she closed the door, he straightened his legs and adjusted himself in his jeans, hoping no one could see him. *Damn*.

She was soon back, and he pawed through the bag and distributed the food and napkins. As they ate, he asked, "What'd you tell J.D.?"

"That I was going to Fort Worth with my girlfriend Suzanne."

He couldn't keep from laughing at the absurdity of what they were doing.

"Don't make fun of me," she said.

"I'm laughing at myself, too. You have to admit it's pretty dumb sneaking around like we're kids doing something wrong. You must be thirty or so and I'm well past. It hasn't been necessary for me to lie to a man about my activities in a helluva long time."

She looked down, intently studying the layers of her sandwich as if she might find enlightenment among them.

"I'm sure. It's unusual for me, too, and it bothers me to do it. I can't explain it. I've never had to lie to Daddy about anything I've done, even when I was a kid. I probably would have told him about this trip if you hadn't asked me not to."

"So?" Her big whiskey-colored eyes met his, and he fixed a truth-demanding look directly into them. "I know why I wanted you not to tell him. But I still don't know why you didn't."

She turned her head and faced the windshield. "I guess it's because . . ." She appeared to be searching for the right words. Maybe she was weighing her loyalties. "Never mind," she said and took another bite of her sandwich.

He hated that. Why did women do it—start something, then say "never mind"? "Say what you were going to."

She hesitated a few more beats. "Okay, then, I will. Were you aware that after your uncle died, my grandfather tried to buy the 6-0 from your aunt?"

Well, that was a gear-grinding switch, but he assumed she was headed somewhere with the remark. His whole family had been aware of Old Man Strayhorn's offer to buy the 6-0 after his uncle Harry's death. He knew his mother had tried to talk her sister into selling it, which had resulted in another big, loud argument between the two women, who had never gotten along well. "Yep."

"But your aunt wouldn't sell to him. Why wouldn't she? I know Grandpa would have paid her a fair price. Did she not need the money?"

"I don't know. I wasn't in that loop. I'm sure she could've used the money. But you see, Aunt Margie was always an ornery ol' gal with her own ideas, especially when somebody pushed her. Guess your granddad must have pushed her a little too hard."

"But if she needed the money . . ."

"There was more to it than money, darlin'. Aunt Margie had ideals. She said it wasn't right that Strayhorns get to own all the land. She believed they already had enough."

Brady had let slip more words about his family than he

intended to. "But all of that was years ago," he added, hoping to kill the discussion. "What's it got to do with you and your being here with me today? Are you trying to tell me your granddad's about to make me an offer I can't refuse?"

"No. I told you yesterday. I just think you need help. And I don't know why I brought up Grandpa. I just wondered if you knew he had once tried to buy your land."

As stories went, that one was leakier than a rusted bucket. If somebody were holding a gun to his head, Brady couldn't have stopped himself from busting out laughing. "Not only are you fibbing to your daddy, darlin'. Now I think you're lying to me."

"Look, can you stop trying to attach motives to me that aren't there? It's starting to be annoying. If you didn't want to put up with me, you shouldn't have said I could come with you."

"You're right." He wadded his breakfast trash into a ball and stuffed it into the McDonald's bag. "I'll keep my mouth shut 'til you're ready to tell me what your granddad's really up to."

He laid the sack of trash on the console for later disposal and reached for the ignition, but before he cranked the engine, she said, "Wait. I have an orange. Would you like half?"

"Sure. You can peel it while we're on the road."

"By the way," she said. "I'm not thirty. I'm still twenty-nine. You must be the same age as Jake."

"Nope. Younger than Jake. Just turned thirty-four."

Jude was happy he cleared up that question. She had wondered about his age. He backed out of the parking space, and they were on the move again. As they merged onto the interstate, she peeled the orange and handed him slices. She hadn't intended to eat it driving up the road, but she didn't complain.

Only a few miles past the McDonald's, they veered onto another exit ramp off the interstate and sped down a state highway, passing through a different landscape—open green pastures dotted with large old oak trees and cedar brakes, all indicative of a moister climate. "I've never been on this road," she said. "This is pretty country, but the bluestem grass in West Texas is better feed than the coastal. It has more nutrients."

"Who said?" Brady asked.

"I say," she answered. "More nutritious grass is why West Texas, even with all its challenges, is better cattle country."

"That sounds like a direct quote from your granddad."

"Actually, it's a direct quote from a textbook and a professor at A&M."

His eyes fixed on her.

"Watch the road," she said, uncomfortable under his scrutiny.

"Just exactly what is it you studied at A&M anyway?"

She didn't miss the you-mean-you've-got-a-brain? tone of the question. "For what it's worth at this particular moment, I have a masters in biology, with an emphasis on genetics. And a bachelors in business ag. In case you haven't figured it out, I'm the future of the Circle C ranch."

"Is that a fact?"

Didn't he believe her? "Yes," she said flatly.

"Your dad and granddad are just going to turn the whole place over to you."

She heard mockery in his statement. "They've never said so. But Daddy and Grandpa refuse to face the facts. I'm the only choice. There simply is no one else. I know it's going to happen someday. So I'm grooming myself every day."

"Trying to replace two ranching legends, darlin', now that's a tall order."

He didn't say "*for a woman*," but she heard the implication. He reeked of chauvinism, in both looks and attitude. "Jake and Cable are the only other heirs, and they have no interest in the place. I'm the only one who cares about the fact that it's been here for a hundred and forty years. It's a legacy to be preserved. And it's part of Texas history. I refuse to see it go up for sale and get cut up into subdivisions."

"So you're telling me if I cowboy for the Circle C long enough, one of these days you'll be my boss?"

"Yes," she said again.

He made no obvious response, but she sensed that the balance between them had shifted, and she regretted it. She never discussed ownership of the ranch and wished she hadn't talked about her role in its future. Before that, she had believed Brady felt no inferiority to her.

They turned off the highway onto a caliche county road. "It's another fifteen miles to my trailer," he said.

Soon they made another turn and bumped along a rugged two-track passage that was little more than a path. A few head of cattle grazed in the distance. At last they came to a gray, single-wide mobile home perched atop a treeless bald knob of a hill. A silver, late-model, four-horse trailer was parked beside it. The mobile home wasn't much bigger than the horse trailer and had probably cost less.

"Is that your horse trailer?" she asked.

"Yep."

"It looks like it has bunk room in it."

"Yep. I figure if Aunt Margie's old house falls down around me, I can always sleep in the horse trailer." He laughed, so she did, too.

The mobile home had no skirting, but it still looked neat and well kept. She saw no trash around it, nothing stored under it or against it. A hundred feet down the hill behind it stood a silver steel barn with an attached iron-pipe corral so white and clean, it almost sparkled.

Jude knew about the outpost dwellings ranches furnished for their hands. The Circle C had a number of houses and mobile homes similar to this one. Except for major repairs, the employee using it was expected to keep the place up. "I'll bet the owner of this place hates to see you go," she said. "Most ranch hands wouldn't keep it this neat."

"I don't like being a slob. I grew up with three sisters and a brother. Everything we had was either worn-out, torn up or not working. At some point, I decided not to live that way."

He scooted out of the truck and reached into the backseat for his hat, then yanked the tarp off the pickup bed. Jude hurried to help him lift out the empty boxes. In the late morning heat and heavy humidity, she began to sweat immediately.

Together they carried the empty boxes up four wrought-iron steps to a four-foot-square wrought-iron porch and on into the mobile. The narrow mobile home was so stuffy and hot, she could scarcely draw a breath. Plastic shades on the windows offered a scant barrier against the relentless sun. And if the place was like most single-wide mobiles, it probably lacked good insulation. It was as neat and clean inside as it was outside, but it smelled like plastic and chemicals. Jude recognized the odor as typical of mobile homes that had been manufactured as cheaply as possible. She had been in all of the Circle C's mobiles at one time or other, either when they were new or when they had been vacated by an employee.

"There's an air conditioner in the bedroom," Brady said and left the living room. She heard the start of a soft roar and he returned. "Everything in here except the furniture belongs to me. I'll pack up the computer and that stuff in the second bedroom, and you can get the living room. That cool air will make its way in here pretty soon."

Jude picked up an empty box. The closest she had ever come to packing to move was when she had traveled back and forth between the Circle C and her condo in Bryan during her college days. Even then, she hadn't had to do the whole chore herself. Daddy had hired a moving company to help her. Turning in a circle, she couldn't see much in the living room to pack: a small TV, a CD player and CDs, a cactus plant and a few other odds and ends. She began to place things in the box.

Soon Brady passed through the living room on his way outside carrying a monitor and a computer, and she wondered what he did with a computer. After that, he carried out two huge boxes of books. He made several trips with books, and she wondered what kind of books they were. He hadn't impressed her as being a reader.

She finished packing everything that was loose in the living room. Looking for the next project, she poked her head into the adjoining room and discovered a bedroom. *His* bedroom. She knew because it looked like him. Spartan and uncluttered. Nothing out of place. Queen-size bed neatly made, plain brown bedspread. One square lamp table, one round, stubby ceramic lamp, one rectangular digital clock radio. A pair of well-worn boots sat side by side near a wooden chair. She caught that scent of cologne again. A small air conditioner, roaring dully, filled half of one of the bedroom's two windows.

She picked up an empty cardboard box and carried it to the beside table. She started by unplugging the clock radio and placing it in the box, then opened the top drawer of the lamp table. Inside the drawer was a paperback book, some loose coins . . . and a box of . . . *condoms.* Jude sank to the edge of the mattress to examine the small flat box. It was a commonly seen brand, but what she found most intriguing was the large *XL* showing in bright white against the black background. *Well, after all, he is a big guy,* she thought. She opened the box and found it half empty. So he had a girlfriend whom he must have made love with here in this bed. An uneasiness trickled through her.

Just then, she heard him come back into the mobile through the front door. She dropped the box back into the drawer, shut it quickly and got to her feet just as he walked into the bedroom. "I, uh, finished the living room," she told him, her voice wobbling with a nervous quiver.

"Mind starting on the kitchen?" he asked. "Before we leave tomorrow, I'll take care of the rest of the stuff in this bedroom. I already took most of my clothes to Lockett, so there's just a few odds and ends left."

"Right." She grabbed the cardboard box and headed for

the kitchen, but her mind was still focused on his bedroom and what it said about him.

She had just started emptying the kitchen cupboards when she heard the sound of a vehicle. Brady came out of the bedroom, went to the front door and looked out. "Shit," he mumbled, and stepped outside.

Jude walked over and looked out the door. A car was roaring up the long driveway. It came to a caliche-grinding halt that kicked up a cloud of white dust. The car, an aged Toyota, was so filthy and faded she couldn't determine the color, but she thought it might have been blue once.

Brady stepped down the four steps and walked toward the car.

A woman with long, obviously dyed auburn hair as straight as string climbed out of the car. She had on skintight jeans and a black skintight tank top that showed ample cleavage and said JACK DANIEL'S in rhinestones across the front. The very air around her trembled with her agitation. She slammed the car door with a loud clack.

"Hi, Ginger," Brady said.

The woman stamped to within a couple feet of where he stood and glared up at him, her hands on her hips. Even from her station at the front door, Jude could see the fire in the new arrival's eyes.

"I can't believe you," the woman barked. "You left town without saying kiss my ass, go to hell, or see ya later?"

"Calm down, Ginger."

"*Calm down?*" She bent at the waist, face thrust forward, eyes bugged. "*Calm down?*" she said louder. "That's the thanks I get for *fucking* you anytime you wanted it? Putting up with your shit? Never taking me anywhere, never spending any money on me? Spending most of your free time on your fuckin' horses?"

She spun on the ball of her foot, yanked open the car's back door and dragged out a small TV. Gripping it with both hands, she raised it to shoulder level and slammed it to the ground. It hit with a clunk and broke into pieces.

Jude's breath caught, but Brady stood there unmoving, one knee cocked, his arms folded over his chest.

The upper half of Ginger's body disappeared inside the car again. Seconds later she emerged with a cardboard box, turned it upside down and dumped the contents—which looked like a dozen CDs—on top of the broken TV pieces.

She stomped around the car's back end and yanked open the other back door. She pulled out a large photo album and loose pictures and what looked like a rolled poster. She threw the album and poster on top of the pile of rubble, then ripped a handful of the pictures in half and threw them onto the pile.

Then she kicked the debris with the toe of her cowboy boot. "Fuck you, Brady Fallon!"

She stomped to the driver's door and jerked it open, slid behind the wheel and slammed the door shut, and the engine ground to life with a loud growl. She backed in an arc, stopped and stuck her head out the window. "I hope you starve to death, you son of a bitch!"

Jude's eyes popped wide. She had never called a man a son of a bitch, and couldn't recall if she had ever heard *any* woman say that to a man's face. For that matter, she couldn't recall ever having a tantrum like the one she had just witnessed. She waited for some kind of outburst or reaction from Brady, but he continued to stand in the same spot, unmoving.

The visitor gunned the engine and roared back down the driveway, leaving a rooster tail of dust and gravel behind her.

Her pulse drumming inside her ears, Jude eased out of the trailer onto the tiny wrought-iron porch. "Brady?"

He turned and looked up at her. "What is it, darlin'?"

"Are you okay?"

"Finer'n frog hair. Sorry you saw that."

If the expression on his face was any indication, he didn't feel that fine. He came up the steps and she had to move aside so he could get to the front door. "Who, uh, is she? A girlfriend?"

"Sort of. But not really."

Jude didn't even try to figure out what that meant. "She's mad, huh?"

Another one of those mysterious soft chuckles that made his eyes crinkle at the corners.

"She spends a lot of her time that way. Her problem is, her presence just doesn't light up a room." He leveled a look into her eyes and winked. "Unlike yours." He pushed the door open. "I think there's still some beer in the fridge. Want one?"

She stood a few speechless seconds and watched him disappear into the mobile home.

9

After Brady went into the mobile home for the beers, Jude stood for a moment looking at the small pile of torn and broken objects. What had she walked into? She had witnessed something not just personal, but probably painful. Who else or what else might suddenly appear? A shard of doubt about the wisdom of making this trip with a man she scarcely knew stole into her good intentions.

Well, the least she could do was pick up the rubble on the ground. She went back inside the mobile home for a trash bag. Brady was nowhere to be seen, so she assumed he was in the bathroom. She carried a black plastic bag back outside and down to the little pile on the driveway, some twenty feet away from the porch's bottom step.

She knelt on one knee and started with the loose photographs. They were eight-by-ten black-and-white prints, and only a few of them were torn in half. As she gathered them, she would have had to be blind not to see that the pictures appeared to be professionally taken and all were of the same subject—an extremely well-built, nearly naked man in various poses. He wore a bandana around his neck, cowboy boots on his feet and a dark thong that barely covered his privates. To her astonishment, even with shoulder-length hair, he looked amazingly like . . .

Like a younger Brady Fallon.

Her mind went blank, as if it didn't want to acknowledge

what her eyes were seeing. "Oh, my gosh," she whispered, letting the shock of recognition seep in. She sorted through the pictures, stealing quick glances at each one. "Oh, my gosh."

Though she knew she was alone, she still looked up and around to see if someone could be watching her. Then she shot a look over her shoulder toward the mobile home to see if that someone could be Brady.

Seeing no sign of him, she quickly shuffled through the pictures again, stopping at a back shot in which he wasn't wearing even the bandana and the cowboy boots. The thong's waistband was visible, but she hardly noticed it. He stood in a he-man pose, his face in profile, arms raised to shoulder level and bent at the elbow, biceps flexed and bulging like melons, shoulder muscles clearly defined. He was beautiful, like an ancient Greek athlete.

Jude hadn't seen a naked man since ending her affair with Jason Weatherby. And Jason in the buff was pathetic compared to the body in the photographs she held in her hand. She couldn't tear her eyes away from the bare buttocks, small and taut, the narrow waist, the broad, muscular shoulders.

On a hard swallow, she stuffed the loose photographs into the plastic bag, picked up the poster and began to unroll it. Inch by inch a full frontal photograph came into view—the same man from the thighs up. Distinct ab muscles rippled beneath his pecs. No hair showed on his body, but a dark shadow peeked from beneath the triangular thong. The thong's silky-looking fabric clung to and outlined the shape and generous size of his genitals.

Her mouth went dry and she had to fight an urge in her fingers to touch the very spot the black triangle covered. Her thoughts darted everywhere at once, including back to his bedroom and the extra-large-size condoms in his bedside table drawer. "Oh, my gosh," she whispered and pressed her unruly fingers against her lips, still unable to tear her eyes away from the photograph.

"Like what you see?"

Her heart leaped. "Oh!" All in one motion she sprang to her feet, thrust the poster behind her and spun toward the voice. Brady stood on the porch. He was holding a small cardboard box. Her eyes dropped directly to his fly, but she quickly angled her attention to a bush beside the step. "Um, I was just picking up this mess."

He tossed the box onto the porch and took the four steps down in two long strides. Without a word, he held out a can of beer for her.

She took it reflexively with her free hand. "I wasn't trying to be nosy, honest. I mean, the pictures were just lying all over the place. Anyone could have seen them."

He neither smiled nor frowned. He set his own beer on the ground and reached around her for the poster. His chest brushed her shoulder and his musky male scent surrounded her. Her heart leaped again and she gave him an uneasy smile, relinquishing her hold on the poster.

He bent at the waist, picked up the plastic bag and crumpled the poster into it. She winced. A wicked part of her hated seeing something as delectable as the poster be trashed. She would love to show it to Suzanne.

He picked up what was left of the photographs, crumpling them into his fist, and shoved them inside the bag, too. The album, then the pieces of the broken TV, followed. He jerked the bag closed and carried the bundle to the bed of his pickup.

Watching him cram the bag into the corner they had designated for trash, she squatted and, with her free hand, picked up the CDs. Even with a task at hand, she couldn't shake the image of the frontal shot. "I wasn't being nosy, honest."

"I believe you."

As a dozen questions and emotions flitted through her head, she held up the CDs. "Did you, uh, want to keep these?"

"That's what the box is for."

She nodded, returned to the porch and picked up the box. She set her own beer can down on the top step and began arranging the CDs in the box, looking at each one as if she were really interested. "Oh, Alan Jackson. I like his music. . . . And Carrie Underwood. I like her, too. . . . Hey, here's one by Josh Turner. . . ."

Shut up, Jude.

She set the box of CDs aside, took a seat on the top step and sipped her beer.

He stood with his arms braced against the edge of the pickup bed, his back to her. He was obviously upset and probably too embarrassed to look at her.

"Those pictures, uh, look like they were taken a while ago," she called to his back, raising her voice so it would carry across the front yard.

He neither replied nor turned in her direction.

"Were you, uh, a model?"

He said nothing, but continued to stand with his back to her.

She dared not put her next question into words. A minute passed, then two, while she waited silently, hoping he would explain. She had never found herself so speechless.

She wondered why the woman named Ginger had those pictures, but instead of asking, she said, "Look, dammit, they're just pictures."

He finally turned and looked her way, his blue eyes hard as ice cubes.

"They look like some kind of publicity shots," she added, unable to read his expression.

He walked over and picked up his beer from where he had left it on the ground and sauntered toward the steps. A visual of those long, muscular thighs free of blue denim and leading all the way up to his groin filled her mind. He sat down beside her, his hip touching hers. Unnerved by the closeness, she scooted to her right to give him more room.

"No, I wasn't a model." He lifted his beer can and swallowed a long drink, the flex of his throat muscles nearly hypnotizing her.

Another minute of silence passed. "You, uh, certainly had a nice body back then."

That was lame, Jude. As if he didn't now.

Shut up, Jude.

She sat there, her shoulders taut, feeling the heat of his body close to hers and wishing she could identify the strange crawly feeling deep inside her.

"Before you ask the next question, I'll just tell you," he said dully. "I was a dancer."

Stripper! Her jaw dropped, but she stopped herself before blurting out the word. "Hey, that's great," she said cheerily. "It's great you can do that. I've got two left feet myself."

He looked across his shoulder at her again with a don't-be-stupid expression.

But even his glare didn't stop her. She had to know about those pictures. "You danced professionally? Around here? Around Fort Worth? Dallas?"

He heaved an aggrieved sigh. "You ever hear of Cowboys?"

"Cowboys? You mean like Chippendales?"

"Yeah," he grunted.

In many ways, Jude was naive and she knew it. But even she had heard of Cowboys. They were a team of male dancers similar to Chippendales who performed to country-western music and wore breakaway Western costumes. When she lived in Bryan, she had even attended private parties where Cowboys had performed. A new visual came to her of Brady with folded dollar bills tucked under his G-string. Then it dawned on her that the thong in the photograph was, in reality, a G-string.

"You were a Cowboys dancer?" She almost burst out laughing, but she could see he found nothing humorous in the situation. "Wow. Those guys can really dance. Where'd you learn how to do that?"

"They teach you."

"Wow," she said again. She had never known a professional . . . *dancer*. She didn't even know if "dancer" was the correct word. There had always been plenty of talk among women about what those gorgeous, sexy men did besides dance. "There's no need to be upset. I won't tell anyone, if that's what's worrying you."

"Darlin', I couldn't care less who you tell. It was a long time ago. And it's not exactly a national secret."

More minutes of silence passed as they sipped their beers, during which time she was finally able to make herself keep her mouth shut.

"I was just thinking," he said, without looking her in the face. "There's still enough daylight. I could go get those horses now and bring them back here. They could spend the night in the corral. Then we could get on the road early tomorrow morning without having to fool with catching them. We could get back to Lockett early enough for me to do half a day's work tomorrow afternoon."

She glanced at the pristine barn and corral. "Why aren't they here already? Your employer wouldn't let you keep them here?"

"He wouldn't mind. But they've always stayed at Ace's. When I left Fort Worth, I didn't have a home for myself, much less three horses. I've been gone quite a bit lately. It's just been easier to leave them at Ace's place. He lives about ten miles from here."

"Ace. I don't think I've ever known anyone named Ace."

"Me, neither. Ace is his nickname." Brady leaned his head back, tilted his beer up and finished it off. "It's initials." He crushed the beer can between his palms as she had seen the Circle C ranch hands do. "His real name's Arthur Charles Earl. But everybody's always called him Ace."

Now she couldn't keep from laughing. The whole afternoon had taken on a comic atmosphere. "That's three first names. I think I like Ace better. But then, he's Ace Earl. That sounds funny, too." She broke into laughter again.

He frowned at her, a deep crease showing between his thick brown brows.

Shut up, Jude. She cleared her throat and wiped the grin off her face. "Bad joke," she said. "Look, I'll help you with the horses. Are they easy to catch?"

"The two geldings are, but my mare's like a lot of women."

Jude let out a strained laugh. "I don't know what that means, but I hope she isn't like the one who just left here."

Brady huffed. "Every horse I've ever been around has a better disposition than Ginger." He got to his feet and started back up the steps. "I'll get us another beer and we'll go."

Jude had drunk less than half the beer she already had. When he disappeared into the mobile home, she poured the remaining liquid on the ground.

As they approached Brady's friend's place, the three horses were standing on a ridge, silhouetted against a sky made golden by the waning afternoon sunlight. The minute the horses saw Brady's pickup, they ambled down the hill toward it.

The two geldings appeared to be strong and solid, what Daddy and the ranch hands called "using horses." But the mare was special. Her superiority showed in her conformation, her size and her attitude. And she was a beautiful grullo color. Jude's curiosity about her sparked immediately.

The horses gathered around them, snuffing and snorting and nuzzling. When Jude reached to stroke the mare's neck, she jerked her head and sashayed backward, snorting and farting as she escaped Jude's touch.

"Watch yourself with her," Brady said. "She's got a mind of her own. And she's in season, which makes her an even bigger pain in the ass."

He started for the barn and Jude followed. The horses clomped along with them and would have come into the barn if Brady hadn't shut them out. Jude followed him into a tiny tack room, where he plucked three plastic buckets and three halters off nails on the wall. In the tack room's close, hot quarters, she felt strangely uneasy, still thinking of Brady Fallon naked. She didn't know if she would ever be able to be near him again without thinking of him in that way.

"I love horses," she said, holding out her hand to receive a bucket and a halter.

"All women love horses. Until it comes to taking care of them."

Jude resented that. But she suspected the remark, along with others he had made, must say something about his past relationships with women, though she wasn't sure what. "What are their names?"

"Sorrel's named Tuffy. The bay's Poncho."

"What about the mare?"

"Sweet Sal. But she's not sweet."

"High-strung, huh?"

"Afraid so."

High-strung horses didn't frighten Jude. She had grown up with spirited horses. Her own horse, Patch, was a power-ful stallion with a mind of his own.

Ace's barn had no stalls, but under a shed roof on one side, it had several mangers attached to the outside wall. Brady dumped oats in two mangers and Jude did likewise in a third. "Ace doesn't have any horses?"

"Not right now. He used to have a rope horse, but he sold him."

They returned to the outside of the fence and propped their arms on the top rail, watching the horses eat. Sweet Sal didn't appear to be the least bit intimidated by the two males. "Sal's a beauty," she said. "I've always liked that grullo color. A grullo's really a black dun, you know. Kind of rare."

His head turned her way and he gave her another one of those how-do-you-know-so-much? looks. "I know." He turned his attention back to Sal. "She looks pretty, but she's a prima donna."

"She looks like she's got some good breeding. Classy. Where'd you get her?"

"A guy gave her to me."

Jude let out a chuff of disbelief. "Just like that? Some guy just up and gave you a classy horse?"

His brow tented. "'Course not. I did some riding for him. I found out too late he didn't have any money to pay me. A horse was better than nothing."

"Is she papered?"

"Yeah. She's out of a King Ranch horse. But I didn't know it when I got her. I almost sold her."

Jude made a mental note of a horse named Sweet Sal, sired by a famous King Ranch horse. At home, she could research the entire bloodline in minutes. "Why? You don't like her?"

"I didn't have a place to keep her. Ace was already boarding Tuffy and Poncho and I didn't feel like I could just put another horse on his pasture. But he said one more didn't matter. I haven't had much time to work with her. That's why she's such a son of a bitch."

"How old?"

"Five."

"Has she foaled?"

"Nope. Never could afford the fee for a good stud. Can't afford AI, either."

"You don't have to artificially inseminate. You could hand breed her or even pasture breed her."

"Like you say, she's a good horse. Far as I know, she's never been bred. Ornery as she is, she might put up a fight. I don't want to chance getting her hurt by a stud that might get ornery, too."

"But all stallions aren't ornery."

He shook his head, dismissing the conversation.

"Once you get settled back in Lockett, you could at least think about it. It's a shame to have a good, strong mare and not breed her. And five years old is an ideal age."

"I don't have time to fool with a baby."

Indeed, a baby took a lot of work to make it grow into a good horse. Jude had raised Patch from a baby and been involved with many of the Circle C's new foals.

The horses finished their grain and sauntered over to the fence. Tuffy and Poncho proved easy to catch and soon were loaded into the trailer. But when Brady opened the corral gate to catch Sal, she dashed past him and out into the pasture before he could touch her with the halter.

"Sal, you butthole, get back here!" He let out a shrill whistle, but the mare continued playing her game of trotting toward him, then, just before she came close enough for either Jude or Brady to get a rope on her, galloping away, tail in the air, mane flying.

"Well, I guess she's showed off enough," Brady said, sighing. "Time to quit horsing around." He handed Jude the halter, walked out into the open pasture and stood there with his hand out, smooching at her and talking horse talk. Sal trotted toward him, taunting him by making him think she would come to him. Just before she reached him, she picked up speed, turned on a dime and started in the opposite direction. Brady broke into a run alongside her, then in a flash, grabbed her mane, hopped twice beside her and threw himself astraddle her back.

It happened almost too quickly to register in Jude's mind. What did register was a warm sense of pleasure that caught in her midsection. And just like that, she realized she could fall head over heels in love with Brady Fallon. Even if he *had* been a stripper.

Then again, maybe what she felt was something else entirely. Something like *lust*. Hell. Brady was the sexiest man she had ever known up close and personal. And she was only human, despite what Suzanne said.

Sweet Sal pranced and danced and sidled and gathered herself to buck once, but Brady gripped her dark mane and stayed on her back until she calmed and lined out. "Bring that halter," he shouted.

Jude quick-stepped out to the horse, and the naughty girl

stood perfectly still, even nibbled at Jude's ear and cheek while Jude slipped the halter onto her head. "You're nothing but a big show-off," Jude told her. "You need to spend a day with me and Patch. We'd teach you how to behave."

Brady threw a long leg over the horse's neck, pushing off her back and dropping to the ground flat-footed. "Let's get her into the trailer. I'm starving."

He gathered his gear from Ace's tack room and threw it in the pickup bed on top of the boxes they had packed earlier. His mood appeared to have worsened, and Jude couldn't tell if it was because of Ginger or the pictures or Sal's behavior. She chose to blame his bad mood on the horse. She settled herself into the pickup's passenger seat. "Horses really want to please us, you know. They just don't always know what we want them to do. We have to show them. I hope you aren't really mad at her."

"Mad at her?" He chuckled, the warmth of it slithering through Jude's system like warm, sweet syrup. "Hell, I'm not mad at her. I'm in love with her."

As they drove away from Ace's place, he said, "We can wash up back at the trailer. We'll go into Stephenville and I'll buy us a steak for supper."

"Listen, there's no need—"

"Darlin', I've got to eat. You think I'm gonna eat and not feed you?"

"No. I just mean I can buy my—"

Brady raised a palm. "No," he said.

"But it's not like you've asked me out on a date or something."

"I'll buy supper," he said.

She expelled a breath of resignation. "Fine."

10

While Jude showered, Brady stood at the corral fence watching his horses chomp on the flakes of hay he had thrown them. His mind was on women—Ginger Thompson specifically. She had been drunk when she had shown up earlier, which too often put her in the mood to fight. He had known Ginger his whole life, and should have known he wouldn't get out of Stephenville without one more of her flare-ups. At least today's tantrum hadn't been as wild and crazy as the one that had prompted him to end things with her several months back. Then, she had taken a pool cue to the front of his truck, denting the fenders and breaking the headlights, leaving him without transportation for several days while the truck underwent repair.

The pool-cue stunt was the eye-opener he needed. It helped him decide that romps in the sack and raunchy sex, the only things he and Ginger had in common, just weren't worth so much chaos in his life. Hadn't he already lived nine years with a woman who was brainless, irresponsible and nuts?

He thought about the photographs. *Those friggin' twelve-year-old pictures.* Would they ever stop chasing him? Jude had put up a good front when she saw them, but she probably had been shocked. After she had seen him nearly naked in the pictures, riding together in the close quarters of his truck to Ace's place and back had been as uncomfortable as traipsing through a bed of prickly pear. Her learning of his less-than-conventional past troubled him. After all, he had that long-ago connection with her family, and even with her in a distant way.

He wasn't ashamed of having held a job as an exotic dancer, not really. It wasn't like he had robbed a bank, although back in those days, money had been the only thing on his mind. His mother had been sick and out of work, and he was the oldest and male to boot. He had sucked it up and done what was necessary at the time.

He made a helluva lot more dancing half naked than he made cowboying for ranches around Stephenville, working on a dairy farm or driving a truck. And he had been able to live at home and help his mother with his three sisters and little brother. In the long run, the pay had not only helped his family and paid for school, the nighttime hours had enabled him to spend his days in classes. He had succeeded in avoiding the lake of alcohol that had been available to him, along with enough recreational drugs to baffle a pharmacist. He had managed to resist the rampant promiscuity and exotic sex. Well, to be honest, he hadn't *always* resisted the exotic sex. But as far as he was concerned, the whole experience had turned out okay.

What troubled him about Jude seeing the pictures, as well as her witnessing Ginger's fit, was that he sensed a certain innocence about his new boss's daughter. J. D. Strayhorn had a reputation for being a tough manager but having a soft side when it came to his only daughter. He had done or would do everything in his considerable power to protect her from worldly evils. Jude might be outgoing and well educated, but Brady knew she had grown up under unusual circumstances. And he suspected she led a sheltered life. He could think of no woman her age who lived at home with her parents. Nor could he think of one who felt a need to sneak around like a teenager.

But what was going on within him was more confusing

than just plain embarrassment at her seeing the pictures. All day, he had felt that familiar tension low in his belly, and he'd had to force himself to keep his eyes to himself. He understood what he felt well enough, but what had him baffled was that he had an almost desperate yearning for Jude to think well of him. When she had first inserted herself into his life yesterday, he had tolerated her because of who she was, but after spending time with her, he found himself liking her. She was more than a hot body with a pretty face. She was smart. She seemed to have enthusiasm for everything and an upbeat attitude that was a balm to his soul—though he sensed a layer of frustration seething within her.

"Hell, who isn't frustrated?" he mumbled to the air.

Frustration was Brady Fallon's middle name.

Sal came over to him and nuzzled him as if he had summoned her, as if she were a well-behaved horse that never gave him a minute's trouble. Her personality truly reminded him of some women he had known. *Scary.*

Horses really want to please us, you know. They just don't always know what we want them to do. We have to show them.

You need to spend a day with me and Patch. We'd teach you how to behave.

Jude's words. Patch must be a horse. Brady wondered what Jude knew about horse training. Something, no doubt. The Circle C ranch was known for having good horses. Only someone with some knowledge would know a grullo was a black dun. Having attended cutting shows in Fort Worth and being acquainted with owners of highbred horses, Brady knew that cutting-horse champions had come from various Circle C studs.

The mare nuzzled his pocket and brought him out of his musing. "No goodies tonight," he told her. She ambled back to the two geldings on the other side of the corral as if Brady had disappointed her by not having a present. He shook his head. Just like a woman.

He plucked his cell phone off his belt and checked the time. Then he punched in Ace's number. When his call went to voice mail, Brady left a message saying he had picked up the horses. It was late in the day on a Saturday, so Ace was probably already out looking for a party.

Brady turned from the horse pen, strolled back up to the trailer and sat down on the tiny front stoop, letting the quiet of the late afternoon and panoramic view of the valley seep into his soul. He had liked living here, perched like a raptor atop this rise. His closest neighbor was Ace, ten miles away.

There had been whole days when he hadn't seen or heard another human being. The solitude and silence were good. If he wanted company, he could drive somewhere and find it. If he wanted noise, he could turn on the radio or TV. He couldn't deny being a loner. Without a doubt, this twelve-by-sixty trailer, anchored in the middle of a twenty-section pasture, had saved his sanity during those first months after his exit from Fort Worth.

His thoughts drifted to Jude again, inside the trailer and naked in his shower. An image of soap and water sluicing over her well-honed body filled his mind and he imagined his hands gliding over her breasts, down to her belly, between her legs. He felt a tightening in his groin. Women who looked like her had always appealed to him. Fairly tall, willowy and well developed. He had never gone for the emaciated look.

Just cool it, hoss, he told himself. None of what he thought mattered. She was his new boss's daughter.

Jude stood in front of the vanity mirror brushing her hair. Since the plan was to go out for supper and relax, she saw no need to braid it. She let it fall free in its natural unruliness.

She pulled her change of clothes from her duffel—underwear, jeans and a green tank top. When she packed yesterday morning, the thought that they might have sup-

per out in Stephenville hadn't occurred to her, or she would
have brought better clothes. She put on the clean clothes,
dabbed her grandmother's perfume behind her ears and
between her breasts, then walked outside feeling refreshed.
"Your turn," she told Brady.

"I won't be long," he said, and went inside.

The high humidity, combined with the ninety-five-
degree temperature, had felt suffocating all day, even with
the air conditioner blasting. Evening brought little relief.
Though she had just showered, she began to perspire. She
sat on the steps and tried to study the landscape, watched
a hawk floating on a thermal, hunting his supper. But she
couldn't concentrate. She couldn't get those images of
Brady out of her mind. The smaller photographs of his
bare back and buttocks hadn't been nearly as evocative as
the larger frontal shot and the blatant shapes molded in the
black G-string's front triangle. In the quiet idleness, all she
could think of was him in the shower and water and soap
flooding over all of that hard, naked flesh. She could even
imagine him leaping onto Sal's back naked. She shook
herself out of such musing. A man had never dominated
her thoughts so completely.

He soon came out of the mobile, pushing his hair back
with his fingers and setting his hat on, tugging the brim
low on his forehead. He was wearing clean starched and
ironed Wranglers and a long-sleeve Cinch button-down
the same color as his eyes. He looked cowboy delicious,
almost too much to take in all at once. She sprang to her
feet.

"Ready?" he asked curtly, turning the lock, then slamming the door.

He seemed less friendly than he had earlier. Maybe he
was still embarrassed, she told herself. "Sure."

He gestured her ahead of him and they went to his
pickup. Inside the cab, his damp masculine smell, with a
hint of shampoo and cologne mixed in, filled the close
quarters. It zoomed to her very core, making her even

more nervous. She was glad for the daylight. "Can I ask you something?" she asked as he pulled out of the driveway and onto the highway.

He made a low grunting sound that she took to mean "Not really, but I know you're going to anyway."

"How old were you in those pictures?"

His eyes stayed fixed on the road, his left wrist hooked over the steering wheel, his right hand splayed on his thigh. "Twenty-two. Or maybe three." He answered without inflection.

"Wow. How did you get in such good shape? Did you play sports in school?"

"Nope."

"People aren't born with bodies that look like those pictures. You had to have put some effort into it. Did you work out in a gym?"

"Nope."

She chuffed. "Look, I know you know words besides 'nope' and 'yep.' " For crying out loud, hadn't Daddy said he was a college graduate? And hadn't Jake said he had owned a business?

"What I did, darlin', was work. Period. I roughnecked for a few years on an offshore rig. That's a job that'll bulk you up in a hurry."

Stories abounded in Texas about the hard physical work, as well as danger, on offshore oil wells. "Oh, my gosh, really? I've never known anyone who worked on an offshore rig. You did that when you were a kid?"

"No, I wasn't a kid. I was eighteen."

Jude envisioned the eighteen-year-olds in her classes. Few of them, even kids who worked on their parents' farms or ranches, had bodies that looked like Brady's. Her curiosity was getting the better of her again. "That's a kid. So why were you doing that kind of work when you were that young? Did you live at home? Had you finished school, quit school, what?"

His head finally turned in her direction. "Why are you so determined to hear my life story?"

"Because I'm interested. I'm interested in everyone who does something I've never done."

He didn't say anything right away, just turned his eyes back to the road. "Okay, here it is. Simple story. We always needed money. I was always big for my age, so I did physical jobs. When I turned eighteen, I answered an ad in the Fort Worth paper. I got hired onto a roustabout crew out of Houston. Eventually, I moved up to roughnecking."

Before she could ask who "we" was, he turned into the parking lot of a low-slung yellow stucco building. A red neon sign on the windowless wall said LUPE'S CANTINA. The building looked like something right out of the seamier parts of Fort Worth—not that she had been to those places, but she had seen pictures. Uncertainty swelled within her, but she tried to dismiss it. For some reason, she felt safe in Brady's company.

"Believe it or not," he said, as if he had read her mind, "this place cooks good steaks. A lot of the old-time locals come here to eat. But the surroundings probably aren't what you're used to." He pulled into a parking spot near the front door,

"I'm not used to anything in particular. Since I left college, I mostly eat at home."

The heavy door opened onto a long, narrow room with dim lighting. It was packed with people. From somewhere country music played. It could barely be heard above the din, but she could make out George Strait singing "How 'Bout Them Cowgirls."

Jude had been in any number of noisy, jam-packed bars and bistros in Bryan and Austin, but the crowds had been made up of college students. This crowd, mostly men of varying ages, was different. Instead of taking her elbow, Brady slid his large, warm hand under her hair and cupped her nape in a firm but gentle clasp as he kept her close to his side and guided her through the throng. The possessiveness of it made her feel small and protected.

Many of the bar customers seemed to know him and spoke to him as they passed. Jude had the impression all were staring at her, no doubt wondering if she had replaced the woman named Ginger. To her annoyance, she felt a smug delight at being seen in that role.

At the back of the barroom was a small dance floor, and there she spotted the source of the music. A jukebox stood like a neon-lit kaleidoscope in one corner, splaying an array of soft, varicolored light onto a small wooden dance floor. A few more steps and they were inside a dining room. A hostess met them with a big grin and hearty greeting. As she led them to a booth, over her shoulder she chattered to Brady about his sisters.

Jude and Brady took seats opposite each other. As they ordered drinks—a margarita for her and whiskey and water for him—the hostess continued to talk local gossip. Soon a waitress joined the hostess and they had a jovial conversation with Brady about his family. In the middle of it, Brady ordered two strip steaks cooked medium, baked potatoes, salads and iced tea.

After the hostess and waitress left, he said, "Steak okay with you?"

Jude smiled. "You bet. My family's in the beef business."

"I wasn't trying to be rude by not asking you what you wanted, but those girls are talkative. I figured if I didn't get a word in edgewise and tell them what we want to eat, we could be here all night. They were in the same grade in school as one of my sisters."

Jude had no idea how it would feel to have several sisters and brothers to chat about. Even her childhood relationship with her cousins wasn't the same as having siblings. "It's okay. Do your sisters all live here?"

"None of my family lives here anymore. We're all scattered in four directions now."

Jude wanted to ask why he had returned if he had no family here, but for once she managed to keep her mouth shut. They sat in awkward silence, her with her hands tucked between her knees, Brady looking around the room. He nodded at a couple who sat a few tables away, and the man returned the greeting.

"A lot of people seem to know you," Jude said. "Are you here a lot?"

"Since I can't cook worth a damn, I'm everywhere a lot if there's food. Stephenville's a small town. Once you get away from the college, there aren't that many places to get a good meal."

"Ah." Jude nodded. A few more seconds of silence, then their drinks came. The cold margarita tasted good, but strong. After the events of the day, Jude needed something strong.

"I want you to know I appreciate your helping me," he said and sipped his whiskey, swallowing on a grimace. "Clearing out the trailer took longer than I thought it would. If you hadn't come along, I'd still be packing boxes."

She had wondered if he would acknowledge that she had been of help. She didn't care so much about being thanked, but she wanted him to say she had been useful. She couldn't keep from smiling. "I offered because I wanted to. Can I ask you something?"

One corner of his mouth tipped into a sort-of grin. "Have I been able to stop you so far?"

"Where did you learn to do that trick, mounting Sal like that?"

"It's not a trick. I just refuse to let an animal that's supposed to be dumber than I am get the best of me. It's bad enough she's spoiled rotten."

"But you did it perfectly. You must have practiced it."

"Darlin', I've been working on ranches, fooling with horses and cows, my whole life. I'm not afraid of them."

She suspected he wasn't afraid of much. What little she

had learned of him in a short time said he had no fear of stepping out of the ordinary. "I'm not afraid of them, either, but I can't jump on the back of a loping horse."

He ducked his chin and rubbed his brow. End of discussion.

"Can I ask you something else? I'm not being nosy, but—"

"I know you're not. What is it you want to know?"

"Why did that woman have those pictures? Where did she get them?"

He gave a rueful sigh. "She bought 'em online. The Cowboys' PR company sells 'em."

"But you look so young in them and—"

"Darlin', the people who sell 'em don't tell their customers they're buying old pictures. And I guess people who want pictures of half-naked men wouldn't care anyway."

"But what if you don't want them sold?"

"I don't own 'em. I get a little bit of royalty money when they sell 'em, but it's very little. These days, believe me, us old guys have been replaced by young bucks wearing even less."

Recalling the thong, Jude laughed. "How could they be wearing less? You mean they're clear naked?"

He looked at her with a crooked grin. "Yep."

"Oh, my gosh." Her hands flew to cover her nose and mouth as she laughed. A new image of him without the thong replaced the more modest one.

"You're not shocked, are you?" he asked. "Lord, look at the stuff out there nowadays."

"I'm a high school teacher, remember? Almost nothing shocks me anymore. But once in a while, something does surprise me."

"Why don't we stop talking about me, and you tell me why a rich, good-looking woman—"

"Hey, Brady." A tall, lean cowboy wearing a black hat and the typical garb sauntered toward them, carrying a beer bottle. "You been out to the place?" His pointed gaze came at Jude, and she saw devilment in his eyes.

"Hey, Ace." Brady put out his hand and they shook. "Listen, I picked up the horses. I left a message on your voice mail. Figure out how much I still owe you and we'll settle up."

"No hurry." Ace's quizzical look came at Jude again.

"This is a friend of mine," Brady said, tilting his chin toward Jude. "Jude Str—Judy Strong. She's doing me a favor and helping me clear out the trailer."

Jude shot a questioning look across the table at Brady, then quickly recovered and decided to go along. She said hello and offered Ace her right hand.

Ace took it and held it a few extra seconds in more than a handshake of greeting. "Where you from?"

"Abilene," Brady said before Jude could reply. She removed her hand from Ace's.

"Abilene, huh? I roped in that little rodeo over there a few times years back. Even won a little money."

"I see," Jude said.

Ace returned his attention to Brady. "You all moved out?"

"Soon will be."

"I'm gonna miss that ornery mare," Ace said on a laugh, stealing glances at Jude. She could tell he was as curious about her as she was about Brady. "I picked up some calves from Jack a couple days ago," Ace said. "Man, he hates seeing you leave, buddy. He was ready to bawl. Says he doesn't know how he's gonna replace you."

"Yeah?" Brady said. He appeared to be embarrassed by the compliment. "So where you headed, Ace? Wanna sit down and eat with us?"

"Nah. I'm going back to the bar to drink tequila with Billy Torrence. I think there's a poker game coming together and I got paid today." He swigged a drink from the bottle, then looked down intently at Brady. "Ginger came to see me a little earlier."

Brady's brow arched as he looked up at Ace.

"She says you've moved up a rung from the rest of us, Brady. Looks like you're cutting all your old ties. Gonna start over with a clean slate, huh?"

"That's the definition of starting over, Ace."

"Cutting ties with your boy, too?"

Brady fixed him with a hard glare that said "back off," and Jude sensed his edginess again. "No," he snapped.

Ace didn't reply for a few moments. Then, "Yeah, well, Ginger's pretty upset. She was drunk and on a crying jag. I took her home and put her to bed."

Jude wondered what that meant and watched Brady's reaction. He nodded but didn't reply. His expression remained neutral. After a few seconds, Ace backed away. "Well, see you around."

Brady put out his right hand again. "If you're ever in West Texas, Ace."

"Sure thing." They shook hands, but it was nothing more than one of those ceremonial things. Jude sensed a low-grade tension between them. She suspected Brady and his friend might never meet face-to-face again.

She waited until Ace passed through the doorway to the bar. "You and Ginger were serious?"

"No. I've known her for years. She gets drunk and goes crazy."

Jude nodded and waited for more. When he said nothing else, she said, "Have you known Ace long?"

"Most of my life."

"Has he always been envious of you?"

Brady snorted. "Of me? Darlin', I don't have much for anybody to envy. Nah, Ace is just being Ace. He's a ladies' man. It's you he's interested in. Couldn't you tell?"

That had been obvious. But she wondered if Ace's attitude toward Brady came from something deeper. "He's jealous over something. Maybe it's your inheritance."

Brady's gaze moved to the doorway. "Huh," he said, as if he'd just had a sudden revelation.

"Why didn't you want him to know my name?"

"Because I don't feel like explaining to anybody what J. D. Strayhorn's daughter is doing in Lupe's Cantina in Stephenville, Texas. It's nobody's damn business."

11

Brady was having trouble with his eyes. They kept straying to the lacy edge of Jude's black bra that occasionally peeked from behind the V-neck of her tight little green top. Or they landed on the black bra strap that sometimes sneaked out at her shoulder. If she was aware of it, she showed no indication. After being around her for two days, he wondered if she would care even if she were aware of it. She didn't strike him as being an empty head who cared about her own looks and comfort above all else.

He was surprised by how she had sized up Ace in a matter of minutes. With that ability to read people, she probably made a good teacher.

He had no doubt Ace envied him inheriting a ranch, even a small one. Brady still remembered how his old friend had been awed and even intimidated by Brady's success at developing subdivisions and building upscale homes in Fort Worth. Ace had always made a living as a ranch hand and had never aspired to do much else. Still, almost every ranch hand had a dream, even if far-fetched, of owning his own place.

Knowing Ace too well, Brady was still annoyed by his blatant attention to Jude. The guy always had his eye out for a good-looking woman, even one who was taken.

Whoa! Just back up, he told himself. Jude wasn't "taken." At least not by Brady. Sure, he was turned on by looking at her and felt a strong need to protect her until he got her back to Lockett safe and sound, but Jude was nothing more than an acquaintance to him, right?

Right.

She did look sexy, though, in that top that hugged her everywhere and highlighted nearly perfect tits with plenty of enticing cleavage. *Cool it*, he warned himself. The last thing he should be looking at was Jude Strayhorn's cleavage.

The waitress appeared and he was relieved to sideline nonsensical thoughts. She set a large wooden bowl of salad, a white crockery pitcher of salad dressing and an array of fixin's in the middle of the table. She added a pair of tongs and two salad plates, then sailed away.

Jude interrupted his thoughts. "Ace mentioned your son. How old is he?"

Brady watched as she used the tongs to pile greens onto a plate. "Nine."

"Where does he live?"

"Fort Worth."

"With his mother?" She handed the heaped-up plate across the table to him.

He took it, leveling a long, querulous look at the pile of salad. Being a meat-and-potatoes man, he typically didn't eat this much green stuff in a whole week. "Yeah," he said.

She was already loading up the other plate. "How're you going to see him if you live in Lockett?"

Dammit, he didn't need to be reminded by someone who had no idea about his life or his contentious history with his ex-wife and father-in-law that he hadn't quite found an answer to that question. "I'm gonna work it out as soon as I get settled."

Holding the pitcher of salad dressing above her plate, Jude gave him a solemn, probing look. "I just wondered. A lot of the time, ex-wives don't like the kids being carted off to a location miles away."

Inwardly, he winced under her scrupulous gaze. Why did her eyes always seem to be probing, looking for something inside him? "You know this from experience? You've got kids?"

"I've never been married. But I know plenty of divorced parents who have kids." She drenched her salad with dressing, then dipped her finger in it and tasted. "Hmm. This is good dressing. Try some." She passed the pitcher across the table to him. The movement of her arm pressed against her breast, raising a soft-looking pillow of flesh above the edge of the black lace that was already spinning fantasies in his mind and groin.

Willing his eyes back to his plate, he dripped a small amount of the dressing onto his salad. "I told you it's a good place to eat," he said defensively.

"More than half my students come from single-parent homes," she said, digging into her salad. Her full lips moved with agility as she munched like a rabbit. His eyes fixed on her mouth. She swallowed with a frown, wiped her mouth with her napkin and tilted her head. "It's a challenging dilemma. The kids with only one parent don't seem to do as well in school."

Brady hated hearing that, though he knew it instinctively. He worried every day about how Marvalee and her new husband were raising—or not raising—Andy. Having grown up without a father himself, he hated not being a part of his son's daily life. "You had only one parent. You seem to have turned out okay."

She looked at him with a smile that made him dizzy. "Oh, wow. I forgot you would know that about me." She returned to her salad. "Actually, I had more supervision than most kids ever have. Besides Daddy, I had Grandpa. And a dozen housekeepers. For that matter, Daddy and Grandpa still want to supervise me. And for a long time I had Grandpa's mother. Do you remember her? Everyone called her Penny Ann, but when I was a little girl she told me to call her Grammy Pen, so I still do when I talk about her." She picked up her glass of tea and swallowed a long drink.

Jude's great-grandmother must have been ancient when

Jude was born. As a boy, Brady might have seen an elderly woman around the Circle C, but after twenty years, he couldn't recall.

He barely remembered the people with whom he had interacted often back then—people closer to his age, like Jake and Cable, and even Judith Ann. "I don't think I do," he answered, picking chunks of tomato out of his salad and placing them on the edge of his plate.

"You should eat those." She pointed her fork at the tomato chunks. "Tomatoes are good for you. They're high in antioxidants. They have lycopene. Everyone should eat either the raw fruit itself—tomatoes are really a fruit, you know—or some kind of tomato product every day."

Somehow Brady didn't think he would win this debate. He jabbed a tomato chunk with his fork and popped it into his mouth. "Is that what *you* do?"

"I try to. And I nag Daddy and Grandpa about it, too. It isn't pop science. It's real. You know that old saying about eating an apple a day? I happen to think it should be revised. I believe a tomato should be added to it."

"I see," he said, and ate some more salad and bites of tomato.

"Grammy Pen passed away just a few years ago," she said. "She was ninety-five. I really miss her. She's the person in the family I want to be like. I'm named after her. Well, not after her only. I'm also named after a cousin who died as a little kid."

Following her chatter took some effort, Brady was beginning to realize. He leaped at the chance to ask a question of his own for a change. "Who died?"

"Judith Ellen Campbell. She drowned in the Red in 1861, when the Campbells first came to Texas. She was the first Judith. I'm the third one."

"The Red."

"The Red River. You know, that long body of water between Texas and Oklahoma?"

"I know where the Red River is," Brady grumbled.

Jude giggled. "I'm kidding you. I'm trying to make you smile. But there is more than one Red River, you know."

To please her, Brady forced himself to smile. "But the others don't count."

"Spoken like a true Texan. You *are* a Texan, right?"

He wondered why she asked but didn't pursue the question. He chuckled. "Yes, ma'am. Born in Stephenville."

She went on talking between forkfuls of salad and more lip action as she chewed. "In case you're wondering how the Campbells got into the Strayhorn act, or vice versa, the founder of the Circle C was Alister Campbell. He was a farmer from Missouri and a Southern sympathizer. That's why all of the men in the family are named after Jefferson Davis. After Alister and his family got burned out by Jayhawkers, they left Missouri forever. Grammy Pen said they thought they would escape the war by coming to Texas."

"So why do you want to be like your great-grandma?" Brady asked.

"Grammy Pen was strong. She was only two years older than I am now when her husband died suddenly. Heart failure, they thought, but they never really knew. There weren't any doctors close by in those days. Some people say he was so mean and crooked, the devil called him to come and be one of his generals."

She sat back, dabbed at her mouth with her napkin and laughed. "You don't ever want to let Grandpa hear you say anything like that, though. He thinks his father was a good businessman, though most people will tell you the guy was a crooked lawyer."

Family lore. Brady had never known his grandparents on his father's side and had barely known his mother's parents. "Humph," he grunted, but he was interested in Jude's story.

"Anyway, after he died, Grammy Pen had the whole ranch on her shoulders. That same year, Pearl Harbor was bombed. Most of the men in Willard County left for the military, including Grandpa. He joined the navy."

For a man who had spent his life in West Texas, where

there were few natural bodies of water, to join the navy struck Brady as curious. "The navy?"

"That's funny, isn't it? Especially since no one in the whole family, including him, can swim. Grammy Pen said he hauled some calves to Abilene and when he passed a recruiter's office, he stopped and signed up."

"Seems like a man would have to be able to swim to be in the navy."

"Grandpa was so scared they would kick him out if he couldn't swim, he tricked them and they never knew the difference."

"You can't swim, either, huh?"

She laughed. "Where would I have learned? I could have taken swimming at A&M, but I couldn't see myself in a beginner's swimming class. I'll bet *you* can swim, though, huh?"

Brady thought again about the sheltered life Jude had led. "Yeah," he answered.

"Grandpa was in the navy more than two years, and he never did learn to swim. While he was gone, Grammy Pen worked right alongside the few hands the Circle C had left. She could ride and rope and do all the work. She managed the business end of things, too. And she gardened and cooked and ran the household. She didn't shirk from anything. A few years after the war, she finally turned management of the ranch over to Grandpa and took up causes."

Every big old ranch in West Texas probably had a similar story, including the part about a crooked ancestor. But hearing all that family history only reminded Brady of the vast differences between Jude's life and his own. Hell. She was Texas aristocracy. A damn princess. He had been a reasonably successful businessman—and had made a lot of money at one point—but compared to her, he was nothing more than a saddle tramp.

Don't let her get to you, horse sense told him. *After you get her back to Lockett, she'll disappear behind that wall of family and money and you'll never see her again.*

While she continued to talk, his mind drifted to the days just two short years ago when he'd had several popular subdivisions under development and multiple construction jobs under way. It had been a mistake for him to move to Stephenville and hole up in a single-wide trailer house, working a low-paying job. After his business fell apart, with his education and experience, he could have done a number of things in Fort Worth, and had even had some good offers. Marvalee's father hadn't succeeded in totally ruining him. But at the time, Brady had wanted nothing more than to crawl into a hole and lick his wounds. Tonight, revisiting his errors in judgment only worsened his mood.

Jude stopped chattering and eating and looked up at him, no doubt having noticed that his mind had wandered. "Am I boring you?"

"No," he answered quickly. "I've never heard the Circle C's history."

"When I get started on it, I tend to ramble. Because I love all of it so much, I forget other people might not be interested. I'm a little bit of a nut. I'm so devoted to Daddy and Grandpa and the ranch that I'm unable to leave for long. People tell me I'd be less frustrated if I just move to Fort Worth or Dallas and get some kind of real job where I can use my education and make a true contribution to society. But I know I wouldn't like leaving the ranch. Or Willard County, either."

"Why is contributing to society so important?"

"Because I was born blessed and I know it. I realize it more every day." She set her fork on the empty salad plate and her mouth broke into a smile that lit her whole face. "I'm afraid if I get too full of it, taking advantage of all that I've been given and not giving anything back, lightning might strike me or something."

Before Brady lost himself in his admiration for her, the waitress delivered their steaks, sizzling on heavy, hot platters, along with huge baked potatoes, sliced open and steaming. He watched Jude heap her potato with a little of everything—salt, pepper, butter, sour cream, grated cheese, chives and bacon bits.

So much for a delicate flower who eats like bird, he thought. But he liked that she didn't come up with the tired I-have-to-watch-my-figure cliché. She seemed to dive head-long into everything she did. He admired that, too.

He sampled a bite of steak. It was cooked to perfection, as delicious as it was tender. From the outside, Lupe's Cantina looked like a dive. Inside looked only slightly better. But he wanted Jude to know he had brought her here because he truly thought the food was good.

"How long were you married?" she asked, cutting into her steak.

Brady's fork stopped on the way to his mouth. He wasn't eager to discuss his former marriage but didn't want to be rude by saying "none of your business." "Seven years."

"Hey, you're right. This is good steak. I don't know how to cook much myself, but I appreciate good food. I eat a lot, but I usually get a lot of exercise, so I don't get fat. You said your son's nine? So he was seven when you got a divorce?"

How did she know when he got a divorce? "Uh, yeah," he answered.

"Was your ex-wife pregnant when you got married? Or was your son born early?"

Brady stared at her, his fork suspended, flummoxed by her intrusiveness.

"Wait, don't answer that." She put down her fork and raised her palms. Her shoulders heaved in a sigh. Her cleavage rose and fell. "I shouldn't have asked. It's none of my business."

Exactly, Brady thought, returning to his meal, glad to concentrate on his plate instead of the soft flesh at her neck-line.

"I apologize. I'm well-known for talking when I should be listening. It's just that I'm interested in everything." She laughed. "Just tell me when to shut my mouth. Everyone else does."

Brady liked that she was able to laugh at herself. In fact, he was enjoying her company too much. And it was beginning to have less and less to do with finding her sexy and alluring. He chuckled to show her he wasn't offended. He knew he didn't have to answer questions if he didn't want to. "I wouldn't do that. So why haven't you gotten married?"

"Oh, I'm a failure in that area. Big-time. Daddy and Grandpa would like to marry me off to someone *they* see as a good match, but I've resisted."

Brady supposed any man marrying into the Strayhorn family would be expected to meet certain requirements, like a husband being chosen by a king for his daughter, the princess. There would naturally be scrutiny and prenuptial agreements. He had been asked to sign one when he married Marvalee. Like a damn fool, he had done it, even though Marvalee was already pregnant and Brady had never quite figured out what the prenuptial agreement protected her from. *He* was the one who had gotten raped financially. "And in your daddy's estimation, who's a good spouse?"

"Someone fertile." She covered her mouth with her napkin and laughed heartily. "They want me to have kids. Sons, preferably. Sort of like one of the cows or the broodmares. If you ever go into Daddy's study, you'll see pictures of all his favorites on the credenza behind his desk. There I am, alongside his favorite bulls and stallions. If there were an auction where he and Grandpa could go and bid on a husband to mate with the headstrong female member of the family, both of them would have seats in the front row."

Is she serious? Brady wondered. He stopped cutting his steak and arched an eyebrow. "You're joking, right?"

"Not entirely. Since I'll soon be thirty, they're getting more worried every day."

Having been married to the only daughter of a wealthy Fort Worth businessman, Brady knew something about Jude's situation. Of course his former father-in-law was not nearly as rich as the Strayhorns, nor was he the overseer of a legend and a dynasty, but he had made it evident at every opportunity that his daughter's husband had to please her father as well as her. Brady stopped his memory from taking him down that thorny path. "Sounds like getting married and having kids is not something *you're* worried about."

"Not really. Although I probably should think about it. It's what Daddy and Grandpa want. I was engaged a couple of times, but things didn't work out. Daddy and Grandpa would have been happy with either one of my fiancés, but they weren't the ones who would've had to live with them. But that's all water under the bridge. Really, right now, I'm more interested in changing the way Daddy and Grandpa do some things at the ranch."

Well, that was certainly two different topics in the same breath. While Brady was mildly curious about the changes she might like to implement at the Circle C, at this moment, he found *her* and her past much more interesting. She seemed awfully nonchalant about two broken engagements. He couldn't relate. Even now, two years later, he was still uncomfortable discussing his former marriage and he wanted to talk about the divorce even less. He couldn't help wondering what kind of men she had planned to marry. "You didn't like the men you were engaged to or what?"

"Not much. The first one was sort of a selfish person. He cared more about marrying into my family than he cared about marrying me. I knew it almost from the beginning, but his parents were friends of Daddy and Grandpa. Webb's daddy is one of those silk-stocking lawyers in Austin. I saved all of us a lot of angst by breaking up with him. My second fiancé was a sissy and sort of a mama's boy. His daddy and mine are friends. Nice enough guy, but kind of helpless. It would be insane for me to marry someone who's afraid of cows and horses."

Brady agreed with her. He had seen men who were afraid of animals. He chuckled.

Staring at the lacy black edge of her bra, his thoughts leaped to sex. Of course she'd had had sex with those two men. He could think of no woman he had ever met who was celibate at twenty-nine years old. Jude was a hot number, the picture of health and vitality, with more than her share of spunk and energy and passion. No selfish bastard or mama's boy would ever be enough for her. He tried not to add "in bed" to that thought, but how could he not when that was the direction his imagination was taking him?

Sex wasn't everything, but a good time in the bedroom went a long way to gluing a relationship together. If the sex with her fiancés had been all that great, would she have been so easygoing about breaking up the relationships? He doubted it.

"My fiancés are long and boring stories," she went on. "The point is, I do understand why you'd get annoyed by my bringing up your relationship with your ex-wife. Some things are just too much trouble to explain to strangers. I've never explained my engagements entirely to Suzanne Breedlove, and she's my best friend."

Now Brady was more curious than ever. Sex aside, her former fiancés must have been upset when she bailed, because if a man were seeking to "marry up," Jude Strayhorn was as good as it got. In more ways than not, she fit the stereotypical ideal. Besides being rich, she was movie-star good-looking, educated, smart and good company. On a scale of one to ten, he might classify her a nine. That is, if he were interested enough to bother with labeling her. Nine was as high as he was willing to rate any woman, come to think of it. He had *never* met a ten.

The voices in the room suddenly sounded louder, and he noticed the jukebox had stopped. He felt uncomfortable without the music in the background. "I'm gonna buy some tunes." He got to his feet, strode to the barroom and added half a dozen quarters to the machine.

When he returned, Jude said, "You're really into music, aren't you?"

"Makes a hard job go faster. I got used to having it around in the construction business. Seemed like every sub on every job had a boom box blasting. I used to wonder if the construction industry would collapse if somebody banned honky-tonk music."

They had finished their meal. She had polished off the good-size strip steak and a baked potato as big as his hand. "Dessert?" he asked.

"No, thanks. I'm full. But I was really hungry. A biscuit and sausage only go so far."

He winced. After their late breakfast at McDonald's, he hadn't even thought of lunch. A fine host he was. And after she had volunteered to help him, too.

The waitress came and cleared the table, and Brady ordered another margarita for her and a whiskey shot for himself. While they waited for them, Jude leaned forward, her forearms on the table, her long hair falling over them like shimmering silk. "Listen, do people ever use that dance floor in the other room?"

"Sure. If they want to."

"Could we, uh . . . could we dance?"

"Dance?"

"I don't get to very often. Dancing's like swimming. Unless it's Cable, I don't think anyone in my family knows how. I'm not very good at it, but I'd just like to, you know . . . dance."

Brady didn't especially enjoy dancing, but he knew how and he didn't mind humoring her. "Okay, sure." He scooted from his seat, stood and offered her his hand. She scooted out of the booth, too, and he led her to the dance floor. No one else was dancing.

Sliding his arm around her waist, he positioned her in front of him. She stood there rigidly with at least two feet between them, looking up at him expectantly, her whiskey-colored eyes filled with a hundred layers. And for a fleeting moment, he wondered what she truly thought of him as a man.

It doesn't matter what she thinks, a voice told him. There were too many differences between them.

He glanced down at her left hand lying on his right forearm. "Well, the first thing you need to know about dancing, darlin', is it's a contact activity."

"Oh. Right." She laughed and placed her hand on his shoulder.

He steered them out to the middle of the dance floor and soon discovered that, as she had said, she wasn't very good at it. After she tripped over his feet several times, he stopped. "How many times did you say you've danced?"

She shrugged. "Three or four. I went with Suzanne to a couple of rodeo dances, but I didn't learn much about dancing. At rodeo dances, most people are too drunk to dance. But they aren't too drunk to drive." She laughed again.

"That's a scary thought," Brady muttered, liking her off-beat sense of humor. He didn't disagree with her assessment of rodeo dances. "Okay, just bear with me here."

He knew not the first thing about teaching a woman to dance, had never even tried to do it, but he placed his right hand on her hip and pulled her against him, at the same time sliding his right knee slightly between her legs. Her eyes flared and he said, "I don't know how to teach dancing, but from this stance, I can force your feet to go somewhere."

Her eyes lit up with understanding. "Oh. Okay." She relaxed her shoulders and wiggled her hips a little. "Okay, I'm ready."

God, she was killing him. "Now I'm gonna just sort of move you around the floor a little. You just loosen up and get the feel of moving backward. When you get to relaxing some, we can work on the steps."

He half led, half dragged her through the rest of the song. Another slow tune began, and she showed no sign of giving up. She wouldn't. He had already figured out she was no quitter. He gave her a few suggestions about what to do with her feet and they went through the exercise again.

Three songs later, they were laughing and moving together fairly skillfully and he was having fun teasing her. He didn't mind having his arms around her, either. The jukebox stopped playing, so he hooked an arm around her shoulder and guided her back toward their booth, intent on sitting down and sipping his drink.

"I've got some quarters in my purse," she said.

"Aren't you tired?"

"I'm just learning. I don't want to give up now." She bent for her purse, dragged it toward the edge of the booth seat and began digging inside.

Yep. He had pegged her personality.

On a sigh, Brady shoved his hand into his pocket and came up with several quarters. "Here," he said. "I've got quarters. If you want to keep at it, I'll play something." He picked up his glass and drained it. She did likewise. Before going to the jukebox to revive the music, he signaled for the waitress to bring them two more drinks.

By the end of a couple more tunes, she was moving with him easily without stepping on his feet. By the end of three more, they were scarcely moving at all, and they had stopped laughing. Her head was resting on his shoulder and his cheek was pressed against her sweet-smelling hair. Her left arm encircled his waist, their bodies were melded together tighter than a sandwich and he was valiantly fighting to keep from wrapping his own left arm around her. She was warm and soft, and that clean, flowery smell that was distinctly hers hypnotized him. The room seemed to be spinning. An erection had swelled in his shorts and he had practically sprained his back trying to maneuver himself so she wouldn't be aware of it. But he knew damn well she had to notice. Yet, she had made no attempt to move away. And the fact that she hadn't was tearing him up.

At the same time, J. D. Strayhorn's face, with hard brown eyes and a scowling mouth, floated in and out of his mind. On the verge of praying for willpower, Brady gripped her shoulders, set her away from him and looked into her face. "Jude. We need to sit down."

She looked up at him with parted moist lips and dreamy eyes that had gone from amber to as dark as coffee. "Okay," she said softly.

A longing profound enough to be mystifying passed through him. *Jesus, get me out of this.*

But even as he prayed, he wasn't sure he wanted out of whatever he was in.

When they reached the booth, four fresh drinks were sitting on the table. The waitress breezed by and said, "Ace wanted to buy y'all a drink."

"Great. I'm thirsty." Jude slid into the booth and picked up a margarita.

Brady sat down, too, but he was embarrassed to look her in the eye. He usually kept his libido under control, especially in a matchup that had absolutely nowhere to go. The alcohol plus knowing she had seen him bare assed in those pictures had mixed in with his belief that she knew he had a hard-on. It had all done something to him. In a matter of hours, she had become aware of him more intimately than had most of the people he knew. He had never been more uncomfortable.

A few minutes later, when he felt some relief behind his fly, he pushed his drinks to the center of the table. "Look, I've had enough to drink and I've got to drive. Let's go on home. I want to get up early and get on the road."

"Right."

Thank God she doesn't want to dance some more.

He signaled for the waitress to bring them the check. He paid in cash. He hadn't had credit cards for two years. Without them, he had discovered life went more smoothly.

Jude gulped what was left of her drink, got to her feet, took a few seconds to steady herself and picked up her purse.

Oh, hell. Is she drunk?

He, too, stood and urged her ahead of him toward the front door. As they passed through the bar again, Ace sat back on his bar stool and reached out. He clasped Jude's forearm, stopping them. "Guess I'll see ya when I see ya, Brady."

Ace didn't fool Brady. The man's eyes, as well as his

hand, were on Jude again. Brady felt a rush of . . . what? Jealousy? *Christ!*

No. It wasn't jealousy. It was responsibility. She was in his charge. He had to make sure she returned to Lockett no worse off than when they left, which meant keeping her away from the likes of Ace.

He nudged her forward again, away from Ace's touch. "I won't be hard to find. Thanks for the drink."

12

The heavy front door of Lupe's Cantina banged shut behind them, abruptly arresting the barroom sounds. It also killed the air-conditioning. Enveloped by the day's lingering heat and thick humid air, Jude felt as if she had walked into a steam bath. She knew she was in a lowland part of the state where the nighttime summer temperature didn't drop, nor did a dry, cool evening breeze relieve the heat. And the air had a swampy odor. Stephenville wasn't far from Bryan and Austin. She hadn't enjoyed the climate there, either.

Brady had parked his pickup a short walk away. He bleeped the doors unlocked and held the passenger door for her. As she brushed past him and climbed inside, she couldn't see his eyes, but she was well aware of his body. He had tried to conceal the bulge in his jeans that pressed against her stomach while they were dancing, but she had felt it anyway.

Without a word, he closed her into the pickup's dark sanctum. Was he angry? Upset? She couldn't tell. What she *could* tell was that his mood had changed and something was on his mind. She couldn't pinpoint the exact moment they had gone from fun to something else, and too much tequila wasn't helping. All she knew was that one minute he had been teaching her to dance, and they had been laughing and joking about her clumsiness; the next they were moving belly to belly, thigh to thigh, and were close to making out on the dance floor. Then he had abruptly brought an end to the dancing.

Jude. We need to sit down.

She watched him round the front end of the pickup, her heartbeat thumping in her ears. She blamed that, too, on the tequila. He scooted behind the wheel, then reached back, picked up his hat from the backseat and set it on his head. He tugged the brim down on his forehead, fastened his seat belt and started the engine, all without saying a word. He pulled out of the parking lot and sped toward the traffic light and the left turn that would take them to his mobile home.

In the darkness, the pickup cab felt more intimate than it had in the daylight. She sank into the buttery leather bucket seat with her thoughts. The image from the poster and the black triangle of cloth barely covering his most intimate parts was back. It had returned to tease her when she felt his hardness against her stomach on the dance floor. From that moment on, the erotic picture of his bare body had returned and fixed itself in her mind, and she became acutely aware of everywhere their bodies touched. Instead of putting distance between them like she should have, she had arched her back and pressed even closer. What was wrong with her?

The question she had pondered yesterday came back to her, and she just had to ask him, "Where do you, uh, plan on me sleeping?"

"My sleeping bag's still on the shelf in the closet. I'll throw it on the couch in the living room, and you can have the bed."

His answer had come so quickly, she could only conclude he must have thoughts similar to hers. And imagining what those thoughts might be did nothing to quell her uneasiness. "I don't mind renting a room here in town," she said. After all, he was more than six feet tall. He wouldn't fit on the couch.

"That's not necessary. And driving in to town to pick you up tomorrow is forty miles out of the way. I'd like to get back to Lockett before noon."

"Oh. I didn't think of that."

He looked at her across his shoulder, his expression unreadable in the cab's dim light, but she could see he wasn't smiling. "Quit worrying," he said, so sharply she didn't need to see his face to know he was irritated. "The sleeping arrangements aren't a problem. I know what you're thinking, but I'm not some horny kid. I'm not gonna jump your bones."

She felt her whole body flush. Thank God he couldn't possibly know what she was thinking. Or could he? "I didn't think . . . that."

He turned his attention to the radio, switched it on and punched buttons until Josh Turner's sexy deep voice cut through the silence with the last half of "Would You Go with Me." Jude kept quiet, gluing her eyes to the dark landscape whisking past them. Tension felt like a blanket around them, so thick and heavy in the pickup cab's close space, she could barely endure it. "I think it would make more sense if I took the sofa. I'm only five-seven. I think I'd be more comfortable there than you would."

"Darlin', I don't expect you to camp out. It's no big deal. I've slept on the couch before."

Now, what did *that* mean? When he was married?

He appeared to be watching something in his side mirror. He stopped for the red light, made the left turn when a green arrow lit up and headed into the moonlit night toward the mobile home. On the radio, Alan Jackson sang "Don't Ask Why."

In the silence, Jude's agile imagination contrived multiple scenarios of her slightly tipsy and overheated body entwined with Brady's perfect one. It was an outrageous notion, but something had freed her inhibitions and replaced good sense. Was it seeing the intimate pictures of him? Was it because she'd had one too many margaritas? Was it as simple as being out of town, away from the scrutiny of everyone who had ever known her? Or maybe none of that was the explanation. Maybe this attraction went back even farther than the past few hours. Since the first time they met, she had behaved so strangely around him, she almost didn't recognize herself. A mysterious force beyond her control seemed to have taken over.

Get real, Jude. It's sex. Bottom line: Mysterious force equals sex.

God, had it been only two days since she drove into Mrs. Wallace's driveway and saw him?

Contemplating sex with any man she scarcely knew was ridiculous, but even more so with Brady Fallon. She could count off, oh, probably twenty good and practical reasons why it would be a monumental mistake. But hadn't she already ignored practicality in the first place by inviting herself to come here with him?

Something deeper than practicality raised its pesky head and set her thoughts on a new course. Sex with the two men she had planned to marry had been far from perfect and not memorable in a good way. The awkwardness that had accompanied it had always made her anxious. She found the idea of sex with someone like Brady both frightening and fascinating at the same time. He had a rawness about him that neither Webb Henderson nor Jason Weatherby possessed. Brady would have certain expectations, and she doubted she would know how to meet them. A man who looked like him probably had untold experiences with women, while Jude hadn't even been kissed in more than three years.

She rarely felt inadequate in any area, but when it came to men and relationships, and sex in particular, she had to acknowledge her limitations. She knew more about mating in cows and horses than she knew about her own sexuality. She might as well be a twenty-nine-year-old virgin. Suzanne was right.

Minutes lapsed with neither of them speaking. Perhaps it was just as well. Her throat had gone so dry, she might not be able to talk, and her chest felt as if a lariat had tightened around it. And her pulse rate seemed to be elevating with every passing minute.

The dash clock showed eleven when they came to a stop in front of the mobile home.

Brady still seemed out of sorts. She didn't wait for him to come around to open her door. She opened it herself and slid out. Preoccupied with all that was going on inside her head, she crashed into him.

His hands sprang out and grabbed her shoulders, steadying her. On her bare arms, they felt as hot as a brand and set off a new tumult within her. Startled, she looked up into his unsmiling face.

He dropped his hands and stepped back. "Sorry," he said stiffly.

He let her pass in front of him, and they walked toward the mobile home. She stood behind him while he unlocked the front door. An unfamiliar rhythm thrummed in her belly, raged in her ears. . . . *Lust* . . . pure animal lust. She could think of no time when she had lusted after a man, but she was convinced that was what had her bumbling and fumbling now.

He stood aside and gestured her into the mobile, then came in behind her and clicked on the overhead light. The room lit up in the dingy pall of one ceiling light. He had turned off the air conditioner before they went to town. The place felt airless and as hot as a sauna, and that trailer-house plastic smell was back, though the mobile had been closed up and locked for only a few hours. Her whole body began to perspire.

"We need to hit the sack so we can get going early tomorrow," he said, lifting off his hat and dropping it onto the only chair in the living room. "I'll get the sleeping bag. Then the bedroom's all yours."

"Okay, I guess, but, really—"

Before she could finish, he tramped toward the bedroom, the heavy thuds of his boot heels bouncing off the mobile home's thin floor.

Before she had time to sit down on the sofa, he returned, carrying a rolled sleeping bag under one arm. "I turned on the air. This isn't like West Texas. Here, it doesn't cool off at night." His speech sounded strained, his tone brusque.

"But what about you? Won't you be too warm on the sofa?"

"I'll be fine."

She didn't believe that. "I was just thinking, the, uh, bed's big enough. We, uh . . . we could both be comfortable."

He looked at her, blank faced. Tension strung between them like a taut rope, even more potent than it had been in the pickup cab.

"To sleep, I mean," she added quickly. Now her heart was galloping.

A few beats passed, then his head shook. "Nuh-uh." Her duffel had been sitting on the sofa since this morning. He moved it to the floor. "You might be comfortable, but I wouldn't." He unrolled the sleeping bag, threw it out to its full length and began smoothing and fitting it to the sofa.

"But I think—"

"Jude," he said, cutting her off bluntly, at the same time straightening and looking at her with fierce eyes. A thin sheen of perspiration shone on his face. "Trying to sleep beside you in a bed would be a torment I don't want to inflict on myself. Get it?"

The sharp tone pierced her. Without warning, hot tears rose in her throat, but she swallowed them quickly. "Oh."

A muscle bunched in his jaw and a few more seconds of loud silence passed. Then he looked away and shook his head again. "I've gotta get a pillow." He strode back to the bedroom.

Was he mad at her? She hated the idea that he might be. People were never mad at her. Tears made it all the way to the rims of her eyes. She blinked to keep them from spilling over. She was behaving worse than teenager. In fact, she had students who could probably handle this better than she was.

He returned and caught her wiping the dampness from her cheeks with her fingertips. He dropped the pillow onto the sofa and reached her in two steps, but she couldn't look at him. She detested having him see her reddened eyes. His arm draped around her shoulder and he pulled her against his side, into the heady space and scent of warm male and woodsy cologne. "Hey, now," he said softly, and gave her shoulder a little squeeze.

With nowhere else to put her hands, she had to place one on his middle and the other on the small of his back. She could feel his heartbeat, and it was pounding. Her eyes landed on the top button of his shirt. A tuft of crisp brown hair and his tanned neck showed in the vee of his open collar. She could see his pulse jumping in the hollow of his throat.

"C'mon now. Don't cry," he said.

"No. I'm not. Really, I'm not. I never cry."

His rough fingers pushed her hair back from her face, and placed it behind her shoulders, as if she were a child. "I didn't intend to hurt your feelings. I just meant . . ."

As his words trailed off, she looked up into his beautiful blue eyes. In the room's dim light they looked like sapphires, and they were staring back at her with what she believed to be desire, saying so much more than words. A wild feeling of arousal charged through her. He was so close, his face only inches away. Her palms already touched his midriff. Her body already touched his. The room's heat and that primal force filling the space around them with an excruciating weightiness pushed her up on her tiptoes, and she pressed her lips to his.

His head jerked back, his hands grasped her wrists. "Jude, what're you do—"

"I—I don't know." Her voice wavered as if it were unwilling to support her actions. His strong hands manacled her wrists, holding her in place.

"I just know I—I . . . The way you were looking at me, the—the way you were when we were dancing, I thought you . . . wanted . . ."

His gaze held hers. "Jude, God, do you think I'm nuts?"

He was rejecting her? With horror, she realized he was.

Humiliation struck like a slap. More tears burned behind her eyes, but she steeled herself. Her pride would never allow her to show him he had hurt her. She jerked her wrists against his grasp. "Let go."

But he held her like a vise. "Jude, wait."

"I said let go of me." She jerked against his strength again. Jaw clenched, she kicked at his shin with the toe of her boot, but he made a little backward hop and she missed. As quick as lightning, he loosened his hold on her wrists and she found her arms pinned to her sides by his and her body pressed tightly against him, as if she were wrapped in a straitjacket. His long legs bracketed hers, and against her belly she could again feel the ridge behind his fly.

She squirmed within his hold, but his strength was too much to overcome. She glared up at him, clenched teeth and hostile eyes her only weapons. "Let. Me. Go."

"Dammit, wait," he said again, only holding her tighter and capturing her eyes with his. "What I said didn't come out right. Jude, listen to me. What I meant to say was what sane man wouldn't want you? You had it right. That last hour of dancing just about did me in."

She tried to move. "Let me go."

"Not 'til you calm down. . . . Jude, stop fighting me and listen."

She stilled and looked up at him again. Though emotions she had never known careened through her, her body remained tight as a stretched rubber band.

"Jude, give me a break here. Right now, I'm your daddy's employee. And I really need that job. I can't afford to do . . . this."

Something even harder to bear than humiliation rushed into her—the realization of her own insensitivity and self-absorption. Hadn't he already told her the job at the Circle C was important to him? And hadn't she made this trip in secret because she knew the consequences if her father learned she was here?

She ducked her chin and gazed at his chest, her thoughts

a blur. His pulse seemed to be beating even harder in the hollow of his throat. The physical struggle and adrenaline, coupled with the frustration she had already felt, had her own heart leaping as if it wanted to escape her rib cage. "I know. Honestly, I do know. Just let me go. Please."

He dropped his arms, freeing her, and stepped back. She couldn't make herself lift her chin and see her own mortification reflected in his face, but she felt his eyes boring into the top of her head, heard his ragged breathing. Her own breath was shaky, but no more so than the rest of her. She barely found her voice. "This was stupid. *I* was stupid. As you say, let's just go to sleep so we can get an early start tomorrow. The sooner I get home, the better."

Gathering her composure, she flung back her hair, walked across the room, picked up her duffel and started for the bedroom. But she had to say something, had to somehow acquit herself. She stopped but still didn't want to look him in the face. "I misunderstood." She swallowed, groping for words. "I, uh, thought you—you were attracted to me in the same way I was"—she drew a deep breath—"attracted to you."

"I'm attracted to a lot of things I know better than to grab on to," he said, his voice still rough.

A humorless huff blurted from her throat, and she started for the bedroom again, all bluff.

"Dammit, Jude . . ." His hand caught her elbow.

She stiffened but let him draw her back and turn her to face him, let him clasp her jaw with his calloused fingers and lift her chin until she had to look up at him. Their gazes locked. His blue-flame eyes burned into hers. She could feel his warm breath on her lips. Seconds passed. Then his head slowly shook. "But God knows," he murmured, "I've been known to take a chance." His mouth lowered toward hers.

She hadn't been wrong about the desire she saw in those eyes. She thought she could hear both their hearts beating in runaway harmony. His fingers moved down the side of her throat until his hand closed gently on her neck. "God," he whispered, "you're so damn . . ."

He leaned toward her again, and this time, she didn't try to escape. His mouth came down on hers and she didn't resist. Just as she suspected he might, he kissed her as no one ever had, making her feel wanted in a way she had never felt. His lips parted hers and his tongue thrust into her mouth. He tasted of whiskey, but not unpleasant. His hands burrowed into her hair until they clutched her head and she couldn't have escaped his marauding mouth even if she had wanted to. Utter bliss exploded within her. Warmth pooled between her thighs and in the tips of her breasts, making them so achingly tight that an unfamiliar sound escaped her throat. Grabbing on to his shoulders as if he were a lifeline, she kissed him back with all her might.

He lifted his lips from hers, dragged them across her cheek and down her neck. "God, Jude," he whispered raggedly, "you're as hot as I am."

He set her away, leaving her mouth feeling swollen and wet and her eyes searching his. Their breath rushed and shuddered, and their chests heaved, His eyes had turned an odd violet color and lost their clarity. They now looked dark and sleepy. He turned away, locked the front door and switched off the light, plunging them into total blackness. He scooped her up, settled her in his arms and carried her toward the bedroom. She clung to his back and neck, buried her face against his shoulder. "I always say the wrong things," she said softly. "I don't mean to."

"I know," he said just as softly.

The bedroom was so cool, it almost felt chilly. It didn't seem possible, but it was even darker than the living room. But he seemed to know the way through the blackness. The air conditioner's low roar overrode sound, but not the echo of her heart thrashing in her ears. He laid her across the bed and followed her down. In a whisper of both their starched denim jeans and the dull thunk of colliding boots, his knee pressed between hers and pinned her to the mattress.

Though she was surrounded by him—his scent, his heat, his strength, his profound masculinity—she still felt a need to explain. "It's . . . it's just that . . . I wanted to . . ."

"Shh. It's okay, sweetheart."

His arm cradled her neck while his mouth cruised over her cheeks, down her throat. His hand skimmed her whole body, stroking, caressing more gently than she would have ever expected from a man of his size and strength. The more he explored, the more swollen and hot her nipples felt inside her bra. All of her clothing began to feel binding. Even her skin felt too tight and too hot. She began to squirm and clutch at his shirt, trying to unbutton it. "Brady, can we . . . ?"

He started to sit up, but she couldn't bear to have him part from her, even for a minute. "Don't—don't stop."

He kissed her again. "Just gonna turn on the light," he said.

"Oh. Do—do we have to?"

"You've never had the light on?"

"No. I mean, well, yes, but . . . I don't know what I mean."

"You're beautiful. I want to see you," he said, softly. "It'll be okay."

"Okay," she said, her voice coming out tiny.

She sat up with him, hooking her arms around his thick biceps and pressing her breasts against it, laying her cheek against his shoulder. With his other hand, he reached over and switched on the stubby round lamp on the bedside table. Light not much better than a flashlight's cast a golden fan on the floor and on the edge of the bed. She watched him open the bedside table drawer, his capable hands spotlighted by the lamplight. He lifted out the black box of condoms she had left in the drawer earlier.

An image of the woman named Ginger flitted through her mind along with the certain knowledge that she and maybe others had slept with him in this very bed, but Jude refused to let a visual form. She wanted this, and nothing else mattered.

His fingers came to her chin and he smiled. "It's a dim light." He kissed her sweetly, then reached for her foot and pried off her boot. His big hand closed around her foot in a caress as he looked at her across his shoulder for a few beats. Now she was glad he had turned on the light, even as a nerve jumped inside her stomach. She wanted to see him, too.

He tugged off her other boot, followed by her socks.

His arms came around her, and he held her for a long moment. He was good at hugging. She wrapped her arms around his shoulders and hugged him back. Then he kissed her, his tongue touching hers tentatively, as if he were testing for her response. They kissed and kissed and his hands moved over her body until an audible soughing sound had replaced normal breathing and her very bones felt like warm liquid.

Eventually, their mouths parted and he tugged at the hem of her top. "Help me take this off," he said. "I don't want to tear it." With no hesitation, she yanked the knit top over her head. Her nipples tightened even more as the room's cool air touched her bare skin, yet her breasts throbbed with heat.

He ducked his head, and his mouth moved over the mound of flesh above the edge of her bra. "I do love black lace," he mumbled against her skin, "but right this minute, sweetheart, it's in the way." He delicately tugged the lacy edge down and exposed her nipple. It was embarrassingly rigid and protruded over the edge of the lace. On a deep hum, he kissed and licked, drew the firm peak deeply into the wet heat of his mouth. Something deep inside her flexed. She curved her hands around his head and held him in place.

"Oooh," she breathed, closing her eyes and basking in knowing he desired her. He sucked rhythmically, and deep muscles she didn't know she had began to clench up inside her. The sensation was consuming and she wanted more.

His hand went behind her and she felt her bra release. In the far recesses of her clouded mind, a voice told her he was awfully practiced at this to be able to undo it one-handed, but she couldn't make herself worry over it.

"Don't ever think I don't want you," he said.

She thrilled at the words. "I won't. No. I won't."

Her bra went away and his large hand cupped her breast, plumped it and molded it while his mouth moved over it, his beard stubble rasping the tender skin. While he teased the one breast, his fingers stroked and pulled at the nipple of the other. On a deep sigh, she tilted her head back and pushed her chest forward, making it easy for him to do whatever he wanted. Her vaginal muscles throbbed, and that deep flex became an exquisite need. She had never felt such emptiness. "Brady, I feel funny. Inside. Can you . . . can you do something?"

"What, sweetheart? Tell me what you want."

"I don't know. . . . Just something."

He chuckled softly against her breasts. "Yes, ma'am." His arm slid behind her and he eased her back on the bed, murmuring soft words made incoherent by the roar of the air conditioner. His hot mouth closed over her other nipple, and he drew hard, his breath humid and warm. Save for the desire for more of the same, every thought fled, and she moaned softly so he would know how much he pleased her. His hand slid down and she felt him undo her belt and tug at her zipper. She began to tremble. The next thing she knew, his mouth was at her ear and he was whispering reassurances and wicked promises and his hand was sliding inside her panties. She felt so swollen and hot and damp. Drenched. Still, drunk with desire, she opened her knees and he cupped her sex. His finger found her opening and slipped inside, "I'm—I'm wet," she said weakly, clenching around his finger.

"That's a good thing." To her dismay, he withdrew his finger and took her mouth in another slow, voluptuous kiss, at the same time working her jeans down past her hips. When they would go no farther, he lifted his mouth from hers. "Lift up, sweetheart." She dug her heels into the mattress and raised her hips. He easily stripped off her jeans and panties. And just like that, she was naked on his bed, and his

eyes and hands were roaming and stroking as if she belonged to him, and he was telling her she was soft as a kit-
ten and beautiful, and heat was surging in every part of her
body.

He sat up again and tugged off his own boots, yanked off
his socks. Shamelessly sprawled, she propped herself on her
elbows and watched as he straightened and pulled his shirt
from his waistband and began to unbutton it, revealing a
strip of his tanned chest an inch at a time. He unbuttoned the
cuffs, peeled the garment off and tossed it away, his muscles
rippling and bunching under his skin. She took in the full
measure of his wide chest, lightly dusted with hair that
trailed all the way to his belt buckle. She had a mental picture of where it ended. . . . But in the poster, he'd had no
body hair.

He stood, unbuckled his belt and shucked his jeans and
shorts, his eyes never leaving her. His erection sprang free,
only inches from her face. He was beautifully made from
head to toe, and perfect. And he was impossibly large.
Something dark spiked within her. She wanted to please him
in the way her first fiancé had taught her. She eased off the
edge of the mattress onto her knees, leaned forward and
pressed her face against his groin. He went perfectly still.
"Jude, don't . . ."

She ignored him and clutched his taut buttocks, breathed
in his musky scent, pressed kisses against the crisp nest surrounding his erection. His jutting penis twitched as her
cheek touched it, and she moved her mouth along the hot,
velvety flesh until she reached the plump tip. She molded
her mouth over it, thrilled at the soft grunt that came from
him. She licked away salty moisture, slid her mouth the
length of him, until she could feel the thick tip of him
against the back of her throat, then she drew back slowly and
circled the rim with her tongue. "Oh, Jesus," he ground out,
grasping her shoulders and pushing himself away from her.
"Sweetheart, I'll come."

He pulled her up and jerked back the covers on the bed.

"Get in," he said roughly, and she crawled between the sheets. Everything changed. In an instant he was hovering over her, bracketing her with his arms and kneeing her thighs apart. He looked down at her with fiery eyes and a hard mouth. "Where'd you learn that?" he said raggedly, and kissed her fiercely.

His mouth moved over her breasts, her torso, down her body. His tongue sank into her navel. She shuddered and arched her back, lifted her belly to him. He nipped at her flesh, pressed hot suckling kisses to the hollows beneath her hip bones, cruised to where her thighs joined her trunk, and all the while his whispery words, thick and broken, played with her mind . . . *climb up inside you . . . never come out . . . come 'til you scream . . .*

Now her heart was hammering. No man had ever spoken such words to her, but they excited her. All of that was what she thought she wanted. He clasped her knees with his palms and pushed her thighs wide, ducked his head and nuzzled her pubic hair, inhaled deeply. From somewhere it came to her that smell was the oldest of humankind's senses, even as panic and embarrassment suffused her in equal measure. She pushed against his head. "Brady, don't . . ."

"Don't what?" His mouth moved over the insides of her thighs.

"Brady, I've never . . ." She felt his breath warm against her most intimate place. "No one's ever . . ."

"Close your eyes and relax," he said huskily. Then his mouth was there, where no man's mouth had ever been, and she was shaking all over and floating in a haze of anticipation.

She forced herself up, braced on her elbows, fisted her hand in his hair, intending to stop him, but the sight of his head between her legs aroused her in a way she had never been before. When his tongue swept the length of her cleft, all she could do was whimper and let her knees fall wide.

She felt herself open. Then his hands slid under her bottom and he lifted her to his mouth. His tongue slipped into the top of her sex, and exquisite pleasure shot through her. With a gasp she braced on one hand and gripped a fistful of his hair, watched his head move as he licked into her again and again. Rational thought left her mind. The flex inside her turned to deep spasms and driving need. Nothing mattered but his agile tongue's point of contact. . . . Her breath turned to quick pants, out of her control . . . *oh . . . oh . . . oh . . .*

He stopped abruptly, leaving her bereft and desperate. "Don't stop," she cried. "Please don't stop." His wet mouth moved up her body and took her mouth again in a savage kiss. Her hips hitched against him. "Please don't stop," she begged again. She sucked on his tongue, licked her own taste from his lips.

He pulled away from her.

"Just a minute, sweetheart." He grabbed a condom off the beside table and quickly snapped it on with trembling hands.

Then he was back, between her thighs, his body hovering above hers, and the wide tip of him was there, nudging into where she felt so hot and empty. "I want to be inside you when you come," he choked out.

"Hurry," she said, lifting herself, her thighs shamelessly open. She ran her hands over his muscled back, clutched at his firm buttocks. He pushed into her in one long, slow stroke, until it seemed he could go no farther. He stopped, groaning softly. Her hungry flesh pulled against his hardness. He felt so big inside her, but she wriggled against him, wanting more. He held himself still. She opened her eyes and saw his face, his expression strained and harsh.

"Lift your knees, sweetheart. Put your legs around me."

She obeyed, taking him until it felt as if he were buried all the way to her heart. "Oh. Oh, Brady . . ."

"Okay?"

"Yes." She lifted her head and kissed him.

"Stay with me," he murmured, his voice gruff. He began to rock in a slow, ceaseless rhythm. His hot, thick flesh moved inside her with melting friction and deep thrusts, tormenting her with utter delight. She lost track of time and thought. Those needy deep muscles grabbed at his penis again and again, and he groaned his pleasure. Then, down there, where they were joined, spasms of the sweetest agony began to wash through her. His mouth locked onto hers. Stars passed behind her eyes as spasms of pleasure rippled through her. Somehow, through the haze that had taken her over, she felt him strain, heard him grunt. Instinctively, she dug her fingers into his buttocks and anchored him to her. He pounded hard up into her, once, twice, until a bark burst from his chest and he collapsed on top of her.

He was shaking and sweating, and she could feel his heart pounding. She was no better off herself. When she found the strength to speak, she whispered, "Oh, my gosh. Are we okay?"

He heaved a great breath and chuckled against her neck. "I don't know yet."

They clung to each other. Soon he started kissing her face and neck and murmuring words of sweetness to her. He stayed inside her for a long time. She didn't move, not wanting him to leave her. Finally, he shifted to her side, but his heavy arm remained draped across her body.

Brady left her and padded to the bathroom. He was shaken in an unexpected way. As he washed himself in the vanity sink, he thought about the conflicting mix that was Jude Strayhorn. She was beautiful and rich, but down-to-earth and funny and fun. She was naive but, at the same time, hot as a pistol and sexy. Every man's dream. And she didn't even know it. He had sensed that primitive passion in her when she confronted him in his aunt's driveway, and tonight he had let it lure him past reason. When she had shown him she had a hunger that matched his, the loss of control had begun to creep in. Then when Ace had blatantly shown an interest in her, even put his hand on her, Brady had lost his damn mind. He had wanted to clock Ace Earl, a man he had known for thirty years, just for touching her.

He had to ask himself if he could bear to ever let her go.

He studied his reflection in the vanity mirror. Those were dangerous sentiments for a man who had nothing to offer.

He returned to the bedroom, crawled under the covers and gathered her in his arms. Her body was smooth and soft and lush, all that he loved about women. She snuggled close to him and fit her head against his shoulder, her hand on his chest. "You're something else," he told her.

"I don't know what just happened. I've never . . . I never was before."

God, she was innocent. He smiled, idly stroking the back of her smooth hand with his fingertips. "You're so good. You're just so . . . special."

"No one's ever said that about me."

He scooted down and turned on his side to face her, belly to belly, burrowed his hands in her hair and held her head for a kiss. Then he drew back and smiled. She looked at him and searched his face with eyes layered with shadows. "You make me feel things I've never felt," she said softly, and he almost stopped breathing. "You're wonderful," she said, and his heart nearly stopped.

"You're wonderful, too." He didn't even hesitate to say it.

They talked. She told him how deeply she had been hurt by learning her first fiancé had used her. Brady barely contained his anger. As an eighteen-year-old college freshman who had always lived in a bubble of parental protection, she would have been a lamb. Luckily she had been smart enough to figure out what was happening before it was too late. She told him how, after that, she had devoted herself to her education, not really reconciling with her dad until after she moved back to the ranch. She told him how much it meant to her to be given charge of the Circle C. He even gave her a thumbnail sketch of his own life.

"If you hadn't inherited your aunt's ranch," she asked, "would you have stayed in Stephenville?"

"No. Before Aunt Margie passed away, I had been planning to start a new subdivision in a small town west of Fort

Worth, where my mom lives. I already had my eye on some land and was putting some things in place."

"What if you can't make the ranch work? Will you leave Lockett?"

"I'll have to."

"Oh," she said.

He was certain he heard dismay in her voice and was ridiculously pleased. "Jude, would you care?"

"Yes," she said. "I just can't say I wouldn't."

13

Jude awoke, her stomach rumbling, but she didn't open her eyes. Though everything in the kitchen had been packed, she knew a plastic jug of milk still sat inside the refrigerator. The idea of cold, soothing liquid sliding down her throat was incredibly enticing.

The only sound she could hear was the low roar of the air conditioner. The room was cold, but beneath the sheet, Brady's skin was toasty warm. She could feel his even breathing on her neck, his steady heartbeat and crisp chest hair against her back. She thought of waking him but decided against it. They had made love all night. The last time, they had emerged from a deep slumber, more asleep than awake, and found each other in the dark. Later they had drifted back to sleep with him still inside her.

Through the gauzy layers of her still half-asleep brain, the conversation she'd had with Suzanne echoed. . . . *You've never had it when it was really, really good. If you ever did . . . you couldn't leave it alone. . . . When you find a guy who does it all, you'll be so hungry for it, you'll beg him.*

She felt silly and girlish. No wonder Suzanne constantly railed at her about her about being naive. Naive was what she was. Up until last night, that is. Would she now be someone who couldn't leave it alone? Would she now find herself chasing after men, as Suzanne sometimes did, just for sex? She shrank from the thought, but at the same time, after what she and Brady had done in this bed, how could her attitude toward men, any men, ever be the same?

Brady. She felt a tiny smile tug at her lips. Sweet, strong and gentle Brady. She had never known such intimacy with another human being. Compared to him, the two men her family would have seen her marry were pathetic.

Finally, she opened her eyes and saw the chilly bedroom bright with sunshine filtering through the Venetian blinds. *Uh-oh.* The clock was packed and she didn't wear a wristwatch, but from the look of the golden light surrounding them, it had to be at least seven. And they had a five- or six-hour slow drive ahead of them, hauling horses. So much for Brady's plan to get back to Lockett by noon.

His arm lay like a weight across her body. She carefully moved it from around her midsection and untangled her legs from his. He stirred but didn't awaken. She sat up and yawned, waiting for her wits to organize. A dull ache throbbed behind her eyes. Her nose felt stuffy, which always happened when she slept in a room with air-conditioning. She was used to open windows and fresh air from outside.

Spying last night's jeans and top in two separate spots, she started to stand up but almost fell back to the mattress. Before last night, she'd had sore muscles from helping him with the barn boards. This morning she had tenderness in new places.

She picked up her clothing and padded to the living room, where she had left her duffel, scolding herself for having four margaritas last night. Even in college, she'd never had four margaritas in an evening. In the bathroom, she washed as best she could with the corner of one of the two towels that hadn't been packed. Then she brushed her teeth and washed yesterday's makeup off with her hands.

Sensitive whisker burns reddened her mouth and chin, even her breasts and stomach. Good grief. Would Daddy notice those on her face? And if he did, would he know what they were? She dug into her makeup bag and found cream. Unfortunately, she had brought only one change of clothing and she had worn it last night. The black lace panties smelled musky, reminding her of how wet she had been before Brady stripped her clothes off. She dug in her duffel and found the panties she had worn yesterday. The old jeans she had worn yesterday were filthy, so she put on last night's jeans, enduring the stiffened inseam that chafed her sore places. Finally, she brushed her hair until it crackled with electricity, then plaited it into a single braid. She left the bathroom and tiptoed past the bed. Brady filled more than half of it.

With no glasses left in the kitchen cabinets, she pulled the milk jug out of the refrigerator and drank directly from it, the cold, smooth liquid easing the gnawing feeling inside her stomach. She had never been a big milk drinker, but if she spent much time around Brady, she might become one.

Spending time with Brady. The idea brought to the forefront of her mind a conundrum she didn't know how to tackle. A courtship—and he hadn't said he wanted that— would be impossible to maintain back in Lockett unless he quit his job at the Circle C. And if he did that, how would he earn enough to hang on to the 6-0? In Willard County, made up of ninety-nine percent family farms and ranches, few real jobs existed.

Even with working at the Circle C, rebuilding his aunt's old place might be impossible. Then there was Grandpa's intention to acquire the 6-0. Exactly how he planned to do that had yet to manifest itself, but she knew her grandfather. He would get it done eventually. As much as she loved him, a secret part of her believed he was his father's son.

She returned the milk to the refrigerator, then, careful to be quiet, opened the front door and went outside into the morning sun. It appeared today's weather would be a duplicate of yesterday's—sunny and pleasant now, until the temperature climbed into the nineties in the afternoon. She placed her palms at the small of her back and stretched, then sank to the porch's top step. The sun hadn't had time to warm the porch's wrought-iron mesh, and one layer of denim didn't protect her bottom from the cold metal.

But that discomfort was nothing compared to the frustration now building within her. She had so much to think about, so much guilt to absorb.

She had never known sex—no, lovemaking was what it had been—as it had been with Brady. She had always known something was missing between her and Webb and, later, between her and Jason. Now she knew what. In Brady's arms, she had been his total focus. He had made her feel as if she were a goddess and his only concern was to please her. She had never been the total focus of either of the two men whose engagement rings she had worn. Strayhorn wealth and influence had always been an elephant in the room. Strange. She hardly knew Brady Fallon, but other than providing him with a job, her family's money seemed to mean nothing to him.

But there was no upside to this story. She and Brady had polar goals and battles to wage—starting with her family and the lifetime caveat Daddy and Grandpa had hammered into her. She had heard it a thousand times as a little girl: *Stay away from the bunkhouse, Jude.*

When she became a teenager, the mantra had changed: *Don't forget who you are, Jude. . . . Don't get involved with one of the hands, Jude. . . . Don't distract the hands from their work, Jude.*

She hadn't heard those admonishments in recent years, but no matter. They were marked in her brain as permanently as a brand. And just because they were no longer voiced didn't mean she could ignore them. She might be a grown woman, but no way would it ever be acceptable to either Daddy or Grandpa, or even to herself, for her to have slept with a ranch employee. She had done something so irresponsible, so against the rules, so unacceptable, it had to be kept a secret. If Daddy and Grandpa ever learned about it, things would be bad for Brady. As sure as the sun rose

and set, they would fire him. Nothing was as unpleasant as
the cold, hard truth. What had she done?

Then there were the lies she had already told her father,
heightened by her father's expectation of a report on the
Boren watercolor from the museum in Fort Worth. A sigh
escaped. She had mere hours and a little over three hundred
miles to make up another believable lie. *Damn.* Lying was
hard.

As if all of that weren't enough, guilt and insecurity fu-
eled a deep-seated anguish. For the first time in her life,
she'd had a one-night stand. She now knew how it felt to
wake up beside a man she hardly knew. She might have
touched every naked body part, but that didn't mean she
knew him. Anxiety wormed into her stomach. How would
he feel about her this morning after she had thrown herself
at him? After all they had done last night?

She thought of her cousin, Jake, and his ability to see
through everyone and every circumstance. His respect
meant more to her than anyone's. What would he think of
her if he knew she had practically forced herself on one of
his good friends? Would Brady tell him?

Dear God, what kind of a mess had she made? At the
sheer awfulness of it, she propped her elbows on her knees
and covered her face with her hands. Suddenly she couldn't
wait to get back home, back to the safety of the Circle C.
Leaving the ranch house's rock walls was dangerous.

The sound of a vehicle caught her attention, and she
looked toward the county road. In the distance, a pickup
turned onto the driveway and sped up the hill toward the mobile, dust trailing behind it. "Oh, damn," she mumbled under
her breath.

The pickup, a newer-model Ford, came to a stop, and a
burly man, belly bulging over his belt, climbed out and
stamped up to the porch in quick little steps. He eyed her in
a peculiar way and planted his hammy hands at his waist.
"Jack Durham's my name. You a friend of Brady's?"

Yikes! Brady's boss. Or, that is, his *old* boss. "Yes."

The man looked around. "Where's he at?" he asked gruffly.

She hesitated. "Uh . . . sleeping."

His eyelids narrowed. "What'd you say your name is?"

Her stomach dropped. It was possible Daddy, Grandpa and Jack Durham were acquainted. "Uh, Judy. Judy Strong."

"You look familiar. You live around here?"

"Abilene. I'm from Abilene."

His assessing eyes pored over her. "Don't hardly ever get to Abilene. But you shore do look familiar. You ever go to the cuttin' shows in Fort Worth?"

"Uh, no." *Another lie.* "I must have one of those faces that looks like everyone else's."

"Huh," he said, continuing to examine her until she began to feel uncomfortable. Now she was certain this man must have seen her before, and it could very well have been at a horse show. If not in Fort Worth, then somewhere else.

"I need to talk to Brady," he said. "Reckon we could wake 'im up?"

She got to her feet, eager to escape. "Sure. I'll get him."

Just then, Brady came out of the mobile buttoning the shirt he had worn to supper last night. He must have heard them talking. "Hey, Jack, what's up?"

"Thought I'd save you some trouble. I come by to get the keys. I figured you'd be close to clearin' out by now."

"Almost. Just have to load up a few more things."

"Well, go ahead and gimme the keys. I got a Meskin gonna move in here and look after the stock in this pasture. I told 'im he could bring his stuff on over around noon."

"I'll get 'em." Brady walked back into the mobile.

"By George, I got it." Jude whipped around toward the voice. To her horror, Mr. Durham's sausagelike finger was pointing at her. "It was Amarillo at the horse sale. You was sittin' with Strayhorn's horse wrangler, Clary Harper. He's a good friend of mine. Known 'im for years. Clary bought that big palomino mare that day."

Jude knew the horse. She thought panic might explode

her skeleton, but before that happened, Brady returned to the porch with a ring of keys. When he handed them over to his former boss, the man said, "Damn, Brady, it pains me to see you go. You done a good job for me here. It's hard to find a man you can trust out here all by hisself."

Brady looked as if he wanted to jump off the porch and run. Jude was beginning to learn that he did not deal well with compliments. He ducked his chin and scratched his eyebrow with his thumb. "Thanks, Jack."

"But I wish you the best. I hope you get that place a-goin'. It was a fine thing your aunt done leavin' it to you."

After more conversation, he and Jack Durham said their good-byes and Brady assured him he would be gone within an hour or two at the most.

As soon as the rancher left, Brady turned to her, the corners of his beautiful mouth tipped up into a wide, white smile. "Morning." He came to her, hooked an arm around her neck, drew her close and placed a smooch on her lips. "You sore?" he asked softly. He picked up the end of her braid and tickled the tip of her nose with it.

He was obviously unconcerned about Jack Durham seeing her here, but Jude's heart was beating like a snare drum. "A little. That last time—"

"Was awesome," he finished, and smooched her lips again. "I woke up hard as a fence rail. If Jack hadn't showed up here, I was planning on dragging you back into that bed."

She was too distressed to think about what he said. "Brady, he knows who I am. At least almost. He's seen me before."

Brady's gaze swung to the departing pickup. "How do you know?"

"He said so. He saw me at the horse sale in Amarillo a few months ago. I was there with Daddy and Clary Harper."

"Who's Clary Harper?"

"The ranch's horse wrangler. He takes care of the remuda. If Mr. Durham puts two and two together . . ."

"Shit," Brady mumbled, then looked down at her, frowning and pulling his lower lip through his teeth. It didn't seem possible, but she felt an invisible barrier spring up between them. "Did you tell him your name?"

"I said Judy Strong. From Abilene." She pulled away from him and sank to the porch, unconcerned about the chill of the wrought iron against her bottom. "I swear to God, if I ever get back to Lockett, I will never tell another lie."

When he didn't say anything, she turned her head and looked up at him. He was gazing out toward the horizon and a clear blue summer sky, not revealing so much as a hint of his thoughts, and she realized again that she truly did not know him. She had no idea what might be going on inside his head. Still, she needed reassurance of some kind from him. She waited for him to sit down beside her and put his arm around her, yearned to hear him say everything was okay.

But he didn't. A long silence passed. Then he said, "I'm gonna get the bedroom cleaned out." His eyes met hers. "Lying's never a good plan." He turned and walked back into the mobile.

Back in the trailer, Brady began to strip the sheets off the bed. *Shit*. This charade he was in the middle of had stopped being a game. What were the odds Jack Durham would appear from out of the blue this morning and have a face-to-face with Jude on the damn front porch? Or that he would have seen her at a horse sale just a few months back? In the almost two years Brady had worked for Jack, the man hadn't visited this remote trailer half a dozen times. When Brady had needed a personal meeting about something, he had usually gone to the Durham ranch house. He had heard Jack say at some point in the past that he was acquainted with the Circle C's horse wrangler, but it was one of those inconsequential facts simply thrown into conversation, and Brady hadn't let it take up room in his mind.

Now he wished he had remembered hearing it. No way would he have brought Jude here. If word of their overnight trip somehow got back to J. D. Strayhorn and the man figured out that his daughter and Brady had slept together, for damn sure, Brady would find himself unemployed. And that would set him off on Plan B, a direction he had neither thoroughly thought through nor wanted to go.

Shit. Women. Just look at the trouble they had caused him. When Jude had come on to him last night, why hadn't he tucked her into bed, said good night and bedded down on the couch? He had been in sticky situations with women before and had usually had wits enough to make the right choices. So where had those wits been last night? He couldn't even blame what had happened on booze because he hadn't drunk that much. His judgment seemed worse now at thirty-four than it had been at twenty-four.

As he gathered the sheets into a ball and stuffed them into a black plastic bag, the smell of sex reached his nose and he couldn't keep from thinking of last night. He had no logical answers for his logical questions, but he sure had some illogical excuses. Last night, he had wanted Jude in a way he hadn't wanted any woman in a long time. When he learned she wanted him, too, his ego had soared and temptation had won out.

Compared to most women he had known, she was practically untouched. Instead of turning him off, that knowledge had been a powerful aphrodisiac. All he had been able to think about was how he wanted her for his own, how he wanted to possess her. And how he *didn't* want some asshole like Ace pawing her. He hadn't had that attitude about a woman, including the woman who had been his wife, in a long, long time, if ever. Indeed, last night, Brady Fallon had wanted to be Jude Strayhorn's man.

But this was today, and reality had ridden the sunrays right into the room, bringing conflict with it. A woman like her could fuck up his life beyond description. She was daddy's little girl who had everything she wanted all the time. He knew firsthand just how hard that was to live with. Jude, despite her inexperience with sex, had her choice of men, no doubt. With all she had to offer, she had only to crook a finger and a dozen salivating bird dogs would follow her anywhere. He had to forget about her.

Could he? Last night she had said things to him, things that made him think he meant something to her. Could he believe her? Did he dare?

Even if those questions had answers, and even if he still wanted her, two facts he couldn't ignore: He simply had nothing to offer her, and he couldn't afford her.

14

I'm gonna get the bedroom cleaned out. . . . Lying's never a good plan. . . .

That's all he has to say? Jude sat on the porch step in amazement and dismay. He had touched every one of her most intimate places. Parts of him had found parts of her that the two other men she had slept with hadn't found. And he knew that, too. She had told him. *And that's all he has to say?*

She sat a few more minutes, fighting back the lump in her throat that felt like a burr. A tear sneaked from the corner of one eye, but she quickly swiped it away with the back of her hand. She was a big girl, wasn't she? She spent a lot of time trying to convince everyone that she was. So she had to take responsibility for her own behavior, didn't she? She clenched her jaw. *To hell with it. If he won't give a damn, neither will I.*

Right, Jude. Just get this whole thing over with and get back home, onto familiar ground.

Right.

She entered the mobile and walked into the bedroom. Brady already had the bed stripped and had stuffed the sheets and pillows into a big black plastic sack and was working at emptying drawers. She went to the bathroom and packed the toiletries she had left on the tiny vanity. She then checked the bathroom cabinets and found them empty.

She returned to the bedroom, carrying her duffel. "The bathroom's all clear except for your personal items," she said stiffly.

His attention was on cleaning out a dresser drawer. "Thanks. I'm almost finished here. Then we can get going. We'll get some breakfast up the road."

At a fast-food place. "That'll be fine."

He looked up at her with that teasing, knee-weakening grin. "Since I know you like to sit down, we'll find a place we can go inside. We're already late anyway."

This morning, reality was far clearer than it had been last night, and her knees had a little more strength. She found herself able to resist his knee-weakening grin. At the thought of lying more when she saw her father again, Brady's timetable seemed less important. "Look, since we're already late, I need a favor."

He smiled and she saw sincerity in his eyes. "Name it."

"I need to go to Fort Worth. I know we're close."

Seeing his mouth open to speak stopped her, but he said nothing, so she went on. "Daddy asked me to check out a watercolor at a museum on Main Street. Since he thinks my girlfriend and I spent the night in downtown Fort Worth, he'll be disappointed if I tell him I didn't go to the museum. I feel I really need to do that. You might not be aware of it, but he's an art collector."

His eyes locked on hers. She sensed words stuck in his throat and she prepared herself to argue if he said there wasn't enough time. Instead, he said, "Okay. If that's what you need to do."

"Great. I think I'm all ready. I'll be waiting outside. If you want, I can feed the horses and hook up the trailer."

He gave her a look.

"I know how to feed horses and hook up a trailer." That wasn't a lie. She had done both many times.

She picked up the plastic sack holding the bed linens and started for the pickup. A cardboard box filled with miscellaneous items sat by the door. Among the assortment was the flat black box of condoms. She stared at it for a few beats, willing away a tightness in her chest, and proceeded outside.

By the time he came out, she had fed the horses a few flakes of hay, hooked up the trailer and backed it down to the corral. "Thanks for doing that," he said.

"No problem. Just trying to beat the clock." She followed him down to the corral, and they worked as a team haltering the horses and loading them. Sal didn't make a fuss, just docilely followed the geldings into the trailer. While he secured them inside, Jude took a seat inside the pickup.

Several minutes later, he climbed behind the wheel, filling the whole pickup cab with his presence, and they were on their way toward Stephenville.

"We're going back to Stephenville?" Jude asked.

"Shortest way to Fort Worth."

"Oh. I'm not familiar with this part of the country. Listen, since we're going back to Stephenville, if we could stop somewhere, I could get something for my headache."

He grinned. "Too much tequila?"

She suspected the cause was tension rather than tequila. Her body felt tight as a bowstring, and her eyes felt grainy from lack of sleep. But she managed a tense smile. "Probably."

Parking a crew-cab pickup pulling a four-horse trailer loaded with three animals was a challenge anywhere. They found no good place until they reached an isolated convenience store on the outskirts of Stephenville. By then the ache in her head had spread to her neck and shoulders.

"Do you want coffee?" she asked, picking up her purse and opening her door.

"I'll wait for breakfast," he said, and she was glad. She didn't feel like debating who would pay.

When she returned to the pickup, country music filled the cab. They rode toward Fort Worth without talking, the bass from the radio's speakers drumming between her temples. It was just as well the radio overpowered conversation, because the burr in her throat had grown to the size of a tumbleweed.

She couldn't keep from watching him surreptitiously, and she couldn't keep from admiring the efficient movement of his capable body, the masculine grace of his hands—hands that had caressed her with indescribable tenderness. She saw again what a skillful driver he was. Fast, alert and competent. She believed that was how he handled every aspect of his life. She waited for him to start a conversation, but he didn't. How could they follow last night with behaving like strangers this morning? How could he say all that he had said while they made love, then not even talk today?

Made love? You had sex, Jude. It isn't the same thing.

She swallowed the thickness that had again gathered in her throat and stared out the window.

As he said they would, they stopped for breakfast on the outskirts of Fort Worth. At a Waffle House, they took up eight parking spaces with the pickup and horse trailer. Over coffee, while waiting for the food, Brady scanned the Fort Worth Sunday paper.

Having no interest in the newspaper, she looked around. Everyone in the small diner looked scruffy, as if they had been drinking and partying all night. Just as she and Brady looked, no doubt. Neither of them had showered and shampooed. She wondered if Brady had even combed his thick brown hair. It had even more curl today than she had noticed yesterday. He hadn't shaved. Dark stubble showed on his jaws, making him look sexy and dangerous. She remembered the rasp of whisker stubble on her intimate flesh. A quickening low in her belly startled her, and she was disgusted with herself. They were in Waffle House, forgodsake.

Jack Durham's arrival had prevented more than their morning ablutions. She wanted to believe that if the man hadn't appeared and reminded them of facts neither she nor Brady wanted to be reminded of, she would have crawled back into Brady's bed and they would have spent another hour having mind-numbing sex.

On a quiet Sunday morning, parking the pickup and horse trailer on the deserted streets of downtown Fort Worth presented no problem. They moved through the museum quickly, stopping only occasionally to look longer at a particularly interesting piece, until they reached the museum's latest Boren acquisition. With the artist being one of her father's favorites, Jude had seen many of his works. Daddy even owned two of his originals. She didn't dislike them, but she didn't have the interest and keen eye of a collector. Brady, on the other hand, appeared to be sincerely interested.

"I'll be damned," he said, bending forward, his fingers stuffed into his back pockets, his elbows cocked. "Just look at that. I've got a pair of boots that look just like that."

She peered closer at the image of a pair of worn boots and spurs. The life-size subjects looked as if they could be plucked from the frame and worn. "I'm sure all working cowboys do," she said.

"That's what I am. A working cowboy. Too bad I can't paint. If I could, I might not be where I am now."

She wondered what that meant. An image of him mounting his horse and riding away passed through her mind. All at once, she realized that image had replaced the one from the poster. Perhaps because a nearly nude picture of him didn't compare to the real thing.

As they left the museum, she picked up a flyer on the new watercolor to take home to Daddy. She felt a modicum of relief at seeing the painting, and her mood lifted. At least she could say truthfully she had been to the museum and seen it. And the two ibuprophen combined with the food had started to ease her headache.

Back in the pickup, as Brady fired the engine, he said, "Since we're going west and the day's already shot, let's stop by that other museum that's got all the Russells and Remingtons. I haven't been there in a long time."

"The Amon Carter?" She had been to the Amon Carter in

January when she and Daddy had come to Fort Worth's annual rodeo.

"Yeah," he said, and started out of downtown Fort Worth on the street that would take them there.

Jude was surprised. Indeed, the Amon Carter Museum had one of the most extensive collections of Russell and Remington art, but Brady Fallon was not a person she would expect to know the names of artists, much less be interested in seeing their work. "What about the horses?" she asked.

"They'll be okay if we don't take too long."

They strolled through the exhibits. She became acutely aware of Brady's hand on her shoulder as he pointed out with his opposite hand that every Russell had a splash of bright red. He slipped his arm around her waist as he discussed the accuracy of the detail in the horses. After observing the paintings, they moved on to the sculptures.

Before leaving the museum, they stood and perused the life-size mural on the wall in the front room—a group of hatless cowboys standing around a wrapped corpse in an open grave. In the background, the artist had painted a sea of longhorn cattle.

"One of those could be my distant grandfather," Jude said. "He drove a hundred head of strays up from South Texas. While his cattle grazed on open range, he lived in a dugout. That was the beginning of the Circle C."

She sensed his eyes on her and looked up. "We need to get going," he said. "I'm sure those horses are getting restless."

When they were on their way again, she had to ask, "How do you know so much about art?"

"I just know what I like. I like the history that Western art represents. I've always wanted to go to Montana. If I ever do, I'm gonna make it a point to go to Russell's hometown."

Jude had never *wanted* to go to Montana, but she had been there. She had accompanied her father to look at some livestock. When they were there, even her art collector father hadn't mentioned stopping by Charles Russell's former residence.

Soon they were on the interstate heading west, a long drive ahead of them. The radio played softly. They talked about music and movies. Brady seemed more relaxed and open, like he had been last night. They stopped at a large roadside park and exercised the horses before the last long leg of the trip.

Her braid had become a weight pulling at her neck, so once they were on the road again, she loosened it, dug a brush from her purse and brushed her hair. Brady's attention volleyed between watching her and watching the road. "I like your hair," he said.

"Thanks," she replied, smiling at the memory of his hands buried in it last night.

They stopped for lunch at a Denny's. As they crossed the parking lot, he caught her hand and held it. That same feeling of being cared for and protected that she had experienced in Lupe's last night came back.

As they started through the Denny's doorway, to her astonishment, Brady dropped her hand as if it were a hot coal and stopped to chat with a man coming out. The stranger discussed the construction business in Fort Worth and even mentioned Brady's divorce and his former father-in-law. They appeared to be more than casual acquaintances. She stood back from the conversation, not wanting to be included. Brady made no attempt to introduce her and she was thankful.

Aware of the horses in the trailer, they hurried through lunch. Brady remained quiet. She suspected he was worried about having run into someone who knew him again. When she asked who the man was, he said the guy was a drywall installer, someone he had known for years in the home-building business, and there was no danger of him knowing J.D. Jude wanted to ask him about his business and what had happened to it, but she was no longer comfortable peppering him with questions.

Then they were driving again, and this time not talking about even innocuous subjects such as movies, as if running into Brady's Fort Worth acquaintance had shoved the mistake they had made—the mistake *she* had made—into their faces again. It loomed larger with every mile closer to Lockett.

Since they weren't conversing, her mind was free to consider again all of the reasons she should never have done what she did last night. She couldn't deny that being with him, then seeing those photos, had ignited something new and different, but that didn't mean she should have acted on whatever it was. She was a disciplined person. How had she lost so much control of the past twenty-four hours, of herself? How could she have handled this so badly?

She was a mess. Her emotions had been in turmoil since this morning, yet she, Jude Strayhorn, who was known for saying what she thought, was unprepared to talk about her feelings, couldn't even define what they were.

The radio seemed to be playing louder. The afternoon sun burned through the windshield, and they both put on sunglasses. With her eyes hidden by dark lenses, she stared at his profile. She might be wallowing in confusion, but one thing was gradually becoming clear. She simply couldn't have a fling in Lockett, Texas, with Brady Fallon. She had to say something, had to clear the air, had to end this before it went any further, though the idea of not seeing him again, not spending time with him, felt as heavy as a stone in her stomach.

When she saw a freeway sign noting that Abilene was fifty miles ahead, she reached over and switched off the radio. "I feel I should tell you something."

His eyes stayed focused on the highway, but she could see a tic in his jaw. She heaved a breath and said, "I don't want you to feel obligated because of last night. If I hadn't started it, I know you wouldn't have—I know *we* wouldn't have—"

"Don't worry about it," he said flatly. No expression that she could discern.

Rattled by his dispassionate reaction and her own chagrin, she forged ahead, letting words fall out of her mouth without forethought. "I know it didn't look like it last night, but, uh . . . I'm not necessarily looking for a, uh . . . boyfriend. Daddy and Grandpa have never allowed me to even go around the bunkhouse. If they knew where I've been the last two days, it goes without saying they would be really upset. I've never . . . I've never even dated one of the ranch hands, much less—"

"I figured out all that before I agreed to take you with me." He looked at her across his shoulder, but with him wearing sunglasses, she couldn't see his eyes. "As for anything else, I wasn't holding up a sign saying I was looking for a girlfriend, either. The last thing I can afford is a woman. I took this whole thing to be a no-strings-attached deal."

She flinched inside. She knew she must mean something to him, because she'd had experience with two men to whom she personally had meant nothing. What had meant something to them was her family's wealth. Being with Brady had felt somehow different. "Right. It isn't like you kidnapped me or something, is it? Or that we pledged undying love."

"That's how I see it," he said.

She wanted to curl up and wail, but she turned back to the sunny day gliding past the passenger window. Gradually that and the dull monotony of the Chevy's big engine lulled her to sleep.

With Jude having dozed off, Brady was alone with his thoughts. And that was damn sure where he needed to be. Jude Strayhorn had sure as hell put him in his place, hadn't she?

He shifted in his seat in an effort to stay awake. Having gotten almost no sleep, he, too, would like a nice, long nap, but he had no time for it today. The interstate and two more hours of driving stretched ahead of him; then he had chores to do at the 6-0.

He went over a checklist in his mind. He had to unload the boxes in the truck bed. The fence around the small pasture attached to the barn was in decent shape, but rust and dry rot had done a number on the gate. The old hinges needed some strengthening. That should take him less than an hour. He would still have time to get in touch with Jake and find out where he could get some extra hay. If they reached Lockett early enough, he might still be able to haul it tonight.

He dared to glance at Jude, sleeping like a baby, her chest rising and falling evenly. She had on the same black bra she had worn last night. Her arm was positioned so that a small pillow of flesh pushed above her tight little top's neckline. A wide strip of black lace lay seductively over it. And today, he knew just how soft that mammary flesh felt filling his hands and how sensitive her nipples were to his fingers and mouth. *Damn.*

He tried not to look at her, but his eyes seemed to have a will of their own, just like last night in Lupe's. She was beautiful. And fearless. And unruly. She had a wildness inside, barely restrained by family loyalty and tradition. She reminded him of Sal. He had kept that horse for those very qualities. But Jude was a helluva lot more threatening to his well-being than any horse.

He turned his eyes back to the road, trying to wrestle his thoughts away from last night. But the effort proved fruitless. The landscape flanking I-20 wasn't much to look at, and it sure as hell didn't compare to the view of Jude's lush, naked body astraddle his hips. She had ridden him as if he were a bucking bull that was hers to conquer. That full-frontal vision of female perfection, her head tilted back, her swollen lips parted and wet, her hands burrowed in her wild and thick-as-a-mane hair, would be branded on his brain for a good long while.

He shifted in his seat again, his pants suddenly too tight.

Shit. Minutes ago, he would have sworn he didn't have the energy for a hard-on.

He thought about irony. Besides the unexpected meeting with Jack Durham, there was the even more unexpected encounter with Mark Howard, one of his former Fort Worth subcontractors and a hunting buddy. What were the chances of running into him at a Denny's halfway between Fort Worth and Lockett on a Sunday afternoon? He and Mark knew each other well enough for Mark to give him an elbow nudge and ask who Jude was. And Brady had answered with a lie, which was just plain dumb. One lie only led to another. With so many sightings, it seemed almost inevitable that his lost weekend with Jude would get back to the Circle C. He puffed his cheeks and blew out a breath.

A small sound came from Jude, and he glanced at her again. She turned toward him and resettled herself, still sleeping. Her shiny hair fell over her shoulder like a silky waterfall, and the black lace continued to peek at him. Looking on the bright side, if one could be found, maybe he had nothing to worry about. Jack didn't know Jude, and Brady could think of no reason for him to call up the Circle C's horse wrangler and discuss her. And Brady was sure she wouldn't be telling her daddy or anybody else around Lockett where and how she had spent Saturday night. Plus, hadn't she made it clear she didn't expect to be seeing Brady Fallon again?

. . . I'm not necessarily looking for a, uh . . . boyfriend.

He should be happy about that. But he wasn't.

Jude opened her eyes to familiar surroundings. A change in the pickup's engine noise had awakened her. They had left the interstate, which meant they were approximately a hundred miles from Lockett. She blinked herself awake. "We're almost home."

"Good thing you were asleep. Dodging all those semis with my eyes closed was hair-raising. I've run off the road four times."

She looked at him with a start. "You have not."

"No, but I sure could use a nap. You ever pulled a horse trailer?"

She gave him a thin-lipped scowl. "What do you think? Would you like for me to drive?"

"Would you mind? I'm barely staying awake."

"I'm refreshed now. I can drive."

He slowed and eased to a stop on the shoulder, and they switched places. Once they were moving again, he turned on the radio and fell sound asleep.

Jude drove into the 6-0's driveway in the late afternoon. They climbed out of the pickup to a pleasant temperature, familiar scents of sage and cedar in the air and the ever-present breeze. After standing in the trailer all day with no water and exercising only once since this morning, the horses needed to be unloaded and watered immediately. Brady went about the task, and Jude felt obligated to help. Together, they led the three animals to the water tank kept full by the windmill, and the animals drank long and deeply.

"I want to check the fence one more time," Brady said, "then I'll get your truck out of the shed."

"I'll help you," Jude said.

Going in opposite directions, they left the horses to drink and began to walk the perimeter of the small fenced pasture attached to the barn. Part of Jude dreaded the end of the chores and going home. Not wanting to go home was a new and confusing idea. She had never disliked going home to the Circle C.

After he was satisfied with the fence, they returned to the front of the house. He opened the pickup door and lifted her duffel and purse off the backseat. As she took them from him, her heart suddenly swelled in her throat again and she glanced up and caught him looking back at her in an odd way. The air shimmied between them, just as it had the first day she saw him in this very driveway. "I appreciate your going out of your way to take me to Fort Worth, Brady. At least I won't have to lie to Daddy about the painting."

"I didn't mind. Thanks again for helping me in the trailer. But I already told you that."

Emotions ping-ponged within her. This distance between them was insane. They had spent hours making love. His hands and mouth had been all over her. Hers all over him, too. He had been inside her, had taken her to places within herself she didn't know were there. "Brady—"

"Don't, Jude. Neither one of us is looking to get into something complicated. We had a good time, but it would be dumb not to end this right now."

A good time? She hesitated, fearing she could be on the verge of an all-out breakdown.

"If you'll give me your keys, I'll warm up your truck and back it out of the shed," he said.

She dug in her purse and handed him her pickup keys. He reached out and brushed her cheek with his rough thumb, his eyes holding hers in a gentle embrace. "Remember, J.D. and your grandpa are waiting for you. I'm sure they want to hear all about that pretty painting."

She tried to laugh, but her nose was suddenly so plugged, she could scarcely draw a good breath.

"I'm gonna go get your truck," he said. "You gonna be okay?"

She nodded and looked away.

He walked off, and soon she heard the clatter of her pickup's diesel engine.

He drove the Dodge over to where she stood and stepped out. A corner of his mouth lifted into a smile. "Guess I'll get initiated tomorrow. J.D. said they're starting to wean the spring calves. Do you help with that?"

She let out a shaky breath. "No. Daddy and Grandpa won't hear of it. Grandpa says a woman doing that kind of work is unladylike. Never mind that his mother did it. And Daddy says it's dirty and dangerous."

"I'd say that's all true."

"Please. Now you sound like them. Those are only surface excuses, anyway. The real reasons go much deeper."

She managed a pathetic laugh. "They don't think I'm totally worthless, though. They let me buy bulls, so in a way I've got some control."

"If a man's in the cattle business, the bull buyer's pretty important."

"Yeah, I know." She climbed behind the wheel and buzzed down the window. The thought of driving out of the driveway and parting from him filled her chest with pain. Why couldn't she just simply go home and tell Daddy she had found someone she wanted to be with, someone she enjoyed more than she had ever enjoyed Webb Henderson or Jason Weatherby? What was wrong with that someone being a ranch hand?

But those were silly questions. She knew what they would find wrong. She had heard it from both of them since she was old enough to know the difference between girls and boys.

Brady hooked his hands on the windowsill. "You take care, you hear?"

She looked him in the eye. "You, too."

He stepped back from the door. She buzzed up the window and drove away. She took forty minutes to make the twenty-minute drive from the 6-0 to the Circle C. Doing it without tears had to be one of the greatest feats of will she had ever accomplished. By the time she reached home, through sheer willpower, she had gotten a handle on her emotions.

It was nearly suppertime when she parked in the garage, but she wasn't hungry. What she really wanted to do was slink up to her room, bathe and bury herself under the covers, but trying to escape supper without hurting Grandpa's feelings was more trouble than it was worth. She pulled down her visor and checked the whisker burns on her face again. They were much less obvious now. The cream she had used this morning had helped. For supper, she could cover them with makeup. Then it dawned on her: She had no bags and boxes from a shopping spree. *Damn.* Now she had to make up another lie.

Daddy and the aroma of Tex-Mex spices met her at the back door. Daddy was smiling and happy to see her. He pecked her cheek, but she broke away from him without a hug, fearing he would detect that she smelled like sex.

"How was your trip?" He took her duffel from her hand.

"Exhausting."

"Where's your loot?" He looked around her, obviously seeking something else to carry for her.

"Oh, we didn't go shopping. There was a good movie playing, so we did that."

She started for the stairs, and he accompanied her. "You saw the painting, though?"

She was more grateful than ever that she had asked Brady to take her to Fort Worth—and that he had been willing. "Yes, we did. And it's beautiful, Daddy. You'll have to be sure to go over there to see it. I brought you a flyer. We went out to the Amon Carter, too." Being able to tell the truth, even if only a half-truth, almost chased away her fatigue.

"You can tell me about the Boren later. It's nearly supper-time. Hurry and get dressed. Clary's gonna eat with us."

That information almost froze her in place, but she managed to breezily say, "Okay."

She showered and shampooed, dressed in a cotton eyelet prairie dress and tan huaraches, then went downstairs to the kitchen. Irene had made enchiladas, and Windy had fried tortilla chips and put together a black bean salad to go with them. He told her that Daddy and Clary were in the office and Daddy wanted her to join them for a drink. She couldn't think of anything she wanted to do less, but she set her jaw and made her way to Daddy's office. As soon as she entered, her father and Clary stood.

Clary nodded to her. "How're you this ev'nin', Miss Jude?" Clary Harper was a middle-aged man who had a deep voice and a strong Texas twang, as did most of the local people. For supper with Daddy and Grandpa, he had slicked his hair back and put on a starched white shirt and a blue silky neckerchief. Familiar surroundings with familiar people. Little by little, Jude was starting to feel comfortable in her own skin again. "Good, Clary. What exciting things are going on with the horses?"

"Just makin' sure our mounts are all in good shape for the weanin'."

Daddy handed her a drink of whiskey diluted with water and she sipped it. "That's good. Wish I could go with you."

"Now, you don't wish that, Miss Jude. It's a man's job. Bein' out in that ol' sun all day would just cook yore pretty skin, and that ol' wind would grind that swirlin' sand clear through you."

"I've told her the same thing, Clary," Daddy said, smiling at her. He held a chair for her.

She sat and he moved to his desk chair. "The new man's starting tomorrow," he said to Clary, and Jude felt a little prick in her intestines. "He's a good-size man, so he'll need a couple of strong mounts. He looks stout, and he's no greenhorn. I expect he can handle a strong horse."

Misery settled within Jude along with a memory of Brady throwing himself onto Sweet Sal's back. Indeed he could handle a strong horse, and he was anything but a greenhorn.

Clary Harper behaved no differently from how he always had. She became convinced that Jack Durham hadn't rushed home and called him to discuss the woman who sat beside him at the horse sale in Amarillo. As much as she was in no mood for company, Jude was glad for Clary's presence. With company for supper, no one would spend too much time asking about her trip to Fort Worth.

Supper ended early in anticipation of rising early to load the gear and horses for the thirty-five-mile trip to the north pastures and the weaning pens. There, roughly three thousand head of prime Circle C mother cows and their calves lived—close to half the ranch's herd. Even Grandpa would be going. He no longer participated in separating the cows and calves, but he could still sit his old horse, and he liked to watch the work.

He made no mention of an evening walk, which suited Jude fine.

15

Jude had been at the 6-0 almost an hour, time enough to walk to the barn and the pasture behind it and look at the horses. A month had passed since she had seen Brady Fallon. He hadn't attended the Circle C's Fourth of July picnic, held every year for the ranch hands. Jude had almost not attended herself, for fear of running into Brady. She couldn't keep from wondering if he hadn't come because he didn't want to run into her.

But not seeing him did not mean he hadn't been a presence in her life. His face with its intense eyes had loomed like a specter in her restless nights. His pickup, parked in the same spot in the big barn's parking lot every day, sat there like a permanent monument. Nightly at supper, Daddy extolled his praises. Daddy thought the man hung the moon, said he was the best hand he had ever hired.

Through all of Daddy's acclimation of Brady's worth, Grandpa had rarely commented or even asked questions, which was unusual. He had always voiced his opinions. She hadn't walked with him much in the past month. The weaning had taken two weeks, and he had been too tired in the evenings. Lately he had complained of not feeling well.

Still, they had walked some, but no matter how much she tried to tactfully pry, he said nothing about Brady or the 6-0. His restraint was starting to make Jude worry about what he might be up to. She hadn't forgotten the first conversation they'd had about his interest in the 6-0 land. All of it reminded Jude of how alone Brady was in his struggle to keep and rebuild his aunt's old ranch. And this was what had brought her here today.

She had taken extra care with her appearance—bathed in skin-softening body wash, washed her hair with cucumber-scented shampoo, taken extra pains with her eye makeup. Luckily, she didn't have to explain why to anyone, because she couldn't really explain it to herself.

Now, attempting to escape the afternoon heat while waiting for Brady to come home, she sat in the shade on the Victorian house's rickety front porch overlooking the caliche driveway. She studied the traces of white paint left on the gingerbread trim that spanned the eaves, letting snippets of her last conversation with Brady tumble through her mind.

. . . I'm not necessarily looking for a, uh . . . boyfriend. . . . I wasn't holding up a sign saying I was looking for a girlfriend, either. . . .

A month since they had said those words in his pickup.

Soon the tan Silverado turned off the highway and started up the driveway. Her heart lifted. The pickup came to a stop in front of the house, and Brady climbed out, one limb at a time. His languid movement told her that he was worn-out.

She watched without moving as he lifted chaps out of the pickup bed, slung them over his shoulder and came toward her in his loose, long-legged gait. With the afternoon sun at his back and his hat set low on his brow, she couldn't clearly see his face, but through shimmering waves of heat and dust, she could see his long, lean body. The late afternoon breeze molded his long-sleeve shirt to clearly defined biceps. A red neckerchief sagged around his neck. Dirty blue denim swathed his slim hips and muscled thighs. His spurs clanked with every step. He was all cowboy, all the time, a man of the West who more than talked the talk. The awareness of that fact and his potent masculinity sweetly squeezed her most secret places. She recognized it now for what it was. She had felt it every time she had seen him. She thought of that day in Stephenville when he had jumped on Sal's back. Her stomach involuntarily twitched.

He was almost to the porch before she could see his eyes, and when she did, her heart turned over.

"Hey," he said in his soft, deep voice. He sat down beside her on the porch, his shirtsleeve touching her arm. He untied his neckerchief, slid it off and dropped it on the porch. "What's up?"

She detected no antagonism. In fact, she thought he behaved as if they were friends who had seen each other only yesterday. Relief flooded her. She hadn't known what to expect when he came home and found her sitting on his porch. He leaned forward and began unbuckling his spurs, his shirt stretched tight across his wide back, emphasizing the flex of his powerful shoulders.

His boots and wash-worn Wranglers were covered with a layer of West Texas red dust. A wide swath of brown stained one side of his blue chambray shirtfront. Jude recognized it as dried blood. "What's up with *you*? You're bloody."

He looked up at her over his shoulder. That mischievous, knee-buckling grin that made creases at the corners of his sky blue eyes and showed his perfect white teeth filled her with warmth. It was even more devastating coming from a dirty face and dark-stubbled jaws. "One of the heifers had a problem. But we fixed it."

She nodded. "Naturally." She looked around. "What's been going on around here? I walked back and looked at the horses. They look to be all settled in."

He lifted his mangled straw hat and ran splayed dirty fingers through sweat-dampened hair. His hair was longer now, she noticed. It curled over his collar. "I've ridden them a couple of times." He set the hat back on and tugged the brim low. "But I've been working in the barn, mostly. When I've had time. Right now, getting the barn fixed up is more important than anything else."

"We didn't see you at the picnic." A fishing question, probably obvious.

"I went to Fort Worth to see my boy."

"Oh." She nodded. "You got through the weaning okay? None of Grandpa's horned Hereford mothers hooked you or anything?"

He chuckled, a low rumble that made her shiver. She remembered the sound from Stephenville. "Nah. Sure is something to see, though. Horned Herefords. Not too many of those old girls around these days." He dropped the spurs onto the porch deck with a clunk.

"I know. They're all purebreds, too. Grandpa loves them. The only things he loves more are the longhorns he keeps as pets. I suppose you've seen those by now."

He nodded and straightened.

"Those Herefords are a mark in time, but they're part of what should be changed. The crossbreeds thrive better and have less trouble calving. Daddy's letting me buy some Angus bulls, so little by little black baldies are starting to show up, but it hasn't been easy with Grandpa's attitude."

"I'm glad to see you."

The words, unexpected, sent a thrill all the way up her spine. He reached up, lifted her sunglasses off her nose and gingerly pushed back strands of her hair that had strayed to one cheek. A proprietary gesture. She didn't even care that his hands were filthy. She smiled. "Me, too."

"But what are you doing here?" He set her sunglasses back on, and the thrill vanished.

"I came to offer you my help."

He looked down, scratching one eyebrow with his thumb. "Lord, Jude. Your help gets risky. What is it you're wanting to help me with?"

She yanked off the sunglasses and pushed to her feet, better able to make her case standing. She propped her hands on her hips. "You know, if horses aren't kept in shape, they forget they're horses. Then they can't be depended on. They need to be ridden. I know you don't have time, so"—she lifted her open palms for emphasis—"I'm offering to ride your horses for you."

He looked up at her with an expression impossible to read, but she knew him well enough to know he was skeptical.

She raised one hand like a traffic cop and tilted her head. "Don't worry. I'm not going to lie to Daddy about it. I learned my lesson on that. I'm going to tell him you've got horses I like the looks of. He knows I like horses. And he thinks a lot of you."

"And where you gonna do this riding?"

"Well, I could ride Poncho and Tuffy here in your pasture behind the barn. It wouldn't have to be every day, and I'd do it when you're at work so I wouldn't be in your way." She bent forward and picked up the manila file folder she had laid on the porch deck. "And I want to work with Sal. I did some research on her. Did you know you're her fourth owner?" She handed him the folder with the printed information she had gleaned from researching Sal's history. "Her dam was a racehorse."

He opened the folder and began to scan the top page.

"I could haul her over to the Circle C and work with her in our big round corral."

He lifted the page and looked underneath, where she had tucked an eight-by-ten color photograph of Patch. "What's this?"

She hesitated before she answered. "My stud, Patch."

He looked up her with an arched brow. "*Your* stud?"

"Grandpa gave him to me a long time ago. He's a tobiano paint."

"What's that?"

"It has to do with his markings. Tobianos have color on one or both flanks, and their heads are usually solid. See, look." She sat down beside him again and pointed to Patch's black flanks and face. "And see, he has white legs and a black shield across his chest. Look how muscled he is in the chest. He's built like a tank. Isn't he handsome?"

Brady shook his head and frowned. Definite negative body language. "Jude—"

Okay, so he had figured out why she had put the photograph in the folder. She charged ahead. "Wait. Before you say no, listen. He has ancient blood in his veins, Brady. He goes all the way back to a Comanche stallion that was given to my great-great-grandfather by Quanah Parker himself. If you go into the dining room at the ranch house, you'll see a portrait of Alister Campbell and Quanah Parker. The paint horse in the background is the distant grandfather of my Patch."

Brady shook his head again. "I don't know, Jude . . ." His voice trailed off.

"Sal's grullo color makes her worth breeding, Brady. It's so rare. Some horse breeders strive for nothing but that color. I went into my files and found data I've collected on the genetics of horse color. The subject's been studied extensively at UC Davis. I wrote several papers on it myself when I was in school. If a black-and-white tobiano paint like Patch bred with a solid grullo mare, the odds are better than thirty-five percent the mare would throw a tobiano foal. It could be black or grullo tobiano. Either one would be great."

"We talked about this in Stephenville. Even if I had the money, I'm not willing to spend it on AI."

At his mention of Stephenville, a nerve began to jump in Jude's stomach, but she concentrated on ignoring it and on keeping her voice casual and normal. She had thought of Stephenville daily, but hearing him say it was different. "I'm not talking about artificial insemination. Most mares aren't bred with AI. It's too expensive. What if we just penned Sal and Patch in the same pasture for, say, thirty days and let nature take its course?"

"You're talking about live cover. Darlin', I leave here at four thirty every morning. Sometimes I don't get back 'til late afternoon, like today. I don't have time to keep an eye on 'em. Or to help 'em."

Jude sniggered. "They don't really need any help, you know. They know what to do."

He shook his head again. "I don't know the fine points of

horse . . . breeding." A frown furrowed his brow. "Why do you want to do this, Jude?"

For you, Brady. Because you need the money. And because I want you to succeed. And I don't trust my own grandfather. "Because you could sell the foal almost the minute it hits the ground for several thousand dollars. Paint-horse aficionados would love to have a horse out of a stud with Patch's bloodline. Sal's, too. All I'm talking about is taking her over to the Circle C and letting her spend time with Patch. No big deal. If anything went wrong, we've got a state-of-the-art veterinary facility. Dr. Barrett is there every day, and so am I. Of course I'd help. Patch is my stallion and I've got an interest in this, too, you know."

"And that would be what?"

"There aren't any of Patch's babies around the Circle C. Doc doesn't even collect semen from Patch. When we've bred him, it's usually been with live cover. Afterward, the mares get hauled away by their owners and I never get to see the babies. If the baby were a paint, I'd buy it from you myself. I just think it would be so cool to have one of Patch's babies around. I might start from scratch and train it to be a show horse."

"I don't know," Brady said again, but she thought he might be seriously considering it.

"Patch has never hurt a mare," she said.

"The Circle C's got damn near a hundred horses. There must be a grullo mare among them."

She shook her head.

"Why would you buy it from me? If your stallion's the sire, you'd already have an interest in the foal."

"But I'd still buy it."

He shook his head. "I don't know, Jude. A pregnant mare and a foal have special needs. My barn's not good enough." He got to his feet. "Look, I gotta get something to eat. Want a sandwich?"

Having not breached his resistance very well, she backed off. "Sure. Baloney and cheese?"

"You got it."

"Thought you'd never ask."

They went inside. The living room was bright with filtered late-day sunlight, and the room was a sauna. Brady turned on the swamp cooler. "I need to wash up," he said, and started toward the bathroom.

"I could make the sandwiches."

He stopped and looked back at her with a grin. "I thought you couldn't cook."

"I can't. But I can fix a sandwich."

And she did. Making herself at home in the kitchen, she found everything she needed including potato chips and pickles and a roll of paper towels. She also poured two glasses of milk and had all of it on the table when he came into the kitchen.

His face and neck were washed clean, his hair damp and slicked back. He smelled like soap and water. "Looks good. I don't have a good-looking woman fixing my supper real often." He straddled a chair at the table and she sat down adjacent to him. They spent the next few minutes eating. "Patch is a stud?" he said. "What are you doing riding a stallion? A stallion's too much horse for most women to handle. Most don't even want to."

"Patch is different. He's sweet and gentle. He's been mine since the day he was born. He loves me. And I love him."

"Sweet and gentle. I'll bet. When are you wanting to ride my three?"

"The sooner the better."

He wiped his mouth with a paper towel sheet and sat back in his chair. "Look, I'll go for the riding. And I appreciate your doing it. But I'll have to think about the other."

Jude stopped herself from debating further. "Fine. I'll start tomorrow morning. Is there a place in the barn for me to leave my gear?"

"I put a new lock on the tack room door."

They moved on to talk more about the Circle C cattle and

her vision for the future of the ranch's herd. Brady expressed his desire to buy a few head of his own as soon as he got a little more money together. He talked about the progress he had made on the barn and she told him about her preparations for the coming school year. He complimented her on doing that job when she didn't need to. And soon they had finished supper. Fearing she might wear out her welcome, Jude said she had to go. He walked with her toward her pickup.

"So you'll really think about breeding Sal?"

He nodded. "Yeah."

She smiled up at him. "Don't take too long, okay? This is July. Prime breeding season."

"Yeah, I know. And Sal's in heat again." He held the door while she climbed in. When she had buckled herself in, he looked at her, a serious expression on his face. "Jude, you're okay, right?"

"What do you mean?"

His chest rose and fell with a great breath. "I mean, uh . . . we, uh, that one time . . . when we weren't so careful. I've been worried about it."

She suppressed a gasp. She knew exactly when he was talking about, but she hadn't worried about it at all. Her period had started right on schedule three days after her return from Stephenville. That *he* would worry hadn't occurred to her. She couldn't keep from smiling. "Are we still talking about breeding?"

He looked away.

"Yes, Brady. I'm okay."

"You'd tell me if you weren't, wouldn't you?"

"Of course I would."

He nodded. "I just wouldn't want to be shut out of a decision."

"Not that it even bears discussion, but if such a thing happened, Brady, there wouldn't be a hair-tearing decision to be made. My daddy and grandpa want me to have kids more than they want anything else for me. "

He nodded. "You said that."

"Even if that weren't true, you think I'd want a little kid to grow up like I did? Missing a parent? With the only female influence in my life coming from an elderly woman and a string of women who couldn't even speak English? Or how Cable grew up? With no parents at all? Trust me, having financial security doesn't make up for a missing parent or two. I know as much as I want to about that subject."

"We both do. I didn't need a lecture."

"I know. And that isn't my intention. I'm just explaining. I know I'm always saying that Daddy and Grandpa did a fine job raising me and having no mother hasn't mattered to me, but it isn't true. But what else could I say, circumstances being what they are? You can rest assured that if I could prevent it, I wouldn't let an innocent little kid grow up like I have."

He nodded. "I'm just saying, Jude, let's not be dumb."

She didn't know what he meant but she recalled she hadn't heard him mention a father. It came back to her how hard it was to get him to express his thoughts in the light of day. In the dark, in his bed, he had been different. Another smile crawled across her lips. "Why, Mr. Fallon. Is this some kind of a roundabout, almost-maybe-but-not-entirely hint that we might do it again someday?"

"I'm just making sure everything's okay." He patted the windowsill. "You better go on home."

By the time Jude reached the highway, she was near tears. It had taken all of her will to babble in that casual banter when she wanted to melt against him and let him kiss her silly. She loved so much about him—even his brutal honesty and his closemouthed stoicism. She wondered whether she loved *him*. She might not know that for sure, but she knew one thing—she couldn't stand the thought of going home and sitting at the supper table listening to Daddy praising him as if he were a son and watching Grandpa sit there in smug silence, with no telling what kind of shenanigans going through his mind.

She hadn't seen Suzanne in days and hadn't been able to reach her by phone. She keyed in her friend's number and waited to leave yet another voice-mail message, but Suzanne surprised her by answering this time.

"Hey, you're home. Okay if I drop by?"

"Jude. Come on over. I've got something to tell you. I'm in the horse pen."

When Jude reached Suzanne's house, she found her just leaving the corral. Jude stepped out of her pickup.

"Hiya, girlfriend," the blond bombshell said, smiling broadly. She seemed to be in an exceptionally good mood.

"Where in the world have you been?" Jude asked. "I've been calling you for days."

Instead of looking at her, Suzanne busied herself latching the gate. "Um, over at Pat's."

Surprised, Jude gave her friend a narrow-eyed assessment. "You've been over at Pat Garner's for days?"

Suzanne looked across her shoulder and grinned. "I finally decided to give him a go."

"Wow," Jude said. "I can't believe you didn't tell me."

"Haven't had a chance. That's why I'm telling you now." Suzanne leaned against the gate, tilted her head back and laughed. "Today's the first day we've come up for air. I haven't even checked phone messages."

Still surprised by the new development, Jude stuffed her hands into her back pockets and looked at her friend big eyed. "So how was it? If you stayed with him for days, it must have been pretty good."

Suzanne chuckled in a low, private way. "Well, he isn't as hot as Mitch." She shook her head and her eyes took on a faraway look. "Ah, Mitch." She sighed. "That man knew all the right moves, if you know what I mean."

Another one of the mysterious statements that often came from Suzanne when she talked about her former husband or lover or whatever he had been. But for the first time, Jude had an inkling of understanding. "The right moves, huh?"

"Let's just say Pat's a little more conservative than Mitch.

But that's probably a good thing. Twenty other women aren't chasing him. And he's eager to please me. He'll learn." She pushed away from the gate. "I was just going up to the house to grab something to eat. Have you had supper?"

"I've eaten, but I'll drive you up there." They climbed into Jude's pickup. Jude started the engine and eased toward Suzanne's house.

"You've already eaten? Is the Circle C kitchen serving supper early these days?"

"I ate with a friend."

A sly look angled from Suzanne. "You're all fixed up. Makeup and everything. You even smell good. Who'd you eat with?"

Damn. Sometimes it was unnerving how well Suzanne knew her. "I ate at Brady Fallon's. I was going over some stuff with him. He's got a beautiful grullo mare. I was trying to talk him into letting Patch breed her."

"Ah. A conversation about horses fucking. Now, that's interesting foreplay."

"Oh, Suzanne. It wasn't foreplay."

They reached the house and Jude killed the engine, but neither of them rushed to exit the pickup. "He's got three horses. I'm going to start riding them for him. He can't afford to hire someone to do it."

"Well, aren't you good. You can't find anything else to do, so you're riding other people's horses?"

"I feel like he's an old friend. He's known Jake and Cable, you know, since we were all kids. And I knew him myself when I was a little kid, though I don't remember him."

"I see," Suzanne said, nodding. A reptilian grin spread across her full pink lips. "I need to get a look at this guy. I'll tell you who's hot for him, big-time. You know Joyce Harrison?"

Jude knew Joyce Harrison well. Like Suzanne, she worked at Lucky's Grocery. She had been two grades ahead of Jude and Suzanne in school.

"He's *all*"—Suzanne pressed the air with both hands—"and I do mean *all* she talks about. I'm telling you, her panties are practically on fire."

An awareness of her own body filtered through Jude. And of something darker. Possessiveness and jealousy. Brady's words from just a couple of hours earlier came at her: *I leave here at four thirty every morning. Sometimes I don't get back 'til late afternoon, like today.* "He works dawn to dark. How does she know him?"

"He buys groceries."

Bologna, cheese, and bread. "But that doesn't mean—"

"They've gone out. Twice. She says they've both got boys the same age. They started talking about their kids one day when he was checking out, and boom. They went out."

A punch couldn't have stunned Jude more. Brady was new in Lockett. The very last thing she expected to learn was that he had acquired a girlfriend. A memory of the Stephenville woman named Ginger ballooned in her mind. Of course he would soon have a girlfriend in Lockett, even if he was new in town. He had too much appeal not to have a string of women interested in him.

"You know how she is about men," Suzanne said. "I don't know if he asked her or she asked him, but she's been swooning and talking about body parts in the break room for two weeks."

The pickup cab began to shrink, and Jude felt as if it might close in on her and crush her. She knew for a fact that cowboying for the Circle C was an exhausting job. Where would Brady, or any man, find the time and energy for much of a social life? "Body parts? Does that mean she's sleeping with him?"

"Not yet. But it's not *her* fault. She's made herself plenty available. A few days ago she went down to Abilene and spent her whole paycheck on porno underwear. She even bought some of those candy panties out of some catalog. Strawberry flavored. She says it'll happen the next time they get together if she has to strip naked and spread her legs in his pickup bed." Suzanne giggled. "I hate to say it, but I can see that happening, can't you?"

"She's a slut," Jude said angrily, remembering how Joyce Harrison had been an issue when she so openly and aggressively pursued Jake during his first campaign for sheriff. "Brady seems like a nice man. I can't believe he'd take up with a slut."

"Jude. He's male. I'm sure he likes to screw as much as the next guy, and how many available women are there around here? Joyce is somebody he can do the nasty with without making an investment."

Jude believed he'd had exactly that type of relationship with Ginger, but she said, "I can't believe he's like that."

"Why are you defending him, girlfriend? You sound like you're interested in him yourself."

"No, I just . . . Well, I don't know. Maybe I'm disappointed he isn't a better person than that."

"Jude. You are so dumb. Which is ridiculous because you're in the animal-fucking business."

"I am not!"

"What do you call breeding cattle and horses for a living? You know your stallion, Patch, the one you were just talking about? Men are no different. They get a hard-on, and the pursuit of a hot female replaces every rational thought they ever had."

"That's cold, Suzanne."

Suzanne shrugged and fluttered her eyelashes. "Voice of experience."

"Humph," Jude said truculently, in such a bad mood, she wanted to break something. "Was that how it was with Mitch?"

Suzanne chuckled. "All I'm gonna say is, Mitch was a champion at more than bull riding. And his reputation followed him."

"Well, I guess we can hope Pat will treat you better."

"I am one hundred percent certain Pat Garner will treat

me better. But he will never shoot me to the moon like Mitch could."

"If you've decided to be with Pat, you should stop thinking about Mitch. And stop comparing."

"*That* is easier said than done. Trust me, my dear, if you ever find a man who does for you what Mitch did for me, you won't have such a prissy attitude."

Jude feared she knew exactly what Suzanne was talking about. And to her horror, she feared she had found one. And she didn't know what to do about it.

"So what's on your mind?" Suzanne asked. "Why do I feel like you came by to talk about something?"

"Nothing. Can't I just stop to say hello?"

"I know how you are about getting home in time for supper. You never come to my house at this time of day unless something's bothering you."

Jude shook her head. A need to talk had driven her to Suzanne's house, all right, but she could no longer talk about Brady to Suzanne, knowing he had spent time with a woman she and Suzanne knew well. Or that it was only a matter of days before he would be doing the same thing with Joyce Harrison that he had done with Jude Strayhorn.

16

Jude raced home, breaking the speed limit as usual. Snippets of Suzanne's conversation turned over in her mind, though one stood out more than the others.

They've both got boys the same age.

He hadn't said much about his son, but she knew he had made three trips to Fort Worth to see him in the time he had worked at the Circle C. At dinner in Stephenville, he had avoided her questions about his son. But then he had discussed him with Joyce Harrison?

She found Daddy and Grandpa still at the supper table with two guests she didn't recognize. Not even the aroma of charbroiled steaks lured her to join them. She said a cursory hello, made small talk, then jogged upstairs to her room. She had to be alone so she could think.

For all of the time Brady had waltzed through her head since the liaison with him a month ago, she hadn't considered the possibility of his being interested in another woman. She had wondered about his relationship with Ginger a few times but dismissed those thoughts. Ginger was in another town. *I wasn't holding up a sign saying I was looking for a girlfriend, either.* Was a *convenience* all Brady really wanted?

She went to bed with a new quandary at the forefront of her thoughts. Before Brady, she had never met a man she wanted, hadn't even considered that when the day came that she did, she might not be able to have him. The realization was as sharp as a spear through her heart. She didn't know what to do. And now she wasn't sure she could rely on Suzanne for help and advice.

Her mind drifted to a deeper truth. When had she ever had a female friend or relative to rely on when she had questions that begged for answers or problems that called for solving? Suzanne had left Lockett after high school, and they'd had little contact until she returned three years ago. Though Grammy Pen had bestowed countless words of sagely advice through the years, really, she had been too old to help with many of Jude's problems.

Jude had floundered through her snags and obstacles alone. She made decisions alone. *The strong are always alone,* Grammy Pen had told her, *because the weak have nothing to offer them.* How many times had those words forced Jude to find the right path through her setbacks? She was strong; she knew she was. And she would be strong now. She would start over, ceasing to let Brady Fallon appeal to her baser urges. But at the same time, she wanted to maintain their acquaintance. They were friends. She was a smart, well-educated woman. She would figure out how to be friends with a man with whom she couldn't be anything else.

The next morning, after a restless night, she loaded up her working saddle and other miscellaneous horse gear. All the way to the 6-0 barn, she told herself she was doing this because she loved horses. The fact that they were Brady's horses was of secondary importance. When she went inside the tack room, she saw the fine fix-up job Brady had done— new boards on the walls, new shelves. The area was small, but it was every bit as clean, neat and organized as the huge tack room at the Circle C.

She rode all three horses, which consumed the morning. They were frisky and rebellious, and Sal threatened to buck, but Jude had no trouble gaining control. She had spent her life on horses. She knew them better than they knew themselves. Brady's horses were healthy, strong animals under ten years old, and she liked all of them. At dinnertime she returned home.

Only she and Daddy were at the table to eat. Grandpa didn't eat the noon meal often anymore. Irene had made them chicken salad sandwiches. The opportunity was perfect to discuss Sal. She gathered her courage and told Daddy she had volunteered to ride Brady's horses as a personal favor. To head off his questioning how she even knew Brady, she added, "He has a grullo mare that's beautiful, so one day when I saw his pickup at home, I stopped and asked him about her."

It was frightening how easy it had become to lie to her father.

"Huh. He hasn't mentioned her." Daddy bit into his sandwich as if he were starved. No doubt he had eaten breakfast with the hands at four forty-five that morning.

"Oh. Well, I've been seeing her in the pasture every time I've gone to town. She goes back to a King Ranch stud and a mare that won on the track. A little high-spirited, but—"

"Which stud?"

"Peppy Sand Badger."

Daddy stopped the sandwich on the way to his mouth. "Hmm. Brady and I talked about horses just a few days ago. Wonder why he didn't mention he owned a horse of that caliber."

She didn't dare tell him she had taken it upon herself to learn the horse's lineage. "I rode her this morning and—"

"This morning? You've already started?"

"I thought I should. In another few weeks, school will be starting. Since I'm going to be helping coach the girls' teams, I need to do something to get in shape."

He nodded, returning to his sandwich.

"Daddy, I was thinking about bringing the mare over here, to work in the big corral. She hasn't had much training, but I think she's got cow-horse potential."

He nodded, still more interested in his meal than Brady's horse. "Clary would probably be glad to help you with that."

She nodded, too, at the same time breathing a sigh of relief. Her father would never have told her she couldn't use the big corral, but she was glad he didn't ask her more questions about the horse or Brady.

Through the next week, she rode at least one of the horses every morning, but saw nothing of Brady, a deliberate plan on her part. After learning he was seeing a woman in town, she would feel even more awkward around him.

Friday morning, instead of riding the horses, she attended a faculty meeting and tea at the high school. It was a social gathering for the new high school teachers to get acquainted and the old ones to get reacquainted before the fall. Willard County High School had three other single female teachers—one Jude's age who had never been married and two divorcées. While the teachers sipped some red punch, which was probably Kool-Aid, and nibbled homemade cookies, talk among the women turned to the new owner of the 6-0, Brady Fallon—how good-looking he was, how well built he was, naughty double entendres about how he filled out a pair of jeans. As Jude listened to the prattle, she thought it amazing how quickly word of a sexy eligible man got around. It was as if he gave off a scent, like a mare in heat.

The last item of gossip concerned Joyce Harrison and how a woman who had been married three times and had three kids managed to be asked out by him. Jude clenched her jaw but said not a word.

"Let's go to my office so we can talk."

Brady had no idea what J. D. Strayhorn wanted to talk about. He couldn't keep from wondering if he had learned about the weekend in Stephenville. He felt a tinge of guilt over having collaborated with Jude to lie to her father, his boss and a man he had no reason to disrespect. His heart beating a little faster than normal, Brady followed him.

They entered the Circle C ranch house through the back

door. Brady hadn't been in this house since he was twelve.
Back then, he thought it a palace. Today, through his
builder's eye, it seemed to be mostly big, old and outdated.
No radio or TV in sight, no voices. He did smell food as they
passed the entrance to the dining room. He tried to steal a
glance into the long room to find the photograph of Jude's
distant relative and Quanah Parker, but keeping up with
J.D.'s quick steps, he didn't have an opportunity.

Brady's clinking spurs echoed off the stucco walls and
high ceilings, but he'd had no chance to remove them before
J.D. urged him into the house. He had barely had time to remove his chaps. Everywhere he looked, Western art hung on
the walls or Western-themed sculpture filled corners. His
childhood memories didn't include seeing any of that.

He followed J.D. into the office. Brady's experienced eye
took in the dark wood paneling, obviously real wood and
old. Even the blinds on a tall window were made of wood.
Hunting trophies were everywhere. Not even a hint of femi-
nine influence showed in the surroundings. The older man
strode toward slatted bifold doors and opened them to reveal
a hidden wet bar. Brady had built many homes with the same
concealed bar feature—in offices, dens, playrooms, living
rooms, even bedrooms.

"How was your weekend?" J.D. asked. "You drove over
to Fort Worth?"

How was his weekend? Truthfully, except for seeing his
son, Brady's weekend hadn't been worth a damn. He felt as
if he had been on the road for a solid three days. He left
Lockett before daylight on Friday, drove six hours to the
home he had once owned in Fort Worth and picked up Andy.
With the nine-year-old distressed about leaving his older
stepbrother behind, Brady picked up Jarrett, too. Andy always wanted Jarrett to be included. Brady didn't mind. He
was the closest thing to a real father Jarrett had. Marvalee
had been glad to unload the two kids. She and her husband
had planned an adult weekend, she called it, gambling in
Shreveport. "Uh, yeah."

"Spent time with your boy, huh?"

Brady had taken the two boys to his mom's house in Weatherford. From there, they went to a calf-roping play day on Friday afternoon. The next day, he took the boys fishing at the local lake. On Sunday, before he returned them to Marvalee, they saw a movie in Fort Worth, and ate at a pizza joint afterward. Then he had made the six-hour drive back to Lockett.

His visits with Andy were always like that, always hurried, as he rushed to cram as much nine-year-old "fun" as possible into a short time. There was usually a tearful goodbye. Leaving the boys behind on Sunday afternoon had been hard, but no harder than it ever was. "Yeah, it was my turn," he told J.D.

"He's okay?"

"Growing like a weed," Brady answered, his hat hanging on the fingertips of one hand. J.D. was dropping ice cubes into two glasses. He couldn't be too pissed off if he was making drinks.

"What's your poison?"

"Whiskey'll do," Brady answered. "Any kind's okay."

J.D. busied himself splashing Crown Royal into the two glasses. Brady didn't often drink high-end whiskey.

"Have a seat," J.D. said.

Covered in red dirt stuck to his sweaty clothing, Brady looked around. He chose a leather-covered chair he figured would be the easiest to clean after he left. He sat down, propping his left ankle across his right thigh, and hung his dirty hat on his knee. J.D. handed him the glass of whiskey and seated himself behind a huge antique desk. Brady recognized the wood as cherry.

J.D. opened a drawer and brought out a wooden box of fragrant cigars. He leaned across the desk and offered them to Brady, but Brady declined with a lift of his hand. "No, thanks. I'm not a smoker."

J.D. took his time snipping the tip of a long cigar. "Nothing I enjoy more at the end of the day than a good cigar." He lit up, and a pleasant, fruity scent filled the air. He picked up his glass, lifted it to Brady and sipped. Brady did likewise, shuddering as the whiskey burned all the way down his gullet.

"I know your day has been as long as mine, so I'll get right to the point," J.D. said, a swirl of smoke rising from the cigar. He rested his forearms on the desktop, the cigar fitted between his thumb and finger. "I don't know if you've been here long enough to know about the nuts and bolts of our operation. In a nutshell, the way it's worked for years, and worked well, I might add, is my dad has handled the financial end of things. He's been sort of the CEO, you might say, and I've run the ranch. A lot of the larger outfits have general managers, but we've never seen a need for that arrangement here. We've gotten along with me and a wagon boss who's in charge when I can't be around."

Brady had yet to see a day when J.D. had not been present. He started to feel a nervous twitch in his jaw. "I see."

"I believe you told me when you hired on you have a BBA?"

"Yes, sir," Brady said. "I thought for a while about going on for an MBA after I moved to Fort Worth, but never got around to it." He had become a father instead, but he had no regrets about that.

J.D. nodded. "So you've got some education in management. And you owned a business in Fort Worth. "

"Yes, sir."

"My daughter's got a business degree. Business ag. She's also got a degree in biology and has a keen interest in genetics." He drew on his cigar and exhaled, then let out a low laugh. "Sometimes I think that girl's got more brains than her pretty head can hold. I rely on her to keep up with our bulls. Does a fine job, too."

By now Brady knew the Circle C owned around three hundred bulls that were constantly rotated. Small ranchers were lucky to own that many cows. Brady suspected that keeping up with so many bulls on a spread as big as the Circle C was a daunting challenge. He couldn't figure out where J.D. was leading him in this conversation. His right leg wanted to bounce up and down, but he willed his heel to stay on the floor. He sipped another drink, hoping for the whiskey to calm his nerves. "Yes, sir," he repeated.

J.D. leaned forward, his chin thrust out. His eyes were friendly, but serious. "My dad will be eighty-five next month, Brady. He's a sharp old guy, but he's slipping. And I think he's tired. He's spending more than half his time in his room. The last year, I've been taking on the biggest part of his responsibilities on top of my own. To tell you the truth, I'm a little tired, too."

"I'll bet," Brady said.

"I've seen you work, Brady. You're low-key, but you get things done. I like that in a man. I've seen you with the men. I can tell they respect you and trust you. That's important in an outfit like this. We have high regard for our hands. We try to take good care of them and keep them happy. It's part of our philosophy and our reputation. Some of them have been with us their whole lives. A couple have brought their own sons into our employ."

"Yes, sir, I'm aware." Brady could think of three father-son teams who worked as ranch hands. He swallowed another sip.

"What I'm getting at is, I'd like to give Dad some relief, and I'm asking you to give me some."

"In what way?" Brady sipped again.

"I want you to take part of my job. In time, perhaps all of it."

Brady swallowed and sat straighter in his chair. "I see, sir."

"I've talked to Jack Durham. He told me he would've had no problem putting you in charge of his whole place."

Brady knew Jack liked him, but handing over responsibility for his whole ranch? That was a damn big exaggeration. Besides that, Jack's operation didn't come close to being as big and complex as the Circle C's. "He did?"

"As I said, we've never had a general manager, but if you're not averse to trying it, I'm not, either."

Statistics zoomed through Brady's head like lightning flashes—cows and bulls and mares and studs and unending acres of land and dollars. He might have a college degree in business administration, he might have owned his own business, but he had *never* had responsibility for something as vast as the Circle C ranch. And hadn't expected to. But he had never suffered from a lack of self-confidence, either, and the very thought of the challenge set his pulse to racing. He threw back the remainder of his drink, the burn making his eyes water. "Well, sir, I don't know," he almost croaked.

"The pay would be commensurate with the added responsibilities, of course. And we usually furnish our upper-tier folks with a house if they need it or want it."

"I see, sir."

"No need to call me 'sir,' Brady. I'm not my dad."

"No, sir. I mean yes, sir."

J.D. leaned back in his chair again and drew on his cigar. "Well, what do you think?"

Brady didn't answer immediately. He couldn't. First, because he couldn't believe what he had just heard. And second, because this was the job Jude wanted—the job Jude thought she was going to get. "I guess I have to say, J.D., it sounds like your daughter's got the education to do the job. And the right. And I bet she'd want to."

"Oh, she thinks she does. She's smart enough, for sure. But Jude doesn't understand. She can't ramrod the ranch hands and do day after day of man's work. No woman could. That girl means everything to me. I don't want to watch her turn into a weathered woman with a back broken by hard work. I have no doubt the day will come when she can oversee Strayhorn Corp, but that's not the same as managing the hands and the day-to-day work. For now, Dad and I wish she would settle down and concentrate on getting married and having a family."

Whoa. J. D. Strayhorn obviously didn't know his daughter very well. Or perhaps he did, but chose to ignore certain things, like Jude's desperate desire to do the very job Brady was being offered.

"Jude's never had much female influence in her life, you see. Fortunately, my grandmother lived a long time and was able to be there for her at times. But on the whole, it's been hard, my dad and me trying to bring a girl up to be a lady, especially one as spirited and bright as Jude." He leaned forward again and smiled. "You know, Brady, I believe the world would be an easier place to live in if people would conform to the roles God intended. Like animals do. You never see mares and cows raising hell about their places in the pecking order. God didn't make mares and cows to be in charge of the herd."

Well, that was an attitude that would make the feminist movement grind its teeth. But Brady didn't entirely disagree with J.D. He had spent too many years working with and around animals and nature to take issue with the point. Life just had more balance when women behaved as women and men stepped up and assumed their roles as men. "Uh, no, I guess He didn't," he said.

"Sometimes Jude and I lock horns over the issue," J.D. said with a smile.

Brady needed something to hide the trembling in his hands that J.D.'s offer had set off. He set his glass on a table beside a stuffed wild turkey. He picked his hat off his knee and sat straight in his chair. "I appreciate your confidence in me, J.D., and I'm flattered. I'll think about it. I'll have to figure out how the increased responsibility here would mesh with my responsibility to myself. As I've said, I'm hoping to get the 6-0 up and operating within the next year. Or two at the most."

"Then a little extra pay should be welcome. Do you have any questions?"

"I do have one. If I decline, what happens? Would you then put your daughter in the job?"

J.D. adjusted his silver glasses. A solemn, direct look

came from his dark brown eyes. "No. I would not. I'd have to look for a manager outside of Willard County."

Brady could tell by the set of J.D.'s mouth and the look in his eye that was exactly what the man would do. A man didn't oversee an empire for all the years J. D. Strayhorn had without the ability to make tough calls. Still, Brady hesitated, trying to muddle his way through to determining Jude's father's attitude about her, but he couldn't quite pinpoint it. "My problem is time, J.D. And speaking of time"— Brady rose from his chair—"how about I give you an answer by the end of the week?"

"Great." J.D. pushed back from his desk, stood and put out his right hand. "Just give me the word and we'll sit down over a drink and talk money."

"Great," Brady echoed, shaking hands. He moved toward the door.

"While you're thinking about it," J.D. said, "I'd like for you to keep in mind I'm not talking about a temporary arrangement. If we can come to an agreement where you're satisfied, I'd expect it to be long-term. If I invest in a man, I want *him* to make an investment, too."

"Yes, sir, I understand," Brady said.

J.D. followed him out to the hallway and they strolled toward the back door together.

Brady took in as much of the artwork as he could absorb. Jude hadn't been kidding about her dad being a collector. And she hadn't been kidding about his approach to life, either. The preceding conversation had sent reservations and caution and worry careening through Brady's mind. "Beautiful art," Brady said casually.

"Besides my cigars, it's my one guilty pleasure. My vice, you could say. Most of my social activity consists of shopping for art." He bent and delicately dusted something off a frame with his fingertips. "I gave up on courting women a long time ago."

As Brady climbed into his pickup, he pondered the meeting with J.D. The offer to manage the Circle C ranch was so unexpected—even unbelievable—he needed to have more time to digest it. His mind settled on J. D. Strayhorn, the man. He remembered him from his boyhood days as somebody who was always busy, who walked in quick steps everywhere he went, a man with little to say. Brady couldn't fault him for that. He didn't say much himself. Now, looking at J.D. through the prism of adult eyes, Brady saw him as not much different today than he had been twenty years ago. He came across as a cordial guy, but also one distant son of a bitch.

If he didn't want his daughter running the ranch, why hadn't he anointed his nephew Cable? Brady knew Jake had no interest, but no one, not even Jake, seemed to know about Cable.

Not once since the day Brady had been hired had J.D. mentioned Cable or Jake or Brady's association with them twenty-something years back. Brady had brought up Jake and Cable a couple of times, but J.D. had glided right past the subject of his two nephews as if they didn't exist. Brady had even discussed it briefly with his mother over the weekend. She had reminded him of the details of the affair between J.D.'s wife and brother, and the car accident that had killed them. Was that incident at the root of J.D.'s attitude?

A tiny voice in the back of Brady's mind told him that after what had happened with Jude, he shouldn't even consider J.D.'s offer, that he should have turned it down on the spot. The lost weekend with Jude was bound to come back to haunt him.

But at the moment, ego and temptation were the more powerful drivers. For a man who loved the outdoors and good cattle and smart horses, being a general manager of one of the largest and most successful ranches in Texas was a once-in-a-lifetime opportunity. He couldn't discount the money, either. Without a doubt, the job came with a six-digit salary.

He saw no point in wasting energy conjuring up questions that had no answers or finding answers that had no questions. His most nagging concern was Judith Ann. He would bet the job he had just been offered that she had no idea her father planned on hiring an outsider to manage the Circle C.

17

Jude loved teaching at the high school. Preparing for the launch of the school year suddenly had her busier than she had been all summer. With the sports teams beginning try-outs a couple of weeks before classes started, she was forced to juggle riding Brady's horses and working with Sal with her obligations at the high school. She had little time to stew over Brady's social life.

She worked with Sal in the big corral on Saturday. The mare had become easier to catch and was more responsive to commands, though the horse suffered occasional lapses and reverted to her wilder instincts. Because it was the weekend, Jude had wondered whether Brady would stop to see how the horse was improving, but he didn't show. Nor did she see him when she worked with Sal on Sunday afternoon.

On Monday, the workouts with the prospective volleyball and basketball players lasted into the afternoon. All week, she had arrived home well after supper and ended up eating in the kitchen while Irene cleaned. Wanting to reach the ranch house in time to eat with Daddy and Grandpa, she decided to pass on riding Brady's horses.

Daddy met her at the back door and told her he and Grandpa had been missing her at the evening meal. She hurried upstairs and showered off the day's dust and heat. She dressed in a full floral-print skirt made of floaty fabric and a simple aqua T. She had bought it especially to wear with a gorgeous necklace made of cat's-eye, mother-of-pearl stones and a huge turquoise cabochon. It was an artist's original purchased during her last trip to Santa Fe. She was too late getting downstairs to meet Daddy in his office for a drink.

She, Daddy and Grandpa took their seats at the table and dined on fried quail with cream gravy and mashed potatoes. Toward the end of supper, Grandpa asked Daddy, "Did young Fallon give you an answer?"

Jude's attention perked up and she leveled a look across the table at her father. He wiped his mouth with his napkin and turned his head toward Grandpa, adjusting his wire-rimmed glasses. "He came and talked to me today. We're going to start on Monday with him spending days with me."

What were they talking about? Jude watched as Grandpa busied himself pushing peas onto his knife. "I hope you know what you're doing, Jasper."

"I have a lot of confidence. The more I see him with the hands, the more I like him. He's a quiet guy. Doesn't say much. Doesn't throw his weight around. When he does talk, he's usually got something to say. He's got leadership skills, too. Can make decisions. No longer than he's been here, the men already look up to him. He gives off an air of trust. I'm impressed."

Jude's fork stopped, suspended over her plate. What *were* they talking about?

"And what about his place?" Grandpa asked.

Daddy shrugged. "He'll have a little more money to spend on it."

"But will he have the time? I'm sure I don't have to remind you, Jasper, that this ranch requires your attention daily, seven days a week. The hands might take days off, but *you* don't."

"I know, Dad. It's just a trial for a few months. Fallon understands that."

Jude's felt as if the hair had risen on her scalp. A knot so large she couldn't swallow another bite of food formed in her stomach. She laid her fork on her plate with a clunk. "What are you two talking about?"

Her father looked across the table at her, his expression unsmiling. "I was going to tell you, Jude, but we didn't get a chance to talk before supper." He put down his fork and dabbed at his lips with his napkin. He spoke without looking at her. "I'm giving Brady Fallon a trial as a general manager."

Jude's jaw dropped. Her heartbeat kicked up, and the very air whooshed from her lungs. "But you—you can't."

"Jude, listen—"

"No. I won't listen. If this ranch requires an additional manager, it should be me."

"Jude, we've talked about this many times. You can't manage the hands. It would just be too hard for a woman."

"You don't know that. The LO is owned by a woman. And she runs it herself. And she—she works alongside the hands." Her pulse was swishing in her ears so loudly, she felt as if she were screaming from the bottom of an empty well.

"And look at her," Daddy said. "She looks more male than female. Caring for livestock is a physical, outdoor job. The years of hard work in the sun and weather have taken their toll on Louelle, Jude. Even on her health. She's had no life. She's had to work twice as hard as the hands just to hold their respect."

A memory of the last time she had seen Margie Wallace alive flew into Jude's mind. Her skin had been tanned to nut-brown and as wrinkled as badly treated leather. She had dressed in men's clothes and, like Louelle Squires, looked more male than female. Jude's mouth opened and closed like a fish out of water. She searched for a rebuttal, but her brain felt as if it had frozen.

"But there's more to it than that," Daddy said, leaning forward, as if pushing his face closer would enhance his argument. "Ranching's a precarious business these days. Every time we turn around, some new radical group wants to put us out of business. We just aren't making the profit we used to."

"But—but we could be. If you and Grandpa weren't so old-fashioned. If you'd listen to some of my ideas and—"

"Jude. We've talked about this."

"Our ways have come from practice over time, Judith Ann," Grandpa put in. "They work as well as any can. Your daddy's seen to that. Change only for its own sake is too costly."

"We can't afford to experiment," Daddy added.

"Experiment!" Her eyes bugged. "What do you think you'll be doing with Brady Fallon?" She held her father's gaze, waiting for a reason, an excuse, anything, but he only looked at her. "I've lived here my whole life. I know every inch of every acre, every section. I know the animals. I've organized my very existence around the management of this place. I've dedicated myself to its future. I've made sacrifices. You can't do this."

"Judith Ann, remember yourself," her grandfather said. "We're at the supper table."

Jude glared at her grandfather. Her heart was pounding and she realized her voice had become strident. She reined in her frustration and tried to compose herself. But she was shaking and her voice felt unsteady. "And—and what about Cable? If you need another management person, why wouldn't you bring him home?"

"We talked to Cable months back," Grandpa said.

Jude stared at her grandfather, blinking. Daddy had never told her they had contacted Cable. He hadn't told her he was even considering giving up management of the ranch. Of course he and Grandpa both had talked to her cousin Cable. He was, after all, *male*.

"He's happy where he is," her father said. "He's got his hands full with his rope-manufacturing company. He isn't interested in coming back here."

"But Jake—"

"What about Jake?" her father said coldly, a muscle flexing in his jaw.

Grandpa cleared his throat and signaled Irene to refill his water glass.

Indeed, what about Jake? Jake had made it clear in no uncertain terms that he had no interest in associating with his grandfather or his only living uncle, but he might be happy Brady Fallon had been chosen to ramrod the Circle C.

Jude was out of words. Nothing she said would matter, anyway. "This is insane," she cried. She threw her napkin on her plate and jerked away from the table.

She charged up the stairs, taking them two steps at a time. Inside her room, she paced, breathing deeply, seeking to calm the thudding in her chest. She would leave here. She would not, could not, stay where she wasn't wanted. Or appreciated. She would leave. She should have done it already.

She went into the bathroom and pulled a clean washcloth from its rack, drenched it with cold water and pressed it to her face. Her cheeks felt as if they were on fire. She sank to the vanity chair, waiting for her pulse rate to slow and her thoughts to organize.

After a few minutes she returned to the bedroom just in time to hear boot steps in the hall. It would be her father. She couldn't remember the last time he had been to her room, but she was sure her outburst had upset him. Ordinarily she, Daddy and Grandpa got along.

Three light raps. *Don't open the door,* a childish part of her said. *You're upset. Let him be upset, too.*

But she couldn't shut out her only parent. She drew a shaky breath and opened the door.

"Hey, punkin, can I come in?"

She threw a palm in the air and jammed the opposite fist against her hip. "You know, Daddy, I really hate that name. I've asked you a hundred times to please not call me that. I'm not ten years old."

He came in and carefully closed the door behind him, a hangdog look about him. In case he intended to hug her or try to cajole her out of her anger, she stepped out of his reach. He walked over to an antique fainting couch that occupied a corner of the room and sat down. He looked up at her and patted the seat beside him.

"I'm not in the mood to sit down," she said, crossing her arms under her breasts. "Or to talk. You're wasting your time coming up here."

She moved to one of the three tall windows and pulled aside the filmy ivory lace that covered it, turning her back on him. She stared out at the garden and trees beyond. Tiny white lights—fairy lights—hung in the trees, like stars in the twilight. She had put them there herself one Christmas break when she was home from college. Doing it had taken her days. At her father's instruction, Irene's husband had maintained them ever since. "You know something, Daddy? I should've never come back here after school. I could've gone on to vet school. Or gone to Dallas or Houston or even back East and worked in research. I came back because I thought I was needed. And I thought the Circle C was my future."

"Jude, it would break my heart to see you leave here." His voice came to her softly, laced with sincerity. "This is your home. And you're the best thing I have to show for my time on this earth."

She couldn't doubt he loved her. She huffed. "If that's true, why treat me badly?"

"I thought you liked Brady Fallon. I thought that's why you were working his horses for him."

"This has nothing to do with Brady Fallon." She turned to face him. He was leaning forward, looking up at her, his elbows propped on his thighs. "Why don't you get it?" she said tersely. "Why don't you understand that I'm an extremely capable, well-educated adult? That I happen to be female doesn't take away from that fact. I can run this ranch."

"I don't doubt your capabilities for a minute," he replied sharply. "Do you think I'd turn management of our bull herd over to you if I doubted your ability? Do you think I don't know how challenging it is to buy and sell and maneuver three hundred bulls? Your knowledge has improved the quality of our calves immensely. And they get better every year. Don't think I don't know why the packers want Circle C stock before any other and why they pay more. My confidence in you isn't the issue."

"It's exactly the issue."

He sighed and straightened, bracing his palms on his thighs. "Most women want to get married and have their own families. That's what Grandpa and I both want for you. What chance do you think you'd have to do that if you were trying to ride herd on all of this?" He made a sweeping gesture with his arm. "I'm not complaining about it, because I love it. It's my life. But, Jude, keeping the Circle C afloat is an all-consuming job."

Jude knew the hours he worked and had marveled for years at all he dealt with single-handedly. Daily, even after he came in from outside, he spent hours in his office. She relented and sat down beside him, but refused to look at him.

His arm came around her shoulders and he pulled her against his side, surrounding her with the scent of cigars and whiskey, the scent of familiarity and home. But she wasn't ready to surrender her anger. And his words didn't heal the slash she felt deep in her heart. She leaned away from him, but he didn't let go.

"Don't be mad at me, sweetheart," he said. "I'm trying to do what's best for everybody. You've seen how your grandpa's slipping. I'm more than a little worried about him. I'm going to have to help him more, which is why I felt a need to bring in another man."

At the mention of the word "man," Jude felt her mouth quirk.

"You could help Grandpa, too, you know. Learn the ins and outs of the ranch's finances. That's important, Jude."

Jude knew that. But that facet of the ranch's operation had always belonged to Grandpa. Sometimes he spent entire days on the phone with bankers and investment types or with the accountant in Abilene. Strayhorn Corp had investments in many venues other than West Texas land and cattle.

As if he knew what she was thinking, her father added, "You know, we haven't been as lucky as some of the other West Texas stock growers. Without oil, the management of outside investment is just as important as taking good care of our land and our livestock."

Jude was well aware oil hadn't been discovered on the Circle C land. At one point years ago, a push had been made to find the elusive black gold and thirty wells had been drilled. Thirty dry holes. Nowadays, the science of oil exploration had vastly improved, and wildcatting was not quite such a shot in the dark. Scientists could know what was under the surface and where. But until recently, the oil market had been so stagnant and government regulation so restrictive, no exploration projects had even been considered.

Under three hundred thousand acres of land in West Texas, fossil fuel had to be somewhere, but Grandpa had said he wasn't pouring any more money into holes in the ground. And that had settled it. If she were managing the ranch, she would reopen those doors. The market had changed, and so had the public need. She shook her head and drew a deep sniff, trying to arrest the tears that kept sneaking up her throat. "Grandpa's never been willing to—"

"He knows he's aging. He's more inclined now to give up some control."

"But not necessarily to me."

"He knows you're smart. He's not excited about your bringing in Angus bulls, and he doesn't understand the new demand for grass-fed beef, but he's impressed with the way you handle yourself. And he likes those big checks after we ship calves." He gave her shoulder a little shake. "If you offer to help him, he won't turn you down."

"I don't know." She shook her head. "Maybe."

Daddy gave her shoulder a squeeze. "That's my girl." He stood and pulled her up with him. "You're a bright spot in my life, Jude. Ever since your mother left, all I've wanted is for you to be happy. I want you to find someone to share your life with."

My mother. Hah! "Why? You've never found anyone."

"See, Jude, this is what I've been trying to tell you all along about this place using up your whole life. My mother died soon after Ike and Karen—"

He stopped, removed his glasses and squeezed the bridge of his nose. Jude stared up at him in awe. She couldn't remember the last time she had heard him say his deceased brother's or wife's names. Or if she had ever seen him on the verge of tears.

He cleared his throat and repositioned his glasses. "Grandpa, uh, needed a lot of support back then. I lost my brother and my wife, but he lost his son, his daughter-in-law *and* his own wife the same year. And I lost my mother, too. And because of what happened, we . . . he . . . also lost Jake. He wasn't able to do much around the ranch for a long time. Depression, I think they called it."

Jude had never heard that her grandfather had suffered from depression. No one would have dared say it. Just the word would have been an indication of weakness. She had assumed her grandfather was made of iron, as all the Strayhorn men before him had been.

Depression was not what Grammy Pen had called all that had happened those twenty-four years ago. She had called it the Campbell Curse.

"Helping him through that took a lot," Daddy continued. "I never had a chance to do much grieving myself. While all of that was going on, somebody still had to take care of the Circle C. So you see, there's really been no chance for anyone or anything else in my life. But as I said, I'm not complaining or making excuses. I'm just trying to help you understand that sometimes life throws detours in your path that you can't get around. I'm trying to give you a better chance at happiness than I had."

Now the tears had sneaked in again, but she sniffed them

away. She had never been a crier and wouldn't be one now. "I'm sorry, Daddy. I don't mean to be hateful. I'm just disappointed."

He looped his arm around her shoulders again, and this time she didn't pull away. "Don't be, Daughter. The day will come when you'll own this place. And your children after that. That's why Dad and I harp at you all the time about getting married and having a family. Have you ever considered what would happen to this ranch if you had no children?

"You must never forget your roots. In 1861, Alister Campbell lost a daughter on his trip to Texas. In memory of her, you carry her name. Eventually, with all the hardship, the work, the war and the uncertainty of frontier life, old Alister lost his wife to madness. But he never lost sight of his goals. Five generations have worked at preserving his legacy. We can't let him down."

Indeed, the family legend had it that Alister Campbell's wife never recovered from her three-year-old daughter's drowning in the Red River and was haunted by the small body never being found. Just a year later, at twenty-one years old, Mary Ellen Roslyn Campbell had hanged herself. Jude sniffed again. "I know, Daddy."

"Tell you what. Let's ride this week. My sorrel isn't getting nearly the exercise he needs. The weaning's all done. Hopefully I'll be able to get away for a few hours. You could take Brady's mare and we could ride over and look at the Spring Creek pasture. The mesquites over there damn near got the jump on us. I've been wanting to check on the job the brush-removal crew has been doing."

Daddy could drive to the Spring Creek pasture in his pickup in less than half the time it took to ride a horse to it. Riding the pasture with her father had always been a bonding experience and normally something Jude loved doing. But today she didn't want to ride horseback to look at mesquite trees at Spring Creek. What difference would it make if she saw them? They were Brady Fallon's problem now.

She would never cease loving her father or her grandfather, but her heart had been severely wounded, her emotions battered. And Daddy and Grandpa were responsible.

"I won't be able to ride," she said. "I'm back to working every day at the school."

18

The next morning, after a fitful night, Jude came to consciousness slowly. Her eyes resisted opening. Instead of bounding out of bed with her typical enthusiasm for meeting the day, she lay there replaying last night's conversation and the latest affront to her dignity and intelligence by those who were supposed to love her.

She searched her mind for words to describe what they had done to her.

Betrayal? That word didn't fit. She had to admit that nothing had ever been promised to her. Not really. Implied, maybe, but not promised.

Misunderstanding? Understatement of the year. Her father and grandfather had never understood her. A disconnect had always existed between her and them. She had often wondered if it was as simple as the fact that they were male and she wasn't. Daddy had sometimes tried to span the gap through the years, but Grandpa hadn't even made an attempt. The outdated belief—and they had never tried to hide it—that a woman couldn't function by herself in a man's world was so deeply ingrained in both of them, it was an insurmountable wall. She should have faced that long ago.

She thought of various points in her life when they had maneuvered her to do their will and how she had tried to be a good daughter and granddaughter by doing what they expected of her. She had gone to college, been a diligent student and earned three degrees. She had shunned many of the pitfalls of college life, such as drugs, alcohol, having fun instead of studying.

She had even been engaged to marry two men—well, boys, really—who Daddy and Grandpa chose. She'd had no great affection for either one. Both of those engagements had been efforts on her part to conform to Daddy's and Grandpa's wishes.

Her mind traveled back to her first year of college, when Daddy had arranged for her to meet Webb Henderson, the son of one of his and Grandpa's political friends in Austin. Though she had never had a boyfriend, she allowed herself to become engaged at eighteen.

Webb had been so eager for sex, he almost forced himself on her. She was a virgin and couldn't have been more naive. She knew plenty about animal sex, but she hadn't known what to expect from men. She didn't figure out Webb immediately, didn't realize the prize he and his father had their eyes on was the Circle C. When it dawned on her that Webb and his parents would like nothing more than for her to get pregnant and force a shotgun wedding, she marched to a doctor in Bryan and obtained a prescription for birth control pills.

She broke the engagement several times. But Webb didn't bow out gracefully. He caused havoc in her life and she made up with him. Eight stressful months passed before the final breakup came, when she called the police to have him removed from her house. His enraged father contacted hers, and Daddy sent for her to come back to the ranch, where a three-day verbal assault ensued. But she had stood her ground and returned to school unengaged, determined that school was for education, not socializing. Daddy had asked, but she had never revealed most of what had happened between her and Webb. Better to let sleeping dogs lie, as Grammy Pen always said.

After earning her master's seven years later, she became engaged to Jason Weatherby. Daddy had done business with

Jason's father, and the two parents had gone out of their way
to force a relationship between their children. Though she
went through the prenuptial motions, she couldn't imagine
spending a lifetime with Jason. From the beginning, she believed him to be spoiled, selfish and snobbish, all traits she
couldn't tolerate. And *he* would have never tolerated her
Willard County friends. She couldn't even imagine him in
Suzanne's company.

Fortunately, she was able to end that relationship in a
mere three months, before Strayhorn Corp's lawyers and the
Weatherby's lawyers had even had time to accrue billable
hours hashing out the prenuptial agreement. But Daddy still
had a ridiculous, even laughable, idea that she and Jason
might renew their engagement.

Daddy and Grandpa's ideal was for her to marry someone
who would become part of the ranch operation, at which
point she would be set aside as the baby maker, like all the
Strayhorn women before her.

Of course Daddy and Grandpa had always meant well. If
she hadn't believed that, she couldn't have lived here and
had an affectionate relationship with them.

But this time they had committed the ultimate offense,
and she could no longer excuse them as having "meant
well." Hiring a general manager was not a short-term decision.

*You can't manage the hands. It would just be too hard for
a woman.*

That statement was the bottom line. If Brady hadn't
agreed to take the job, she suspected Daddy would find
some other outsider. Then the Circle C would be going the
direction of most other dynastic spreads around Texas—run
by outsiders while the owners found other things to do, or
even lived in faraway places. The realization had broken
something within Jude that would never be mended. She no
longer felt herself a part of the ranch's inner circle. In a matter of hours, she had become a different person.

Her next thought was of Brady Fallon, the man who had

usurped her place in the universe. But her good sense kicked in and wouldn't allow her to go there. Brady hadn't taken anything away from her. He had simply been standing behind the door when her own father closed it on her expectations.

She forced herself out of bed and stood in front of the vanity mirror. Her eyes were swollen from crying half the night. She hated crying. She had grown up in a world of men who didn't cry. Trying to show them she was as stalwart as they, she had learned as a child to quash her female expressions of emotion. All night she had fought the sobs that built in her chest, but she had finally given in to them in the wee hours.

She had also spent part of the restless night recalling her plan to buy the 6-0 ranch with her trust-fund money. She had abandoned the idea, but now she could think of no reason not to return to it. And she could do it now without so much as a pang of conscience.

She showered and dressed, leaving the house without eating breakfast, her raw, pitiful-looking eyes hidden by dark sunglasses. She headed for the 6-0.

Brady was already outside when she arrived. She knew because she could hear Toby Keith singing about his "Whiskey Girl" at high decibels from behind the house.

Her feet felt as if they weighed a hundred pounds as she walked past the house toward the barn and saw him standing on an upper rung of a tall ladder braced against the barn wall. He was beautiful, so strong and lean. That quickening of her heartbeat that always came when she saw him rushed through her. The arcane feeling was even more powerful than what had happened at home or what she had come here for.

He had a hammer in his hand. When he saw her, he looked at her for a few beats before starting down the ladder with graceful masculine agility. By the time she reached him, he had stepped off the bottom rung. He smelled of clean sweat. She sensed a wariness about him. He probably feared she might break into a tantrum and take off a strip of his hide or something worse. She shoved her hands in her back pockets. "You got a minute?"

"Sure." He tugged off his leather gloves and stuffed them into his back pocket. He had on faded Wranglers and a faded gray T-shirt, the arm holes ragged where the sleeves had been ripped out. His tanned, defined biceps rippled as he dropped his hammer into a toolbox on the ground, then squatted and latched the box. Sweat had made a damp wedge down the middle of the back of his shirt. The fact that they'd had sex she would never forget just six weeks ago felt as if it had happened in another life. "You riding this morning?" he asked.

She shook her head. "I rode Thursday. Sal's still at the Circle C. I was planning to work with her this weekend, so I didn't bring her back yet."

He nodded.

"I want to make you a deal," she said.

"A deal." He lifted off his cap and wiped his forehead with his forearm, thick dark underarm hair showing when he raised his arm. A visual of him lying in bed against brown plaid sheets with his arm cocked behind his head came to her, and she almost shuddered. "I found out last night that starting Monday, you'll be dedicating your life and your future to the Circle C, so—"

"Jude, I didn't . . . I tried to tell J.D. you'd be—"

"Disappointed? Disillusioned? Let down?" She twisted her mouth into a horseshoe scowl and raised a dismissive palm. "Nah, not me. I'm Judith Ann, the model child. I'm used to being shunted aside for the sake of the Campbell legacy." She wished she could quell the sarcasm, but today it wasn't possible.

Concern showed in his eyes. He reset his cap. "I was going to try to talk to you."

"It isn't your place to talk to me. Look, I've got a question for you. My daddy, the man you'll be trying to replace—which I assure you will be no easy task—works twenty-four-seven. How do you figure you'll have any time to give to the 6-0?"

"I'm still thinking about it. No hard-and-fast decisions have been made."

"Oh, Daddy's determined. I saw it in his eye. Believe me, he's made hard-and-fast decisions even if you haven't. Here's an idea. While you're thinking about running the Circle C, maybe you can think about this, too. You need money. I need land. I've got one, you've got the other. Somewhere in that scenario, there's a place for us to meet. I want to move forward with some of my ideas."

"Jude, I'm not interested in selling—"

"I'm not talking about selling. Do you want to chat out here in the sun, or can we find some shade?"

He drew in a breath and gestured toward the barn. They walked inside the wooden building together, into the dim murk that felt almost cool without the press of the direct sun. He pushed back the bill of his cap and leaned his backside against a stack of hay bales. He crossed his ankles and hooked his thumbs in his pockets. "What's on your mind?"

The casual pose in his tight jeans made her eyes drift toward his fly, and she thought of Joyce Harrison. She quickly jerked her thoughts back on track and her eyes up to his face.

"Can you take off those sunglasses?" he said. "I like seeing your eyes."

She hesitated, then yanked off the sunglasses. His mouth tightened as if he were surprised by her appearance. She must look even more awful than she thought.

"Grandpa expects you to fail here, you know. And after you do, he expects you to come to him, hat in hand, begging him to buy you out. Then he expects you to sell to him at a rock-bottom price."

The words felt strange to say. Twenty-four hours ago, she wouldn't have dreamed of spouting something Grandpa had told her in confidence.

Brady's shoulders lifted in a shrug. "So? Nothing new

about that. Years ago, he tried to buy the place from Aunt Margie."

"And you're willing to work for him as a manager knowing what I just told you?"

"What do I care what he expects? Just because a man expects something doesn't mean he gets it, even if he's Jeff Strayhorn."

"Well, you obviously don't know my grandfather."

"Look, Jude. This is a good opportunity for me. A job I can do. Something I believe I'll like. That doesn't mean it or they will own me. Besides, it might not work out. It's a trial at first."

"Oh, you'll work out, Brady. I might not know you that well, but I can see you'll work out."

"Jude, I don't blame you for being upset. If I were in your shoes—"

She raised her hand again and stopped his words. "Don't say that. You can't possibly know anything about being in my shoes."

He straightened to his full height, propping his hands on his hips and looking down at her with those laser eyes. "Then let me put it this way, Jude. If I thought your family was really going to give you what you want, I wouldn't have taken the job. I damn near turned J.D. down on the spot until he told me he would hire somebody from the outside if I didn't take his offer. And I think he was as serious as a man can be. You need to believe me on that. I guess you could look at it as better me than a total stranger."

She did believe him. She knew her father, for all his gentleness at times, was capable of being as ruthless as he felt he had to be. She felt an involuntary wry smile crawl to the corner of her mouth, and she fastened her eyes on his. "And you think you're not a stranger?"

His hand rose as if he might touch her, but then it quickly fell. Instead, he touched her with his eyes. "No. To some people I'm a stranger, but not to you. You've already trusted me with . . . You know you can trust me."

What had he almost said? Trusted him with her virtue?

Emotions she didn't understand filled her chest like a great balloon, and for a moment she couldn't breathe. Surely she was too young to be having a heart attack. "None of that is what I came here to discuss."

"Then speak your piece."

"You've got fifteen sections here, right? More than enough dry land to run a couple hundred cows."

He gave her a look.

She refused to let the glint of caution she saw in his eye deter her. *In for a penny, in for a pound,* as Grammy Pen would say. "I want to lease it from you at the going rate. I'll put my cows on it and some bulls. If more cross-fencing is needed, I'll do it out of my pocket. And I'll be responsible for removing the brush."

"Why would you want to do that, Jude? J.D. and Jeff—"

"I have some ideas about crossbreeding and finishing out calves that Daddy and Grandpa won't let me try. I told you that in Stephenville."

He ducked his chin and looked down. Obviously he didn't want to discuss Stephenville any more than she did.

"Part of the deal is we don't talk about my father or grandfather. And when you're with them, you don't discuss me and what I'm doing here."

He crossed his arms over his chest and just kept looking at her.

"There's one more part. If the day comes you decide to sell, you don't let my grandfather be the buyer. If you sell, you sell to me."

His laser-sharp eyes bored into her as if he had read her mind. "I know you're hurt. I know that right now, you think you want to hurt them back. But going off on your own like this isn't the answer. I think you'll be sorry."

She didn't need to be told that what she was doing would affect her father and grandfather. And she didn't intend to be told how she might feel later. "You need the money," she said. "It's a good deal. The brush cleanup alone makes it a good deal."

"I'll think about it."

Brady watched Jude drive away. She had brass balls. He had to give her that. But that wasn't a new discovery.

One of the hardest things he'd had to do lately was keep his mind from wandering to the hours they had spent together.

Now he had even more to think about. Jude's offer had more positives than negatives. Though he and J.D. hadn't yet sat down for a serious talk about money, Brady knew that even with good pay, he could still be years away from getting enough money together to stock the 6-0 with a cattle herd. A short-term land lease could help him toward that end. He didn't really expect Jude to pay for removing the brush. On the other hand, he couldn't afford to do it himself, and if she wanted good graze, it had to be done.

Of course she knew that. She was too smart not to.

He had only her word that she knew a damn thing about cattle raising. But his instinct told him not to doubt her. He had questioned what she knew about horse training, but she was doing an outstanding job with his horses. Hell, she had almost turned Sal into a disciplined animal.

But if he took her up on her offer, what would he be stepping into? How would the Strayhorn men feel about his making a side deal with Jude?

He stared out across the pasture where his two geldings had sought shade under a shed roof attached to one side of the corral. Not even noon, and the day was already scorching. Given the circumstances, he doubted Jude would return to ride the geldings, and he knew he wouldn't have time to do it himself. They were good horses. He probably should sell them while they were young enough to bring top prices. He had hung on to them, believing the time would come when Andy would be with him, but with every visit to Fort

Worth, his hopes for that grew weaker. He was starting to notice more distance between himself and his son.

Horses as pets made no sense. If the day ever came when he had the time and need for them, Texas was full of good horses. If he started working as the Circle C's manager, he would sell the geldings for sure.

Then it dawned on him. He had told Jude no decisions had been made, but had she been right? Had he already unconsciously agreed to J.D.'s offer before the trial period even began?

19

A few days later Jude sat at the computer in her office at one end of the ranch's veterinary clinic. The original intent for the spacious room was for it to be the ranch's business office. But Daddy conducted most of his business from his office in the house, so Jude had appropriated the space in the veterinary clinic for her bull-management tasks.

She liked being in the veterinary building, close enough to Doc Barrett to know what was current with the ranch's various studs and the broodmares. She liked the idea of walking into the clinic when she wanted to, checking things out and talking to Doc about which studs to breed with which mares. She liked being included in the insemination process. In the past few days, being around the horses and the ongoing breeding operation had helped her gain control of her emotions. The certainty of science had a way of bringing her back down to earth and reminding her of the insignificance of her problems in the scheme of things.

Today she was pleased with the online transaction she had just completed. She had bought a handsome, square-built, beefy Black Angus goliath from an Angus farm in Minnesota. He had a long formal name, but she called him Batman. He had a pedigree even longer than his name, and his stats were impressive. Going outside to buy pedigreed bulls was too expensive to do it often. Most of the time, the ranch raised its own bulls. But she wanted to establish a high-quality Angus strain in the Circle C's herd. So far, the ranch had few Angus cows, but Batman would produce good, solid, black baldies out of the Herefords.

Staying busy with something that interested her profoundly helped keep her mind off Brady and the bruising her psyche had absorbed this week. At least she felt she was making a valuable contribution, and inch by inch, she was adding diversity to the Circle C's stock.

She heard familiar voices from the hallway and looked up and out the door. Her father was standing in front of the reception desk with Brady Fallon, talking to Amanda Brown, who manned the desk. Jude had known it was only a matter of time before Daddy brought Brady into her office. She closed her computer program, logged off and started gathering her things, hoping to escape while her father gave Brady the cook's tour of the rest of the facility.

But the tour didn't happen. Daddy made a beeline for her office, with Brady behind him.

"Jude," he said with exaggerated enthusiasm, coming around to her side of the desk and placing an arm around her shoulder. "I know you're acquainted with Brady Fallon."

"Yes, I am." She directed her gaze at Brady, but he played it cool, standing there holding his hat on his fingers and smiling in a noncommittal way. "Morning, Jude," he said.

Daddy looked down at the picture she had printed of Batman and picked it up. "What's this?"

"That's Batman. I just bought him."

Daddy chuckled and looked across the desk at Brady. "Jude has her own names for the bulls. Sometimes I have a hard time keeping up."

Brady gave her that knee-buckling grin that had become way too familiar. "Sounds like fun."

"Sweetheart, we've got this little problem," Daddy said. "Brady needs an office."

He almost said the whole string of words in one breath. Instantly she knew what would come next. She felt the heat of anger creep to her cheeks, but she tamped down her urge to scream. An outburst would be childish, and her protest would be meaningless. "Oh," she said with exaggerated cheeriness. "Well, he can have this one. I'll just move my things into the house."

"Do you mind?" Her father gave her a smile that displayed more relief than joy.

Since she had scarcely spoken to him in several days, hadn't eaten dinner with him and hadn't dropped into his office for a drink at the end of the day, he had been tiptoeing around her. He might be expecting a tantrum, but apparently he didn't even know her well enough to notice that invective wasn't her style.

"That house has ten extra bedrooms," she said. "Surely there's one that will suit my needs." She began stacking items from the top of her desk into a neat pile. Her arms felt as if they were as disconnected from her shoulders as her mouth was from her feelings. Her hands moved in little jerks.

"Okay, then," Daddy said. "That'll work out great. Look, I'll leave you two to handle this. I've got to get to Abilene. I'm already late."

And just like that, he walked out, leaving Brady looking sheepish and standing in front of her desk. For a few seconds, she, too, stood there in stunned silence. It wasn't enough that Daddy had denied her the thing she wanted most. He also expected her to be his assistant in compounding her own wretchedness? Dear God, could he be any more unconscious?

"Jude, I don't expect you to move," Brady said. "There must be some other place I can find around here for what little space I need. I told J.D.—"

"Nonsense. I'm only in here because Daddy isn't. No, this room was built to be the ranch manager's office, so you should take it. I assure you, this will be much easier on everyone than having your office in the house." *Oh, damn.* She sounded like a shit. She closed her eyes and pressed her fingertips between her brows. "That is, I didn't mean—"

"I know what you meant," he said. "And you're right. I would be uncomfortable going and coming in your house."

"Fine. I'll just go get some boxes." She moved from behind the desk and walked out to the receptionist's desk on shaky knees, not looking at him and putting on a front of nonchalance. But inside she was trembling. She couldn't tell if she was upset over her office being hijacked or because Brady Fallon, doused with his sexy cologne and wearing his starched and creased Wranglers and his Cinch button-down, was standing within feet of her. "Amanda, would you do me a favor and see if you can find some boxes for me to pack some things in?"

Of course Amanda Brown knew Brady had been given the job as general manager. Amanda's husband, Travis, worked as a ranch hand. Brady was now his boss.

When Jude returned to the office, Brady had laid his hat on a lamp table in the corner of the room and was holding a stack of framed photographs in his hands. "Good-looking bull," he said, looking down at a profile picture of a curried and combed champion Hereford in all of his male glory.

Jude glanced at the enlarged snapshot, then turned her attention to removing pictures from the wall. "Yeah, he was. That picture was taken just before he went to the sale. He was a great bull, but he got too big. His weight was hard on the cows."

"I can see it would be," Brady mumbled. "Not to mention his own back legs."

A memory shot through her mind: *Brady hovering high over her, braced on his hands, his hips pumping and pumping, the thrust and drag deep inside her, driving her toward an elusive need . . .*

She shook herself mentally and jerked her head toward him. His expression was solemn. His glacial blue eyes were focused on hers, but she couldn't tell what was going on behind them.

Amanda broke the spell by coming in and setting four cardboard boxes on the floor.

"Great. Thanks," Jude said airily and picked up a box. Her stomach was tied in knots.

Brady's hand gripped the other side of the box. "I'll help you," he said softly. Her chin lifted and she saw a flicker of gentleness in those orbs of blue ice. She considered saying "no, thanks," but she couldn't hear herself being so petty. Instead she jerked the box to wrench it back from him, but he held it tightly. "I said I'll help you," he said.

She heaved a great breath, closed her eyes and released her hold on the box. *Damn.* She was a wreck. She picked up another box and turned her attention back to the pictures on the wall. "With a little help, at least I'll be able to get out of here faster."

While he placed the items from the desk in the box, she began to pack her personal gallery—portraits of special bulls, a picture of her mounted on Patch, a picture of a younger Jake and Cable laughing together, an eight-by-ten of Daddy that had been made when he appeared on the cover of a magazine. She and Brady worked in silence until awkwardness, like a rampaging fire, sucked the last bit of air from the room.

Brady, too, must have felt the need for some kind of communication because he said, "I took a peek at Sal before your dad and I came in here"

"She's looking good," Jude replied curtly. "She's very smart."

"I checked out your paint, too," he said without emotion.

Jude's suggestion to breed Patch to Sal had taken such a backseat to everything else going on, she had given it little thought. She stopped her busy hands and looked up. "Oh?"

"I've never paid a lot of attention to paint horses, but Patch is one of the prettier ones I've seen. I like that his eyes are brown."

Jude liked that about Patch, too. With his solid black head, she thought he would look odd if his eyes were blue like some paints' were. She felt a tiny surge of excitement. "So you've decided to breed Sal, then?"

"Maybe next year. When things get a little more settled and I've gotten a chance to get ready for it."

"If you don't intend to do it, why even bring it up?" she snapped.

He opened his palms defensively. "I wanted to let you know I'm not ignoring you."

She chastised herself for being a bitch. At the core of things, none of this was Brady's fault. "Well, whatever. I suppose waiting makes sense. I'd still be willing to buy the foal. For that matter, I'm sure Daddy would buy Sal for a broodmare if I asked him to."

Brady shook his head. "I'm not ready to sell her."

Jude hadn't intended to bring up the offer to lease his land, having decided the next move was his. But the opportunity seemed golden. She gave him a direct look. "What about the other offer I made you?"

"I'm still thinking about it."

"Now's the time to be breeding for spring calves. That window's almost closed."

"I know."

Her cell phone trilled from the top of the desk. She walked over and picked it up. The caller was Windy. She listened for a few seconds, then turned to Brady. "Windy almost has dinner ready, but there's no one to eat. Daddy's gone to Abilene, and Grandpa says he wants to stay in his room."

Brady said nothing, only looked at her expectantly. Tension hovered in the air around him, and she sensed he was a dam holding back a torrent of words.

"Would you like to eat dinner in the house?" she asked. "The food's cooked. It would be wasteful not to eat it." Okay, so it was only a halfhearted invitation to dine.

He must have sensed her lack of keenness, because he didn't reply immediately.

What the hell, she thought. This whole thing was stupid. She turned back to the phone. "I'll come, Windy. And I'll bring our new GM with me."

Brady had mixed emotions about eating lunch in the Circle C house. If Jude hadn't committed him, he would have begged off. That uncomfortable feeling of being an interloper she was only patiently tolerating stuck in his craw.

Then again, maybe he was wrong. After all, she was the one who had invited *him* to eat. She didn't have to.

And he was the one who hadn't said no. Just like he hadn't said no that night in Stephenville. Christ, would that one mistake keep on picking at him for the rest of his life?

They walked side by side across the grounds to the house. Jude looked especially pretty today, he thought. She had on tight jeans, a Western-cut formfitting shirt and boots made of something exotic and, no doubt, expensive. And silver hoop earrings as big around as beer cans. She looked much better than the last time he had seen her, when her eyes were swollen from crying and she had spoken to him from soul-deep bitterness about her plans to start her own herd.

On the one hand, he was pleased for the opportunity to talk to her without the flurry of activity in the veterinary building, though she was touchy as a rattler and he didn't blame her. He couldn't believe how tactless her father was about her feelings. When J.D. had suggested that he take her office in the veterinary building, Brady had feared it might be the proverbial last straw.

They went into the house through the back door. He had been in the ranch house several times by now. Every time, he'd had to fend off a profoundly lonely feeling that hung in the air like a heavy drape, though he knew there had been a time when the place was alive. A president had actually slept here and hunted the Circle C acres. Brady couldn't imagine what it must be like—two old men and a young woman—trying to fill up this much space. The builder in him calculated a minimum of fifteen thousand square feet.

Jude directed him to a seat opposite hers at the long, rustic oak table in the middle of the dining room. He angled a glance toward the end of it, counting the chairs—five on each side of the table and one on each end. There must have been a time when every chair's leather seat had had a butt on it, but he would bet that had been long ago.

Soon a Mexican woman brought in the food—barbecued brisket, pinto beans, cole slaw, and a cast-iron skillet of steaming cornbread. He had eaten breakfast with the hands at four thirty this morning, and his stomach was cheering at the aromas filling the space around them.

He looked at the empty armchair at the end of the table. The throne. Jude caught him. "That's Grandpa's chair," she said. "He doesn't always eat dinner. He says three meals a day make him feel too full. His digestive system sometimes gives him problems."

Brady's gaze moved up to the wall behind the patriarch's chair. The portrait hanging there had to be the one Jude had mentioned—the one of Quanah Parker and Jude's distant grandparent. Sure enough, in the background was a paint horse, just as she had said. A sudden feeling of time passing and dynasties dying swirled around him like a dry wind and made him even more uncomfortable than he was before he came in here.

"Grandpa's getting old," she said, offering him the platter of thinly sliced beef brisket.

Despite the American Heart Association's cautions, Brady suspected beef was the daily fare in the Strayhorn house. "He and I used to take walks in the evening after supper," she said, "but we haven't been doing that lately."

He watched as she served herself. She was still a hearty eater, just like that night in Stephenville. "Why not?"

"I don't know exactly. It's sort of like we're headed in opposite directions. It's okay, though. Pretty soon, I have to start getting ready for school anyway."

"I've heard you're good at teaching school."

"Who told you that?" *Joyce Harrison?*

"I don't remember. I've just heard it around."

Joyce Harrison, Jude thought. "I am good at it. And I get a thrill out of it. I like helping people. If I can light a spark in some kid and he or she goes on from here and gets a good education and does well, that makes me happy."

"That sounds like a good thing you're doing. Why not concentrate on that?"

"I do concentrate on it. Most of the time."

He looked up from buttering half a slice of cornbread. "If you're good at teaching school and you like it, why would you want to give it up and put a bunch of cows on my place when you don't have to?"

"But I do have to. Now more than ever."

"To prove what, darlin'? Maybe that's why your dad can't see your point. He doesn't understand what you're trying to prove."

"Are you lecturing me? After I've invited you to dinner?" She gave a little laugh that sounded insincere. "Now you're starting to sound like Daddy."

He could tell she had tried to allay her sharp tone with that phony little laugh, but she was still uptight and uneasy—a different woman from the seemingly carefree one who spent two days with him in Stephenville. "I'm not lecturing. I just see you and your dad caught in this tight jar, and neither one of you seems to be able to get a breath of fresh air or climb out."

"We usually get along. In spite of him not appreciating me. He doesn't value my education. He doesn't even know who I am."

"You've got control of the bulls around here, right? How much is that bull herd worth?"

"I'm not sure."

He didn't believe her. Bull rotation was an ever-evolving part of ranching, large or small. Bulls were good for only six or seven years max. He suspected she could tell him to the penny what had been paid for the bulls if they had been bought, what had been invested in them if they were home-bred and what they would sell for when the decision was made to move them out. "Then I'll guess. I'm gonna say a million dollars. And darlin', where I come from, that ain't chicken feed."

Her mouth pursed. "So what?"

"I'm saying a cowman doesn't put the future of his herd, and consequently the ranch, in the hands of somebody he has no faith in. Especially now, when he's about to turn management over to a tenderfoot like me. What would I do without your support and your knowledge?"

She had stopped eating. "What are you getting at?"

"I'm just suggesting that if you agree to help me out a little, maybe I'll be so backward and needy, you won't have time to go off half-cocked and start your own little herd." He met her eyes and captured them. "I'm gonna need your help, Jude. And I'd be really grateful if you weren't distracted by something else."

She sat back in her chair and pushed her hair back, then crossed her arms over her chest. A long, assessing gaze from those wide, whiskey-colored eyes came his way. Something was going on in that pretty head, but he wasn't gambler enough to try to guess what.

"Why do I feel like I'm being manipulated?" she asked.

"No, darlin', you're not. You wanted to make a deal? Okay, here's my counteroffer. Postpone your plans to start your own herd for a while, make up with your daddy and help me do this job. Later on, if you still feel like you have to go in your own direction, then I'll agree to lease you my land and we'll sit down and work out the details."

She continued to stare at him, and he held her gaze. He believed he had her respect. He couldn't risk losing it by letting her get the best of him.

"Like with Sal, huh? Maybe next year? You're trying to force me to stall."

He shrugged. "It's damn near too late to start on a spring calf crop anyway."

"I don't know. I'll think about it," she said, throwing his own words back at him.

He suppressed a smile as he remembered something a wise Fort Worth businessman had once told him: A smart man could always use the help of a smart woman.

20

Jude was hot. She had been hot all night. The temperature hadn't dropped as it usually did. She had also been awake half the night, but not only because of the heat.

Yesterday's events had scrolled through her half sleep at least two dozen times. After they had eaten dinner together, she and Brady had returned to the veterinary clinic and packed the remaining items in the office. He had been disgustingly obsequious, as if he expected her to break into screams any minute. Ginger flashed in her mind. Maybe tantrums were what Brady expected from all women. Maybe his perception of women was as warped as her father's.

Already, mentally, Jude no longer called the space in the veterinary clinic "her" office. She had moved on. Amazing how quickly one thing could change to another. Margie Wallace's death, for instance. Who could have ever foreseen the bizarre chain of events one elderly woman's dying would set off?

Irene's husband had helped her and Brady carry the packed boxes and computer into the house, where they left everything in the hallway near the back door. Jude had been caught so off balance by the reason for the move, she had been unable to think of where else to put her things. In a house with more than twenty rooms, she could think of nowhere to place a few boxes. How strange was that? After all the commotion had settled and she was left alone, she roamed every floor, looking for a new place to locate. For the first time in her entire life, she had felt out of place, as if she didn't belong here.

Then Windy had unwittingly reminded her of who she was. It had happened as she stood in the doorway of the large room behind the kitchen pantry, considering it for an office. Its shelves were piled with flotsam and jetsam. Junk. Miscellaneous items that probably could be thrown away.

Windy came up behind her. "Whatcha lookin' for, Miss Jude?"

"Just wondering if this would make a good office."

"It's a nice big room. When you was a little girl, it was wall to wall with home cannin'. You 'member that?"

Vignettes flashed through her memory of shelves brimming with glass quart jars of peaches and apricots and tomatoes and jams and jellies of every kind. No one canned fruits and vegetables or made jam at the ranch any longer. Windy probably wouldn't know where to start. "I remember," Jude replied.

"I was just a tenderfoot in those days," the aging cook said. "I didn't work in the house, but I recollect seein' all those jars. Yore Grandma Penny Ann loved to garden and she loved to put up vittles. Nobody could do a better job than her."

And just like that, Jude had remembered whose granddaughter she was and she had determined where her new office would be.

Now she made herself get out of bed and perform her morning ritual. For the sake of comfort and convenience, she put on athletic shoes. Before going downstairs, she prowled a huge storeroom on the third floor and found a solid oak table to use as her computer desk. Brady might have taken the office in the veterinary clinic, but Jude had kept the computer with the software she needed. All of her records were stored on the computer's hard drive, which forced Daddy to buy Brady a new machine. A small price to pay for uprooting her, she figured. At some point in the future, perhaps she would go down to Abilene or over to Lubbock and buy a real computer desk.

Or not.

This morning, she felt insecure enough to wonder if she would even be living here six months from now.

It was nine o'clock before Jude reached the ground floor. As it always was at this hour of the morning, the house was empty except for Windy and Irene in the kitchen and Lola Mendez fussing about with a feather duster. Jude declined breakfast.

She stood in the doorway of the octagon-shaped sunroom located just off the hallway that led to the back door. Six of its eight walls had tall, narrow windows covered by wooden blinds. The air had a golden hue to it, and pale yellow walls made it feel sunny even on cloudy days. A fat, red enamel woodstove hunkered in one of the wall's angles and would keep her toasty on cold days. The room was still furnished as her great-grandmother had originally bedecked it more than fifty years earlier—tan wicker furniture with red-and-yellow-striped cushions that looked like Mexican serapes, a desk Jude viewed as being tiny, but Grammy Pen had called a lady's desk.

The room hadn't been used in years. As far as Jude knew, it looked today just as Grammy Pen had left it the day a massive stroke had taken her life. Her great-grandmother had had it added on to the house so she could sit in the morning sunshine while she drank her coffee and read a stack of newspapers and made phone calls to senators and congressmen.

Jude had never been political, but she supposed politics was a subject she should learn something about. Daddy constantly talked of how large-scale cattle ranching was being pressured and legislated into extinction.

But today, Jude didn't have to worry about politics. She conscripted Irene's husband and a helper to carry the heavy table down from the third-floor storeroom, then haul Grammy Pen's lady's desk back up. As she busied herself hooking up her computer and its devices, she remembered sitting on the settee with Grammy Pen and listening to her read stories of Peter Rabbit.

When she started unpacking the box holding her pictures, she realized the sunroom had limited wall space, so she returned to the third floor. In one of the seldom-used bedrooms, she found a long dresser and called on Irene's husband and his helper again. This was the way her life had always been. For as long as she could remember, if she needed help, if she couldn't manage something alone, she'd had to rely on hired people. No family member or friends had ever been available.

Once the dresser was in place, she set out her favorite things, save the picture of her father. That she laid face down in one of the dresser's drawers.

All in all, she didn't dislike the new surroundings. From one of the wicker chairs positioned by the window, she could look outside at the big red barn with a white encircled *C* painted on one end of the loft. All of the hands' vehicles were parked in front of the barn, including Brady Fallon's tan Silverado. Now, with him present at the ranch some part of every day, even her comfort zone in her own home was threatened. Still, it wasn't in her nature to carry a chip on her shoulder. Just because she had lost a battle didn't mean she had lost the war. For now, she tamped her stewing intentions down to a frustrated simmer.

Dinnertime had come and gone by the time she finished, and she hadn't eaten all day. Daddy had peeked into the sunroom and reminded her it was time to eat, but she had made an excuse that she was too busy. Suzanne got off work at the grocery store at two, so Jude shoved her feet into her boots, picked up her purse and drove to town.

Entering Lucky's Grocery was like stepping into some grocer's poorly organized attic. A combination of the outdated and modern met customers in every overstocked aisle. If Lockett had had a real fire department, Lucky's would have been ticketed heavily for multiple fire code violations.

The first person she ran into was Joyce Harrison at Lucky's only cash register. Jude hadn't seen Joyce in months. Today she studied her. She was slightly overweight. Her hair was dark brown, styled in an outdated curly do. Bows or barrettes usually adorned her hair, but today, little red hearts were somehow attached. If Jude were asked to guess her age, she would say forty, but Jude knew the woman was only two years older than she and Suzanne.

"Why, Jude Strayhorn," Joyce said. "I never see you in here. You slummin' today?"

Jude wasn't sure how to take Joyce's remark. She had always guarded against appearing uppity to her Willard County friends and neighbors, constantly aware that most of them struggled to get by. It was true she didn't often go to the grocery store. She had no need to. "I'm looking for Suzanne."

"She's in the back room. I'll page her."

Joyce pushed a button on an intercom mounted on the wall and paged Suzanne to come to the front of the store. While Jude waited, she thumbed through one of the tabloid papers she picked off the rack beside the cash register. "How have you been, Joyce?"

"Just fine. Guess what. I'm dating a guy who started working for y'all."

Jude saw the edges of the newsprint pages begin to tremble and realized her hands were shaking. "Really?"

"His name's Brady Fallon. Have you met him?"

Jude looked up, schooling her expression to bland. "Yes, of course." *A few weeks ago, I spent an entire night having wild and crazy sex with him. And I just gave him my office yesterday.*

Joyce closed her dark brown eyes and shook her head. "He is so dreamy." Her eyes popped open and a direct look came at Jude. "Listen, y'all furnish houses for some of your hands, don't you?"

"Some of them."

"The school bus comes out there and picks up the kids, right?"

"It comes to our front gate. It doesn't come onto the ranch."

"So if somebody lived in one of those houses, they'd have to drive their kid to the front gate?"

"Yeah," Jude answered cautiously. "Why are you asking?"

Joyce angled her head and gave Jude a coy smile. "Oh, just collecting information. In case it's needed."

Before the conversation could go further, Suzanne appeared. "Hey, girlfriend. What're you doing in town?"

"I came to buy you lunch," Jude said, sliding the tabloid newspaper back into its slot.

"Uh-oh. The cook quit?"

Jude laughed. Windy would probably be the Circle C's cook until he could no longer function.

Suzanne clocked out and they strolled up the sidewalk toward Maisie's Café, the only eating place in Lockett. "Joyce just asked me about the school bus coming to the ranch," Jude said as they walked. "Why does she want to know that?"

"Oh, honey, she's planning a wedding. She's got the hots for Brady Fallon that bad."

Jude felt a start within her and warned herself about reacting. "Daddy hasn't mentioned that. He keeps up with what everyone's doing. I'm sure he'd know if one of the hands was getting married."

They reached the café's plate-glass entry door. Inside, Maisie's looked as dated as the grocery store, with the exception that Maisie had deliberately striven for the nineteenth-century look. At midafternoon, Jude and Suzanne were the only customers. Over hamburgers and iced tea, Jude told Suzanne about the recent developments in her life, all the way back to her trip with Brady to Stephenville. Afterward, she felt as if a yoke had been lifted from her shoulders.

Suzanne had listened as if she were spellbound. "Good

grief," she said. "I ought to be insulted you didn't tell me about any of this. Is J.D. retiring?"

"Daddy will never retire. He's taking over some of what Grandpa does."

"And you're okay with all of this?"

"Even if I weren't, there's nothing I can do about it." She pushed her plate away, planted her elbow on the table and rested her jaw on her palm. "I think deep down I knew Daddy was never going to let me have much control over what goes on."

"Nothing ever stays the same, Jude. These are major life changes for you. What are you gonna do now?"

"I don't know. I'm trying to get my wits about me so I can make some decisions. Decisions I should have made a long time ago."

"You aren't planning on leaving town, are you?"

"I should. I wonder if I could be like Cable. Just leave and never come back. Or if I could do what Jake does. Pretend the family and all its warts and history don't exist."

Suzanne's hand came across the table, and Jude felt the touch of friendship—and the intensity of her friend's gaze. "Don't do it, Jude. If you *want* to leave, that's one thing, but don't do it because you're mad at J.D. You know he loves you. He's just dumb. Hell, he can't help it. After all, he's male."

Jude huffed a humorless laugh. "It isn't exactly anger that I feel." She sighed and shook her head. "I don't know what I feel. Nothing I've tried has gone well lately."

"It's that old Chinese philosophy. Maybe you're entering a cycle."

Jude frowned, wondering how Suzanne would know anything about Chinese philosophy. "What Chinese philosophy?"

"Oh, you've heard it. You know, seven years of good things followed by seven years of bad things?"

"Hmm, that better not be true," Jude mumbled.

"So what's with this guy, Brady Fallon?" Suzanne asked.

"I mean, is he a cockhound or what? My God, it isn't enough that Joyce Harrison is practically chasing him up the street with her tongue hanging out. Jude Strayhorn, a Texas version of the Virgin Mary, went off and had hot sex for a weekend with him? Some planet must be in retrograde or something."

"I know. It's so weird. I'd never really thought of sex before."

A mischievous look angled from Suzanne's blue eyes. Her mouth tipped into a sly grin. "So how was it?"

"How was what? The sex?"

"Hell, yes, the sex. How was it?"

Jude turned away and frowned. "It was okay."

"That's all? Just okay?"

Jude felt the heat of a blush crawl up her neck. "All right. Better than okay."

"Um, better than that first guy? What's his name—Wes?"

"Webb. Yeah, better."

"Better than the second guy your daddy still wants you to hook up with?"

Jude laughed and nodded.

"Better than both of them put together?"

Jude nodded again.

"I swear to God, getting information out of you is harder than pulling hen's teeth. You aren't gonna give me details, are you?"

"It was like you said it used to be with Mitch."

Suzanne heaved a huge sigh. "Wow. This is really something. And something tells me you really like this guy."

"But I don't think he likes me. After we came back from Stephenville, I panicked. I said something I wish I hadn't."

"Now, there's a news flash. Jude Strayhorn putting her foot in her mouth. What did you say?"

Jude repeated what she had said about not looking for a boyfriend.

"What'd *he* say?"

"He said he wasn't holding up a sign in search of a girl-friend, either."

A little laugh burst from Suzanne followed by a sigh. She shook her head. "Jude, Jude, Jude. What else would he say? I mean, you burst his little ego bubble."

"Do you think he's really sleeping with Joyce?" Jude asked, a quaver in her voice.

Suzanne's shoulders lifted in a shrug. Her eyes grew serious. "I doubt it. She's such a blabbermouth, I feel like she would tell the world if it was really happening. "

"Forgodsake, don't tell anyone about this, Suzanne. Now that Daddy's made Brady the general manager, I don't know what would happen if he found out about Stephenville."

"Oh, you know I'm not gonna say anything. Have I ever?" Suzanne sighed and looked earnestly at Jude. "Back to my original question. What are you gonna do now?"

"For the time being, until I get it sorted out, I'm just going to keep helping Doc Barrett breed mares. We're in the prime breeding season, and we've still got broodmares in heat. I'll keep fiddling with bulls and looking for high producers. And hope Brady changes his mind and lets me breed Patch to his grullo mare. I'm really excited about the idea of a baby paint. It would give me a project for next summer."

Suzanne smiled slyly at her friend. "And you said you never think of sex."

21

The following Monday, Brady approached his driveway with his truck's air conditioner blasting to the max. It was the end of July, and the sun could cook the hide off a rattlesnake in the treeless West Texas plains. He had spent most of the day on horseback, with only his hat for shade. He was worn-out, but working in the sun wasn't what had made him tired. He was used to hard work outdoors. What had him longing for sundown and the evening's cool breeze was that he hadn't returned from Fort Worth until midnight and had slept only four hours before getting up this morning. His weekend had been another one of those marathons: Lockett to Fort Worth, to Weatherford, and back to Fort Worth. Another hard farewell with Andy, then back to Lockett.

Though he didn't enjoy so much driving, he had resigned himself to this trying regimen two weekends every month. It was all the Tarrant County domestic court had granted him, and he intended to give Andy every minute of time allowed.

A shift in the wind had been revealed over the weekend. Marvalee's husband, Drake Lowery, was a class A commercial builder who had built many of the multistory structures in the metroplex area, as well as other cities inside and outside Texas. Besides being a high-end builder, he liked the high life—skiing in Vail, hopping up to Las Vegas for a little gambling, and escaping at the last minute to Cabo for some marlin fishing and Mexican-style partying. Marvalee had hinted that their social activities were being cramped by the two boys.

Brady could read his ex-wife like a large-print book. Any day, now, she would ask him to take Andy off her hands and possibly even Jarrett. And now, thank God and Aunt Margie, Brady had a place to bring his son if Marvalee made that request. And even his stepson. But more than that, he had something to pass on in the future. All Brady had to do was hang on to the 6-0 and keep improving it. He might be tired, but he wasn't unhappy.

As he pulled into his driveway, he saw a newer-model Ford SUV he didn't recognize parked in front of his house. He slowed, wondering who the hell could be visiting him and what they might be selling. Besides the ranch hands at the Circle C, he knew fewer than a dozen people in Willard County. Easing closer, he saw the silhouette of a man wearing a cowboy hat inside the SUV.

Brady was in no mood to be cordial to strangers. He came to a stop, and even before he popped the latch on his door, the SUV driver's door opened and a slight-built middle-aged man stepped out. The man walked purposefully toward him. Brady slowly climbed down from his own rig. He stood in the shadow of his open door as the stranger introduced himself and handed over a business card. FRED WHITMORE, REAL ESTATE BROKER, RANGELAND SPECIALIST. "I'm from Abilene," Whitmore said. "I've got a buyer for your place."

Why would anybody assume it's for sale? Brady wondered. Were his dire circumstances more obvious than he realized? His eyes narrowed. "It's not for sale."

He handed back the business card, stepped around the real estate broker and started for the front door.

"Now don't get too hasty," Whitmore said behind him. A second later, the guy was beside him, quick-stepping to keep up. "My buyer's offering a good price. You oughta look at this offer."

Old Man Strayhorn was Brady's first thought. His second thought was of his deceased aunt's attitude about the Strayhorns owning more than half the county. He stopped and looked down at the real estate man. "It's not for sale."

The Realtor held up a finger. "Let me show you." He turned and started back to the passenger side of the SUV. Brady lifted his hat and wiped his brow with his shirtsleeve, watching as the man dragged out a black portfolio that looked like an oversize notebook. He unzipped it and scanned the contents for a few seconds, then came back, adjusting papers inside the portfolio. "I've brought a signed contract with me, Mr. Fallon. Drove all this way from Abilene. I've got an earnest-money check in my safe in my office." Whitmore looked up. "Could we go sit down somewhere and just talk about it?"

Real estate transactions, both as seller and as buyer, weren't new to Brady. And neither were real estate brokers. In his career as a land developer and home builder, he had sold hundreds of homes and bought hundreds of acres of land, though he hadn't been near a real estate deal in more than two years. He looked out over the pasture, at his two geldings grazing in the distance. Looking east, he owned everything his eye could see. The rolling acres of grass and knowing it was his touched the deepest place in his chest, and he thought of Andy. "But it's not for sale."

Brady started for the front door again, but the land man dogged his heels. On a sigh, Brady unlocked the front door, looking down at him with an arched brow.

"You really should look at this offer, Mr. Fallon."

On yet another sigh, Brady let Whitmore inside the hot, airless living room. The afternoon sun poured light and heat into the room as if the cheap shades on the windows didn't exist. Brady felt even hotter. He hooked his hat on a hat rack he had put on the wall beside the front door, then walked over and switched on the swamp cooler. "Gets hot in here with the house facing west," he said. "It'll be cooler in the kitchen."

He gestured his guest into the kitchen and invited him to take a seat at the round table. Brady had learned to live with the kitchen's deficiencies. He paid little attention to trappings anyway, but Whitmore seemed to be staring at every corner of the dingy kitchen. "Want a cold drink, Mr. Whitmore?" Brady opened the refrigerator and grabbed two bottles of water.

"No, thanks." The Realtor removed his straw hat and placed it on the table, then reached into his back pocket for a handkerchief and patted his brow. The man opened his portfolio on the tabletop and removed a pen from his shirt pocket. *A real optimist,* Brady thought, suppressing a laugh and putting one water bottle back in the fridge. He dragged a chair from the table, turned it around and straddled it, resting his forearms on the back and hanging on to his water bottle. "How would somebody in Abilene even get wind of my place? And why would they think I want to sell it?" He unscrewed the cap on his bottle, tilted his head back and swigged a long, cold drink.

"That I couldn't tell you, Mr. Fallon."

"Well, show me what you've got. I've got to eat and get to bed. I've been up since four a.m."

The Realtor slid a contract across the table until it lay directly in front of Brady's chair back, its white surface and tiny black print a vivid contrast to the shiny brown of the tabletop. Brady craned his neck and scanned it—and almost did a double take when he saw the purchase price. What he didn't see was a buyer's name. Suspicion streaked through him like a wild horse. *Jeff Strayhorn.* "Whoa. Somebody's offering me a million dollars?"

The real estate broker looked him in the eye, holding his pen over the portfolio. "That's the offer. There's some financing involved, but it would be cash to you."

Brady's mind reeled. Most of the people in Willard County didn't have two nickels to rub together. He could think of absolutely nobody local who could pay a million dollars for grazing land. Nobody except Jeff Strayhorn. But Brady was now a Strayhorn employee. Why would the old

man play games by hiring an Abilene real estate broker?
"Who's the buyer?"

"The buyer wants to remain anonymous until the closing," Whitmore said. "As you can see, the closing date is
thirty days from acceptance. You could have your money in
your hand before winter."

Brady shook his head and slid the contract back to Whitmore. "This is bullshit, Mr. Whitmore. There's nothing here
to be secretive about. If somebody wants to buy this place,
they need to be up front about it. Even if I wanted to sell, I
might like to have a say in who I sell to. But like I told you,
the place isn't on the market. I've got my own plans here. I
am interested in knowing, though, what somebody has seen
here that makes them want to buy it."

"A good-size chunk of good bluestem, all cross-fenced,
with windmills and stock pens, a house and outbuildings.
All of that in one package isn't easy to find in this part of the
country, sir."

As far as Brady knew, bluestem grass had been here since
before the American Indians. It wasn't that rare. He wondered how this guy knew about the cross-fencing or the
windmills or even the stock pens, unless he had been out
snooping over the place in Brady's absence. He didn't trust
Mr. Fred Whitmore entirely. He had dealt with too many real
estate brokers not to have instincts and biases. "If all that's
true, Mr. Whitmore, then that price sounds a little low."

"It's a good, clean deal," Whitmore said. "I urge you to
consider it. The way things are these days, you'll be a long
time getting this kind of offer again."

Well, the guy had slid right past the comment about the
price. So it *was* a low offer. Still, even if it was a little lower
than market, it was a million dollars. Brady had nothing invested here except the money he had paid out of pocket for
the taxes and a few dollars he had spent on the barn. A million dollars cash would solve damn near all his short-term financial problems and even put him on the road back. It

would enable him to start over, if in a smaller way, and re-build.

When he first learned he had inherited this place, hadn't his very first thought been to sell it for any price he could get for it? Of course, that was before he got a fool notion to fix it up and reestablish it as a cattle operation. If he had known back then that he could get a million dollars for it, he might have sold it and never looked back. But that was before he got the idea of someday bringing Andy here to grow up. "How long's the offer good for?"

"Not long. I'd be remiss if I didn't tell you, if you don't take the deal right off, it can be withdrawn at any time. Things happen, you know. People's minds change. In the real estate business, we often say time is of the essence."

Indeed. How many times had he heard that? Brady wondered. "I've got a lot going on right now. And this isn't a decision I'm willing to make overnight."

After the Realtor left, Brady made himself a bologna and cheese sandwich, poured a glass of milk and walked outside. Not a tree grew near the old house. The only shade was from the roof of the small back porch. But the pleasant breeze that always kicked up late in the afternoon touched his face and brought a bouquet of smells—clean, fresh air, fecund barn-yard aromas and the scent of rich earth growing good grass. He sank to an aluminum folding chair he had put beside the back door. The capriciousness of life had flummoxed him again. With somebody hiding behind the curtain of anonymity waving a million dollars at him, Brady had to think.

He set his glass on the porch deck and sprawled in the folding chair, perched on his tailbone, one long leg thrust straight in front of him. His view from the back porch was mostly of the barn and tumbledown outbuildings. All he could see around him was work and more work. New un-painted boards showed on the sides of the barn, making it look like a checkerboard. The old thing stood straight now, as a result of a prodigious effort. Strengthening it and shoring it up had taken a whole month of only brief snatches of time, and he wasn't even finished with it yet.

Were his circumstances so tenuous that he had to consider *any* offer and make the practical decision about it? If he were working as the general manager at the Circle C, there was no telling when he would get around to really fixing this old place up or getting his own cattle. Or even if he ever did own his own herd, he wondered if he would have the time and extra energy to take care of it. As for a place to live, the Circle C would furnish him a house. In fact, if he worked at the ranch, living on it would be more convenient.

He had to delve deeper. He had to consider what he really wanted. He was thirty-four years old and suddenly didn't have a clue what he wanted to be when he grew up. Just a couple months back, he had wanted to be a cattle rancher. A few years back, he had wanted to be a successful home builder. And before that he had wanted to be a college graduate. He hadn't planned on being a father, but after he became one, he had wanted to be that, too. Eventually he had become all that he planned, though the cattle-ranching goal still had hurdles to overcome.

But all of that was superfluous fluff. His life had followed more paths than most young men's, he suspected. But in the bone-deep part of him, he had always known what he wanted most of all: security and a decent home. A house that wasn't overcrowded with too many dwellers or that was never clean because everybody who lived in it worked at menial jobs from sunup to sundown just to eat. He wanted a loving woman who cared about him in a way he had rarely seen in real life, a woman who was glad to see him come home at night. He took pride in being a caretaker, but he wanted somebody in his life who was eager to be his helpmate. A woman who was faithful.

Unbidden, his thoughts turned to Jude Strayhorn. Why couldn't he get somebody who met none of his criteria out of his mind? Was it because he couldn't figure her out? For sure, she'd had him scratching his head from the first minute she showed up in his driveway. She had come on to him like any number of barroom babes he had run across in his life, then showed herself to be less experienced with men than today's teenagers. Then after he had followed her into a petty deception against her family and endangered his own plans, she had brushed him off like lint on her shoulder. As if all of that hadn't left him confused enough, just when he had almost concluded that the weekend in Stephenville had been a figment of his imagination, she had showed up at his house looking sexy and smelling like flowers and offering to ride his horses and lease his land.

Yet, despite the confusion, he instinctively knew why she appealed to him. She was a fierce warrior and didn't even know it. Though she'd had every material advantage life could offer, she was a lonely heart struggling to find a place to belong. Like him, she was a loner, but she had the same deep yearning as he. And the fact that she was rich and he wasn't had nothing to do with it.

Brady had learned a lot about the Strayhorns in the short time he had spent with J.D. Jude might think she had traditional relationships with her family, but that was bullshit. They treated her like a possession. Brady didn't doubt J.D. loved his daughter. But he loved her from a distance, as if he feared reaching to her across his desk might bring an emotion he couldn't handle.

Jake Strayhorn had the same quality about him. Such was the shroud that hung over the whole Strayhorn family, Brady suspected. The darkness of its past. The Campbell Curse.

A low grumble escaped Brady's throat, the sound of him chastising himself for letting his mind wander from the question at hand. He straightened in his chair, picked up his glass and finished off the milk. Now he had a decision to make. To sell or not to sell.

Early the next morning, Jude's father left for an AQHA conference in Amarillo. Soon after, Jude departed for the Dickerson ranch, northeast of Fort Worth, to pick up a pair of prizewinning bulls. Spike and Charlie Brown, she had already named them. Those weren't their registered names, but their registered names were boring. It was the wrong time of year to be bringing in new bulls, but these two had piqued her interest, and she hadn't wanted to miss the opportunity to acquire them.

Early afternoon found her standing in the Dickersons' driveway, readying to leave. She could see a deep purple cloud bank, massive and ominous, spanning the width of the western sky. Heavy air pressed down on her shoulders. The storm rolling out of the Rockies had been forecast for several days and was expected to be vicious. She had intended to be back in Willard County with her cargo before bad weather arrived. Hauling three thousand pounds of beef on the hoof through a West Texas thunderstorm would be a challenge she wouldn't relish. She had a six-hour drive ahead of her.

Now she realized she should have left Lockett earlier this morning and given herself more time to make the round-trip. Mr. Dickerson had insisted on giving her a tour of his ranch, which had used up an hour and a half. Then he and his wife wanted her to stay for dinner and it would have been too rude to tell them no.

She merged onto the interstate at three o'clock in the afternoon. On the last day of July, the day should be bright with sunshine, but the sky had already turned to greenish purple and the storm had chased away the light. Just west of Fort Worth, the wind picked up, buffeting her one-ton pickup and the loaded double-axle trailer behind it as if they weighed no more than a compact car.

In a matter of a few more minutes, the first fat raindrops splattered against the windshield. An instant later, an earth-shaking clap of thunder exploded directly overhead. The heavens opened and great sheets of water poured from the sky, pounding on her pickup roof, beating against the sides in a roar and erasing visibility. Her windshield wipers whipped and thumped, but barely cleared a fan large enough for her to see a foot or two ahead of her. Adrenaline surged, her heart began to race.

Just then her cell phone broke into the "Aggie War Hymn," but she didn't dare try to dig it out of her purse. She leaned forward, gripping the steering wheel with both hands, her eyes plastered to the dim images in front of her. Thunderclaps cracked and boomed overhead like cannons. Jagged streaks of lightning bored into the pastures all around her. The hair rose on her arms as one zigzag struck with a crack near the pickup.

She could feel Spike and Charlie Brown constantly shifting, rocking the trailer. They were terrified. All she needed was for them to unbalance the trailer and cause her to wreck. She slowed her speed in an effort to combat the swaying.

Then the sky lightened slightly, the wind relented and the storm diminished to a steady, drenching rain. She was able to relax her white-knuckle grip on the steering wheel. She found a country-music station on the radio and settled in for a long, slow drive. She began to think about all that had happened to her in the past two months.

No question that Brady Fallon's presence at the Circle C had changed her life. An interesting part of her day had been eliminated because she no longer felt she could move freely around the veterinary clinic for fear of running into him. For the same reason, she no longer helped Doc Barrett with breeding the mares. Doc had noticed her absence and asked her where she was keeping herself. She had told him she had to prepare for the beginning of school.

She had stopped joining Daddy for a drink prior to supper. It was Brady who shared cocktail hour with her father. Jude could live without the liquor, but a part of her missed her daily drink with Daddy. In the past, that had too often been the only chance she had to talk to him during the day.

She felt as if her only ally in the house was Grandpa, and lately, he didn't feel well. A part of her worried about that.

When she rode Patch or Sal, she often found Brady with his arms hooked over the fence rail watching her, which made her so uneasy, she usually stopped the workout early. Everything about him affected her—the way his body moved; the way he slouched against a door, his hip cocked, his thumb hooked in his jeans pocket; the way he peered intently at something that interested him; the crinkles at the corners of his eyes when he smiled.

Maybe what affected her most was knowing he had seen her without her clothes on. And she had seen him. And they had touched each other in the most intimate of ways.

Then there was his supposed courtship of Joyce Harrison, which needled incessantly. Jude was going to the school daily now, and she heard the stories. One of her peers was Joyce's cousin, who talked endlessly about what a quiet, gentle man Brady was, how good he was with Joyce's son, how crazy Joyce was about him, how lucky for Joyce that she had met him. Hearing it was almost more than Jude could stand.

Even when Brady Fallon wasn't in her sight around the Circle C or being discussed at school, he was in her head, especially at night. She revisited that one conversation in his pickup at least once every night.

I'm not necessarily looking for a, uh, boyfriend. . . . I've never even dated one of the ranch hands.

And every time she thought of those words, she wished she had never said them.

All at once, thunder rumbled across the sky like a wagonload of rocks, bringing her thoughts back to the present. The rain bulleted down on her, and she could feel the lug of Spike and Charlie Brown shifting in the trailer again. The farther west she traveled, the worse the storm grew. Thunder became a rumble so constant, it echoed in her very body. Sheet lightning lit the air like camera flashes. The radio had become useless white noise. It didn't matter, anyway. She dared not divert her attention from driving long enough to search for a broadcast. Night was coming on. She began to look for a service station to pull into, but visibility was so poor, she could scarcely read the freeway signs or see exits until she was upon them and it was too late to turn.

She slowed her speed to a crawl and stuck with the far-right lane. Semis passed her, the force of their massive moving weight rocking her, their giant tires spewing rooster tails of water onto her windshield and into the trailer. The trailer had a roof, but the sides were open steel rails, so the bulls were being deluged by every passing truck. She gripped the steering wheel tighter and prayed to be able to stay on the paved surface. She had no idea what might await her if she veered off the highway onto the shoulder.

An hour and a half later, she had driven deeper into the mouth of the beast and conditions had only worsened. Rain continued to pour without letup. A tight knot had formed between her shoulder blades. Soon she recognized signs that she was nearing Abilene. By a miracle, and because she was moving at a snail's pace, she spotted the exit that would take her to Lockett and the Circle C. A hundred more miles and she would be home. "Yes," she cried out. She made the turn onto the state highway.

Now that she was heading northwest, the west wind blasts blew full force against the sides of the pickup and trailer. Keeping the pickup on the road took all of her strength. She couldn't clearly see familiar territory, but she sensed it and her heartbeat slowed. She passed through Lockett and felt her shoulders and neck relax a little for the first time in hours.

Only a few more miles before she reached the Circle C's gate. Suddenly a monstrous gust blasted the side of the trailer and pickup. She felt herself moving to the right, toward a deep barrow ditch she knew ran alongside the highway. Frantically she yanked the steering wheel to the left, but to no avail. She could hear nothing but the roar of the rain and wind, but she felt the road's soft shoulder grab her tires and pull her even farther right. The pickup's forward motion stopped with a *ka-whump!* The rig tipped to the right, and her body slammed against her seat belt. Then everything stopped but the engine, the headlights and the rain. Like a million silver needles, rain drove horizontally through the headlights' blaze. She couldn't see the horizon, but she knew the pickup was lying on its side in the ditch.

And so was the trailer.

The bulls!

She grabbed the door latch and pushed against the door, but the wind defied her strength. She waited for a lull between gusts and pushed again, succeeded in opening the door only partway. She was trapped. She buzzed down the window and looked out. Cold rain pricked her face. As nearly as she could tell, the pickup lay at a forty-five-degree angle against the side of the ditch, and she was five feet off the ground. She killed the headlights and switched off the engine, then squirmed in the driver's bucket seat until she had the window to her back. She climbed out, one leg at a time, hanging on to the windowsill and sliding down the wet door until her feet hit the ground.

Now, even above the roar of the wind and rain, she could hear the anxious bawls of both bulls, could hear their bodies thumping and bumping inside the trailer. With the trailer laid on its right side, she couldn't see into it from where she stood, so she forced her way against the gale to the trailer's back. She peered through the double gate, but in the pitch blackness of the stormy night and blinding rain, she couldn't see the bulls. She could only smell them and hear them. She had to get them out. Their feet and legs could be caught in the trailer's side rails. They could be injured. Or if not, they could injure themselves in their fear.

She needed help. Spike and Charlie Brown needed help. She remembered that her cell phone was inside the cab, but no way would she ever be able to get to it.

She looked around, seeking her bearings, looking through the blinding rain for any sign of a landmark. When she figured out where she was, she realized she was no more than a mile from Brady Fallon's house.

22

Brady had been sleeping so soundly, he thought the knocking on his front door was a dream. When it continued even after he was awake, he opened his eyes. Then he realized the noise wasn't merely knocking; it was pounding, and a hellacious storm was raging outside. He roused himself, pulled on jeans, padded barefoot to the front door and switched on the porch light.

"Jude!" She was soaked to the skin and shaking like a cold dog. Her arms were folded over her chest, and she clutched her elbows. He pulled her into the house. "Jesus, you're freezing."

"I n-need h-help," she said through chattering teeth.

Water poured off her as if she had just stepped out of a pool. Her hair hung in dripping clumps. He knew she had gone east to pick up bulls. He couldn't imagine how she got from that to this.

"Come on." Still gripping her arm, he dragged her to the bathroom and grabbed a handful of bath towels out of the cabinet over the toilet. He handed them to her, then took one himself and began roughly scrubbing her bare arms dry. "What the hell happened?"

"I t-turned over," she said, her voice weak and broken, her whole body quaking. She looked up at him wild-eyed and bedraggled. Dark smears of eye makeup circled her eyes. "I've g-got the bulls. I've g-got to g-get them out. Ph-phone."

"Where are they?"

"In the t-trailer. In the d-ditch."

A sick fear surged in Brady's gut. "Are they hurt?"

"I d-don't know. I c-can't tell."

Even if they weren't hurt, they must be trapped. They had to be freed ASAP. "Let me get some clothes on."

Still shaking and babbling about leaving too late and her pickup sliding off the road, she followed him into the bedroom as if she had been in it a dozen times, her wet boots and jeans leaving a trail of water behind her. Only half listening, he dug toward the back of his closet and came up with the only bathrobe he owned, a thick thing that looked like a horse blanket. "Get those wet clothes off," he said, handing her the robe. "Hell, woman, you'll end up with hypothermia. Or pneumonia."

He pawed through his dresser drawers and came up with socks and a sweatshirt, then dropped to the edge of the mattress and quickly pulled on the socks and his boots.

"What're y-you g-going to do?"

"Saddle Tuffy and get 'em out of there."

Managing two massive, half-wild bulls already panicked by a wreck and a roaring thunderstorm would be impossible on foot. It could end with a sorry result even from horseback. He shrugged into the sweatshirt. "You stay here and warm up."

"No. It's too hard for one p-person. I'll go help."

"You're freezing. Do what I tell you. Get those wet clothes off."

"No. You don't know where the truck is. I'm going." She left the room, her boots squishing. He sighed and shook his head. If the past two months had taught him anything, it was that Jude was not a woman easily thwarted. He turned back to the dresser and found another sweatshirt.

Before leaving the bedroom, he dug in the back of his closet again where he kept a gun safe and brought out his holstered .45 pistol and fastened it on his belt. Worst-case scenario, those bulls would have to be put down.

He caught up with her in the kitchen. "At least put on a dry shirt," he said, offering her the fleece garment.

Her gaze zeroed in on the pistol. She looked up at him, her brow tented with anguish. "Just in case," he said quietly. Her chin dropped to her chest. She was a rancher's daughter. She knew what he knew.

She tried to unbutton her shirt, but her hands were shaking so, she couldn't. He unbuttoned it for her and helped her peel it and her wet bra off. Hardly noticing her nakedness, he pulled the sweatshirt over her head, then plucked his hat off the coatrack by the back door and crammed it over her wet hair. "Okay, let's go."

Wind whipped and rain pelted as they dashed to the barn. In a matter of minutes they had the two geldings saddled. Jude had to be in misery, but she voiced not a word of complaint. He said nothing, either. He had already made the point and didn't intend to belabor it in the middle of the night with two of the Circle C's bulls in trouble.

A well-used slicker hung in the tack room. He grabbed it and tossed it to her. "If you've just got to go, put this on."

"But what about you? What'll you wear?"

He shrugged into his old barn coat and crushed his old felt barn hat onto his head. "I haven't been out in the weather yet."

He picked up a flashlight, lifted two extra lariats off a wall peg and hooked them over his saddle horn. "Let's go." He shoved his boot into a stirrup and swung into the saddle. "Lead the way."

Together they left the comfort of the dry barn. Brady stopped at the cowboy gate that opened into the pasture beside the cattle guard, the easiest place to try to pen the bulls—that is, if they got far enough to need penning. He dismounted, unhooked the wire latch and laid the wire gate back, leaving a ten-foot opening. Then he loped behind Jude through the slop of the 6-0's quarter-mile caliche driveway to the highway. The gale from the west drove the chilling rain like needles against his cheeks.

They crossed the slick highway in a walk, then slipped and slid on the rain-slicked grassy side of the ditch, but neither Tuffy nor Poncho balked. Water ran like a fast stream through the narrow ditch bottom. They trotted through it, and soon, Brady saw the vague outline of the trailer through the rain's haze. They were approaching it from the back. *Thank God,* he thought, because if the truck and trailer had been facing the opposite direction, he didn't know how he would have gotten around them in the deep ditch with its muddy, slick sides.

At the trailer gate, he dismounted and shone the flashlight beam into it. A wind gust pushed him off balance, but he was able to see that the bulls were penned by a partition inside the trailer. They were soaked and pissed off, but both were on their feet, a good sign. They glared into the light and bellowed long and loud. Then he saw the problem. On the side of the trailer that lay against the ditch bank, their feet were thrust through the trailer's open side rails. Trying to force them out could cause a broken leg. Or two. In which case, he would have to put them down. "Aw, shit," he mumbled.

He went back to where Jude sat astride Poncho, covered neck to ankle by his yellow slicker, water sluicing off the brim of her hat. He yelled to be heard above the roaring wind and rain. "I'll get loops on them, then open the gate. When they see the opening, with a little urging, I think they'll come out on their own. But don't force them. If they don't come, if they blow up, at least we'll have some control." *Maybe.* Cattle functioned more from instinct than intelligence, but sometimes they surprised him.

He lifted one of the ropes off his saddle horn and unlatched the divided steel trailer gate. The first bull backed up and swung his wet, woolly head left and right. Brady shook out a small loop, tossed it over the behemoth's horns and snugged it tight. He carried the other end of the lariat back to Jude and handed it up to her. "Keep the tension on your rope," he yelled. "Don't let 'em fight it." He made a circular motion with his fist. She nodded that she understood, stayed Poncho and dallyed the end of the rope.

He grabbed the second lariat and tramped back into the trailer. He looped the second bull's horns, then dropped the partition. The first bull bellowed, then stood motionless as if assessing the new situation. The bulls were large and in their prime. Brady could see that if this plan didn't work, things could turn ugly in a hurry. He backed out of the trailer, mounted up and tightened his own rope, but Jude's rope was the one tied to the first bull's horns. "Just give him a little tug," he yelled to her, confident she knew how to use her horse's strength. "No more than that. See if he'll find his way out." Mentally Brady had his fingers crossed. If the first bull came out on his own, the second would follow if his legs weren't caught.

He watched, holding his breath, as the rain beat them without mercy. After a few seconds, like a woman in high heels, and as if he didn't weigh fifteen hundred pounds, the first bull slowly and delicately stepped through the trailer's steel side rails to freedom, and the second one came behind him. Brady felt the fear leave his chest. Before this minute, he hadn't even noticed it was there. He dallyed his own rope, and then positioned himself beside Jude, their stirrups touching.

She was grinning. "I can't believe they did that so easy," she yelled.

He wasn't sure he could believe it, either. If the bulls were not relatively tame or used to horses, the whole episode could have had a sorry end. The worst part was over. He grinned, too. "We'll go up the ditch until we find a place where the bank isn't so steep, where we can get out without slipping in the mud and grass. When we're out, you keep to the rear and I'll ride flank. We'll drive 'em along the fence and turn 'em into that gate I opened." He trotted ahead to take the lead, holding his bull close behind him. Jude added enough slack to her rope for the second bull to follow on the tail of the first. They moved single file along the ditch bottom, which had turned into liquid red gumbo.

A few feet past the 6-0's driveway, the ditch became shallower and he was able to lead his little column in an angle up onto the highway. They traveled up the wet pavement until they reached the 6-0's driveway and the barbed-wire fence along the left side. He yelled back at her, "Keep 'em against the fence."

They herded the two bulls into the pasture without incident, then released their loops, and Brady closed the gate behind them. "In the morning, I'll check 'em to see if they're okay," he yelled up at her.

Back inside the barn, he helped her strip off her wet gear. He couldn't see clearly in the flashlight's dim glow, but her lips looked as if they had turned blue. He was chilled to the bone himself. "Go inside and get warm. I'll take care of the horses." She nodded and started away, but he stopped her. "Hey." Her head turned in his direction. "You did all right, Jude."

Without a word, she left him and dashed through the storm toward his back door.

In Brady's house, shivering almost to the point of being in pain, Jude spotted the robe he had offered her earlier. She had thrown it across the back of a chair in the kitchen. Now Jude grabbed it and headed for the bathroom. She stripped to her skin and wrapped herself in the robe's warmth and Brady's scent. The thick garment swallowed her. The hem dragged on the floor, and the sleeves hung to her fingertips. As she belted it tightly around her waist, she shuddered from the release of the tension that had held her chilled muscles rigid for so long.

She carried her wet clothing and a towel back to the kitchen. She was met by a powerful wind gust slamming the old frame house and rattling the kitchen window above the sink. She shivered and hung her wet clothing over the backs of the two chairs at the table.

The cookstove was gas, so she rolled the robe's sleeves back and turned on all four burners. It wasn't enough. She had to have warmth *inside*. A sparkling-clean coffeepot sat on the kitchen counter. She searched the cabinets for coffee. Finding none, she turned on the hot-water tap and ran it until steam rose up to her face. With shaking hands, she filled a mug with the hot water, but it still wasn't warm enough. Desperate and still shivering, she rummaged in the cabinets again until she located a pan that would hold at least a quart of water. She filled it from the faucet and set it on a burner to boil. She might not be able to cook, but she could boil water.

While she waited for the water to heat, she sank into a chair at the table and began to towel dry her hair. Not only was she colder than she had ever been in her life, but every nerve in her body felt as if it had knotted into one giant ball between her shoulder blades. Adrenaline had her jumpy and anxious and full of energy, yet she was exhausted. When the water began to rustle in the pan, she poured herself a mug of boiling water.

Brady came in the back door, which opened directly into the kitchen from the outside. He was as wet as she had been. He stamped water and mud off his boots onto a mat at the door and pried off his boots. His face was red from the wind and rain. He shivered and rubbed his palms together. "Son of a bitch. I can't believe it's this friggin' cold in July."

"Welcome to the Panhandle," Jude said, managing to laugh.

He detached his pistol holster and laid it on the table, and she said a prayer of thanksgiving that he hadn't had to use it. "I'll light the fire in the living room," he said.

Jude hadn't even noticed a stove in the living room, but of course, this house would have a space heater. In most of the older dwellings in Willard County, space heaters were the only source of heat. "I boiled some water. I saw the coffeepot, but I couldn't find any coffee."

He smiled. "Don't have any. I rarely drink coffee at home." He picked up the towel she had used to dry her hair, roughed it over his own wet hair, then dropped the towel back on the table. "I'm gonna get some dry clothes on." He walked toward the living room and squeezed her shoulder with one hand as he passed her. A frisson of indefinable emotion passed through her chest.

He was gone a long time. Just as she began to wonder if she should check on him, he came back into the kitchen wearing sweatpants and a long-sleeve snap-button shirt. Pulling a pinch of knit fabric out from his thigh, he smiled almost apologetically. "I don't have a lot of these jogging kind of clothes. But since I don't jog, I guess I don't need them."

Jog. From what Jude knew of Brady, a jogger couldn't keep up with him. She forced a smile, too, thinking how out-of-costume he looked, and studying him as he scuffed about the kitchen in old fabric house shoes. Seeing them aroused a profound sense of intimacy, and she thought about those weeks ago when she had spent the night in bed with this man and she had done things with him she had never before done in her life. They had touched each other everywhere in every way, even shared secrets. Tonight it seemed as if none of that had ever happened. That is, except for the awareness that she was naked under his robe. And from how the soft fabric of the sweatpants clung to his genitals, he, too, appeared to be without underwear. She couldn't make herself stop looking, as a visual of the poster from that day in Stephenville slid through her memory. "Sweatpants don't suit you. I see you as a Wranglers kind of man."

"I've got other clothes besides Wranglers. I just don't wear them."

She looked up and realized he had caught her staring below his waist. Their eyes met, and an edgy silence stretched between them. It was like the unbearable tension that night in the mobile home in Stephenville.

He broke the spell and went to the cupboard. "How about some hot chocolate?" Before she could answer, he dragged out a box of instant hot chocolate mix and used the hot water remaining in the pan on the stovetop to make two mugs. "You hungry?"

"Not really. But I'm curious. What did you wear other clothes for?"

"My other life."

"Can I ask you another question?"

"Sure."

"Would you tell me about your other life?"

There was a long pause while he stirred the chocolate. "Not much to tell. I was a land developer and home builder. Fallon Ranches. Medium to upscale homes on ten to twenty acres outside the city." He lifted a fifth of some kind of whiskey from the top shelf of the cupboard and poured a dollop into each mug. "The homesites weren't really ranches, obviously. More like big lots, but they were what a lot of people wanted. Country living. I was doing pretty well for somebody who started with nothing. Homes sold fast as my crew could build them." He came to the table and smiled as he handed her a steaming mug.

The sharp smell of whiskey touched her nostrils. She looked up and their gazes locked again, and that same longing she had felt that night in Stephenville rushed into her. It was stunning, the power he held over her emotions.

"Thanks," she said softly, and took the warm mug.

He sat down adjacent to her, leaving no more than two feet between them. As it had before, that heady current swirled up between them. It felt like the storm she had just driven through, and was just as unnerving.

Jude suspected he had done better than "pretty well." "I can't imagine you not doing well." She propped her elbow on the table and rested her chin on her palm, ready to listen all night if he would talk. "I suppose getting a divorce ruined everything."

"It was sort of the beginning of the end," he said in his

soft, deep voice. She loved his voice. He fiddled with his mug handle as he talked. "But there was more to it than that. It took me a while to work my way through it, but living on that hilltop in Stephenville, I finally realized all that went wrong. I was too hungry. Tried to move too fast. I was stretched way too tight and had been for a long time. I owed a lot of money to banks. To keep things on an even keel, I needed to give the business all my attention, all the time."

"Then why get a divorce? And I'm not being nosy, Brady, honest. I—I just need to know. I mean, you must've known a divorce—"

"It was Marvalee who pushed for the divorce, Jude." He paused again, his beautiful blue eyes locked on hers. "If she hadn't, I probably would've just kept fighting the battle. She'd found somebody else and wanted out. I was so wrapped up in the business and in trying to be a good father to our son, I didn't even know until she told me."

"Oh," Jude almost whispered. A thousand new questions sprang into her head, but she restrained herself from asking them. "That must have been painful."

A weak smile tipped one side of his mouth and he shrugged. "Actually, the divorce itself wasn't a big trauma. Marvalee and I never did have that love story like you see in the movies. I was okay with ending the marriage. But I wasn't okay with giving up Andy."

"Your son?"

"Yeah. And he's a pistol. He needs me. Marvalee had already started ignoring him before we ever split up. I figured she wouldn't be that upset about giving him up, so I asked for full custody. She said no, so I sued. That's when her dad got involved. You see, he's a big-time real estate man in Fort Worth, with a lot of money, a lot of influence and a lot of friends. He didn't spend much time with his grandson, but he didn't want to let go of him, either."

Daddy would be the same way, Jude thought.

"When her dad entered the picture," Brady said, "everything went downhill for me in a hurry. Fighting for custody of Andy is what finally broke me. Lawyers cost a lot of money. Lawsuits use up a lot of your mental energy. In plain words, with all that was going on, I took my eye off the ball." He picked up his mug and sipped, then gave her another long look across his shoulder. "But it isn't over. I'm looking for things to go in a different direction. That's why I'm trying to hang on to this place. "

Jude felt as if a rock had dropped in her stomach. She had to say something. "Brady, I—"

"Feeling better now?"

"Yes," she said and pulled the robe tighter around herself. She was still cold, but she no longer feared she might die from it. And she really didn't want to say what she had started to.

"Last I heard, you were planning to get home ahead of the storm," he said.

She told him about succumbing to the Dickersons' hospitality because she didn't want to be rude to friends of her father. When she stopped talking, except for the wind whistling around the corners of the old house, silence filled the room.

"This storm's supposed to be gone by daylight," Brady said finally.

"Unusual weather for this time of year," she said.

His beautiful mouth widened into a slight smile. "That's the nature of these tempests that blow in from the mountains."

Discussing the weather. God, how lame could we get?

But discussing the weather was easier than saying what was going on in her head or voicing what she thought she saw in his eyes.

The warmth of the spiked chocolate began to trickle through her system. And so did her father's words from the night he had announced he was installing Brady as the ranch's general manager: *Caring for livestock is a physical, outdoor job. The years of hard work in the sun and weather have taken their toll on Louelle.* "Brady, I couldn't have gotten those bulls out of that trailer all by myself."

"Luckily, you didn't have to."

"But *you* could have done it."

His shoulder lifted in a careless shrug. "I'm bigger and stronger."

"If you hadn't been here, they might have been injured to the point of uselessness or even died. If—if they'd had to be shot . . ." She looked away, hating to admit she might have difficulty doing what would have had to be done. "Do you know that in all the years I've lived at the Circle C, I've never put down an animal? When it's been necessary, it's always been done by someone else." For the first time ever, an inkling of the point her father had been trying to make for years trickled into her obstinacy. "When you own animals, the responsibility of caring for them never relents. Never goes away, day or night, rain or shine."

"That's the essence of ranching, Jude. You try to make life as good for the animals as you can."

"I know. Of course I know that. I've lived with it since the day I was born. I've just never thought about it in depth."

More of her father's words came to her. *It's man's work.* And she had always been satisfied to let certain aspects of ranching be man's work, she realized. But one couldn't separate it, could one? If you were in charge, you couldn't pick and choose which tasks you liked and ignore those you found unpleasant. What had ever made her think she was mentally and physically prepared to take on the job that had been given to Brady? So what was left? She could do the job Grandpa did. Just as her father had said.

She felt a shifting within her, a letting go of some of the anger at her father and indirectly at the man who had just saved two of the ranch's bulls and maybe even her. And she felt guilt. Since Monday, when Daddy had asked her to give up her office, she had been circling and pacing—the house, the barns, the vet clinic—spoiling for a fight. For a week, everyone but Grandpa had avoided her and spoken to her in mollifying tones, which had only escalated her ire and frustration. Even Windy had given her a wide berth. She had volunteered to haul the bulls to escape the heaviness of her own stew. She couldn't recall ever behaving so badly.

She looked into the eyes of the man who had snatched away her plans. It was no wonder her father had put his faith in Brady Fallon. He was much more than a pretty face and magnificent body. He was smart and capable and caring. "I don't know what I would've done if you hadn't been home tonight."

He was looking back at her intently, as if he were studying her. "You would've done what you had to. Everybody usually does."

"Maybe. But not everyone *can*." She closed her eyes and rolled her shoulders against the ache in her back and neck. "People might have good intentions, but they have . . . limitations."

The next thing she knew, Brady's hand had crossed the two feet of distance between them and cupped her nape. He began to rub her neck with his thumb. "I know it was a hard day. It was a bad idea for you to make that trip alone, especially with the weather forecast we had."

She let out a great sigh and tilted her head to the side, relishing the gentle massage of his fingers. "I always do things alone. It's no big deal. I was so scared for a while, though. I know those bulls were, too. I just hope they aren't hurt."

"I didn't see a limp. But they probably think they've been hauled into five kinds of hell. It'll all be better tomorrow when the sun's shining."

His fingers moved to another tender place, and she tilted her head in the opposite direction, letting her shoulders sag and her hands relax in her lap. It felt wonderful to have someone care that she had been tied in knots all afternoon and evening. "I hate to say this, but I don't have a way to get home."

"Jude," he said softly. She opened her eyes just in time to see him lean toward her. He placed a kiss at the corner of her mouth. "Unless you want to, you don't have to go. The fact is, I wish you wouldn't."

Her breath caught and her eyes focused on his mouth. She sat perfectly still, almost not daring to breathe. His hand ran down her arm until it found her hands in her lap. He picked up her hand and rested his elbows on his thighs, his head lowered to where she could see a swirl of wavy caramel-colored hair around his crown.

"I haven't been able to stop thinking about that night in Stephenville," he said softly, fingering her hands. He looked up, his brow arched, his face only inches away. Like blue flames, his eyes burned into hers. "Have you thought about it at all?"

Only every second of every day and night. "Sometimes."

"We're good together, Jude. I know there would be a lot to deal with. But I think we could handle it."

She saw hunger in his eyes, the same as she had seen that night. Her breath suspended as her chest grew heavy and aching and memories bombarded her. She could feel the blood surging through her veins. She could see the stubble of his late-day beard, see a tiny mole near his earlobe, feel his breath on her lips. "But . . . what . . . about . . . Joyce?"

"Joyce? What about her?"

"Everyone in town's talking about her . . . and you. Joyce herself is talking about it."

His eyes held hers. His head slowly shook. "There's no Joyce. Not in the way you're thinking."

Are you sure about that? she was so tempted to say. But she wanted to believe him. And most of all, she didn't want to go.

He stood, which placed his genitals at her eye level. He was hard and of course he knew she was staring. She tried to remember how he looked in his masculine glory, but she really hadn't gotten a thorough look at him aroused that dark night in Stephenville. He offered her his hand. Her heart began to pound as she placed her hand in his and rose to her feet. Then she was in his arms, where she had thought she would never be again. Her head was resting on his shoulder, he was holding her against him and she was no longer cold. She felt lazy and deliciously warm.

"You feel so good," he murmured, his hands moving over her back.

Even through his thick robe, she could feel his erection pressing against her stomach. He caught her hand and moved it between them, placed it against him. He felt hot, even through the fleece cloth. Touching him through the sweatpants' soft fabric was almost more erotic than having him naked in her hand. As she slowly rubbed the length of him, clasped him as best she could, she rose to her tiptoes and sought his mouth. He kissed her hungrily, his tongue sinking all the way into her mouth. In a quick movement, he dropped his sweatpants, and his hard, velvety, naked penis filled her hand. He felt so much bigger than she remembered. Hanging on to him, she tore her mouth from his and pressed her cheek against his shoulder. "Oh, my gosh," she whispered.

"See what you do to me?" he said huskily, then his hand burrowed into her hair and tilted her head, and his mouth was on hers again, setting her on fire. She wrapped her arm around his waist and savored the burn, the subtle taste of chocolate and whiskey. His lips dragged over her face, her eyelids. "God, I want you . . . so much."

She swept her thumb back and forth across the smooth tip of him, feeling his moisture. The scent of sex rose between them. He leaned back and tugged the tie at the robe's front. "This has been driving me nuts," he said roughly. "Worse than that black lace bra."

The robe easily came undone. His hands came inside it and his arms encircled her body. She could feel the warmth of him, skin to skin, feel a fine tremble in his body. He removed himself from her hand. "You'd better stop. Or this'll be over before it starts. Come on." He stepped out of the sweatpants and looped an arm around her shoulders. She slid her arm around his back. This wasn't what she expected

on this dark and stormy night, but she had no objection.
Without a word, they walked to his bedroom.

The bedroom was only dimly lit by the living room light
spilling through the doorway. At the edge of the rumpled
bed, he kissed her again. Her eyes drifted shut as one strong
hand cupped her nape, the other her bare bottom. His tongue
urgently explored her mouth, savagely delved in and out in
a sensual rhythm. Desperate need began to build inside her.
Then both of his hands were on her bottom, kneading, and
he had anchored her to him, pelvis to pelvis, and hot blood
was raging through her veins like fire. Instinctively she
moved herself against his erection. "Brady . . ."

A low hum came from his throat and he became more aggressive, nipping and teasing her lips, his tongue dancing
with hers. The robe slid off her shoulders and hit the floor
soundlessly. She felt his big strong hands on her thighs beneath her bottom. He lifted her off her feet and eased her
back on the bed, at the same time parting her thighs. The
room wasn't so dark that she couldn't see the crown of his
jutting penis peeking from beneath his shirttail. Filled with
sweet anticipation, she lay shamelessly sprawled before his
eyes.

He leaned away from her for a few seconds, and dug a
familiar-looking black box out of his bedside table drawer.
She watched, fascinated, as he rolled a condom onto his
swollen length. She felt dreamy and feverish, as if this
weren't quite happening, but she knew from the hours she
had spent in bed with him before, every inch of him was
real.

Then he was over her, braced on one hand. The other slid
between them and his fingers played in her pubic hair,
stroked her sex. The deep muscles inside her began to
clench. "Brady, please," she murmured.

"Please what?" He lowered his head and kissed her,
licked into her mouth while his fingers gently parted her
drenched folds and stroked and teased.

"You know," she murmured. "Touch me . . ."

"Here?" He worked his fingers up into her slick emptiness.

But his fingers weren't enough. "Yes, but . . ."

"Lift your knees," he said softly. She obeyed. His fingers left her and she felt the wide tip of him push into her, felt her flesh stretch around the thick head of him. "Oh," she said on a sigh. He stopped. Even in the dim light she could see his face fierce with passion. For her. A thrill coursed through her. "Okay?" he said huskily.

"Yes," she breathed, lifting herself to him for more.

As much as she wanted all of him, a little gasp escaped when he pushed all the way in. He felt so hot, and impossibly hard. The pressure of his thickness sent utter pleasure skittering through her.

His eyes opened and their gazes locked as he began moving inside her. So slow. Too slow. "You feel so good," she whispered.

"So good," he echoed. "So sweet." His head lowered and his mouth took hers again in an all-or-nothing kiss. And she gave and gave. All that she was. She was his, forever.

The slow, steady rhythm was agonizing and delicious and wonderful, but that strange need took over her mind and taunted her in the far reaches, and all she could think of was letting it break out. "Brady, please . . ." She hugged his hips with her thighs and tried to urge him to move faster.

"More?"

"Yes."

His tempo picked up. His thick penis thrust into her deeply, heat and friction building a coil of desire low in her belly. Her hips hitched. She began to pant. His chest heaved, his breath gusted. A rough growl rumbled from his throat. His arms hooked behind her knees and he pushed them high and wide, pinning her. He braced himself on his hands and drove deeper, the root of him rasping there where she wanted it. "Oh, don't stop."

"Is that a good spot?"

She began to spasm. "Please don't stop." He didn't, not

until pleasure tore through her in waves. A sob crawled up her throat and became an outcry. He bucked hard, and her name burst from his mouth as he climaxed.

Then it was over and he was lying on top of her. They both gasped for breath, and neither of them was entirely on the bed. She lay beneath him, sprawled and boneless, her palms open beside her head. She wanted him to stay inside her forever. "Wow," she said. "Foreplay must not be all it's cracked up to be."

He lifted his head and smiled weakly. "I was just so friggin' horny. Foreplay comes next."

23

Brady stayed where he was for a long time, buried in Jude's sweet warmth. *Foreplay*. Oh, man, he had been too hot for lengthy foreplay. When he had walked into the kitchen and seen her in his robe, he just knew she was wearing nothing underneath it. There had been more he wanted to say, but all he could think about was her lush body beneath him, his cock buried to the hilt. If he admitted the truth to himself, that's all he had thought about since they spent the night together in Stephenville two months ago.

His strength gradually returned. *Foreplay*. He might be lousy at conversation, but foreplay he could do. He rose above her, pinned her wrists beside her head and looked down at her. Even in the room's poor light, he could see her nipples still peaked and dark. He ducked his head and licked them. She moaned softly, and the sound shot straight to his groin. But he was more in control of himself now, so he took his time teasing and circling her nipples with his tongue. Her vaginal muscles flexed against his penis. "You'll make me hard again."

She laughed softly, and her muscles flexed again. She squirmed against him.

He, too, gave a soft laugh. "You're ornery." He pulled out of her, instantly missing her tight warmth.

"Oh, don't," she said.

"Shh . . . You wanted foreplay." His mouth moved down

her middle, flicking with his tongue and nipping her soft skin with his teeth. He felt her strain against his hands as he smoothed his mouth over her silky body's peaks and valleys. Her scent filled his nostrils and he felt a stir in his belly again, but he told his head to ignore it.

Her back arched. "Brady . . ."

"Hmm?" He released one wrist and slipped two fingers into her as far as they would reach, found her creamy and slick. While he licked her belly, he drew out her moisture and languidly opened her and stroked every sweet, wet petal. Her free hand gripped his biceps and she made sweet little sounds. "Good?" he whispered against her springy woman's hair, burying his nose in her scent and working his fingers inside her.

"Brady . . ."

She was moving restlessly. He quickly pulled out his fingers and slid to the floor on his knees. At the same time he gripped her hips and pulled her with him. He parted the swollen lips of her sex with his thumbs and slid the tip of his tongue into her. She gasped and her hips lifted. And no wonder. Her clit was so firm it was easy to feel with his tongue. He pulled back. Her knees fell wide, opening herself for him. "Oh, don't stop," she whimpered, her hands clasping his head. "Please. Make me—"

"Not yet," he murmured against her slick layers. He took his time. He licked deeply, tasted profusely, avoided giving her what she wanted, while he worked his fingers inside her. Her hips began to pump, she panted and whimpered and when he believed she'd had enough, he drew her hard little clit into his mouth and sucked her as if he were a hungry babe. Her hips came off the bed and she screamed. He held her in place and didn't stop until she came and came and came. Her hands clutched his head and hair and pulled him up her body until his mouth reached hers. She was crying, but she devoured his mouth, wildly licking her own taste from his lips and tongue. "Come inside me," she begged. "Please come inside me. I need you inside me."

"I can't, darlin'." He kissed her hard and fast. "I don't have another rubber."

"I don't care."

"Yes, you do." He kissed her again, giving her his tongue and taking hers. When he felt her begin to calm, he lifted his mouth from hers.

She gasped a great breath, released her grip on his head and flopped her arms against the bed. "Wow," she said.

He chuckled against her neck. He loved giving her pleasure. He got to his feet, heaving a great breath. He pulled her off the bed and up beside him, then turned back the bedspread. "Get under the covers," he said. "I'll be right back."

He padded to the bathroom, disposed of the rubber and washed himself. He hated rubbers. Married sex had spoiled him. He didn't know if he would ever learn to like making love wearing latex. Fucking was one thing, and it called for latex, but making love called for flesh-to-flesh contact.

On his way back to the bedroom, he detoured by the living room and switched off the light, then returned to the bedroom, stripped off his shirt and tossed it, and crawled in bed beside her. "We've gotta get some sleep," he said, and gathered her into his arms.

"I know." She wiggled against him until she found a comfortable place.

He was exhausted, and she had to be, too. He was already drifting into sleep when he thought of something. "Jude? You thought I was sleeping with Joyce Harrison?"

"Just gossip."

"I haven't been with anybody, Jude. Only you."

"Me, neither. But you already know that." He heard her sigh. "I'm an open book."

He smiled.

Brady awoke at four thirty. Of course he had to because breakfast was served in the cookhouse at four forty-five. Jude awoke long enough to kiss him good-bye. He told her he would return after daylight to check on the bulls and deal with the pickup and trailer. Indeed, he had made good on his promise of foreplay. Jude wrapped her arms around his pillow and went back to sleep.

But she was up by six o'clock, smiling and even humming. And noticing a few new sensitive places. She had never even imagined sex could be like it was with Brady. It just proved that when the choice was up to her, when Daddy and Grandpa stayed out of her love life, she did much better on her own. How had she lived without a true loving man for so many years? And why had she?

She slipped into Brady's robe again and padded to the kitchen.

She switched on the radio on top of the old refrigerator and turned up the volume. Country-western music twanged into the room. Honky-tonk music, Suzanne called it. Jude had been in honky-tonks only a few times, always with Suzanne. She moved through a couple of dance steps Brady had taught her as she put water on to make more hot chocolate.

While she waited for the water to boil, she gazed through the kitchen window. With diamondlike brilliance, sunlight glistened off the outbuildings' metal roofs and the moisture on the blades of grass. Summer had returned. This was West Texas at its best, alive and glowing just after a thirst-quenching rain.

She had difficulty imagining the crisis that had beleaguered her only a few hours earlier. This morning, the sky was breathtakingly blue. As blue as Brady Fallon's eyes. She was in awe of the order of things. A month ago, she would have said his eyes were as blue as the sky, but today, in her mind, she saw Brady first. And she saw his square jaw and lean cheeks and the half smile that caused the corners of his eyes to crinkle and dance with a hint of his dry sense of humor.

She touched her jeans and shirt and underwear, which had been left hanging over the backs of two kitchen chairs. They were dry but looked as if they had been trampled by the bulls. Fortunately, with Daddy being in Amarillo, he wouldn't see her when she went home and wonder where she had spent the night. Clumps of mud covered her custom-made boots. They had been soaked from sole to shaft and smelled of wet leather. They would take days to dry out and were probably ruined. She sighed. She liked those boots.

She helped herself to the shower, one of those fiberglass units that had been installed well after the construction of the house. She brushed her teeth with her finger and Brady's toothpaste, used his he-man deodorant and borrowed his brush and comb. She even found some fragrant cream to rub on her face and body. It smelled woodsy, like him. She kept smiling like a loon as she rubbed some everywhere and relished the idea of being enveloped by his scent all day.

Back in the kitchen, she was dumping a packet of instant hot chocolate into a mug when the warble of a phone surprised her. She didn't know he'd had a landline installed. She looked at it on the far end of the counter. She almost answered it but thought better of it at the last minute. Instead, she poured hot water into the mug and waited for the answering machine to pick up. A woman's voice left a message.

"Brady, honey, this is me. I woke up wanting to talk to you. I'm so grateful for the time we had Sunday evening. It meant more to me than I can ever tell you. I've made so many mistakes, Brady, and I don't want to make another. You were right in that Andy loves you so much and he needs you. I know Jarrett isn't your son, but he loves you and needs you, too. Just want to let you know I'm trying to arrange a trip over there. I'm eager to see your aunt's old house. As smart as you are, I'm sure you'll be able to turn it into a mansion. I don't want to interfere with your job, so just let me know when your days off are so we'll be able to spend some time together and work out some things when I come. I'll call you tonight, honey, and we can talk some more. Or if you want to call me, you have my number."

Click!

Jude set the hot pan on the stove, her mind a blank.

Honey? . . . Time we had Sunday evening . . . Work out some things when I come?

As she listened to the message a second time, thought came charging back, bringing the certain knowledge that this was the voice of Brady's ex-wife. But what did this call mean? Were they in the middle of a reconciliation? Other than knowing he went to Fort Worth to visit his son, Jude knew little else about his relationship with his son or his ex-wife. Of course he was devoted to his son. Otherwise he wouldn't drive all the way to Fort Worth so often to see him.

Jude's stomach began to churn. She crossed her arms and gripped her elbows to stop it, but the sick feeling didn't go away. She must be hungry, she thought. She opened the refrigerator but saw nothing but a package of bologna, a package of sliced cheese, a loaf of bread and a gallon of milk. She slammed the refrigerator door and started pacing, trying to put two logical thoughts together.

Brady was a decent man. If he had been planning to reconcile with his ex-wife, surely he wouldn't have had sex with her last night. And he had said things—loving things—as if he cared about her. Had he been lying to her? She could hardly stand to think of him with someone else the way he had been with her last night.

An overwhelming desire to get out of this house overcame her, a desire to go home, to bury herself in familiar and safe surroundings. He had told her to wait for him until he found a chance to come back, but who knew when that would be? All sorts of mishaps and unplanned events could occur at the Circle C. What she had to do was check to see if Spike or Charlie Brown was hurt, then get her pickup and trailer home.

But as she began to get ready to leave, a new dilemma plagued her. If she called on anyone at the ranch to come get her and her pickup, she would have to explain why she was at the new general manager's house in the early morning in filthy, wrinkled clothing. She reiterated her vow to never again get caught up in a web of lies, however petty they originally seemed.

A new Abilene phone book lay on the counter by the phone. She thumbed to the yellow pages and found the tow-truck listings. The dispatcher at the first number told her he would have a truck on the scene in an hour and a half. It was nice when a company needed work enough to provide real customer service. Throwing out her last name had done no harm, either. The Circle C owned a virtual fleet of pickups, trucks and trailers, and sundry other equipment. Once back at the ranch, she could find some kind of rig and return to pick up the bulls without having to explain anything. Brady might return before the tow truck arrived; then again, maybe not.

She pulled on her wet boots, donned her wrinkled clothing and tramped through the mud and sunshine to the soggy pasture behind the barn. Unlike most of the Circle C's bulls, Spike and Charlie Brown were gentle and used to people. They gave her no trouble as she examined their hooves and legs. They had a few scrapes, but nothing that wouldn't heal. Still, she would ask Doc Barrett to look at them.

She went outside to wait for her rescuer. But it wasn't Brady Fallon she waited for. Her knight in shining armor this morning was a tow truck from Abilene.

It was midmorning, and to Brady's annoyance, he hadn't been able to get back to his house, nor had he had a chance to arrange to have the bulls hauled. He had gotten tied up in the vet barn behind the clinic, assisting Doc Barrett and Clary Harper. The peak horse-breeding season was coming to an end, and they were in the middle of teasing a stallion, set to collect semen. He had learned that with having an office so near to the ranch's veterinary operations, he often was called on to help the doc or Clary. He didn't mind. He was learning more about horse breeding and AI than he had ever expected to know, though he was having difficulty concentrating this morning. Because he and Jude had been awake all night, he was tired.

The roar of a large truck engine caught the attention of all three men. Brady left the barn to investigate. He saw Jude's truck, its right side plastered stem to stern with red mud. The passenger door and bed were caved in. A blue-and-white tow truck followed it, pulling a mud-encrusted stock trailer. Brady stopped midstep and stared. Why hadn't she waited for him?

Clary came up beside him. "Is that Judith Ann?"

"Yeah," Brady answered.

"Where the hell has she been?"

Well, Brady couldn't give the horse wrangler an entirely truthful answer, could he? He was still nervous over the fact that Clary and Jack Durham were friends. "Over by Fort Worth. She went to get bulls."

"She had a wreck?"

"Looks like it."

Clary shook his head and sighed. "Well, let's finish what we're doing."

Following the horse wrangler back into the barn, Brady angled a furtive look back at Jude and saw her scoot out of her truck and talk to the tow-truck driver. *Why the hell didn't she wait for me?* he wondered again.

Jude bounded up the stairs, two steps at a time. She intended to shower Brady Fallon's scented cream off her body. She could no longer stand smelling like his woodsy scent all day. While she showered for the second time and shampooed her hair, she replayed the phone message the woman had left on Brady's voice mail. She had to give him the benefit of the doubt. Surely he would explain what that phone call meant.

After drying her hair and dressing in clean clothing, she returned downstairs, to the kitchen. Irene was making tamales for supper. Grandpa loved tamales. Windy said Grandpa wasn't eating dinner, so Jude told him not to bother making the noon meal for just her. She made a peanut butter and banana sandwich. From Windy Jude learned that she and Grandpa would be the only ones at the supper table. She would make a point to walk with him this evening. She should have already offered to help him as Daddy had suggested, but she hadn't found the right moment.

After finishing her sandwich, she peeked out the back door. She had seen Brady and Clary and Doc doing something in the barn. Probably collecting semen from a stud. As soon as they left the barn, when they wouldn't be able to see every move she made, she would hook a trailer to one of the pickups in the equipment storage lot and return to the 6-0 to get the bulls.

Meanwhile, she went to her new office and pulled up the stats on Spike and Charlie Brown. She had to decide where to put them. But she couldn't concentrate. The memory of last night filled every pocket in her brain. She couldn't imagine that Brady would use her and just toss her aside. But because he was so decent, she could also imagine she would lose hands down in a contest between her and his son.

She tried to refocus on the two bulls' stats, but all she could think about was Brady reconciling with his ex-wife. If he did that, how would she endure it? But she wouldn't let herself jump to conclusions. She would continue to give him the benefit of the doubt.

Her cell phone blared the "Aggie War Hymn," yanking her from her obsessive thoughts. When she checked caller ID, she saw the caller was Fred Whitmore. Her stomach lurched. She let the call go to voice mail. A few minutes later, she keyed into her voice-mail box and listened. "Miz Strayhorn? This is Fred Whitmore. Tried to call you a couple times yesterday."

Oh, damn. She remembered ignoring the cell phone while she had been driving in the storm.

All at once she felt bone-deep weariness. The sandwich she had just eaten lay like lead in her stomach. Living the past twenty-four hours on an adrenaline roller coaster and having no sleep had caught up with her. She had no energy for returning Fred Whitmore's call. She had no patience waiting for the men to leave the barn. And she doubted if she had the strength to hook a trailer to the back of a pickup and handle two headstrong animals by herself. She couldn't stop thinking about the woman on Brady's answering machine. She was at a crossroads of some kind, and her mind was too tired to decide what to do. Her bed upstairs beckoned. She ignored Fred Whitmore's message, walked out of the office and trudged upstairs to sleep.

Since his oldest sister was born, thirty-two years ago, and except for the three years he had worked on offshore drilling rigs, Brady Fallon had spent most of his life around women. Yet he didn't claim to be an expert on female behavior. Not even close. But he had taken one look at the tilt of Jude's chin and the resolve in her stride as she walked across the equipment storage lot and had recognized that something was wrong. He had knocked and asked for her at the house but was told by the housekeeper she was napping.

So he had climbed in his truck and headed home, intending to go to bed himself. He had now gotten ten hours of sleep total in three nights. He was running on fumes.

In his kitchen, the red message light on the phone blinked like a beacon. He grabbed a bottle of water from the fridge and leaned a hip against the counter edge as he listened.

"Whoa," he said a minute later.

Would Marvalee really let him have Andy? He had proposed it over the weekend after she had cried on his shoulder that she and her husband were having constant arguments over the kids. But he had never dreamed she would actually let them go or that her father would stand for it. If she really intended to let him have their son, Brady's entire life was headed in a different direction. Again.

He checked the time the message had been recorded. Seven a.m. *Uh-oh.* Now he figured he knew what had set Jude off. The message had the distinct tone of him kissing and making up with his ex-wife. Was Jude pissed off? Probably. Would she listen when he explained what was going on? Maybe. But his immediate concern was for his son. He rifled through a cabinet drawer, found the address book with Marvalee's unlisted number in it and punched it in. She answered on the first ring, as if she had been sitting by the phone.

"Got your message," he said. "What's up?"

"Brady, Drake and I have separated. He's moved out of the house."

For a moment, the words didn't register. Marvalee had been so enamored with Drake Lowery, she had married him within days of her and Brady's divorce. She'd had an affair with him for at least a year before Brady had learned of it. Brady recalled moving out of the house while Lowery moved in, almost on Brady's heels. But he was dead certain Drake Lowery hadn't been nearly as affected by leaving the five-thousand-square-foot house Brady had built for himself and his family as Brady had been. And he was equally sure Lowery hadn't relocated to a single-wide trailer house, worried about how he was going to eat. "Yeah?" Brady said, taking the phone to the table.

"I don't know what's going to happen. Daddy's ready to kill him."

Been there, done that, Brady thought. "Too bad, Marvalee. Sorry it didn't work out for you."

"The kids aren't all that upset, though, thank God. Drake didn't have the same relationship with them that you did."

No news there. "So why are you calling me, Marvalee? You want me to take Andy off your hands?"

"Brady, have you ever thought about the mistake we made, getting the divorce?"

Brady's gut clenched. *The mistake you made,* he thought. "Can't say I have, Marvalee." He had never been madly in love with Marvalee, wouldn't have married her if she hadn't been pregnant with his child. But he cared about her and he would have lived with her, wouldn't have cheated on her. He adored the son they made. He even cared about Jarrett, the son she'd had before they met. She had never married Jarrett's father, and the man had no interest in his son.

"Oh, Brady, don't be callous." Brady couldn't recall anybody other than Marvalee ever calling him callous. "I've been thinking about the fun we used to have," she said. "Remember when I was pregnant with Andy and you were so worried about—"

"Marvalee. Don't do this. Let's don't whip a dead horse."

She didn't say anything for so long, Brady began to wonder if they had lost the connection. "I guess I deserve that," she said at last. "Listen, Brady, if I drive out there this weekend and bring the boys, you'd have time to spend with me, wouldn't you? So we could talk?"

"What is it we're gonna talk about?"

"Things. Andy. Life in general."

An alarm went off in Brady's mind. He knew how manipulative his ex-wife could be. She had grown up the only child of a manipulative father and had learned all the tricks from him. "You already know how I feel about Andy. I don't know what else there is to discuss."

"Well, Andy really wants to see you," she said cheerfully, as if he hadn't flat-ass closed the door in her face. "The little guy went to bed crying just last night, and I told him I would take him to see you. Do you have a place for us to stay?"

"I've got one bed and I'm working every day. I don't know yet what the weekend holds. I guess you could stay in Abilene."

They hung up, with her assuring him she would show up tomorrow. He sat sprawled in the chair, his eyes closed, his thoughts darting everywhere at once. One of his thoughts was of Jude.

24

At four a.m., Brady awoke with his son and Jude moving in and out of his thoughts as if his mind were a revolving door. Marvalee had called him back and told him she, Andy and Jarrett would be at the Embassy Suites in Abilene. The boys could swim and play games there while he and she "talked." A part of him felt as if he should meet her clad in armor.

But before the meeting occurred, he had to see Jude. He didn't understand it, but he needed to keep seeing her. Maybe he needed more than that. Last night had only confirmed what had been going on in his head and the ever-growing feelings in his heart since they went to Stephenville together.

At first, he had been intimidated by who she was as well as the fact that she was the daughter of an overly protective father. It was all too reminiscent of Marvalee and her father. But Jude was nothing like Marvalee. Jude was unselfish and caring and didn't flaunt her family's wealth. In fact, the whole Strayhorn family was low-key. If a person met J.D. on the street, he would never guess the man owned more than half a county. Brady no longer cared that Jude was rich and he wasn't. They were alike in the ways that counted.

The importance of his job at the Circle C ranch had faded behind his desire to spend time with Jude. She was the only woman he had been drawn to in any way other than carnal since his divorce. Hell. Since long before his divorce, maybe since before his marriage. He wanted her yakkety mouth telling him stories of Texas history and reminding him to eat his vegetables, wanted her willingness to help him do whatever he thought needed doing. And he wanted her loyalty. He wanted her in his life. But he didn't want to sneak around and spend nights at his house as if they were doing something wrong.

Having almost slept the clock around, he felt energized and upbeat. He arrived at the Circle C on time and ate breakfast with the hands.

Jude awoke with real estate and Fred Whitmore on her mind. She wished she had never pursued the idea of owning the 6-0 ranchland. That one desire had caused her too much grief. Anything that was as much trouble as that land had become had to be steeped in bad karma. She no longer wanted any part of it.

Her mind churned all through showering and shampooing her hair. Perhaps Fred Whitmore had not yet presented the offer to buy the 6-0. Last night, Brady hadn't mentioned it or even hinted that something like that might be in the wind. But considering how closemouthed Brady was, *would* he mention it?

On the other hand, perhaps Fred had presented the offer, but Brady had turned it down flat. Or, since Brady didn't know the buyer's name, perhaps he simply hadn't wanted to discuss it with her. That was the most likely scenario.

For all her dithering, she came to only one conclusion: If the offer to purchase had been presented and Brady had known she was the anonymous buyer, last night wouldn't have happened. She had to return Fred Whitmore's call ASAP and officially kill her offer to buy the 6-0. She watched the morning news and waited impatiently for eight o'clock. At five minutes after eight, she returned Fred Whitmore's call.

"I got your message yesterday," she told him, "but this is

the first chance I've had to return your call." She steeled herself and asked, "Did the owner, uh, accept my offer?"

"He's thinking about it. I haven't heard from him, but I haven't given up."

"Well, I'm giving up. I want to withdraw the offer."

"You can do that, Miz Strayhorn," he drawled. "Would you mind if I ask why?"

"I've changed my mind. You're sure you didn't reveal my identity?"

"No, ma'am. You asked me not to."

"I'll come by your office in the next few days and pick up my earnest-money check."

By the time Brady finished breakfast and met with the wagon boss to plan the workday, daylight had burst to life with brilliant sunshine and a sky so clear and blue, tiny black specks danced in his sight. The downpour from Tuesday night had washed the red dust off everything, and the landscape shone and smelled like cedar and sage.

He walked over to the ranch house's back door, knocked and asked for Jude. The housekeeper let him in, and he removed his hat as she led him to the breakfast room. Jude was sitting alone at the table eating cereal. *I always do things alone. It's no big deal.* He remembered her saying those words Tuesday night, but seeing her alone at the big round oak table dramatically emphasized the point. He suspected "doing things alone" was a bigger deal than she let on.

She looked up when he walked in. She didn't exactly smile, but she didn't frown, either. Now he knew for sure she had heard Marvalee's message. She looked so beautiful, the sight of her almost took his breath away. Her long thick hair framed her face. Gold highlights shone in the morning sunlight that poured through a wall of French doors. She had on another one of those tight little T-shirts that made his mouth water. Would he ever get tired of just looking at her?

As he approached the table, Windy brought him a mug of steaming coffee and set it on the table. "How ya doin' this mornin', Mr. Fallon?" the grizzled old cook asked. "What'd ya think o' that rain? A real frog-drownder, wasn't it?"

"And we sure needed it," Brady replied.

"Yes, sir, we did," Windy said. "But the boys tell me it didn't bring us much relief from this dang drought." He ambled back to the kitchen.

Conversation about rain and the lack of it was never ending in West Texas. Like a sponge, the thirsty ground had already sucked up Tuesday night's drenching. Brady fixed his eyes on Jude and pulled out a chair adjacent to her at the table. He wanted to kiss her good morning, wanted to take her in his arms, wanted to hear her say she shared his feelings, But he could hardly have an intimate conversation with her with the kitchen help so close. He noticed her bowl was empty. "Want to take a walk?"

She picked up her own coffee mug and they walked outside to the terrace. The wide expanse of red limestone slabs took up half of what was considered the backyard, a bigger footprint than the whole 6-0 house. He set his hat on and they began to stroll the length of the terrace, squinting in the bright sunlight, their boot heels clunking against the solid stone.

"No one really comes out here anymore," she said, gazing at the orchard a hundred yards away. "A long time ago, there were parties out here. There would be politicians and businessmen. A few celebrities. People would fly in. Cable used to bring all of these rodeo people. Even some country-western musicians. I don't know what happened to all that. It just sort of went away."

As far as Brady could tell, there was little time for partying at the Circle C. Routinely, J.D. worked sixteen-hour days. It wouldn't be easy to party hard going to bed before sundown and rising before daylight.

And Jeff Strayhorn, even at his age, worked long hours, too. Brady had heard J.D. say that on some days, the old man never came out of his office until supper. Brady had been surprised to learn that the ranch's money—outside of

the huge cow and horse operations—came from Jeff Strayhorn's astute investing sensibilities.

He thought again of someone Jude's age living in this environment with two old men and a few Mexicans employed
as household help. It reminded him of some fairy-tale
princess in a tower, protected from the outside world. "I
wanted to talk to you," he said.

She stopped walking and looked up at him with those
wide, wondering eyes, and he felt it again—that spinning
sensation, as if they were caught in a vortex. "What about?"
she asked, keeping distance between them. Her tone was
matter-of-fact, unemotional.

"You must have heard my ex-wife's phone message," he
said.

Her shoulders lifted in a shrug, and they began to walk
again. "That's what you want to talk about?"

"No."

They had reached the end of the patio. A rectangular concrete table with two benches sat at the edge under the shade
of a giant old tree. The tree roots had heaved up the limestone slabs in several places. Tufts of grass grew in the
cracks. "Let's sit down," she said, and stepped up on the
bench. She sat on the tabletop, placing her feet on the bench.
He seated himself beside her, his hip and shoulder touching
hers. The concrete had already been warmed by the sun and
he felt it against his bottom. He rested his elbows on his
knees and wrapped his hands around his mug. "What I'd
really like is to kiss you good morning, but I don't suppose
you'd want me to do that."

"Windy's probably spying on us through the breakfast
room doors. He and Daddy have been friends their whole
lives, you know. He tells Daddy everything that happens.
They don't call him Windy for no reason."

He clasped her thigh and pulled it next to his, letting his
hand linger between her legs. He just wanted to touch her.
"What I came to say, Jude, is this. If we're gonna continue
to spend time together, I think we need to come clean with

J.D. We need to stop all this sneaking around and lying to him. I don't want to have to hide."

"*Are* we going to keep seeing each other?"

He smiled. "Jude. We've slept together, darlin'. And it was pretty damn good for both of us. You think we just ignore that like it never happened?"

She leaned forward, too. "I don't know. You slept with Ginger, too. Apparently for a long time. She had your things. Your friends thought you were together."

Uh-oh. This might be harder than he had hoped. He stopped and swirled the liquid in his mug. How could he explain Ginger without sounding like an asshole? "She was, uh—"

"A convenience? Is that the word you're looking for?"

"We were convenient for each other," he said, throwing the remainder of his coffee onto the grass. "Life's like that."

"Not *my* life. . . . You and I have never exactly talked about anything serious."

"You don't think Tuesday night was serious?"

"Well, yes, but—"

"As far as I'm concerned, that was about as serious as I get. I care about you, Jude. And you care, too. I think we've got a chance. I haven't felt that way in a long time, maybe ever. This is why I say we tell your dad, so we can be open and up front. Then you and I can talk about anything you want to, for as long as you want to. I don't like lying."

Coming from him, all of that was an oration. A plain-spoken sonnet without rhyme. Her chest filled with emotion, more than she had ever had to deal with so quickly. Now she was the one who was speechless, a handicap she had rarely suffered. She swallowed, waiting for her voice. "You're the one with something at risk if we tell Daddy."

"I'm willing to take a chance. When we went to Stephenville together, if I had known your dad like I know him now, I wouldn't have asked you to keep the trip a secret. I wouldn't have thought he'd be upset over your going with me. I believe he's a reasonable man."

"Hmm. He has selective reasonableness." She set her mug on the tabletop and laced her fingers. "You have to understand that for my entire life growing up, I was told by him and Grandpa and Grammy Pen to stay away from the ranch hands."

"I can see why they'd say that, Jude. This is a world of men around here, some of them unruly. If I had a young daughter growing up in this environment, I'd do the same thing."

"It's a moot point now. I'm friends with most of the hands. I've taught their kids. They respect me. Let's say I agree with you about telling Daddy. I don't like lying, either. But now that we've come this far, how do you think we should go about informing him?"

"You can leave it to me. I'll take care of it."

"No. It's really been bothering me to keep something like this from him. I should be the one to tell him. In fact, I'll do it today. He's due back from Amarillo this afternoon. I'll make it a point to have a drink with him before supper. I need to discuss Spike and Charlie Brown with him, anyway."

"Who?"

"The bulls."

Brady studied her a few seconds, then chuckled, remembering that J.D. had told him Jude called all the bulls something other than their registered names. "I forgot their names. They're okay, by the way. I sent one of the hands over to my house to pick them up. Doc looked them over."

"I heard."

He looked at her across his shoulder and grinned. "So now that we've settled on telling your dad, there's something else I want you to know. I'm heading down to Abilene. I'm meeting my ex-wife. I'm hoping she's gonna let my boy live with me."

She looked at him, and he couldn't read her expression. Finally she said, "Well, that'll be nice. Then what happens to us?"

"You don't have any objections to kids, do you?"

She gave him one of those are-you-crazy? expressions. "Of course not. I teach kids."

"Then we don't have a problem. Hell. We might even have one or two of our own someday." He draped his arm around her, pulled her close and planted a kiss on her lips. If Windy was spying, so be it.

"Stop that," she said, pushing against him with her elbow. "Windy's probably looking."

Brady got to his feet and stepped off the concrete bench. "I gotta go. I'll be in touch soon as I get back."

Jude was in such a good mood, she marched into the kitchen and began making a sack lunch. Windy was peeling potatoes and whistling, and she just knew he had seen Brady kiss her out on the terrace. For now, she wouldn't worry about it. Daddy wouldn't even be home until late afternoon. She grabbed a bottle of water out of the pantry, then took her lunch with her to the tack room and saddled Patch. She hadn't been paying nearly enough attention to him recently.

She rode through the barn lots and corrals until she reached the vast range that butted up to the back of the ranch compound. She rode through thick, sunbaked grass, taking in all there was around her, all that she adored. She loved the endless expanse of the rolling plain that stretched until it collided with the brilliant blue sky. So much unobstructed space represented a special kind of freedom only a chosen few ever saw for themselves. That fact was never lost on Jude.

A flock of quail burst into flight in her path. Patch shied, but she controlled him and kissed to him and assured him he was okay.

She rode past the old rock fences—layers of flat limestone pieces stacked without mortar. They had been built at the very beginning of the Circle C, before barbed wire. She reined Patch into the depths of Rimrock Canyon, where layers of prehistoric strata looked as if someone had painted stripes on the canyon walls. The canyon's sandy floor was still damp from the rain. She rode to where she knew a pool of rainwater would be standing and saw deer tracks in the soft soil that surrounded it. She stopped for Patch to rest, loosened his cinch and let him drink. There, on a flat outcropping of red limestone, she ate her lunch.

On the high canyon's rim stood the deteriorating walls of an old rock house that had been built before Grandpa was born. The roof had been gone for years. It had been a dwelling for an outpost cowboy who kept an eye on the fences and the cattle herd. The Crowell house, it was called, after its occupant. These days, with pickup trucks and four-wheel drive, there was no need for someone to live this far away from the ranch for that sole purpose.

Rested, Patch easily carried her out of the canyon on a steep trail. At the old rock house she tied him in the shade of an ancient chinaberry tree growing at a corner of the walls and walked inside the rock shell.

She had been here many times. Once, when she came here with Daddy, he had killed a rattlesnake in the tall grass near the front stoop.

Weeds and grass had taken over the floor. Little mounds of sand lay where the floors joined the walls that faced west, deposited there by the ceaseless wind. There had been three rooms, delineated by rock walls. Other than erosion, the walls showed little sign of weakness. They had defied all that nature could throw at them. To Jude, they were a symbol of strength and endurance.

She tried to imagine how it must have been to live here a hundred years ago. How had a lone cowboy stayed warm when a blue norther swept across the plains in January? What did he do when a wicked tornado blasted through in the spring? Or when the relentless August sun seared everything under its canopy?

She had to bring Brady here, to show him what it meant to be Alister Campbell's descendant.

25

Jude returned to the ranch late in the afternoon and saw her father's pickup parked in its usual place in front of the garage doors. She could hardly wait to see him. He wasn't often gone for four days. At the same time, though she was glad he was back, she dreaded having to tell him about her and Brady.

She unsaddled and brushed Patch, thinking through what she would say first. She tried several opening sentences on Patch, but he only snorted and kept eating. If only she could get the same reaction from Daddy.

She entered the house through the back door as she usually did. The housekeeper, Lola Mendez, intercepted her, obviously nervous. "*Su padre. Está* waiting *en* he *oficina.*"

"Thanks, Lola." Jude hurried toward Daddy's office, wondering what had the housekeeper in a dither. She found her father standing behind his desk reading a document. He looked up when she stepped in. The tension in the air was palpable. Lola had been right. He was uptight about something. "Hey, Daddy. Good trip?"

"Come in." He turned to face her, dropping the document onto the desk. He leaned forward, pressing his fingertips against the desktop. "Please tell me, Judith Ann, that you don't really have something going on with Brady Fallon."

He hadn't even said hello. Though she was standing and the wide desk separated them, Jude had the distinct impression he loomed over her. She held his gaze but didn't answer right away.

"Do you?" he shouted, and she jumped.

He never yelled at her. She had hardly heard him raise his voice to anyone, ever. His aggressive attitude was as painful as a slap. Reflexively, she shouted back. *"Yes!"*

Seconds passed. Unmoving, he glared at her, his face redder than she had ever seen it. "Sit down," he said sharply but more calmly. He gestured toward the leather wing chair in front of his desk. She dropped into it, still stunned by his outburst. He took his seat behind his desk. "My God, Jude," he said quietly, as if shouting at her had shocked him, too. "You know the rules. Why would you take up with *him*, of all people?"

She set her jaw. This was not how, or when, she had expected this conversation to occur, but here it was. Time to fish or cut bait, as she had heard Jake say. "Because I care about him," she said firmly.

Her father drew a deep breath. His head shook. "Jude, we've entrusted him with the management of this place. And it looked like it was going to work out. Do you think I can have you playing . . . playing whatever the hell you're playing at in front of the men? In front of their families?"

Jude had already anticipated those words—not precisely, but close. "No one knows. We haven't—"

"How long have you been seeing him?"

Still flustered after having been caught off guard, she couldn't decide how much to tell him. She didn't answer.

His head shook again as if he were still working his way through his shock. "My God. That's what all of this horse riding and training has been about, isn't it?"

Jude winced. "I was trying to help him. I thought he needed help."

More silence. Then, "Are you sleeping with him?"

She almost shouted "none of your business," but faced the fact that her lies had finally caught up with her. More silence passed. She inhaled deeply, shoring herself up to deliver the final blow. "Yes," she admitted softly.

Her father sat back in his chair and turned his face away. After another even louder silence, he heaved a sigh and leaned forward, placed his forearms on his desk and laced his fingers. "How do you think I should deal with this? What do you think I should do about him?"

"What do you mean? He's a grown man. There's nothing you can do about him." She, too, shook her head. "I mean, you can fire him, but . . ." A frown tugged at her brow. "Why—why do you have to do anything? Why can't you just let things be?"

"Because *things*, Jude, are not that simple. He needs to have the respect of the hands and their families to do the job we've given him, not to mention the people who live in Lockett and Willard County. The man we put in charge of all this"—he made a sweeping gesture with his arm—"needs to have enough self-discipline to keep his nose clean and his pants zipped. Do you think the hands and their families won't have fun at our expense behind our backs? Especially yours, Jude."

"I don't know what they'll do," she snapped. But she did know. They would do exactly what Daddy said. Gossip was a pastime in Willard County, and the Strayhorns had always been prime targets. How did she think her father should deal with this? She had no idea. She stood, turning her back to him, grasping her chair back with a white-knuckle grip.

"I don't know how I can keep him in the job I've given him," Daddy said matter-of-factly. "I don't have to tell you that this ranch is one of the most important agribusinesses in West Texas. It's an entity crucial to the economy of this whole area. To be perfectly blunt, Jude, the hands, their families, the whole county, will assume I've turned management of it over to a man whose only qualification is he's . . . he's having sex with my daughter. I don't know if I can even keep him on as a hand. Is he prepared for that? Are you?"

She flinched inside. He was right. If his reasons, other

than love for her, for trying to run her life had been in doubt, they now became painfully clear. As for Brady, he hadn't said he had considered the consequences, and she didn't want him to have to. She turned back with a direct look into her father's troubled eyes. "Daddy, please don't fire him. I won't see him anymore. Just don't fire him."

Her father shook his head again. "I swear I don't understand you, Jude. You were engaged to two fine young men from good families. You found something wrong with both of them and went off half-cocked and broke those alliances."

She gave an audible sigh. "Alliances? Maybe that was the problem, Daddy. They were *alliances*."

"Then you take up with a—a damn saddle tramp who works for the ranch," he went on as if he hadn't heard her.

"Don't say that about Brady. If you thought he was a saddle tramp, why did you hire him to run the place? Especially when you knew *I* wanted to?"

His head cocked and his eyes narrowed. "Is that what this is about? Are you trying to come in through the back door with this guy? Is this a mutiny?"

"A *mutiny*?" she cried. "Forgodsake, please spare me the melodrama." She willed herself to stay calm. "Why can't you just accept that he's someone I like? Someone *I* picked out?"

"So how serious is this? You're not pregnant, are you?"

"No, I'm not pregnant. But what if I were? You and Grandpa are always yammering about me having kids."

"Kids with fathers, Jude. Kids with legitimate fathers. Do I have to say it again? This family sets an example in this county."

"Oh, really? We should talk about that. What kind of example, Daddy? The whole state of Texas gossips about this family's scandals. They even write books about them. My uncle Ike and my stepmother. My uncle Ben—"

Her father sprang to his feet and stabbed the desktop with his finger. "Ben Strayhorn died a hero. Don't you dare disrespect him."

"I was going to say my uncle Ben's wife, Daddy," Jude said as calmly as she could, though her stomach was shaking. "She could hardly be called a hero, could she?"

Ben Strayhorn's wife, Cynthia, had passed from a cocaine overdose soon after Ben's death in combat in Vietnam, leaving their infant son, Cable, an orphan. More of the Campbell Curse, Grammy Pen had said. Daddy and Grandpa had raised Cable, too.

Her father came around the desk and draped an arm around her shoulder. "Look, let's calm down. Let's not fight, Daughter. Listen to me, now. Let's think through this and make the right decision. I'll speak to Brady. I'll—"

"Daddy, no!" Jude shook her head fiercely. "I don't want you to speak to him. Can't you understand? I'm not a kid. And I care about him. And I think . . . no, I *know* he cares about me. Not the money, not the ranch." She stabbed her breastbone with her thumb. "*Me.*"

"All right, Jude." He closed his eyes and raised his palms. "We'll let this all rest for now. We'll talk again when I'm less upset. After I've had some time to think."

She studied him. As surely as she knew her name, she knew he would confront Brady. Because that was the way he was. Nothing she could say would change that. The only thing she didn't know was when. But she no longer believed he would arbitrarily fire him, either. "Could I ask you something, Daddy?"

"What?"

"Was it Windy who told you?"

"Windy's a friend of mind. Has been since I was sixteen years old."

Jude had no one to blame but herself. She had known better than to sit on the terrace and let Brady kiss her. And she had known better than to get involved with a ranch employee in the first place. "I intended to tell you myself. It would have been nice if I'd had that chance." With nothing left to say, she started to leave.

As she put her hand on the doorknob, he said, "Jude."

She looked back at him. He adjusted his glasses and gave her a long, solemn look. "Here's something for you to consider while you're *caring* about Brady Fallon. Your grandfather still wants that 6-0 land. And I'll tell you right now, he intends to get it. When he finds out about this, I don't know what he'll do."

She couldn't resist a sardonic smile. "Looks like the easiest way for him to get what he wants would be for you two to figure out a way to marry me off to Brady. Why not? You've tried to marry me off to everyone else."

Jude found Suzanne at home. Barefoot, red faced and sweating, she was just standing a dingy string mop to dry against the wall on the back porch. "Thank God you showed up," she said. "Now I can sit down and have a glass of tea."

"What're you doing?" Jude asked, taking in the oversize chambray shirt that hung to her girlfriend's thighs.

"Mopping the kitchen. Dad's due in tomorrow night. He's on the road so much, I want the house to look like a home when he gets here."

Jude knew Suzanne worried about her father while he trucked across the country—the places he slept, the food he ate. One of the bonds she and Suzanne had was that they both had only fathers. Suzanne's mother hadn't been absent in body in her daughter's youth, but she might as well have been.

Suzanne picked two glasses from the cupboard and a pitcher of tea from the refrigerator. Jude seated herself at the phony-wood table in the small eating area off the kitchen, watching and listening as Suzanne dropped ice cubes into the glasses. She didn't quite know where to start. She leaned an elbow on the table and propped her chin on her palm. "What's new with you and Pat?"

"Aww. He's the sweetest man. Treats me like a queen." Suzanne came to the table and placed a tall glass of tea in front of Jude. "But he doesn't say much about himself. I still don't understand why he's divorced. The people I work with at the grocery store said his ex took up with some dude from Lubbock."

"She did," Jude said. "She wanted to live in the city." Jude remembered well when Pat Garner and his wife had split. It had happened before Suzanne returned to Lockett. She stared out the large window at the end of the room, trying to divert her attention to anything besides what had happened at her own house. "Daddy found out about me and Brady," she said. The words just came out.

"Oops," Suzanne said. "And then what?"

Jude shook her head, continuing to stare out the window. "I haven't seen him this mad since I broke up with Webb Henderson. I think he might fire Brady altogether. Then again, he might not." Her heart heavy, Jude turned her attention back to her friend, her *only* friend. "I've made the biggest mess. It started out as something so simple. I was just going to help out someone who I thought needed help. Somehow everything got out of my control."

Suzanne leaned forward, her hand clasping Jude's forearm. "Did your dad say he was gonna fire Brady?"

"At first. Then he backed off a little. I still don't know exactly what he'll do." Jude told Suzanne about making the offer on Brady's land, the crisis with the bulls in the storm, and the unbridled sex at Brady's house. She even talked about her grandfather's interest in acquiring the 6-0.

"What was Brady's reaction to your dad?"

"He doesn't know yet. He's in Abilene meeting with his ex-wife. He thinks he might get custody of his son." Jude shrugged and sipped her tea. "He doesn't like sneaking around. He wanted me to tell Daddy. He thinks my father's a reasonable man. But Windy told him before I got a chance to, which only made things worse." Suddenly overwhelmed by all that had happened in such a short time, she dropped her face into her hands. "Oh, God, Suzanne, sometimes I feel like I'm in jail."

"Well, it's a damn nice jail," Suzanne said. "I'd share a

cell with you just to get to wear your jewelry." She sat back and sipped her tea.

"I used to think Daddy and Grandpa would eventually tire of trying to run my life. But I just realized driving over here, I'm never going to have a life as long as I live at the ranch. I couldn't even move into town and get away from them." She sat back in her chair and sighed. "I think I'll go to Fort Worth. I should be able to do something there. Teach, maybe. I could teach in one of the colleges."

"You're going to just up and abandon Brady? After he took a risk for you?"

"His life is here in Lockett now. He might not be working for the Circle C in the future, but he still has the 6-0. Even if he wanted me to be with him, how could I, with Grandpa so greedy for that 6-0 land? Even Daddy doesn't know what he might try. Grandpa's a shrewd old guy. Ruthless, too."

"I can't believe your dad and your granddad would do something to hurt you, Jude."

"They've already done things to hurt me."

"But not deliberately. Not maliciously."

"What difference does it make? The results are still the same. Do you know what my life would have been like if I had married Webb Henderson? Or Jason Weatherby? Miserable, that's what. And I don't think either Daddy or Grandpa has ever considered that. Webb's a horrible human being, and Jason isn't much better. But now, in the irony of ironies, Daddy has no compunction about damaging someone who's a good person—someone I care about."

"Does Brady know you're the one who offered to buy his land?"

"No. And God willing, he never will. Brady's proud. He would be so pissed off. I've withdrawn the offer."

"I suppose the bottom line, here, girlfriend, is how do you really feel about Brady? Are you in love with him?"

Jude looked into her eyes, her throat tight. "I don't know. I just know I think about him all the time. No matter what

I'm doing, he's in the back of my mind. I turn to jelly when I'm close to him. But no more than I know myself these days, it might be just the sex I like. It's so incredible with him, like nothing I've ever known."

"See?" Suzanne said softly. "Now you know why I stayed with Mitch about five years longer than I should have."

They continued to talk, moving on from discussing Jude's unsolvable problems to more talk about Pat Garner. Soon the suppertime hour at the Circle C had passed. Suzanne put a pizza in the oven and they ate it and drank beer on the back porch. When Jude mentioned going home, Suzanne said, "Stay here tonight, girlfriend. You know we've got an extra bed."

Jude stayed. For the first time in her life, she stayed away from home in anger.

When Brady showed up at the Circle C cookhouse for breakfast the next morning, J.D. was already there. Breakfast talk concerned the coming fall sale and a new stud J.D. had negotiated for in Amarillo. After breakfast, J.D. caught up with him outside and they strolled toward the corral attached to the big barn where Clary Harper was working with a one-year-old.

"Good trip?" Brady asked, chewing on a toothpick. He wondered if Jude had talked to him. They reached the corral fence and hooked their arms over the top rail, watching Clary work with the colt. "I sure like the looks of that colt," J.D. said. "He's one of Sandy Dandy's."

Brady nodded. "He's a catty thing. I like that in a horse."

"I need to talk to you about something, Brady." Yep, Jude had told him. Brady angled a look at J.D., but J.D stared straight ahead. Brady could see only his profile. "To tell you the truth, Brady, I don't know where to begin."

"Try the beginning," Brady said.

"My, uh, daughter, um, mentioned that . . ." He cleared his throat. "Uh, mentioned that, uh—"

"Want me to make this easier, J.D.? Jude and I want to see each other. And we don't want to do it behind your back."

"Right. And I'm grateful. And Jude's what I want to talk to you about. She didn't come home last night. I, uh, thought . . . well, I thought—"

"You thought she was with me? Well, she wasn't. I didn't get home from Abilene until late."

Jude's meeting with her dad obviously hadn't gone well. Brady wished he had been the one to tell J.D.

J.D. turned and gave him a blank look. "Well, then, where is she?"

Good question, Brady thought, now starting to be concerned. His heartbeat kicked up. "Beats me."

"She and I had a, um, disagreement yesterday afternoon. She left here upset. She's probably at Suzanne's house." He plucked his cell phone from his belt and punched in a number. Brady watched and listened as J.D. confirmed that Jude was at her girlfriend's house. J.D. asked her about coming home, as if she were a teenager. He soon disconnected and hooked his phone back on his belt. Brady hadn't seen a grown man so flustered in a long time.

"She spent the night at Suzanne Breedlove's house," he said, obviously relieved.

Now Clary was trotting the colt in a circle. "I guess I'd like to, uh, know your intentions toward my daughter," J.D. said, his eyes on the yearling.

What did a thirty-four-year-old man say to a father who asked that about his twenty-nine-year-old daughter? Brady wondered. "I intend for us to spend time together. Get to know each other. Jude's a wonderful person."

J.D. turned and faced him, resting his elbow on the fence rail. "That's all?"

Brady looked at the colt, not knowing what to say. What did J.D. expect?

"Look, let me be candid, Brady. For you and Jude to be, uh, to be—well, this presents a helluva dilemma for me and for this ranch. I've put you in a position of trust. You can see how it looks, you taking up with Jude and, uh, the two of you—"

"Sex" was the word J.D. was having a hard time wrapping his mouth around. But he surely must have known she'd had some kind of sexual relationship with the two men she had been engaged to. Perhaps those affairs occurring outside Willard County made a difference. Embarrassed, Brady would allow this conversation to go only so far. "I won't insult your intelligence, J.D., by telling you Jude and I haven't been close."

"I know. I know. She told me. Look, I don't know how much you know about her past. She's immature where men are concerned. She's been engaged twice. To men my dad and I thought would make good husbands, but—"

"J.D., your daughter's not some kid. She's a smart woman able to do her own thinking. Old enough to decide what she wants."

The man gave a great sigh, then faced Brady with a wide, insincere grin. "She certainly is, and you seem to be what she wants."

J.D.'s behavior gave little indication of how he felt about that. Brady waited for further comment, but J.D. turned his attention back to Clary, who was leading the colt into the barn. He reset his hat and adjusted his glasses. "I've been thinking on this, Brady. I thought about it all night, in fact. The easiest solution for all of us would be for you and Jude to just get married. As you say, she's smart and she's attractive. I'm sure she'll make a good wife. She certainly comes with a dowry."

Brady's felt his brow shoot up. "Did you say dowry?"

"Cows. I know you want a cattle herd of your own. I'd be willing to set you up with breeding stock, no strings attached. Margie Wallace's place ought to easily feed a couple hundred head. You can take your pick. I'm sure my dad would go along with that. We'd just call it a wedding present."

Brady could scarcely believe his ears. "J.D., I'm in no position to take a wife. I'm not saying the day won't come, but—"

"Fallon, you're in no position not to." J.D.'s demeanor and expression had changed quicker than a snap. "Not if you want to continue an association with this ranch. This is my daughter's home, and Lockett is her hometown. As well as mine. If you're going to . . . going to continue to enjoy her company, you're damn well going to marry her."

Fury crawled up Brady's spine, along with sympathy for Jude. "Since we're being frank, J.D., I'm gonna leave this conversation with this. Your daughter shouldn't be a bargaining chip in a negotiation for a husband. And as for my association with this ranch, I took on the job as general manager in good faith, intending to be a loyal administrator. My interest or disinterest in Jude had nothing to do with it."

They faced off for a few seconds, glaring. J.D. broke first and stalked toward his house.

Several minutes later, J.D.'s truck passed on the way to the front gate. Clary Harper walked out of the barn. "Where's the boss going? He upset about something?"

"Don't know exactly," Brady lied. "Listen, Clary, I'm gonna go to my house and get my horse trailer and haul Sal home. She's been here long enough."

"Whatever you want to do, Brady, but she's not any trouble. Fact is, I like having her around. Jude wants to breed Patch to her. I was hoping you'd consider doing that. We haven't had a baby paint around here in a long time."

Just then, Jude's truck came up the road, and Brady wondered if she had met her dad as she came in. She parked in front of the garage and walked into the house without so much as a look toward the barns. "I might just go over and have a talk with Jude about that now," Brady said, and headed for the ranch house's back door.

26

Brady knocked on the back door and asked for Jude. Lola Mendez let him in and told him she was in her office. He removed his hat as the housekeeper led him up the short hall and pointed to a doorway. Peeking inside, he saw a bright, cheerful room in disarray—a couple of unpacked cardboard boxes, a framed picture on a chair, flat surfaces scattered with papers and documents. Jude was standing behind a desk, her long hair pulled back and clipped at her neck. A memory of her standing in his kitchen wearing his bathrobe sprang to his mind and he had to resist the urge to take her in his arms. "Hey," he said, and smiled.

She looked up, her eyebrows rising. "Brady. I wasn't expecting you." Fatigue showed on her face. He suspected she'd had a sleepless night. She had waged a battle that might appear simple to some, but to her, it was an outright rebellion.

"Stopped by to say good morning," he said, entering the room.

"Have you seen Daddy?" She had yet to smile.

"Just talked to him over at the round paddock."

"Was he . . . mean?"

He would never tell her that her father had tried to use her to strike a marriage bargain. "I'll just say we didn't part seeing eye to eye on much besides Sandy Dandy's colt. But he's okay."

She nodded, but he could feel the tension emanating from her, almost as visible as summer heat waves.

He looked around the room, then cautiously glanced back in her direction. She had that taut, fragile look, like she might break into pieces. He hated empty talk, but he said, "I like your new spot. It looks like you."

A weak smile passed over her full lips. "Well, I haven't put everything away. And I don't exactly have a real desk yet."

He nodded, noticing now that her desk was a table. A familiar-looking piece of paper on the corner caught his eye. He didn't mean to snoop, but the paper looked so familiar, he couldn't not look at it. It was a real estate purchase contract. It looked like the document that had been presented to him by the real estate broker from Abilene. Just to be certain he wasn't seeing things, he laid his hat on the table and picked up the contract.

Jude looked across the table at him, bug-eyed, then grabbed for the contract. But he moved it to the side, away from her reach. "You have no right to take something off my desk," she said sharply.

He looked more closely at the document. To verify what his eyes had already told him, he thumbed to the back page and saw Fred Whitmore's signature below the typed phrase "Buyer's name to be disclosed on acceptance."

"What is this?" he asked, looking up at her and schooling his voice not to sound harsh.

She stood still, her wide-eyed gaze glued to his, like a deer caught in headlights.

"Brady—"

"What is this?" he asked again. "You're trying to buy the 6-0? . . . In secret?" As this revelation sunk in, bitterness and distrust spread through him. "And I thought it was your granddad I had to worry about."

"Brady, I can—"

"Don't. Just don't."

He tossed the contract back onto her desk, picked up his

hat and walked out, hanging on to the hat brim to keep from wrapping his hands around her neck and strangling her. He had trusted her, had taken risks for her. Had she been scheming behind his back from the start?

Setting his hat on, Brady strode across the barn lots. *Women.* A man couldn't trust a single damn one of them. It didn't matter if you were married, shacked up or just fucking one—they were all the same. Jude was no different from Marvalee. And J.D. was no different from Marvalee's father. Hell, the Strayhorns were more dangerous than Marvalee's father. They had more money and influence than Marvin Lee Erickson.

He walked into the vet clinic, on into the office that had never really been *his* office, found a blank piece of paper and wrote out his resignation. He placed it on top of the desk in plain view, weighted it with a horseshoe and walked to his truck.

He had just moved on to Plan B. Not his plan of choice, but he could see now it was a helluva lot less complicated than Plan A.

Women, he thought again. On the day of his divorce two and a half years ago, he had vowed never to make another commitment to a female. He should have remembered that before he stepped into Jude's trap.

Jude clutched her elbows tightly as if letting go might make her fly apart. She made no attempt to chase after Brady. What could she say? How could she ever explain? She wilted to a wicker chair and stared outside at the barns. And that's where she was when her father came through the back door. He had a piece of paper in his hand.

He saw her from the hallway and came into the room, looking around. He was obviously uncomfortable.

"This looks nice," he said, as if trying to sound normal. "It'll be comfortable and pretty when you get organized. Penny Ann would be pleased you're using her room, punkin."

"Daddy, please do not call me that silly name. I hate it."
She stood.

"I worried when you didn't come home last night."

She snorted. "I'm surprised you didn't have Jake out
looking for me."

"We don't need the law to resolve our family issues,
Jude."

"Right. And we don't want to have anything to do with
Jake, anyway, do we?" She started for the doorway. She
didn't know where she was headed, but she had to get away.

"Jude, wait. We need to talk."

"No, Daddy, *you* need to talk. *We* . . . never talk. You talk
and I listen. And more times than not, I've always done what
you said. You need to know that has changed."

"Jude, listen—"

"See? This is exactly what I just said. I do not want to listen. Listening to you and Grandpa has caused me nothing
but grief." She turned to leave the room again.

"Jude," he said, his voice elevated and hard. "Come back
in here and talk to me." She stopped and leveled a heated
glare at him. "I have some things to tell you," he said more
softly.

She heaved an exaggerated breath. Nothing could have
kept her from scowling and snapping, "What?"

He sat down on the serape-covered cushion of the wicker
love seat and laid the paper he had in his hand on the tiny
wicker coffee table in front of the love seat. Her eyes narrowed, moving from the paper to his eyes. "What is that?"

He peered up at her but hesitated a few seconds. "Brady's
resignation."

Now she thought her insides really might just go ahead
and fly apart. "He's quit? Did you ask him to?"

"No."

She huffed a bitter laugh. "Then why would he?"

"I want you to know, Jude, I'm trying to salvage this
whole thing." Her father slashed the air with his flattened

hand. "I'm trying to make a deal with him. I've made him a fair offer."

Her brain felt as if a javelin had passed through it. Her brow tugged into a frown. "Offer? What are you talking about?"

He stood up and planted his hands on his belt. "I told him I couldn't have the two of you, uh . . ."

"Sleeping together, Daddy." She wanted to say *fucking*, but she couldn't bring herself to say that to her father.

"I told him if that's what he, er, you, uh . . . both of you want, then you two should get married. I told him you'd been engaged to other men and it hasn't worked out. I told him I realize he's apparently the one you want."

Jude was stunned speechless. Her eyes bugged so hard, she thought they might pop out of their sockets.

"I told him you don't come without a dowry," her father went on. "I said I'd set him up with a small cattle herd. I figure that Wallace place will support two fifty, maybe three hundred head."

Jude fisted her hands. "A bribe? You bribed someone to marry me? My God, Daddy. You didn't sink to that depth even with Webb and Jason. Are you out of your mind? Are you so self-absorbed here in this . . . this limestone fortress that you don't even know how a normal human being would react to that?" Her head throbbed. "Brady wouldn't consider something so outrageous."

"He didn't turn it down." Her father's brown eyes held hers. "He resigned from the GM job, but I think he could be thinking about the offer."

Suddenly Jude couldn't breathe, couldn't find words, wondered how she even remained standing. She unclenched her fists and splayed her fingers. "This is insane. I feel like I'm living in an asylum." She started for the door again.

"Where're you going?"

"Upstairs. I'm worn-out."

"You go on. Get some rest now. It'll soon be dinnertime.

I think we're the only ones here to eat. We can talk then, after you've settled down."

"I will not be settling down. And I will not be eating dinner."

She tramped upstairs on shaky knees. Brady's smile loomed in her mind all the way to her bedroom. She would never stand in the light of those sky blue eyes again. For the first time in her life, she had wanted something more desperately than she wanted to run the Circle C. And her father had destroyed it. But worse than that, she had helped. She thought of her great-grandmother, Penelope Ann. This could only be more of the Campbell Curse.

She hadn't been in her room more than fifteen minutes before she heard quick, heavy boot steps in the hall. She opened the door to see her father standing there with the real estate purchase contract in his hand. His face was a thundercloud. He shook the contract at her. "Jude, what are you doing?"

A week later, Jude's life at the Circle C had changed in ways she would have never thought possible. She had shredded the real estate contract. Her father again had the reins of the Circle C firmly in hand. On the surface, in an overstated display, the household appeared to be calm—but underneath, the ambience was as brittle as dried sticks. She no longer had drinks with her father at the cocktail hour, nor did she walk with Grandpa in the evenings. She didn't even eat dinner and supper with Daddy and Grandpa. She excused herself by saying she had to do work for the start of school. She rode Patch every day, exploring parts of the ranch she hadn't ridden to in months, if not years. She spent her evenings constructing her resume but had difficulty filling a whole page, even when she adjusted the margins.

Suzanne called her every day, trying to persuade her to go here or go there. She did go to town every day to eat at Maisie's. Sometimes Suzanne accompanied her. Jude listened as her best friend raved about Pat Garner. But while she was glad for Suzanne's happiness with a new boyfriend, hearing about it only worsened Jude's mood.

In her mind, she saw herself going to Brady's house and explaining away her attempt to buy his land behind his back for a below-market price. She would park in front of the rickety old porch. He would hear her pickup engine and come outside. There, the fantasy ended because she knew that in reality, he would probably ask her to leave.

Brady was now headed in a different—and less desirable—direction. He had applied for a line of credit at an Abilene bank, using part of the 6-0 land as collateral. He was waiting for an appraiser to arrive and assess its value. Once he had the money, he figured he would start out with two hundred head of cows. Bad time of year to be starting, but he had to make do.

Next week, Andy and Jarrett would be showing up to spend the week with him before the beginning of school. He was still negotiating with Marvalee on custody, but he believed that his ex-wife, now that she would soon be single again, was tired of being a parent.

He was painting one of the bedrooms, getting it ready for the boys, when he heard the clatter of a diesel engine in his driveway. He walked outside just in time to see Jude's truck come to a stop. He had tied a bandana on his head to avoid paint spatter in his hair. He peeled it off and shoved his hand through his hair.

"Hi," she said, looking up at him, her hands stuffed into the back pockets of her jeans. She had on those damn sunglasses that hid half her face, but she looked pretty and sexy. He stuffed the bandana into his hip pocket. "What's up?"

Her shoulders lifted in a shrug. "Nothing much. I just dropped by."

He nodded.

"How're the horses?"

"Great."

"I'll bet they . . . miss me."

Her head turned and she looked out over the pasture where the horses grazed in the sun. His jaw clenched, but he stepped down off the porch. She removed the sunglasses and squinted up at him. "Brady, I—I came to say I'm sorry."

He didn't want to hear her apology. Hell. What he wanted was to have never gotten his own life crossed up with the Circle C in the first place, but it was too late for that. "Don't worry about it. Sh— Stuff happens."

"Can I tell you how . . . or why I wanted to buy the land?"

It made no difference to him that she wanted the land. By now, he had seen that coveting land was in the Strayhorn blood. He supposed she was no different from the rest of that family. Her method was what had him bewildered. And the fact that she had broken their trust. But after she had come to apologize, he wouldn't be so bad-mannered as not to let her talk. He crossed his arms over his chest. "You've got the floor."

"When I first made the offer, it was after Daddy had given you the general manager's job. I was so angry. I've wanted to do something on my own for a long time. And I knew Grandpa wanted the land. I realized it was a mistake later. For what it's worth, I eventually canceled the contract."

It just wasn't enough. How could he forgive her? Given the same opportunity again, she would do exactly what she had done. He had seen nothing to convince him otherwise. "I appreciate your telling me."

She nodded. "Well, I guess that's that. I'm headed for town. Guess I'll go on."

"Yeah, I need to get back to my painting."

"What're you painting?"

"The back bedroom. My boy and my stepson are coming next week."

"Oh. That's what you wanted, isn't it?"

"Yeah."

It was what he wanted, but he had also wanted more that he obviously couldn't have, at least not on his own terms.

The lesson to be learned was that a man shouldn't want—or expect—too much.

The next morning, Jude left the house early and went to town to eat breakfast and run errands. She returned to the ranch midmorning to see a Life Flight helicopter sitting in the parking lot. Her heart nearly leaped from her chest. She slammed to a stop in front of the garage and raced toward the chopper. Doc Barrett met her and stopped her. "Is it Daddy?" she cried, trying to pull away from him.

"No, Jude, no," the vet said, gripping her shoulders and holding her back. "It's Jeff."

"Grandpa? Wh-what happened?"

"We don't know. Maybe a stroke. Maybe a heart attack."

Just then, her father's pickup came to a skidding stop beside her and the vet. "Jude. Get in."

They made the hundred-mile trip to the Abilene hospital in under an hour. Neither of them spoke. Jude sat as rigid as a statue, her teeth clenched. At the hospital, they learned that her grandfather had passed away in the helicopter. When the ER doctor told them, Daddy's eyes teared, as did her own. She stood in the hallway watching him pull his handkerchief from his back pocket, take off his glasses and wipe his eyes. Then he replaced his glasses, pulled his cell phone off his belt and began making phone calls. That was who her father was—the man who always did what needed doing, no matter what. She didn't know who he might be calling. Cable perhaps. Or other distant relatives.

When he finished, he spoke to the doctor again, then a nurse at the nurses' station, after which Jude and he started back to Lockett.

Of course arrangements for Grandpa were already made, had been for years, no doubt. His funeral would take place in the church in Lockett founded by his mother's father. He would be laid to rest beside his wife, who Jude barely remembered.

The tension in the pickup cab was intense. Jude's chest

carried so much weight, she could barely breathe. She wished she hadn't had the wicked thoughts she'd had about Grandpa the last few weeks, wished she had walked with him a few more times. She had, after all, loved him, and he had loved her. She felt bereft and empty. She had to ask, "Did he know about my trying to buy the 6-0?"

"No. There was no reason to tell him that. If you had gone through with it, he would have known then."

She nodded, looking down at the Kleenex she was shredding.

Except for road noise, they rode in silence for another little while. Then Daddy said, "I suppose you'll never tell me why you did that."

She shook her head. "It just seemed like a good idea at the time."

More silence. Then, "Obviously some things at the ranch have to change," her father said, "I don't know if Dad's passing will make a difference to Cable. I'm sure Jake's attitude won't change."

"Cable hasn't lived at the ranch in years. He never did have a great interest in the operation of it. He mostly just liked the horses."

"Before the house fills with people, Jude, I want to have a meeting. With you and Brady Fallon, the three of us together. I want to set things straight."

She looked at him and frowned. "Why?"

"Because I have to think of the future of Strayhorn Corp. And I have to put a new survival mechanism in place. When I hired Brady, I thought I was on the way to getting that done. I still believe in him."

"So why include me in a meeting?"

"Because you and your children are the future of this family's legacy. Maybe Webb and Jason were bad choices for husbands. But I think Brady cares about you. You care about him or you wouldn't have . . ."

When his words trailed off, she said dully, "Slept with

him, Daddy." It felt otherworldly to be having this conversation at this moment.

Unfortunately, her father's belief in Brady and his notions of romance wouldn't undo what she had done. She shook her head again. "Brady's so angry over me trying to buy the 6-0, he barely speaks to me. I doubt if he's interested in breeding. Of course, if you throw enough money in front of him . . ." She twisted her mouth into a horseshoe scowl and bobbed her head.

"Jude. We're talking about the future of the Strayhorn dynasty. Neither one of us can take that lightly."

She stared out the window and made a bitter noise. "Well, we know he isn't sterile. He's already sired one offspring. But I assure you, he isn't available for stud service."

Her father sighed. "You're being mean, Jude. And don't put words into my mouth. The idea is not for you to just have children. I want you to be happy with someone who loves you and who'll look out for you. I want for you what I've never had. There are so many things money can't buy."

The meeting took place the next day. Brady offered his condolences, then listened stoically to what Daddy proposed: Brady would return to work as the general manager, with Jude assisting where it was needed. A romantic relationship between them wasn't a requirement, but if one were to blossom again, Daddy wouldn't oppose it. Jude was amazed when Brady agreed to it, but after all, his choices were limited and he was smart enough to know it.

It all sounded so simple on the surface.

And so ridiculous.

27

In the days following Grandpa's funeral, Jude found herself in a strange state of mind. She focused on doing what she normally did, even helped Brady a little as agreed. She had less time for it because school had started, which kept her busy all day and some evenings.

She and Brady were polite to each other, even complimenting each other when called for, but a solid barrier existed between them. They never discussed the 6-0 or Brady's son. That part of his life seemed off-limits. Brady fit perfectly into Daddy's and Grandpa's proclivity for minimal and selective conversation.

Brady reestablished himself in the office in the veterinary clinic, and she returned to putting things in order in the sunroom. Daddy and Brady began having drinks every evening in Daddy's office. Jude had attended on two of those occasions but had opted out after that. The chauvinism was too blatant, the testosterone too deep.

She decided to ride the young horses to get away from the ranch and people on the weekends. She was a daughter of the earth and had always fared better in life when she remembered that.

The Saturday after school started, she packed a lunch, took a six-pack of bottled water from the pantry, saddled a three-year-old gelding named Pokey and set out for a day-long ride. Before she left the house, Daddy cautioned her about riding out alone on a green-broke horse, but she had no fear of horses, even green-broke ones.

She swung into the saddle and started for the big gate that opened onto the pasture. Brady was there waiting to open the gate for her, and she felt that odd little stir in her stomach when she saw him. No matter what had happened, he was still the best-looking man she had ever met. As she waited for him to open the gate, he gripped Pokey's bridle, looked up at her and wrapped his right hand around her ankle. She made herself not jerk her ankle free of his hand.

"You be careful out there," he said. "Pokey's known to crow hop a little."

She smiled down at him. "We're buds, Pokey and me." She nudged the gray through the gate and didn't look back.

It was morning, but the sun already blazed from a white-hot sky. She was glad she had thrown a long-sleeve shirt over her tank top. The August sun could fry an egg.

A sudden memory of her childhood darted into her mind. Back then, the kitchen help had kept hens for fresh eggs. Cable and Jake had stolen a hatful from the nests, and she had followed them up to the big barn's loft, giggling as they dropped them out the second-story loft window onto the neighboring barn's metal roof and watched them fry. Grandpa had been so mad at them. Even now, thinking of it made her laugh. *Cable*. He had come for Grandpa's funeral. After not seeing or hearing from each other for so long, they'd had a warm reunion. She still had him on her mind.

As she topped a rise, a hot wind swept her cheeks and threatened her hat, causing her to cram it tightly onto her head. The wind's motion even pestered Pokey. He walked with his head down, and she could sense his edginess. The wind had been gusting for several days, only further drying out the already baked pastures and turning the grass crisp. Dry windstorms weren't new occurrences, but they were always nail-biters. No greater fire hazard existed than the combination of dry grass and low humidity.

She rode a familiar trail that led to Rimrock Canyon. Her

destination was roughly eight miles from the ranch house
over mixed terrain, a good workout for a horse. She remembered reading that in the old days, a good horse might travel
twenty miles or more in a day. By the time they reached the
canyon, she and Pokey both were sweating. She found that
the canyon's sandy floor was damp, kept that way by an un-
derground water source. Riding into it felt almost like entering an air-conditioned room. Within the canyon's steep
walls, the wind became a zephyr rather than a gale.

Noon had already passed, so the tiny pool where she usually watered Patch lay in the shadow of the canyon's steep
wall. She loosened Pokey's cinch and let him drink his fill.

She laid out her lunch on the flat limestone outcropping
where she usually ate when she came here. She had packed
an apple, a hunk of Gouda cheese and some Ritz crackers
and a bottle of water. Save for the chirr of insects and the
call of distant birds, no sound penetrated the solitude.

After eating, she lay back on the flat rock and closed her
eyes, thinking about how no matter the day-to-day changes,
life moved on. Just two weeks ago, Grandpa had been carried to his grave in a pine box, on a nineteenth-century buck-
board, escorted by ranch hands wearing work clothing and
riding good horses. A graveside eulogy had been delivered
by Windy. Afterward, there had been grief and whiskey and
speeches by pompous politicians.

And now there was nothing. Except for Brady's presence,
nothing had changed at the Circle C. Constancy. The funda-
mental element of dynasty. It was bigger than all of them.
Daddy knew that. She knew it, too, but had temporarily forgotten it.

She thought about her father sitting at the long dining
table eating alone. She decided to go home. Maybe tonight
she would eat supper at the family table. She cinched her
saddle, mounted Pokey and reined him toward the steep trail
that would take them out of the canyon to the old Crowell
house. Pokey was a flatland horse. She was sure he had
never climbed a steep, zigzag trail. To keep him from pan-

icking, she kept him close to the inside wall, stopping often to let him rest. At the top, just as she always did with Patch, she tied Pokey to the chinaberry tree near the Crowell house, dismounted and walked inside the old walls.

And that's where she was when a hard gust of wind brought a faint whiff of something—something burning. Suddenly she noticed that the sounds of nature had stopped—no whirring insects, no calling birds. An uneasiness slithered up her spine. She walked outside the old house's walls and looked around. Now the smell was stronger. To the northwest, she could see a faint smear of what looked like fog against the sky.

Grassfire!

Her eyes darted to Pokey, tied to the chinaberry tree. He was circling restlessly. She had to get out of here. She quick-stepped to Pokey and loosened his halter rope, took the reins to the saddle horn and lifted her foot to the stirrup. On a nicker, he twisted away, jerking his head and yanking the reins from her hands. He trotted off, dragging the reins on the ground. *"Shit!"*

She eased toward him, holding out her hand, trying not to add her own panic to his. "Pokey, come back here." He was only feet away, but he kept just enough distance between them to keep her from grabbing him. She kissed to him, talked horse talk in low tones, trying to coax him to her. He lowered his head and munched, but jerked away every time she reached for him. "Pokey, you're really trying my patience."

Meanwhile, the wind continued to gust and the smell of smoke grew stronger. From the corner of her eye, she saw that the smear in the distance had grown into a billow, and she could tell it was headed in their direction. Pokey's head began to saw and he began to dance. She said a prayer he didn't run.

As if in answer to her prayer, he stepped on the reins, bringing himself to a halt. She lunged for the reins. His rump wheeled and he sat back on his haunches, pulling against her. Now she could see panic in his eyes.

In a quavery voice she whispered to him, called him sweet names, and at last she was able to calm him enough to get near him. The minute she shoved her boot into the stirrup, he began to twist and nicker, but she hung on and managed to mount. The entrance to the canyon trail was a football field away. She could get there. She urged him to a lope, toward the canyon trail entrance.

A blast of wind and smoke hit her face and filled her nostrils. Her chest tightened and her eyes teared, but she forged ahead. As she fought Pokey to the top of the hill, a line of fire and a wall of blinding, suffocating smoke met her, and she had nowhere to go but back from where she came.

A helicopter landed in the Circle C's parking lot. J.D. climbed out and charged into the clinic. Brady met him at the door. "Fire's in the north pasture," J.D. said breathlessly. "Brady, let's go." He turned and dashed back to the helicopter.

Panic darted through Brady as he hotfooted behind J.D. "Jude's out there!"

"I know," J.D. yelled back as they climbed into the four-seated chopper. "I think I know where."

They lifted off and headed north. In minutes they were looking down on a creeping fire that had already left thousands of charred acres and dead cattle behind it. J.D. directed the pilot, and sure enough, through openings in the smoke, they saw Jude and Pokey inside the walls of an old rock structure. The walls were surrounded by smoke and fire. The wind changed and the fire moved away at an angle.

Jude stepped out to the center of the roofless walls and waved frantically. Brady looked around and saw that the structure sat on the edge of a steep rock bluff. "How the hell did she get there?" he yelled.

"There's a trail," J.D. yelled back. "It comes up out of the canyon." He pointed to the north. "Over there."

Brady spotted the trail. The fire had already moved past it and was rapidly closing in on the structure. J.D. leaned closer to the pilot. "Can you set down somewhere?"

The pilot shook his head. Brady scanned the landscape and spotted a huge rock plateau, the only area not charred. "There," he shouted and pointed. It was a good quarter mile from where Jude and Pokey were trapped.

"What good will that do?" J.D. said, all of them gazing in the distance at the rock.

"Put me down there," Brady said. "I can get to her."

Instantly, the pilot turned the chopper away from the structure toward the flat rock. Brady unlatched his seat belt, preparing to exit the minute the machine touched down.

"Don't worry about the horse," J.D. said.

Brady leaped from the helicopter and landed on the run. He dashed across the charred ground. Ahead of him, the fire moved away from him, but toward Jude. The air had turned to smoke. It filled his lungs. His eyes teared as he searched left and right for a gap in the flames. Suddenly the wind changed and an opening loomed like a corridor. He dashed through and he was there, inside the old rock structure.

Jude fell into his arms and he hauled her tightly against him. "Jesus Christ, Jude. I thought I'd lost you."

She was hanging onto the horse's reins with one hand, but she clutched his shirt and buried her face against his neck. Pokey was stamping and nickering and throwing his head. "I couldn't tell which way to go. What can we do?"

"We're gonna get out of here."

"Pokey, too. We're going to take Pokey, right?"

J.D. had said not to worry about the horse, but Brady couldn't stand the thought of leaving the horse behind. He spied her shirt. "Pokey, too. Gimme your shirt."

Without debate, she whipped the shirt off. Brady grabbed it and approached the anxious horse, holding the garment down by his side and talking sweet. He clutched the horse's ear, twisted it and brought his head down, eased the shirt over his eyes and tucked the arms through the headstall.

"Okay," he said to Jude, grabbing Pokey's reins and the lead rope. "You hang on to my belt. The wind's changing directions every minute. We just have to find an opening. Let's go."

He led them back in the direction from where he had come. Pokey whinnied and fidgeted and shivered all over, but Brady kept a tight grip on him. They passed through the creeping line of fire and onto charred ground. Heat seeped through his boot soles and he moved quickly, sometimes leading, sometimes guiding the blinded horse back toward the flat rock where the chopper had touched down.

Through the smoke, he couldn't spot the trail that led down into the canyon. As if Jude sensed his dilemma and knew his plan, she came from behind him and took the lead. They stopped at the trail entrance and he breathed easier. They weren't safe yet, but the situation was no longer dire. He yanked the shirt from Pokey's face.

Still hanging on to the horse's reins, he looped his arm around Jude's shoulder and felt her body shaking. His eyes locked with hers. Her face was dirty with soot. Tears were streaming down her cheeks, and her nose was running. "You know something, darlin'? If I'm gonna have to keep saving you, we need a more permanent association."

"Oh, Brady"—her voice broke—"I'm so sorry for everything."

He kissed her fiercely. Her arms slid around his waist and she kissed him back just as fiercely. Pokey snorted in his ear. "Let's get out of here."

"The trail's steep. Pokey's only been on it once, coming up."

"We'll make it." He set her away. "You lead the way. Pokey and I'll be right behind you."

Jude pushed herself away from the comfort of his embrace and started down the steep trail. Brady had saved her again. His voice came from behind her. "I'll always have your back," he said.

She knew that. He had just told her he loved her. She knew that, too. She smiled and wiped her nose on the back of her hand.

FROM

LUANN MCLANE

"An author to watch."
—*New York Times* Bestselling Author
Lori Foster

TRICK MY TRUCK BUT DON'T MESS WITH MY HEART

Rumor has it that Candie Montgomery is to blame for
her twin sister's broken engagement. But how can she
be the other woman without even knowing it? Now, she
needs an insta-boyfriend to put a lid on the gossip.
Damage control comes in the sexy form of Tommy
Tucker, who was supposed to be a quick fix. But Candie
might just be in this for the long haul...

**Available wherever books are sold or at
penguin.com**